Novels by Breakfield and
www.Enigma

M000281973

The Enigma Factor

The Enigma Rising

The Enigma Ignite

The Enigma Wraith

The Enigma Stolen

The Enigma Always

The Enigma Gamers
A CATS Tale

The Enigma Broker

The Enigma Dragon
A CATS Tale

The Enigma Source

The Enigma Threat

SHORT STORIES

Out of Poland

Destiny Dreamer

Hidden Target

Hot Chocolate

Love's Enigma

Nowhere But Up

Remember the Future

Riddle Codes

The Jewel

Kirkus Reviews

The Enigma Factor In this debut techno-thriller, the first in a planned series, a hacker finds his life turned upside down as a mysterious company tries to recruit him...

The Enigma Rising In Breakfield and Burkey's latest techno-thriller, a group combats evil in the digital world, with multiple assignments merging in Acapulco and the Cayman Islands.

The Enigma Ignite The authors continue their run of stellar villains with the returning Chairman Lo Chang, but they also add wonderfully unpredictable characters with unclear motivations. A solid espionage thriller that adds more tension and lightheartedness to the series.

The Enigma Wraith The fourth entry in Breakfield and Burkey's techno-thriller series pits the R-Group against a seemingly untraceable computer virus and what could be a full-scale digital assault.

The Enigma Stolen Breakfield and Burkey once again deliver the goods, as returning readers will expect—intelligent technology-laden dialogue; a kidnapping or two; and a bit of action, as Jacob and Petra dodge an assassin (not the cyber kind) in Argentina.

The Enigma Always As always, loaded with smart technological prose and an open ending that suggests more to come.

The Enigma Gamers (A CATS Tale) A cyberattack tale that's superb as both a continuation of a series and a promising start in an entirely new direction.

The Enigma Broker …the authors handle their players as skillfully as casino dealers handle cards, and the various subplots are consistently engaging. The main storyline is energized by its formidable villains…

The Enigma Dragon (A CATS Tale) This second CATS-centric installment (after 2016's *The Enigma Gamers*) will leave readers yearning for more. Astute prose and an unwavering pace energized by first-rate characters and subplots.

The Enigma Source Another top-tier installment that showcases exemplary recurring characters and tech subplots.

The Enigma Beyond the latest installment of this long-running technothriller series finds a next generation cyber security team facing off against unprincipled artificial intelligences. Dense but enthralling entry, with a bevy of new, potential narrative directions.

The Enigma Threat Another clever, energetic addition to an appealing series.

the
Enigma
Factor

Breakfield and Burkey

BOOK 1: Award Winning Techno Thriller Series

The Enigma Factor
By Charles V Breakfield and Roxanne E Burkey
© Copyright 2020 ICABOD Press

Published by

ICABOD Press

ISBN: 978-1-946858-27-6 (Paperback)
ISBN: 978-1-946858-01-6 (eBook)
ISBN: 978-1-946858-02-3 (Audible)

Library of Congress Control Number: 2013916948
Cover, interior and eBook design: Rebecca Finkel, FPGD.com

Second Edition
Printed in the United States

Acknowledgements

We want to thank our families, editors, cover and interior design specialists for making this second edition of *The Enigma Factor* a reality.

Our readers and reviewers have been instrumental in helping us determine how to best reshape the story. Again, our sincere thanks to all for your continued support.

Specialized terms are available beginning on page 368 if needed for readers' reference.

When time runs out ...

Her watchful eyes followed rapid movements across the bright flickering monitor as each piece of the puzzle moved to its assigned location. Her subdued smile increased as each piece was transmitted. She knew that Q on the other side would have them captured and reassembled seconds after they arrived at their destination. This was the last of the updates for the communications interceptor routines.

She always kept her word and honored her family responsibilities. Complex communications were her specialty, and her adaptations kept the family business ahead of the world governments. Even her day job of creating programs with the U.S. telecommunications leader was not at this level due to the bureaucracy they operated under. Over the years she had tried to enlighten them, but it was a slow road of acceptance. This was a part-time outlet for her creativity and it helped her maintain balance.

Pulling her eyes away, she returned to her primary work screen, verifying that the recompiling of those programs was almost finished. The documentation for her departmental changes was already completed, with updates to her team members also issued. Her ability to compartmentalize the two efforts, both for good causes, spoke to her genius. She was slightly distracted by the vibration of her cell phone, which she retrieved from her pocket with the same efficient fluid motion.

"Hello, Julianne here."

"Dobry Wieczór!"

"English please, Father. Good evening to you too."

"Of course, make it harder for me. Q is telling me you are sending the final versions as we speak."

"Yes, they are finished, Father. I need to focus on an upcoming project for work over the next few months, so requests need to go elsewhere."

"Why not quit that job and come home. I would like to spend some time with you as well as get to know your son. How is he doing with his studies? Is he ready for our family now?"

"He is doing well and working hard. He is far more brilliant than any of us. But he knows nothing of the family business as I've repeatedly told you. Not yet. I want him to have a chance to make his choices rather than the family make them for him. My son, my choice. You promised me, Father, and you have never broken a promise to me."

"Yes, you're right. We continue to watch out for you and him, but I want to know him before I die."

"You will next year. I will bring him over, and we will explain things to him together. Just as we agreed. You will be so proud of him. I have only taught him to be the best, to be cautious, and to trust little in a world of bits and bytes. Keep in mind he may choose not to be a part of the business. He is his own man."

"Speaking of careful, have you heard any more from the Sergei character, or has he finally stopped trying to recruit you?"

"That prick! He has not come around for several months. He doesn't think I can help him after the crap programs I provided to him. He actually called me here at work and told me I couldn't program my way out of a paper bag. I believe I threw him way off track. You are still monitoring his activities?"

"Yes, of course we are, along with several others. He is up to something, we know. He will eventually defeat himself."

"Good. As it should be for garbage such as him. Is the rest of the family good? Any new marriages or births I need to know about?"

"No changes. We are all sad that none of your son's generation have fallen in love or found a way to make the next generation. And you, my darling girl, do you need anything? You know I would gladly pay for your efforts on our behalf for these programs."

"I make a good living, Father. I have never asked for family money. My contributions are out of love, as you well know, and the belief that you help make the world better. I need to finish up here and get home to my son. Dobranoc, Father."

"Dobranoc, Daughter. We will talk soon."

Julianne finished wrapping up her efforts and closed down her work machine and her laptop. The laptop she stored in her briefcase, as it was always kept within reach. Turning off the lights as she stepped out and locked her office door, she wasn't surprised to see the others had already left. Putting on her jacket, she took the elevator to the lobby and smiled as she thought of getting home and having the weekend to relax. Maybe she and Jacob could take in one of the Off-Broadway shows. They both deserved a little fun.

It was dark and the street deserted, though damp from heavy dew. Setting her gait for the twenty-minute walk home, she felt herself relaxing as her legs stretched out after sitting at her desk most of the afternoon. Her thoughts wandered to the preparation of supper as she crossed the street. As usual she was intently focused on reaching the destination and not her immediate surroundings.

Over the years she'd learned to focus all her intellectual power on single issues or problems, to the exclusion of all else. This ability to focus her mind had served her well, but tonight it betrayed her. She didn't even notice the car starting up, then aggressively revving the engine. The car lunged out with its high beams focused directly toward her face, leaving her disoriented and blinded, causing her to freeze mid-stride. All those lessons delivered to her son while he was growing up about looking both ways and being aware of your surroundings completely failed to register in her paralyzed state.

Just like the spell cast by an experienced poacher with a high-intensity search light designed to blind and pause a deer, so too did the car's high beams render her immobile. The sound of the squealing tires was not due to a concerned driver trying to stop in time, but rather a predator accelerating the machine to lethal speed. In that all-too-brief window of time that she froze, all possibilities of her future life had only one outcome. The car viciously struck her, killing her as it rolled over her body, crushing her briefcase as well. Her last thought was of Jacob.

The predator brought the car to an abrupt stop and studied the scene for any signs of life in the rear-view mirror. No amount of medical treatment would change the life pooling onto the pavement from the brutal crushing. Satisfied with a job done right the first time, the predator laughed like a madman. The car sped away with no pause and a driver with no remorse.

The investigating detective could find no evidence to change the finality of a random hit and run. She was interred with a quiet service attended by her priest, her son and his friend.

Life has infinite possibilities, but human beings are hopelessly predictable.

"I've got you now," Jacob rumbled at his screen. "And you're mine."

The blue-white glow of his flickering screen provided the final elements of the solution he'd stalked for days, or rather nights. His instincts were right on target. He'd found what he could now see was a bigger problem than the hacker chat rooms had thought. He was damn lucky to have found this one.

Jacob methodically reviewed all his traces to verify that his tests were valid. The door had been wide open. He muttered to himself about the vulnerability of Open Source and applying it without thorough testing. Yep, he had the proof. Good. He had found it for himself but felt the moral necessity of giving back so that others could avoid a pitfall. Jacob did not like seeing others taken for a ride because they foolishly over-trusted. Humans were so vulnerable.

Shifting windows on his screen, he worked through the code corrections he had begun ten nights ago. Satisfied with his recommended modifications, he completed two more extensive tests, just to be sure. Not only did he demand programs that worked correctly every time when his name was on the line, he insisted on them being better than perfect. Nothing could replace the overall sense of accomplishment Jacob felt for a job done right.

As he waited for his program changes to compile, his thoughts drifted to his mom. She had taught him that if it was worth doing, then excellence was the goal.

"There could be lives at stake," she'd always said.

He never could get why she always made it a life and death thing, but as he had grown older, he'd guessed it was for emphasis. It was just her way, opinionated and firm, as well as how Granny had raised her. Boy, he missed their discussions. Both of the ladies that had raised him were fine programmers and communications experts in their own time. His mom's recent passing pressed into his thoughts. He pushed away the anger that came with that thought. After four months, he had only started to be able to concentrate again. He couldn't go there now. This find he had made was too important.

The recompiled fix was retested, and he wrote up the required narrative. Perhaps a little more formal than some other posts, but his name, at least his cyber name, was on it. No one was left to take pride in his name or his ability but himself. He could be true to himself. Mom and Granny would be proud.

He was a hacker. By definition that could be stated as a person who breaks into computers and computer networks for profit, in protest, or because they are motivated by the challenge. Today the subculture was actually part of the open community. Plus, there was the whole White Hat versus Black Hat controversy. Jacob considered himself a White Hat, part of the group of security experts who referred to Black Hats, or computer criminals, as crackers rather than hackers.

His machine chirped. He paused and opened the chat window.

```
Buzz: ping!
JAM: hey, Buzz. Whatcha need
Buzz: Hey man, need some help with some code. I believe
      I know what is needed, but I will take your opinion
JAM: Little busy here Buzz, really don't have time.
Buzz: Loser! What's the matter, not up for real work?
      So much for being a bud
JAM: Ok, ok send it to me, I'll make some time
Buzz: Good man. Need by early morning, see ya!
JAM: Where is my P.O. for this work? ☺
Buzz: lol
```

"Why do I let Buzz suck me in every time?" Jacob muttered.

Going back to the task at hand, he finished his commentary and then posted it and the corrected program to the website. Maybe someone would notice his penchant for detail. Today, at almost thirty, he had a good job with a leading information security company, PT, Inc., as a security penetration-tester, helping companies avoid information compromise. Some would say he was too focused on work.

Laughing to himself, he jumped over to his email account window. He found the note and attachment from Buzz. Great, Buzz wanted him to review the coding routine for interest calculations in a new program for his bank. Reading the requirements, picking through the code Buzz included, Jacob saw error after error.

"His effort here is so junior," Jacob muttered. "Buzz tries, but he is so out of his league. Granted we were college buddies, but this is really bad."

Jacob had been lucky with his scholarship to MIT, whereas Buzz had basically bought his degree.

"Why is it he seems to just try to copy old errors and then fails to work through them to make them right?" Jacob mused. "Okay, more help just like during school. Geez, I can't believe he used that old crap." Opening the chat window, he pinged back.

JAM: Buzz, did you even try man.

Buzz: What do you mean, that is great code, just different style from you.

JAM: Did you copy and paste from somewhere else, rather than code to the requirements? There is a trap statement in here that comes from the open source I fixed two months ago for you, it is wrong here.

Buzz: no man, maybe you opened the wrong file.

JAM: I will fix it, I will also add a file for routines you should look out for in other code. Could cost your bank a fortune.

Buzz: Thanks bud, drinks/food Friday!

Jacob continued for the next few hours correcting Buzz's code and redoing portions to meet the requirements. Too bad he hadn't landed the job Buzz had. The money was so good. Of course, Buzz also had the family influence. It hadn't hurt that Mr. Buswald was connected in the bank and financially set. Buzz did not have the head for finance like his dad. He was educated and liked the idea of being a great programmer, but in all reality, he was only good enough for basic programming. Actually, he might be better at running a team if he wasn't such a pain to be around. He still pulled goofy high school tricks and made cutting comments that tended to alienate people. Ah well, Buzz did help him when his mom was killed. Jacob owed him.

Giving himself a pep talk, Jacob thought he had nothing to complain about. He liked pen-testing, considering it one of the best jobs he'd had so far. Jacob liked the idea of trying to get in the head of a Black Hat who beat down the paths to breach the security. He liked encryption and security aspects of computer programming that his mom had introduced him to, as well as logical system overlaps. He firmly believed in a layered defense approach to data access and securing the resources of a company.

Jacob was very into systems and the various overlapping systems at play. If he could understand the system at play, he could make it work for himself. The age of information was really heady when you got into the bits and bytes like he was. Stopping bad guys from wreaking havoc made him feel like a cyber cowboy.

He checked the requirements one more time, going down the list to make certain each portion was correct to the specifications. Good, one more testing run and trace verification and it would be done. He would send it to Buzz with notes on process that would likely be ignored.

As the test was running, he again drifted to thoughts of Mom and her dedication to him, passing down her knowledge on things like her logical approach to systems and her belief that there existed systems on top of systems as technology achievements continued to evolve.

It had been just the three of them for much of his life. After Granny passed, the two of them remained in this house. Such a pair of focused and secretive ladies he doubted he would ever meet again. He had little idea about his European family roots.

The story he'd been told was that Granny came from Poland as a young woman at the tail end of WWII. Granny lived in Switzerland for a time and raised Julianne. When Julianne moved to the United States to have Jacob, Granny came along to help. Neither of them volunteered any information nor answered any questions on how they got into this country.

The only thing Granny would admit to was that Julianne was her proudest achievement. Of course, she said it in Polish, German,

French or English, depending on which language she wanted him to work on. As such, the household had always been multilingual in reading, speaking and writing. It had helped him though, and he missed the conversations with them. Programming was always in English, always with process, and always focused. Like mother, like daughter. Where Granny had left off training him, Mom continued until her last breath. But the family, their involvement in the war, and his other relatives were totally unknown to him. Jacob had tried some Googling, but he simply didn't have enough information to go on.

Jacob had been told that Granny was born in Poland in 1925 and moved to Switzerland with her family for a time escaping the Germans. She came to America to support Julianne and her baby, Jacob. Very little was discussed about Granny and her time post WWII. Too many years of working, programming, struggling, prior to coming to New York, he suspected, caused the silence on her past. There were no details about her early life and definitely no mention of family. Granny was strict in wanting her daughter Julianne and then Jacob to learn the right way of doing things. She was delighted with Jacob's ability to let fingers fly across the keyboard of his earliest computer. She taught him a lot about working through various programs. She had learned from the ground up, so her teachings were invaluable. Mostly she loved him and let him find his own way from within a grounded framework.

Mom was a carbon copy of Granny. She taught him even more as her work took her to different levels in systems design and security aspects. She too never spoke of his father but indicated that Jacob was a product of an intense love affair during an extended trip to Europe in her twenties. Granny had sent her to a special learning symposium, not to fall in love, she'd often mentioned as she hugged her daughter. Jacob was taught to save money, and together they lived a frugal, efficient lifestyle, which Jacob continued to subscribe to. College without a loan debt had been the focus for Jacob for a long time. The one bump in the road was during his college application where his birth certificate only listed Julianne. The discussion on that was a wall of silence that never collapsed despite repeated queries.

The testing completed as he glanced at the screen. He zipped it up and sent the files to Buzz, confirming the Friday payment of drinks and dinner. Actually, he was looking forward to a night out. He rarely went out, feeling that dating was a bit expensive until he could provide for a lady. Plus, no one had really caught his eye other than a mild appreciation for pretty, intelligent women. Besides, now Buzz would buy and he could continue to save.

Jacob crashed into a dreamless sleep. He awoke a scant four hours later to an unforgiving alarm. Jacob dashed through the shower and as he shaved off the morning shadow, he stared at himself in the mirror. He had helped Buzz last night, or this morning rather. Chuckling, he imagined the look on Buzz's face, likening it to biting into a lemon, when he reviewed the code and commentary. Maybe Buzz would learn a bit, Jacob thought, with the final comb of his thick dark hair.

He grabbed a fast breakfast of orange juice and Cocoa Puffs, typical bachelor fare. Stuffing a couple of apples and a water bottle in his backpack, he loaded up his work PC and locked up the townhouse. The morning was crisp and clear for New York in the summertime so he jumped on his bike, adjusted his backpack and began the twenty-minute ride to work.

CHAPTER 2

We do not look for fame! Fame is only vanity. Outcome is the goal.

Jacob arrived at work with enough time to grab some tea at the coffee shop in the lobby of his building. Julie behind the counter had been here every day since he began this job. She was a pretty girl who always had a nice smile for her customers. Jacob thought she was sweet, even if she was a little too perky for him at times. She always recognized him, though truth told, he essentially took her for granted.

"Morning, Jacob, do you want your usual tea?" Julie asked, throwing him a smile that should have dazzled him but which he totally missed.

She gave him the daily once-over. She liked his six feet plus athletic build and strong, determined jaw, and had often fantasized about the possibilities of a night with him outside these inter-actions. What she wouldn't give to run her fingers through his thick dark hair and see if it felt as rich as it looked. He was nice enough even though he was oblivious to her flirting.

"Ah well!" she sighed.

"Hey, Julie. Yep, that would be great, thanks." Jacob smiled at her but mentally went back to organizing his morning. He knew he had to finish up the Citybankers review project and review Tom's pen-test for World Bank. A team meeting was also on his morning agenda.

"Here you go, Jacob. That'll be two dollars and twenty-six cents," she said as she handed him his tea and a fresh muffin along with another dazzling smile.

A little extra notice would be nice, she silently screamed. Some guys were just too into their thoughts to see what was right in front of them. Someday, he will notice me, by hook or crook, she smiled.

"Here you go, Julie, thanks," Jacob handed her three dollars and picked up the tea and muffin, not acknowledging that he was truly getting a deal. He turned to walk away toward the elevators when reality aligned.

He turned and smiled at Julie, "Hey, thanks for the extra snack. You're sweet."

She beamed and gave him one more megawatt smile and returned to the grumpy customer next in line.

Entering the elevator with a few folks, he punched the 28th floor. The elevator stalled until he inserted his access card, and then the doors finally closed. The group inside was quiet, obviously all still waking up or focusing on their day ahead. Exiting on his floor, he used his security badge with biometric hand scan to enter the PT office space. He was still a bit early and most of his teammates weren't in yet. He did say hi to his boss, Brian, as he passed his office headed toward his own cube.

He had no sooner connected his PC when Brian leaned over the cube wall.

"There's a team meeting today at nine-thirty in the big conference room. I am handing out projects for the next month,

Jacob. I wanted to warn you in advance that I expect you to head up the team review for the major New York bank project. We need to put a bow on this one and finish it this week for billing out. I really don't have a long-term project for you yet, but there is nothing to worry about." Brian's confidence was catching.

"Sure thing, Brian," Jacob stated with the same level of conviction. "I'm always happy to work on any project assigned."

Jacob wanted to mention his success in locating the problem with the Open Source programs, but it really was not applicable to work. Jacob didn't think Brian would even be interested. Brian was so ready to retire in a couple of years that he always seemed to simply want to keep things upright and on course. In Jacob's mind though, Brian had been supportive, like a mentor.

Jacob finished up his current project just in time to attend the team meeting. Jacob was the newest member of the PT team, and he felt like he was still being tested and measured in his performance on the team. He said little during the meetings and pretty much kept to himself, outside of team projects. Granted, the other team members accepted him and often sought his opinion on specific items, but the camaraderie was work-related, not personal. He knew that was his choice, at least for now. Yep, too much work and too little play made Jacob a dull boy.

He liked pen-testing as it provided a way to use his imagination to think like a bad guy and then apply practices to prevent bad guy security breaches. Over the last two years he had found and fixed many potential breaches. Being a part of PT, Inc., meant he was in a fairly elite position, which was a great boost to his career. But PT was smaller than he had originally thought, and they were so regimented in process and procedure that at times it felt like the team was not getting ahead of the curve. The leaders within the global financial community frequently used PT to check out problems in advance, but Jacob felt they could do more. Early on, he had offered some suggestions on how to be more proactive. For the most part Brian had smiled at the suggestions and asked him to keep the ideas coming but had maintained the accepted tried and true procedures.

Initially, the other members had tried a bit of interaction at a more personal level. Jacob had declined most of these offers to pursue his long-term interests. He was what was considered a full-fledged geek. When he wasn't working on project assignments with due dates, he continued personal learning to hone his skills.

As Brian had forewarned, Jacob did not get any of the new projects, and a couple of them sounded like a lot of fun. He wasn't disappointed per se, just wanted more challenges. He knew he received the review assignment because it would be polished and turned over to the customer on time. This had been Jacob's trademark thus far with PT, Inc. Brian seemed to like setting him up to interact with the rest of the team, collaborating on different projects, yet not be directly in those projects. Jacob always found this difficult unless someone on the team came to him. Dipping in others' projects uninvited was not in his DNA, unless he saw a potential problem.

The remainder of the week he completed his projects and turned over the final deliverables, putting the proverbial 'bow' on the New York World Bank Group project. Jacob had the ability to focus on his work projects and tune out the personal, except when things were slow. This week had been busy enough that nights were spent eating at home and crashing. The ten plus hours per day meant he hadn't had time to visit many of the chat rooms he frequented or find another issue to track down for the Freeware World chat room.

Buzz of course had emailed his thanks for the suggestions to his project and had commented that he did not appreciate the jibe. He confirmed meeting up at Elmer's for beer on Friday evening.

Jacob thought briefly about the software program fix with the detailed discussion paper and code he had submitted last weekend, wondering if anyone had a chance to review it yet. He laughed to himself. It was so unlikely that he would even know, outside of comments from the chat rooms, if anyone took his submittal seriously. It was the fourth such submittal he had made. To date he had heard nothing back on any of them. Perhaps that was the way it worked. He had been anonymously praised with the second find through a chat room, but it was a mere blip within the ongoing conversations. Cyber chat was a lot like conversing in the middle of the floor of the New York Stock Exchange, and the old adage still applied. If digital conversations fell on the information forest floor, would anyone even notice?

Refocusing on work, the remainder of Friday was spent on items that were needed for other projects to close out. Brian seemed pleased with his project submittal for the major New York bank project, indicating he had done a great job. Wrapping stuff up and thinking of the new hunts for problems that he might take on for the weekend, he headed home. As he passed by the coffee bar in the lobby, he gave Julie a wave, telling her to enjoy the weekend. He totally missed her flash of smile with good wishes for his weekend, when a text on his cell phone said Buzz would meet him at seven at Elmer's. Jacob smiled at Buzz's timing, knowing he could take his backpack home and catch a cab. He liked being on time, another thing Mom had insisted upon.

CHAPTER 3

It's easier to hide when you are not on the information grid.

Buzz was already in place as Jacob walked into Elmer's at 6:45. The music wasn't too loud, and this was not a place considered "in," so the crowd was sparse. However, the beers were cold and the appetizers were affordable and delicious.

"Hey, Buzz," Jacob said as he slid into the booth. "How's it going in your world? My world thankfully has been relatively quiet for a busy work week."

"Nice of you to show, buddy," Buzz said, obviously in a funk. "I thought maybe you would stand me up like usual."

Apparently, Buzz had been here a while and was more than one beer into the evening. Something seemed just a bit off.

"Never could pass up a free beer, Buzz, especially when you owe me," Jacob said lightly. "Plus, we haven't caught up in a while, and I was looking forward to a bit of your storytelling. How did your project go, man?"

Buzz was on board with his buddy's light response. "Everything is good. I am the hero for the day, but there is this new project I may be assigned, which has me a bit worried. I submitted the project fully documented, thank you very much, and it was so well received that they said I was getting something I could really sink my teeth into. Just means more work and less time to chase the babes."

Jacob grinned. He knew that Buzz was always on the make and for the most part he attracted pretty girls, all the way until he opened his mouth. They had tried a couple of double-dates during college, but Jacob really wasn't into short-term relationships, and with school, he was far too busy to devote himself to a relationship. Though women often approached him, none so far had captured his imagination. His single-mindedness was finding software bugs and chasing bad guys in cyber space.

They discussed the newest viruses that were making the rounds and the newer defense mechanisms for an hour or so.

Then Buzz asked, "What would you think if someone asked you to create a round-up diversion program to the sixth decimal point?"

"What? Are you serious? Is your company asking you to do that? Are you nuts, man?"

This was one area that Jacob had no tolerance for. In finance, someone was always trying to divert rounding decimals, as in taking advantage of rounding past the second decimal point. The stories had been circulating for years about various programs for diversion inside and outside of the rightful institutions. Worse, many of these simply diverted the cash from the individual. Both Granny and Mom had warned him that this was where his integrity really counted. The power of computer technology and programs, in financial places especially, were such that programs could move seemingly miniscule amounts of funds and yet accumulate great wealth. This was common practice for financial institutions for dispensing interest on individual accounts, but past three decimals it was increasingly difficult to audit through as a diversion.

"Boy, are you in a bad mood. I didn't say anyone asked me to. I merely said, what would you think?" Buzz said, looking more dejected. "GEEZZZZ. Never mind the question. I was just sounding you out about some discussions from the chat rooms last night. I should have known better than to bring it up to you. No biggie. I know you are not into making big bucks. Too bad too, you have great abilities that are being squandered with just pen-testing."

As usual Buzz knew just the buttons to push, but Jacob was determined not to let him get under his skin tonight.

He looked hard at Buzz and then said, "You're right, too much reaction." Grinning, he continued, "I guess I was thinking about the little program I sent you with the flaws that I corrected so you could see the right approach and jump too high."

"Ahh, it's alright, man, I understand. You have your White Hat on. Let's talk about DEFCON. Have you decided to go this year or not?" Buzz grinned, but the damper comment had slightly shifted the fun of the evening.

"I haven't had a chance to ask for the time off. With taking time off for my mom's affairs, I think I might be denied. I will try to ask early next week and let you know. We still have almost two months until the event."

Jacob didn't say how much he wanted to go to broaden his face-to-face networking with like-minded folks.

"Hey man, I gotta go. I wanted to do some side studying this weekend. It also looks like this cute redhead has you in her sights," he added with a grin. "Hi Patty, have my seat. I was just leaving."

Patty was one of the regulars at Elmer's and had sat with the guys often over recent months. She didn't do much for Jacob, but she seemed to have her sights set on Buzz. She smiled at him and slid into the bench with Buzz.

Buzz said to Jacob, "Hey, don't go so fast. I haven't showed you my new tattoo!"

Jacob responded, "Sorry, perhaps another time." Now he was really motivated to leave. The last tattoo showing almost got them thrown out, based on where the ink was located.

"Buzz, you have really gotten into this body art thing, haven't you?"

Buzz said, "I sure have. Patty has been making some interesting suggestions. I am sure she'd help you out, man. We need to get that ugly small tat on your arm covered up. Maybe a nice dragon sleeve? All the other coders and hackers I know have some nice body art. You need to expand your horizons, man."

"Yeah.... uh, let me take that under advisement," Jacob replied as he tried not to roll his eyes.

Body art was frowned upon at his job, and he didn't need anything to put him out of favor.

To change the subject, he asked Patty, "How's the catering business?"

"It's doing great, Jacob. Happy to cater a party for you whenever you want." Patty winked as she flipped her shiny red hair behind her shoulders.

"Jacob buddy, we'll text later this weekend. Have fun, I know I will." Buzz focused on Patty.

Jacob found the door, grabbed a cab and went home. He tipped the cabbie a modest amount and received a sarcastic comment in reply, which he ignored. As he walked up the steps, he stopped and picked up all the mail out of his box, opened the door and released the alarm. Walking into his study he flipped on the lights and reached over for the power button on his PC. His movements were fluid and practiced. Jacob was an organized man who liked to make certain he wasted no movements, like a tightly choreographed dance. He entered his password and reached for his mail while his PC continued booting up completely.

The usual complement of advertisements he carefully eliminated for the recycle pile. The last item was a grey envelope with

no return address, postmarked NYC. He couldn't be sure it was
an ad so he opened it. The weight and embossing of the enclosed
paper struck Jacob as expensive. Unfolding the letter, he noticed
the fine print of the font, bold and unassuming. Starting out as
Dear Mr. Michaels, it went on with congratulating him on finding
a significant hole in their bank program and provided him a pass
to the upcoming DEFCON event in Las Vegas. It also included a
reference that his t-shirt was coming under separate cover.

"Yes!" he shouted for no one but himself.

He was invited to attend DEFCON with a benefactor. This
was a great sign. As many times as he had attended DEFCON
with his mom, this was somehow sweeter as he did not have to
purchase the ticket himself. He was amazed, proud and even more
excited than he thought possible. He searched the letter again,
reading every word very carefully. No sign of who actually sent
it by personal name or organization. No worries, he thought.
In answer to Buzz's earlier question, he had decided to attend
DEFCON. Now all he needed was time off from PT. Heck, he
would simply take the time off, approved or not.

He started doing a quick online search to see what the
airfare was from New York City to Las Vegas and to check hotel
costs. He would wait to purchase that ticket and book the hotel
until next week. He was well within the advance purchase airfare timelines. Jacob could easily afford the airfare, but it was a
game to get the lowest fare.

He still banked most of his money in his diversified investment portfolio. This, combined with the money left to him by
his mom, meant he really didn't have to worry. However, not
one to waste funds, he was ever prudent with his spending. The
townhouse was his, so his bills were modest with utilities, cell
phone and taxes.

With a new sense of determination, Jacob began trolling
the chat rooms looking for comments on dubious code that he

might sink his teeth into. He navigated through a couple of chat rooms and ended up stopping at one room where the conversation was about a problem at an unnamed New York City bank and questionable comments. He studied the conversation for a while, hoping it would help him understand where the vulnerability was located and when it had started. The best he could determine was that it was very recent, possibly even today. The extent was not yet defined, nor was the actual bank involved. Just chatter for the moment. He bookmarked it to check later and went to a few other favorite rooms.

He tried to IM Buzz, but he wasn't online. Probably still hooked up with Patty for the evening. Jacob smiled and hoped his buddy had more sense than to treat Patty casually. Pretty Patty seemed like a serious girl who shouldn't be taken for granted.

Of course, Jacob's mom always said girls should be treated with care and not just as casual flings, no matter how tempted he may be. He was a fully functioning, red-blooded American boy, but he had tried to honor Mom's wishes in his treatment of the ladies for the most part.

He always wondered what had happened between his mom and dad. Apparently, Dad had never caught on to the whole relationship thing. He quickly dismissed the thought as he had no basis for any conjecture, just a dim wish that he might understand what kind of man his father had been. Jacob would never desert his offspring, so it bothered him that his dad had done just that.

He fixed supper, ate and cleaned up before going back for another round of chat room review. Though he hardly ever commented in general chat rooms, he did like to see the exchanges. The questionable issue at the bank apparently was a hoax and several hackers were making comments about the lack of clever coding and full testing. It seemed a non-event, especially when he caught sight of a new chat comment from Buzz.

Buzz: Ping?

Buzz: Hey man, you still on line?

JAM: Yeah, what's up with the bank chatter?

Buzz: Nothing. These dorks are just so behind. It was the deal that your team worked on two weeks ago and resolved. It seems fine. Couple guys are hunting for specifics, probably feds.

JAM: Ah, good. You spent some time with Patty?

Buzz: Yepper, she'll be here in a bit to continue the weekend. She's really fun.

JAM: So it seems. You have fun. I am going to do that online tracer course and call it a night, but I'll be on early. Also, I am going to DEFCON, received a pass in the mail today

Buzz: Awesome you obviously rate, who sent 'em?

JAM: Unknown but I'm not looking for extra lives in Angry Birds! No flights yet will let you know.

Buzz: Cool later. Patty just rang the bell. See ya!

Jacob closed the window and went in search of the online tracer course he had signed up for earlier. This course would extend his tool set to help him trace for rootkits installed in firmware, hypervisor and the kernel. He was already an expert for those placed in the user-mode applications. This course would enable him to see more sophisticated exploiting, as in serious malware intended for stealing anything from identities, corporate secrets or funds from financial institutions. Jacob wanted to stay current on tracing these issues. All the headline cases of hackers were at these levels.

Jacob spent the next six hours completing the web-based course, picking up a few tidbits he hadn't seen before. Tired of looking at his screen, he cleaned his cyber tracks and shut down his PC. Crashing onto his bed, he fell into a dreamless sleep.

CHAPTER 4

Subtle exploitation only occurs when you think you are watching closely.

Jacob was tracking a new potential vulnerability that he had discovered. This one was so interesting that after work most days he was focused on breaking into the code. He normally didn't do this during the work week as he tended to lose track of time. But this one was fascinating. Something was just not right. He kept at it nightly, making notations on the avenues he had tried, methodically working his way through the program.

This was a very large program, and it took major concentration to follow the lines of code from one end to the other. There must have been more than a hundred threads to follow. He estimated this one would take him several weeks to finish reviewing. Perhaps there were no issues here, but it was nagging at him. The format was definitely old school. Much more like Granny's or Mom's coding structures.

Asking Brian for the time off to attend DEFCON was easier than Jacob had thought. He'd reach out to Buzz tonight on logistics and to set his air travel. He wrapped up his project review for the day and gave Brian the information on a thumb drive on his way out. Another project completed.

Throwing on his backpack, he waved to Julie on his way out the door. She flashed her usual smile and waved back. Unlocking his bike, he mounted up for the ride home. The weather was really nice, and since he was leaving on time for a Friday, the traffic would not be difficult to maneuver around. He made it home in good time, pulled his bike up the steps and secured it with the lock. He immediately noticed the soft-pack protruding from the mailbox. The package was opened at one end, making it look like the postman had taken a bite out of it before leaving it in his box. He smiled as he recalled the promised t-shirt.

Opening the package, Jacob was not disappointed. The front of the shirt read 'Better to have hacked and conquered', and on the back it read 'Than never to have hacked at all'. Perfect. This was definitely in his wardrobe for DEFCON. Then he noticed the soft-pack also had papers stuffed inside. He reached in and pulled out First Class airfare from New York LaGuardia to Las Vegas. Wow, that was so not expected. He examined the package again and found there was no return address. Who was this benefactor and what was their expectation? Jacob hated owing anyone, especially someone unknown, but the feeling of having reached this pinnacle won out.

This time there was no letter, but the airline tickets had his full name and even his reward number. There was a paid in full voucher in his name for the Las Vegas Hilton as well. This pulled him up short. Jacob took great pains in concealing his identity, and though the forum he had submitted to with the code changes and program had asked for an address, he never filled in his full name, only JAM as an online identity. As Alice in Wonderland would say, "curious-er and curious-er". First the invite and pass to DEFCON addressed to JAM, now airfare and hotel in his full name. Airfare had to be in your full name for ID checking at the gates, thank you Homeland Security. He was definitely involved with an unknown class of folks to have this much detailed information on him. His immediate concern was to reinforce his identity concealment. Obviously, he had more work to do in this area. Something was exposed. He fervently believed cyber thievery and the prevalent identity theft was no joke.

Still frowning as he booted up his PC and began organizing for his evening activity, he first reviewed his identity concealment barriers and routine password changes before going back to the problem program. None of his investment or banking finances were set up online under his real name but rather a pseudo-name. Jacob added a few layers to his identity concealment and also added a tracking program should someone start hunting his personal information. He felt a bit better with this in place and returned his focus to the newest Open Source program under his review. He wanted to try out some new ideas on reorganizing the program. Being Friday night, Jacob had the whole weekend to focus. Jacob had his rhythm going when a familiar chirp sounded. He opened the window to see Buzz asking for help.

> Buzz: Hey JAM man, you in?
>
> JAM: Right here, what's up?
>
> Buzz: I need some of your expertise buddy. New program due Monday and it's really a bear.
>
> JAM: Come on Buzz, I am off the clock Also got my shirt today and it rocks.
>
> Buzz: Cool. White Hat intact. So 'bout helping out your old buddy? This could launch me big time man.
>
> JAM: What is it you're stuck on maybe I can IM you through it.
>
> Buzz: Nope it is bigger than an X-Box. I need the programs to interact for ID positive in five places
>
> JAM: argh! What are you doing breaking into Fort Knox? Ok send me the info and the IDs for testing. You need to learn more.
>
> Buzz: lol. thanks buddy, I promise I always learn from you.

Okay, he'd ignore that for a while as he returned to his hunt through the program. With so many crackers from all over the world in the financial sector either doing identity theft or simply moving monies around, there were many places to hide unscrupulous code. Open Source, by the sheer nature of its broad availability, was the primary target.

With all the budget cuts across U.S. businesses, the idea of freeware to save spending was often used for what was termed lower level needs. The problem with lower level needs is they inevitably interacted with something at a higher level, thus opening the doors to malware breaches. Much like Buzz's request, integration to multiple databases is clearly a way to rapid access other information. With the success rate climbing for social engineering into company data, security continued to be a problem and these types of programs simply exacerbated the risk to company proprietary information.

Humans liked being flattered and asked for their opinions, often not taking care to notice who was asking. That, along with the challenging global economy, was forcing increased Open Source use, which led to increased vulnerability in companies and to individuals. Discussion rooms were filled with APAC and EMEA government-sponsored crackers, plus the rogue individual wannabes. This new breed seemed to be prevalent and annoying but fortunately not as experienced and destructive as they could become, especially with the good guys watching. As Buzz had previously suggested, his White Hat was intact.

Jacob kept running through each of the program threads until the first hour of Saturday when he decided to take a break and look at Buzz's newest request. The guidelines Buzz provided were pretty straightforward, but the access to the various areas that were a part of Buzz's notes didn't totally make sense. He reviewed the notes and texted Buzz a few more times until he felt he had a good understanding of the need. Using his standard formats, he hammered out the code required and began localized testing. Once the localized testing was completed and the changes reflected in his code, he accessed the remote data sources and tested all the sequences again.

Yep, he thought, he was going to have to review with Buzz, again, the nature of complex password interactions to multiple data sources. Perhaps a few hours at DEFCON could be set aside for this activity, and others could chime in as well. If Buzz was really going to move up, he had to do it on his own two brain cells. Jacob resolved that he would not continue to prop Buzz up. The bank was in the big league, and Buzz could either make the cut or fail on his own. Testing completed, he wrapped up all the code and committed it to a thumb drive. This was entirely too big and too sensitive to email. He would run it by Buzz's place later this afternoon.

Jacob crashed for a while and woke up starving. He ate a hearty breakfast of his own creation and loaded up for a quick bike ride which would also take him by Buzz's. The weather was beautiful, and the ride around Central Park was just what he needed to clear his head. He noticed folks out walking, kids playing, families picnicking, and the ever-present tourists. After completing his 60 miles, he headed over to Buzz's place.

Buzz answered the door, looking almost awake with coffee in hand. Jacob heard the noise of the TV in the background. Buzz invited him inside and as he entered the kitchen, he saw Patty at the stove.

"Hey Patty, I sure didn't expect to see you here. What's cooking? It smells great." Jacob smiled at his buddy.

"I am just finishing up creating pasta with shrimp and Caesar salad for a late lunch, early dinner thing. If you want to share, there is more than enough," Patty offered.

Her glance to Buzz indicated it was okay for the invite as well.

"Sure, that would be great, thanks. Hey, Buzz, while she is finishing that up, can we chat in your office?"

"Sure, come on," Buzz said as he moved toward his home office. "What's up that we need to chat in here? You know Patty is oblivious to most technology talk."

"I know, but this is more about you, Buzz," Jacob continued. "I fixed all the programs and ran the testing. We need to review this, and you need to understand so you can work on your own. I don't have the time to do your job and mine. Plus, man, you should never provide me the access to your test systems. That is such a security breach. Granted I am a great guy, your friend and a wonderful programmer, but this needs to stop."

"Come on, man, you know that I can do it, just not as fast and flawlessly as you. Okay, okay, I will take a deep look and stop asking favors," Buzz said as he took the thumb drive and dropped the contents onto his hard drive. "Wow!" He exclaimed. "You broke down each of these into individual programming modules that can be reused, complete with directions and testing routines."

His eyes continued to scan the content of the notes. Buzz was a fast reader; slow programmer but fast reader.

"Okay, I see what you mean by your framework methodology now; this is what you were saying your mom taught you. I've never seen it put together into this type of structure. Man, this is so easy. Yep, I can take it from here. This will take me to the big time. I can reuse the modules for other routines. That's how you get stuff done so fast."

"I don't know about big time," Jacob smiled, hoping Buzz really did get it. "But I am glad you have the whole end-to-end example to use as a go-by. Heck, with the programs in here you could make or keep a fortune for your company. Keep your own White Hat intact rather than trying to wear mine."

"Yeah, right," Buzz thoughtfully replied, momentarily lost in his dreams of grandeur. "Okay, let's eat. All this work on top of last night with Patty is making me extra hungry."

The next couple of hours the threesome ate, laughed, and told some great stories. Jacob thanked Patty for her efforts and headed home. He was grateful he was back on his bike after eating so much food. He thought the whole afternoon was good and that Buzz could work on his own. And it was interesting that Patty was becoming a more permanent fixture for Buzz. Perhaps she could keep him on the straight and narrow.

He hit the townhouse and spent the remainder of the weekend testing each of the threads of the problem program. He was certain there was something there, but so far, he could not put his finger on it. He saw a small routine in the middle of a thread that looked out of place but that turned out to be a dead end. Nothing else popped out as a warning. After completing roughly eighty percent of the review, he was a bit disheartened to have found nothing significant.

CHAPTER 5

The rules always favor those willing to risk getting hurt!

The next two weeks screamed by at work. Jacob still did not have a big project, but he had been assisting with several projects and felt some of his contributions made a huge positive impact. Brian was happy when the billable items were all completed prior to his departure to DEFCON on Thursday afternoon. Four days in the midst of geeks, hackers, feds, programmers and who knows what kind of fun. After all he was headed to the land of no time and no tales, Las Vegas.

Buzz was not going to arrive in Vegas until the next day because of a work issue. When they had last talked, Buzz was definitely on a high for something he had done. Perhaps Jacob could pry the details from him. He walked up to the check in counter at the Las Vegas Hilton with his reservation confirmation in hand. He was giving his name to the clerk when a movement on his right caught his eye.

A female was also checking in with another clerk. What caught his eye was her shirt. She had a shirt just like the one he had received in the mail. The same grey with black lettering. He had not worn his shirt on the flight since he was saving it for the main event tomorrow. Yep, as she moved her backpack to access her wallet, he clearly saw the words, *Than never to have hacked at all*. He smiled as he took in details about her. Hair worn in a severe bun, but dark and light colors swirling together, dark framed glasses, big brown eyes he imagined, and slight build. Not much of a shape per se, definitely compact and on the short side. Nice legs, he grinned. He was definitely a leg guy. He doubted the top of her head would reach his shoulder. No quick smile either. She glanced his way with a serious expression as she finished her check in process. Not even the hint of a smile passed her lips.

The check in clerk pulled Jacob from his perusal to have him sign for the room and suggested some sights to see in Las Vegas. By the time he was finished and had picked up his backpack to move, the woman had vanished. Jacob shrugged, assuming he might run into her at the event. Perhaps he could discover how she had received her shirt. The idea was gently planted in his mind, making him grin and shake his head.

Jacob's room was amazing. It contained not only the usual amenities of bed and bathroom but also a separate sitting area and workspace which he could make use of while attending the convention.

DEFCON is a convention that brings together the high-end hacker and cracker community to discuss and share information regarding Open Source, security, technology changes and associated technology shifts. A very broad range of folks attended, some of whom he might know from previous events and some simply by reputation.

While looking at the convention offerings and deciding what he would attend, he laughed when he came across the titles of a couple of seminars, *Mamma, Don't Let Your Babies Grow Up to be Pen-Testers*, which touted the other side of the penetration-testing business, and Lock Picking, designed for the younger up-and-coming cracker crowd. He could have used DEFCON when he was eight even though Granny and Mom had already made sure he was well-coached in technology.

He registered for several sessions which interested him, including *Staying Connected During a Revolution or Disaster, Traps of Gold: Hacking the Global Economy with GPUs or How I Learned to Stop Worrying and Love Bitcoin, Owned Over Amateur Radio: Remote Kernel Exploitation in 2011* and *Covert Post-Exploitation Forensics with Metasploit.* He received the summary of his selections with his badge. Jacob really wanted to attend all the forensic sessions as he could apply this information to his work and to his personal endeavors. The first session was scheduled for early morning.

Wandering around the floor, he saw many vendors and their products. Like any convention, there were sellers, buyers, observers, and personal networking opportunities. It was a place to be seen. The best of the best good guys or bad guys attended this event. Even the FBI had a booth for recruiting folks. He knew from his three-month internship at the FBI, while in his final semester at MIT, that they recruited from the top one percent at all the technology schools. They had made him an offer, but he really didn't want to work for the government, at least not yet. His mom had suggested he get a wide range of experience domestically and internationally before considering a government position. She didn't trust the government, but Jacob suspected that was more from her time in Europe than her life in the U.S. Of course, that was purely speculation on his part. Too bad she was so secretive about her overseas exploits and family history.

He ran into a few guys he had seen in prior years. Outside of possibly tripping on one another in a chat room, they rarely communicated. Funny, they all seemed to have instant recall on prior discussions, so it was to a degree like seeing old friends. These were all brilliant guys with a passion for technology and information security and basically White Hats. Like him, they mostly hated social media postings, like Facebook or Twitter, as that was viewed as great fodder for social engineering and often resulted in identity compromise or out-and-out identity theft. They took their financial, personal, and family security very seriously. One of the grey beards, a term for anyone in the technology field for over ten years, tag name Quip, had brought his 12-year-old nephew. Quip said his nephew was getting really good at finding vulnerabilities, and Quip was glad that some sessions at this year's DEFCON would help keep the kid on the good side of the fine line.

To help keep some semblance of order, the DEFCON organizers had launched some fun but harmless hacking exercises for the attendees rather than let them amuse themselves. Complaints about PC and cell phones being hacked in prior years for sport was something the organizers were trying to avoid. Many guys he knew signed up for a few of the onsite contests that were taking place, then regrouped in a central spot for lunch and serious people watching. Comments about passing folks, as well as speculation on their status and predisposition for good or evil, made for lively conversation. Jacob suspected the group was correct ninety percent of the time. He saw one guy pass with a shirt like his, and the group made some positive comments about the guy and his abilities. Jacob could only imagine what they'd say when he wore his shirt tomorrow.

You could identify the long-term hackers by their skin, which usually resembled fish underbellies, their only color being from creative tattoos which covered all genres and in many cases much of their exposed skin. Even at a convention like this, the Feds were spotted with their well-cut suits. There were very few females in the crowd, and yet the younger set seemed about split between girls and boys. Then he caught sight of the woman he'd seen at the check in desk coming out of the exhibit hall.

Quip made a low whistle and said mostly to himself, "Well, lookie here, Petra decided to make an appearance after all. That makes this just a whole lot more interesting now."

Jacob was about to make a comment when the woman named Petra seemed to make a beeline to Quip. He rose and gave her a hug hello, which she returned along with a quick whisper in his ear.

Quip turned to face the group and said, "Guys, want to introduce you to Petra, one of the best encryption gurus in Europe on a special six-month assignment here in the States. Glad you could make it and class up this event a bit, Petra. These guys are regular Joes like me, except for number one in his MIT grad class, Jacob over there."

Petra nodded to each of the guys in turn.

With a longer look at Jacob and quick appraisal, she said, "Hi there, Jacob" and quickly turned back to Quip.

She sat down with Quip, a little too far away from Jacob to engage in casual conversation. She spoke in quiet tones with Quip while the others resumed discussions on the foot traffic.

Quip was never who he seemed to be, mostly because you could never get a straight answer out of him. Once while standing with a group of other propeller-heads, Quip was asked who he worked for, and he answered that he did mostly volunteer work.

When the individual pressed him for more information, he said, "I work with a group of volunteers that likes to destabilize third world dictatorships and oppressive military juntas. I like to cater the heavy weapons for them. The load order of the equipment and weapons into the C130 Hercules is critical to a successful deployment, particularly when you're under fire."

Most of the group wandered off right after that description. He frequently sported a limp, supporting himself with a walking cane. His colleagues had learned that invariably someone would ask what had happened to him, and no one wanted to miss his explanation. So once again someone wandered into the group, this time a female, and she had to ask what had happened. He did not fail to provide an outrageous answer.

With all due seriousness, Quip lamented, "I fell and hurt my leg while trying to stand and fuck in a hammock."

The poor woman, trying to recover some of her dignity while turning nine shades of red, responded, "Well, I guess it was fortunate that it was only your leg that got hurt."

Quip retorted with a grin, "Wasn't it though? Of course, if it had been something else, I wouldn't be limping now."

Jacob listened to the lively banter as well as heard small parts of the exchange between Quip and Petra, though nothing that made a lot of sense. He did take the time to observe her. He again noted her slight build, though she was taller than he had first thought. He suspected the lack of more feminine distinction had to do with her choice of professions rather than her inability to look like a lady. An encryption guru was an elitist. He wondered if her focus was on one thing such as desktop, data, software, or email encryption. He had heard some chat room discussions about current encryption software developed to prevent snooping on smart phones and SIP technologies. Open Standards like Open Source were easier to adopt into an environment but typically with less security than companies needed to protect their customers and information.

He sat there and observed her in profile. It was impossible not to admire her fine bone structure, porcelain skin, unadorned eyes of brown with long lashes, and with her hair up in a bun, her thin neck was straight and strong like her posture. She wasn't giggly and quick with a smile, like Julie at the coffee bar, or Patty, but rather focused. His observations continued for the next half an hour or so when the group finally got up and all went their separate ways. Petra, he noticed, went back toward the exhibit hall. Jacob decided he needed to take a look at the exhibits as well after saying goodbye to the others. Plus, he found her very intriguing and wanted to know more.

Jacob entered through the main door of the exhibit hall to all the banners and noise. The crowd was relatively dense which was fully expected for the introduction day. Jacob knew from experience that the crowds would thin out after the seminars began and folks focused on specific areas of interest. This afternoon was more of a reconnaissance on what was available to attendees, as well as opportunities to troll the vendors and reconnect with folks. Petra was nowhere in sight, having been swallowed up by the crowd. Jacob decided that he would work from the right side of the hall to the left, thinking she would be working the hall left to right. For some reason he wanted a chance to speak to her alone, which was both annoying and compelling. Surely, he had no other interest in her, other than what he might learn from her regarding encryption. For now, that was his story, and he was sticking to it.

Jacob made his way down each of the vendor rows. Some were selling software tools, others additional products, and some services for contract. It covered every contingency and every experience level. Even the kids, in tow with their parents, were finding booths of interest. Conversations that he caught in passing also covered the "how to do thus-and-such", through to the "I did this-and-that". Some of the conversations were fairly detailed, and the speakers made it clear that they didn't care who might be listening. It was amazing that people thought they had anonymity, especially as packed as this hall was. He stopped to speak to a few fellow programmers and pen-testers he had associated with at one time or another, catching up on stuff. Jacob did more listening and encouraged them to talk rather than bragging from his side. By the time he rounded the last row he had not caught sight of Petra and was ready to retire. It had been a long travel day, and he wanted to be fresh for the morning sessions he'd signed up to attend.

Jacob returned to his room and ordered room service. After eating he fell into bed, travel finally catching up to him. As he slept, he dreamed of conversations with his mom, specifically focused on protecting himself, keeping his personal information private, covering his tracks, his passwords, and his internet dealings. Even his choice of internet handle in JAM had not been to his mom's liking, as it was too close to reality. They had disagreed about hiding in plain sight and those philosophies. She also admonished him, in his dream, for letting someone find out enough about him to provide a plane ticket to this event. In the dream they worked out a plan to modify his personal security even further, and he agreed when he returned home to reinvent his internet persona.

He woke up early with resolve on several fronts. He suspected that those nagging details about his personal security had been in the back of his mind all along, and it had taken complete relaxation to help move them toward a solution. He connected from his room and again carefully changed passwords and moved accounts from one place to another. He was pleased to see that nothing had crossed the border security he had established when he had first received the specifically named airline tickets. He also took a quick view of his work email and saw nothing that required his attention.

He ordered room service again for breakfast and dressed. He wore his prized t-shirt, hoping that he would meet others of like mind. Maybe he would locate Petra and have some serious discussion about encryption. With the way that Quip had reverently referred to her, Jacob felt she would be a great contact to include in his personal experts' network. Networking with like-minded folks at his level had been beneficial so far in his career, though he always felt he was providing the answers rather than asking the questions. He locked his PC into the room safe and grabbed his badge, and then went to the meeting room area on the convention level.

CHAPTER 6

Once the train is in motion, you can only stop it from inside.

Jacob worked his way with the herds through the security process. He attended his first session on new security tools for Unix and Open Source. He picked up a few tips but was disappointed that he was already fully versed in most of the information covered, although a little extra knowledge was always welcome. It was tough trying to stay current with technology that changed so fast.

Jacob ran into Buzz at the Traps of Gold session. After the session, which was quite insightful on various hacker and cracker techniques, Buzz pulled him aside.

"Nice shirt, man. Is that the one anonymously sent to you? Very cool, buddy." Buzz seemed envious.

"It is and I actually saw two yesterday walking around. I really didn't get a chance to hook up and talk to them but perhaps later today. It feels cool to be part of something. I'm just not certain what that something is yet," Jacob grinned.

"Hey man, I wanted to thank you for the programs and information you brought over the other day. I get what you were referring to with the framework and even found a very creative

40

way to deploy those subroutines." Buzz smiled and shook his hand. "You are still my best friend and I appreciate your kicking my butt, as it were. I'm trying to get more structured."

Jacob invoked with an even tone, "I know you believe what you are saying at this moment. But it's important for you to pay attention to the details, Buzz. You are dealing with a great deal of financial information for thousands of folks, and being careless or sloppy will bite your ass. You have to be responsible with your program interactions. I won't always be around to bail you out."

Laughing slightly, Buzz justified, "I know that you always think I oversimplify or take the easy route, but this time I have found a way to move forward. And I owe it all to you. You are really my oldest and best friend, man, so thanks. I will be happy to buy dinner and drinks tomorrow if you are free. Just call my cell."

"Alright, buddy. Gotta go to the Hacking the Global Economy session. I think I signed up for the last seat."

"You must have cause I couldn't buy my way into that session. Let me know all the ways to improve my fortune, okay? Don't say it. I'm just kidding. I'm being responsible. Promise."

Jacob went down the last hall, entering the room for the session. It was nearly full, but people were still milling about chatting. He saw a couple more folks he knew and tipped his head. He looked around for a seat near the back, when he spotted Petra. He convinced two people to move over so he could sit next to her.

"Hello there, glad to see you again, Petra."

She gave him a serious look and an almost smile, "Hi, Jacob, thought I might see you here. I was hoping we might have a chance to chat. Quip seems to think highly of you. It might be good to see what kind of common ground we have on programming structures, testing, and encryption methods."

"That'd be great." He smiled, eager for the discussion. "I was hoping for that very discussion with you. Especially after Quip gave you such a strong endorsement yesterday. He said you were in the U.S. temporarily but left off where home is. I can't place your accent."

Petra looked at him intensely, then said, "My home is in Luxembourg, but I work all over Europe and some in Asia Pac, depending on the needs of my customers. I have a smattering of many languages as needed for work, but over the years have worked very hard to remove any accent. My first language was Polish though, then English. I had private tutors until I attended college."

Surprised, he said, "Funny, that was my first language as well, but I have not used it much. Interesting though it . . ."

He abruptly stopped as the session was brought to order, and the speakers commenced their presentation. The information was very detailed and focused on programs that protect financial transactions that span global commerce. There was some extensive discussion about digital currency, which was fascinating.

Speaker 1 opened with the history, "Bitcoin was created in 2009 as a method to enable payment or micropayments without the need for a central authority, more of a peer-to-peer currency. People interact with Bitcoin using a "wallet," which can be stored on their computer by the Bitcoin software or hosted on a third-party website. It has enjoyed good and bad press, trying to be the internet currency or else global currency alternative.

"The problem with Bitcoin is the same thing that people love about Bitcoin: it leaves no trace. It takes an incredible amount of computing power to create new Bitcoins with a PC. You can, of course, just buy them on an exchange, which is what most people do. A complicated algorithm keeps the total supply steady. Once these digital coins are created, they're still just a handful of bits and bytes, a little piece of encrypted code. There is no fundamental value. It is an idea that in today's shaky economy is considered risky by many. There was also reference to another digital currency that was gaining some ground in Asia called SECcoin. It appeared to have limited distribution, but the reports were more favorable than those of Bitcoin."

The questions and answers segment of the session were really digging deep into the information and possible negative impact of technology hackers on the overall global economy. Then discussion ventured down to crackers and their negative impact on the economy, and the value of multiple security layers and increased complex encryption. The continuing rise of problem groups out of Eastern Europe and APAC, especially China, were also touched on and some loudly protested the attack. Individual discussions continued as the session ended and folks were exiting.

"What session did you sign up for next, Petra?" Jacob hoped it was the one he had picked.

"I didn't. There is nothing in this hour or the next that I found interesting."

"I signed up for a session to fill the time, but if you'd rather go and find a place to talk, I believe I would enjoy learning more about encryption from your perspective and what you are seeing." As well as learning a bit more about you, he thought.

"That sounds good to me, Jacob. I would like to learn more about your work. I like your shirt. I did not wear mine today, but I know what it takes to get one, so you interest me. Perhaps we can share information, like humans with talking rather than machine talk. There are times when I tire of electronic communications, though I do it all the time. Voices are nice." She smiled nicely, but not too openly at him.

"Totally agree," he chuckled.

They found an area on the same level with no one around. The chairs were comfortable as they settled in to chat. Jacob was admiring the fit of her jeans, mentally removing her garments and speculating on what he might find underneath, when he snapped back to reality. He was attracted to her, but she was a new professional contact. He could not explain why he was drawn to her like few women ever before, so he tossed it up to hormones. She was becoming too fascinating.

"Jacob, what is it that you do? Quip mentioned some of your talents yesterday and seems impressed, but I would like to hear your story." She looked at him straight on with no guile.

"Really? Quip is a great guy that I have known for some time. Mostly online, but we have crossed paths in person three or four times. Funny he has never mentioned you until the introduction yesterday. Actually, he talks very little about himself or people he knows, just security stuff."

"As I would expect, for a poor conversationalist like Quip. I too am very private until I fully trust someone," she said with a slight smile. "So please tell me a bit about Jacob."

"I work for a pen-tester organization, PT, Inc. The firm supports requests from the financial industry. We do a lot of system and access checking across their networks, reviews of programs, changes, and upgrade plans. With banking institutions there is always the fear that the bad guys will get into the systems, take passwords, extract money and cause problems."

"And do you like the work?" She asked with penetrating eyes.

"I do like it. Especially when I find something that others have overlooked. I like getting to the source of the problems, closing gaps and knowing that the institution is safe until the next time. It is a funny business in that we are called when a problem is suspected. I find in some of the freelance work I pursue I like to find the source of the problem before the problem has had a chance to create issues for organizations. Open Source seems to be the potential soup de jour on that front."

He thought of the efforts he'd made to earn the shirt, yet he was not comfortable revealing the details. Some people did not appreciate volunteered program changes distributed on the Internet.

"So, what you are saying is that you like to get ahead of the curve? Do you consider yourself a good guy or a bad guy in the technology field? As in, do you create programs that cause problems or just fix and remove ones that do?" As she spoke her eyes seemed to be trying to reach his soul.

Jacob chuckled, "I can build programs that cause problems and that has a certain appeal, more for catching others. But I'd have to say I'm essentially a good guy. My mom taught me right from wrong when I was very little. She is actually a very large part of what I am today. I guess you could say I am, to a degree, following in her footsteps as well as her mother who migrated to the U.S. from Poland. I recently lost my mom, which makes me want to work harder to continue her legacy."

"I'm sorry for your loss. I can hear in your voice that you must have loved her a great deal. Was she a pen-tester as well?" Concern and sympathy showed on her face.

"I did love her, and no, she wasn't a pen-tester. She was a programmer and telecommunications specialist. However, back to your question, I can do programming that could be interpreted as bad or modified for bad behavior. I just couldn't deliver them with that in mind. After graduation, I wanted to find different ways to use my talents outside of simply programming. I find this industry is filled with people that are talented, though easily corrupted. Money is a great driver for unsavory activities. I like to find the bad guys and make things right. And you, Miss Petra, what is your depth of encryption algorithms? Quip seems very impressed with your skill level." He was surprised at the depth of his interest.

"I've worked in this field for several years. I came up through the ranks, starting very early with programming and knowledge of interpreting other code sets. Recently I've spent a lot of time with rootkits from a malware perspective. Like you, I guess, I like to discover the bad and eradicate it. I have found though in my years of programming and slicing and dicing others' programs apart, that the talent of folks today is either very sloppy or very, very good. I mostly freelance for customers depending upon the need.

"Currently, I am working with an institution in the U.S. in New York City, which is being considered for purchase by a firm in Switzerland. I am checking out their technology infrastructure overall and seeing if they have any problems with their security and the nature of their encryption levels. It is a bit dated, but so far effective. In fifteen years, they have never had an information breach. This is a good thing considering the firm that is thinking of the purchase. For this job, I am actually working for both firms. Both firms will benefit from my knowledge and the information I provide. More consulting, though at a very in-depth level from multiple perspectives, and I am providing summaries to both companies." She smiled with the obvious next question forming in his mind.

"Interesting. So how long have you been freelancing, and most importantly, can you make a good living doing that? You hardly seem old enough to have been doing this for years." He grinned, thinking that the depth of her sentiment might align with his.

Petra laughed, "Yes, I make a good living. I actually have for the last four years doing this type of activity. Trust me, I am old enough, especially when my papa started me at the ripe old age of ten. He did not want to have me question what I would do, so he started early."

"I have found in the U.S. that a freelancer alone, without rock solid credentials from the Feds, is likely to starve waiting for jobs, hence my joining PT." Jacob was opening up to her in a surprising way.

They continued discussing several items of technology and programming. He looked her over again, pleased at what he saw. He was apprehensive at the growing attraction as well as the sudden need to reveal a bit more about himself. Disconcerting. After discussing several subjects, he was astounded that an hour had passed.

Jacob continued, "At some point, I would like to have my own organization to help protect financial institutions. I feel that they are at the greatest risk as the world gets smaller and smaller. I want to help make certain that the average Joe feels their monies are protected and that they can trust their institutions with their livelihood. Political powers come and go, but financial well-being cannot afford to be corrupted. I suspect that there are very powerful men, no offense, who think they can rule the world. Most threats these days I believe are from those gaining in technology knowledge that think stealing is the proper avenue. Those who have no moral compass are on the rise, and the headlines seem to agree."

"No offense taken." Petra looked long and hard at Jacob, then continued, "However, technology knows no gender, nor does corruption. Women simply have other avenues to exploit than men. People have been greedy forever for land, possessions, riches, and enslaving others. The wars of the past have been fought for these things. Are you suggesting that you could create such an organization and meet that goal? I would not have suspected you were so naïve, Jacob, to think that you could wield that sort of power."

Jacob swallowed a bit and then said, "No, I think that is the case. However, there are so many rogues out there willing to do anything for a buck. Maybe I'm jaded at this point, but good guys need to form up versus the bad guys without country boundaries, but rather technology safeguards. I have recently come from a deal where someone tried to add in some really poor malware to extract passwords. It was done so badly, I picked it out easily and blocked the problem. Just looked like someone trying for quick funds access. I think the lines are blurred these days in finding the bad guys. The speculations in the blogs, news sources, and underground are all over the map."

"Oh, there are some folks out there trying to get the dollars, and then there are others trying to get the millions and absolute control in the same process. Take care that you do not find the obvious and ignore the hidden. This is today's current game, and the sophistication is becoming better all the time. On that I agree with you. You just surprise me with your view, considering you work in New York City.

"Enough of that. What did you do for the shirt you are wearing?" Her face becoming calm and her eyes not as piercing, she smiled slightly and seemed to be interested in him as well.

The pride was evident on his face as he explained, "I was able to find a problem in a Unix-based program that was available in freeware, Open Source. It had some structure issues. I corrected the issues and posted my findings with a lot of detail and program revisions. At least with the new programming changes I added, folks that use this particular freeware can have confidence that breaking it will take an extremely high talent and only from the inside. At least that is what I think I did. Hard to tell when all you get is a shirt, hotel accommodations, and airfare tickets. And yours, what did you do?"

"What?" Petra's voice was rising, and irritation was suddenly present as she continued with a tightened expression. "Are you saying you received a shirt as well as hotel accommodations and airfare tickets? How can that be? Someone has to know your information quite well to do airfare post-911. I would have thought with your background you would take better care of concealment from identity theft."

"Well, yeah, I thought it was odd. I received a note to my JAM presence that my shirt would arrive in a few days. When it did there were airline tickets and a prepaid room here at DEFCON. I thought it was odd as well and modified my personal security settings everywhere." He quickly moved into defense mode, feeling angry that their fun discussion was ended.

"Jacob, you are compromised. Quip had indicated that you were very careful and that he really had not been able to find out much about you over the years. I thought even from talking with you now, that you understood how bad the bad guys can be. They know you and your details. You are obviously a target or at the very least at risk." She looked angry and sad at the same time.

The thought that she would pity him pissed him off.

He tersely added, "Don't you think you are being just a bit over the top with someone you only recently met? Who do you think you are talking to?"

"I am not overreacting and you, Jacob, are far too lax. I am telling you; you need to leave here now. Go home, Jacob. You are not yet mature enough to play in this world. I had presumed you were better prepared and better taught." Her entire being seemed to dismiss him.

"Better taught? We've been talking all of thirty minutes and you want to judge my mom and her training of me? Well, thanks for the free advice, however, I will finish the show here. I have lots to learn and still some folks to speak to." He calmly spoke while rising to his full height as if to bully her.

"No, you will go now. I will see what I can find and fix for you. Technology is good and bad, always. You simply must know what side you are on. Go home, Jacob. I guess I can say, almost great to meet you. Perhaps another time in the future, we can speak more when you have grown." With that outburst, Petra rose and stomped away quickly, leaving Jacob with his mouth wide open.

Jacob admonished himself for revealing so much to Petra. He was thoroughly angry and bewildered at her outburst. Where did she come off telling him to grow up? He was still bristling from the taught better comment. How dare she criticize his mother? Obviously she was a nut case, and he would catch up with Quip and get some extra details about this female. And to think he even considered looking at her legs. Argh! He had no intention of leaving DEFCON with two more days to go.

He rushed off to his last session of the day, but had a hard time keeping his focus on the information presented. He saw no one he knew. After the session he returned to his room and logged in to check his security for all of his accounts. Everything was in order with nothing breached. Feeling a bit better and wanting to put Petra out of his mind, he ordered room service. Once it arrived, he decided to browse around a few sites and chat rooms.

After a few hours of working on various little things and some remote chats to help a few buds, he signed off and crashed. His dreams were filled with replays of his conversation with Petra that had gone south so quickly. He even tried changing the conversation in his dreams, but the result was the same. She insulted him and told him to go home, like some child.

CHAPTER 7

Dreams and nightmares
so closely related,
yet opposite spectrums.

A screeching alarm thankfully pulled him from his lousy sleep. He wasn't in a good mood. Jacob wanted to find Petra and find out what her problem was and why she had reacted the way she did. He showered but decided breakfast could wait until he went downstairs to DEFCON. There was a meager breakfast served for attendees before the first session. Perhaps he would be able to locate Petra, or at least Quip. At the last minute he decided he would take his PC with him for notes on the two sessions he looked forward to attending today.

Just when Jacob thought things couldn't get any worse, the DEFCON security check point refused his entry. His badge would not scan as recognized.

Jacob protested, "I've already been attending this event, and you passed me through yesterday without a beat. Come on, man, don't you remember me?"

The bruiser at the door laughed and said, "That's what they all say, Mac. Your badge is invalid, and you don't enter. End of story."

Jacob was pissed. "I have been here. I'm signed up for a session. And I am entitled to breakfast, so move out of my way."

"Mac, you are not going in here on my watch. I was hired to keep out the riffraff. With an invalid badge, you are considered riffraff. Step away, unless you want the casino security guys headed this way to escort you outside."

Jacob glanced over and saw two very large guys in dark suits approaching. Security in casinos is not a laughing matter, so he walked back toward the registration desk. He asked the pleasant woman running the registration counter to look up his name and hoped it was simply a matter of reprinting his badge. She was unable to locate his name and indicated he must be mistaken. He was not registered. She agreed that the badge he had looked right, but obviously it wasn't valid. The lady was sorry, but registration had closed last night. No additional attendees could be registered as all the classes scheduled were full.

Trying to justify the situation, he reasoned it wasn't like he'd paid for his ticket. Of course, that meant he didn't have a receipt. Petra's comments came back like a sledgehammer. Jacob turned and walked away toward the nearest restaurant. His empty stomach and the security bruisers were not improving the lousy mood that had started his day.

He sat down and ordered breakfast. The waitress brought his food quickly, and he consumed it with a vengeance. He was feeling much better and felt ready to find Quip and Petra, although he had no real way of reaching either of them unless he saw them. Jacob signed the ticket with his room number, printing his name as indicated.

The waitress returned several minutes later asking Jacob if he could rewrite his room number on the check. When Jacob confirmed he had written down the correct information she began shaking her head with a weak smile, saying that he must

be mistaken about the room number because he was not registered in the hotel. She asked if he had another form of payment
for the meal.

"You need to go check again," Jacob was beginning to get
really angry, though he knew that taking it out on the waitress
was pointless. "If that doesn't work, then I want to speak to your
manager."

The waitress went away to recheck and returned a few
minutes later with her manager in tow. The manager conveyed
the same information that the waitress had provided and asked
for an alternate form of payment. Jacob handed over his credit
card, signed the check and left in search of someone he knew.
This was beginning to look like another bad dream rather than
a new day.

Jacob wandered around for a while near the DEFCON
entrance hoping to catch sight of anyone he knew, as well as to
walk off his anger. Mulling over the weirdness from this morning
was getting him nowhere. Unless someone was entering or exiting,
he had no view of the attendees. After an hour or so of loitering,
he decided that he wouldn't see anyone until the end of the session.
Frustrated, he went back through the casino. He found a bit of
luck at the slots, but gambling was not his thing. Even the cutie
that tried to pick him up couldn't spark his interest. His thoughts
unexpectedly went to Petra. Frustrated, he decided to return to
his room and pack. If he couldn't get into DEFCON, then he was
going home. Without the conference Vegas held no fascination
for him.

At the door to his room, he repeatedly ran his door keycard
to access his room but was getting no green light. The cleaning
lady was servicing the room across the hall, so he asked if she
would be so kind as to open the door since his key wouldn't work.
She indicated this was not permitted but would be happy to call

her supervisor for approval. Reaching her supervisor, the cleaning lady exchanged information with her, but much like the restaurant earlier, the conversation ended with the same result. He was not registered.

Jacob was practically yelling at the poor cleaning woman when a strong hand latched onto his shoulder. Turning him around, the security guard suggested that Jacob accompany him. Jacob knew better than to cause a fight. These guys meant business.

As they walked toward the elevators, Jacob said, "Hey man, all I want to do is get my belongings from my room and leave the hotel."

The guard was kind but stern. "We are going to the security chief and see what the next steps should be. You've been flagged from an earlier incident in the restaurant near the event halls and by DEFCON security guards. Let's go talk to my chief nice and quiet."

CHAPTER 8

Random events having no dependencies and yet an interrelationship upon reflection.

Arriving at the security office of the casino, Jacob was escorted to a small conference room. The Security Chief, Charles Moore, joined them a few minutes later. They talked for almost two hours with Jacob relating all the events of the day, providing identification, and listing all the items still remaining in the room, including some cash he had locked in the room safe.

With the discussion at a standstill, Mr. Moore got up to leave the room.

He glanced back at Jacob from the open door. "Sit tight, son. I'll be back in a bit."

Jacob reflected on everything that had occurred with this trip to Vegas. The events were odd, i.e., being blocked out of DEFCON, the issues with his room, and the overall unsettled rest the night before. He was trying to tie all the issues together, and it seemed to all circle back to his discussion with Petra and her abrupt dismissal of him the day before. It kept echoing in his mind when she said, "Go home, I'll see what I can find and fix for you."

He kept examining the different aspects of his morning and felt that there was some unaccounted detail. Jacob was frustrated over cooling his heels in the security office and just wanted to get back to New York City. He called the airlines and was able to reschedule his flight for late that afternoon into LaGuardia. At least changing the flight hadn't been a problem. He'd just gotten up to start pacing, sick of sitting in the uncomfortable chairs, when the door opened and Mr. Moore re-entered.

"Jacob, I did a little background check on you. Your story is checking out even to the point of our being able to confirm your arrival at the hotel. It is odd though. There seems to be a virus of some sort on the hotel registration system that removed your information, along with a couple of other guests. We still have not been able to do anything about your DEFCON registration, but that is really not connected to the hotel systems. I've reactivated your room key card, but I could not change your check out date from today. It seems your room has already been allocated to another incoming guest, but it has not yet been cleaned. You have about thirty minutes to retrieve your belongings and check out. I'm sorry, but at this point we have no vacancies, so we cannot move you to another room either. To be honest, I wasn't sure that would even interest you. I also spoke to the hotel manager, explaining your situation, and he has provided this voucher for your next stay, which includes two nights free here at the hotel and two meals at any of the hotel restaurants."

Jacob smiled, knowing he could at least leave this nightmare.

"Thanks for your efforts," Jacob stated sincerely. "I guess I will be going back to my room then and retrieving my stuff. It is good to know that I checked out for you guys. I will certainly try to return soon, and overall, the accommodations are really nice here. I hope you get the virus under control so that not too many other guests are bothered."

"Yeah, well, I think we have it in hand. It is very tough to get into our systems as you can imagine. Quite honestly, with DEFCON hosted here we took some special precautions. In my ten years here, I cannot recall any similar incident. On behalf of the Las Vegas Hilton, we appreciate your understanding." Mr. Moore smiled as he shook hands with Jacob.

Jacob moved toward the door and, turning just before walking away, said, "Hey, thanks again."

Jacob hurried back to his room. He packed his bags, retrieved the stuff from the room safe and was walking out just as housekeeping was going to knock on the door for cleaning.

Jacob headed down to the front desk to check out. He was always amazed at the number of walk ups set up for folks to check in or out in Las Vegas hotels. This one had probably 20 different walk up stations staffed and waiting for customers. Lots of people, lots of noise, with the beginning of the casino floor, which he had just passed through, directly off registration. The noise and lights of Las Vegas were unique to this world and not just for the rich and famous by any means.

The lines were not long, but every station was busy as he glanced down the line. Freedom to the outside was simply a check out away. When he finally got up to the counter, Jacob listened and responded when needed. The clerk was figuring his tally and verifying with Jacob the charges for Internet access, room services, etc., when out of the corner of his eye Jacob caught sight of a woman that looked just like Petra.

He could only see a side view, and she was wearing a short leather jacket with a backpack. Her clerk handed her a piece of paper, and she turned slightly, bending down to get the handle of her luggage. With that slight turn Jacob could see clearly that it was Petra. Funny, it looked like she was checking out too. His clerk was trying to hand him his receipt while he was trying to track Petra through the growing crowd. He snatched the paper from the clerk, offhandedly thanking him while trying to gather his bag, slip on his backpack again, and keep Petra in his line of sight. He started to walk away when the clerk called him.

"Mr. Michaels, sir. I have a letter that was left for you."

Distracted, Jacob turned his attention back to the clerk and returned the few steps to the counter. "Hey, sorry, did you say you had something for me?"

"Yes, sir. Someone left this letter for you a bit ago. We had thought since you were checking out, we would keep it at the desk."

"Ok, great." He grabbed the letter and said, "I am in a bit of a hurry. Thank you again."

He stuffed it into his suitcase as he hurried past the line of people. He had lost sight of Petra but felt he might catch her in the taxi line as he rushed out the door. Outside he located the taxi line in time to see Petra disappear into a waiting taxi. He heard the doorman say "airport" to her driver as he entered the line at the end. He estimated that ten folks were ahead of him for a taxi. His turn arrived, and he too took a taxi to the airport. One thing about Las Vegas, there was only one main airport, though it was big enough that finding someone would be a challenge. He mulled over how he might locate Petra. He recalled that Quip said she was working in New York. Wouldn't it be funny if she was on his flight?

Arriving at the airport, he picked up his boarding pass and proceeded to the security checkpoint. He and about a thousand of his unknown friends going through the itty-bitty security funnel. What a pain in the backside, he thought, as he removed his shoes, PC, and one-quart clear plastic baggie. Finding Petra would be like the old needle in a haystack.

He proceeded to his gate, and even though he kept scanning he was not able to catch sight of her. She was not in his waiting area, so likely she was not on his flight. His flight was called for boarding. Suddenly he felt very tired and ready to go home. He set up his computer when the flight was airborne and reviewed the notes, he had taken in the few sessions he had attended. It would be good manners to provide some summary write-ups on the sessions to others on the team in the office. Just part of the easy permission he received to attend DEFCON. How to explain why he hadn't stayed for the full event was a discussion he was really hoping to avoid with Brian. On second thought though, Brian might be interested in what happened and have some insight as to how his selective removal from every data source might have occurred. Jacob certainly had his ideas, but gaining Brian's perspective might be insightful.

During the flight he finished his summary, ate a nice meal served in First Class and had just dozed off when he felt the plane touchdown. Jacob grabbed his stuff, no checked luggage, exited quickly and grabbed a cab for the short ride home. After he paid the driver with a nice tip, he picked up the mail and entered his place. Then he headed for the shower and bed. Technically, he was not due to work until Monday, so he thought he would sleep in as he drifted off.

His dreams were all over the place, like snippets of bad B-movies. Dark characters, covert discussions, hidden things all jumbled together. His Mom, Petra and Buzz all prime characters, in and out of the dream. He woke up with vague memories of disjointed dreams and no answers.

CHAPTER 9

Distorting the facts is not valuable, but influencing the decision is.

Jacob debated going into the office. He lingered over coffee and breakfast. He knew he'd have no way of figuring out what actually occurred in Las Vegas. He also failed to make heads or tails out of his dreams from the night before but knew there was something important in the jumble. Perhaps a discussion with Brian and some new work projects would free up his mind to find some answers.

He repacked his backpack for the day, ignoring his suitcase on the floor, and secured his townhouse. Quickly he mounted his bike and found that he was soothed by the ride to the office. The weather was agreeable, and he felt great after he had pedaled the short distance. Outside the office building, he secured his bike then headed straight to the coffee bar.

"Hey Julie, how are you today."

Giving Jacob one of those thousand-watt smiles, Julie replied, "Great, thanks. Nice to see you, though I thought you were out of town. What can I get you today? Your usual tea?"

"Yeah. Well, I'm back a bit earlier than I planned. I will take a latte with a double shot of espresso today rather than tea, please."

"Sure! That will be four dollars and seventy-five cents, please," Julie said as she cranked up her smile.

"Thanks!" he frowned as he handed her a five-dollar bill. "Now I remember why the tea is better for me. It's my wallet. You have a nice day, Julie."

"You too, Jacob, and here is a muffin to go with it, on the house."

"Hey, thanks again, Julie," he said as he placed an extra dollar in the tip jar.

Jacob made his way to the elevator and then to the PT offices. He headed toward his cube, passing Brian's empty office. The light was on so Brian was somewhere on the floor. Jacob booted up his computer and signed in, waiting for all the programs to load and his authorization for entry into PT corporate WAN space. He launched his MOC client and changed his availability. Brian was showing available, so he opened a window to ping him.

Jacob: Just thought I would let you know I was in Brian

Brian: Wow, good timing Jacob, bring your PC and come into conference room A. You were about to be called anyway.

Jacob: K, on my way any problem?

Brian: Yep, explain when you get here, customer is present.

With that, Jacob pulled his PC with the power cord and headed to the room with latte in hand. He opened the door, and Brian turned to him.

"Great, Jacob, take a seat. This is Mr. Larry Cornwall of International Banks LLP. He was just beginning to discuss a problem that exists at the bank. Larry is head of their IT group."

"Nice to meet you, Mr. Cornwall." Jacob extended his hand.

"You as well. Please call me Larry. Brian here was just telling me about your background in security and testing for unauthorized access. I am here to engage your team to help me find a problem. I was just telling Brian that my guys stumbled over this event in our logs that can't be explained. We don't see any breaches, but it makes me uncomfortable. I don't believe in random events or coincidences. My guys have tried, but at this point they think the log file has been tampered with which should not be possible.

"PT has experience in our environment, and we are about due for a review. I just think it is worth having it now rather than in sixty days. We did find some code that appeared so odd that I brought a copy of it or you to review in advance. It doesn't appear to be connected to any other programs so my guys didn't recognize it and quite honestly it is a bit complicated for their skill levels. Most of our programming is contracted with all new code validated by PT before being placed into production. This program doesn't show PT's validation markings, which may or may not be a problem. We have teams that are working on changes, and this was found within the secured sector, thus isolated from sensitive information."

Larry handed Jacob a thumb drive which he plugged into the side of his machine and waited for his PC's acknowledgement of the device. He had reviewed programs before and knew that PT validation marks were always inserted within the first five lines of all validated programs. That was likely as far as Larry's guys went into review of the code.

Brian took up the conversation before Jacob could speak. "I was telling Larry that you were attending DEFCON and perhaps would be ideal to take the lead when you returned. With your arrival this morning, we won't have to put off the services. We do have a standard service contract that we can modify for starting tomorrow if you can be onsite then, Jacob. With their security firewalls, there is no way to access via remote support. The location is in Manhattan at their main office."

"No problem," Jacob said, then faced Larry. "What time would you like me to start and what do I need from your security folks to access the building?"

Jacob knew that post-911 buildings in New York, especially in Manhattan, were very hard to enter without proper authorization. No way to bluff one's way into most buildings in New York these days unless it was retail space.

"If you can arrive at seven-thirty, I can meet you in the lobby, square the security with a day badge and request at least a two-week badge for your access on your own. I will get my guys in place by eight with all the information we have and your system access information. Of course, you will be given full access, but I would like one of my guys to shadow you at least part of the time to learn a bit more. Brian, I think that is already in our agreement, right?"

Brian glanced at his machine, "Yep, it sure is. However, if our team, mainly Jacob, has special routines confidential to PT, then he will alert your guys at those points to leave or whatever the approved process dictates. The machines that Jacob will use will not have any screen capture software on them, which we check as a matter of routine in advance. Agreed?"

"Yes, Brian, that has been the standard agreement in the past, and I didn't think you guys changed policy. Sounds good. Jacob, I will see you in the lobby in the morning."

"Yes, sir. I will be there by seven-thirty with my ID in hand. Thank you, Larry, I am sure we can track it down. I will take a look at this today and perhaps have some information to share with you in the morning. Thank you for bringing it with you."

They shook hands and said their goodbyes. Brian escorted Larry out while Jacob returned to his cube and started reviewing the program he had been given. Jacob had only begun reading the code and starting to annotate when Brian peeked over the cube.

"I am not sure why you are back early, but your timing is great. Get to a stopping point and come to my office."

Jacob knew that his stopping point had been reached, so he followed Brian to his office. He closed the door and sat in the chair.

"Correct me if I am wrong, but DEFCON is still running? Yet here you are in the office. I suspect there is a story here, right?"

Jacob grimaced slightly before responding like a whipped puppy dog. "Yep, there is a story, but it is straight out of *Grimm's Fairy Tales*. Let's just say that it was like an out-of-body experience that I'd sooner not relive. I already started to review this program; it will likely take most of the day. Then tomorrow I will be with Larry and his team, rather than stop in here first, if that is ok with you."

Edging his eyebrows up with a questioning look, Brian said evenly, "Okay, I get it. The story can wait until another time as long as you are good to go. I wanted to let you know that Larry is likely more concerned than he is letting on. This bank is important to his livelihood, and he doesn't want anyone messing with his baby. I need you to keep me posted, and if it is something hairy, you might want to make certain you bring me into discussions with Larry. I've known the guy a long time. He is a straight shooter and hates being out of the loop."

"I do recall you having a history with Larry. But I always work with the customer and their customers' interest in the forefront. Let me get started and see if we can determine what's up. I will make certain his team is aware each step of the way."

"Works for me. Thanks, Jacob, glad you are back." Grinning, Brian added, "We'll discuss Vegas when it stops stinging you."

CHAPTER 10

Opportunity is only good if you exploit it.

Once established in the Manhattan office of the bank bright and early, Jacob started by looking at the server activity. Review of the cobbled program was inconclusive and likely connected to another program. He noticed the server was running at ninety plus percent and was trying to do outbound contact to a remote system. After he questioned the local techs, they confirmed that the remote system call was not to one of their machines, so Jacob unplugged the server from the network, and it tried relentlessly to reestablish contact.

Jacob located the program that was making the attempt at remote contact and copied it onto his thumb drive. He was unable to see all of the code since it was encrypted and resisted his attempts to figure out what it was doing, so he rebooted the server.

All the rogue programs vanished when it came back up and started behaving normally, with the exception of a sporadic attempt to reach an external system. He was sure it was infected but could no longer find the rogue executables he had seen earlier. He suspected that the server intrusion had gotten a computer virus, and the rogue program was now operating cloaked, like a rootkit program.

A rootkit program is nearly impossible to remove from a computer. One of his early professors, in discussing rootkits, stated that "the only way to eliminate them was to take off in a low earth orbit and nuke it from space." He doubted that the bank would agree to this approach. He disconnected the server from the network so that it could do no harm. It was a non-essential system, which was always the best attack starting point.

While doing the forensics on the attack, Jacob saw some excellent efforts to hide malicious code, actually making it cover its own tracks. When Jacob poked it, it changed its signature and adapted. The shadow tech that Larry had working with him hadn't said a word though he watched everything Jacob did. Obviously, he wasn't an expert at this type of effort.

Wow! Jacob thought to himself. Self-aware code that is reasonably sophisticated and not typical of a financial institution.

He then focused on the malicious code to adapt password progression as it mutated. Taken aback, Jacob spotted the password coding assignment that he had done as a favor for Buzz. The coding assignment turned out to be part of a rogue computer virus now present on the bank's corporate network. As he realized what he was looking at, he was stunned.

"What the hell! Buzz, you SOB," he mumbled.

As he reviewed the rest of the code he was trying to remove, he realized it was part of an algorithm that was too sophisticated for Buzz to do on his own. Though he racked his brain, Jacob knew there was nothing else that he had provided to Buzz that could enable the characteristic behavior that he was seeing. He started to test his tracking fixes on the safe system, and by all appearances it seemed to be working. After he finished his notes, he closed down the safe system, loaded up his PC, thanked the tech that had shadowed him and headed home.

Once home he quickly connected one of his machines to the Internet. He recognized that this was really not the usual type of program within his sphere of expertise. Perhaps Quip could assist, at least with a good approach to take. Checking, he located Quip online.

> JAM: Hey man are you there? Need some help!
>
> Quip: Hey JAM sure missed seeing you at DEFCON after day 1. Work called you back huh?
>
> JAM: That is a story requiring beer and time man. Have another issue though that I could use some advice. Got time?
>
> Quip: Sure, what's up?
>
> JAM: Working for a customer and think I have rootkit at work. Some of the code I follow, but it vanishes.
>
> Quip: Yeah, those things can be a bear. But that is not me man, Petra maybe. Reach out to her.
>
> JAM: Yeah well, don't know how and she left me fairly peeved in Las Vegas.
>
> Quip: Really, last I saw you were in a cozy discussion by yourselves. I figured you had hooked up.
>
> JAM: Nope, not so much. How can I find her?
>
> Quip: Don't have a number, but you might reach her at this chat room with a different persona securecyrptographerroom.net Just supply some fresh blood problem and the sharks will whirl into a frenzy, then she'll show. Use my alter ego, Brutus if you want. She has responded to me sometimes.

Jacob went to the chat room using the non-standard persona Brutus. He began to supply a crazy problem that was not related to his issue. A few of the visitors exchanged with him, and he kept growing the fictional problem. Quip was on target with the frenzied sharks. After an hour of rapid-fire comments exchanged, and about when he thought Petra must be sleeping, his cell phone rang. As he connected the call, he heard clicking which he recognized as a layer of encryption on the call.

"Hello?" he questioned, all senses on alert.

"Hello, Jacob," she quietly said. "You seem to have one very wild problem that everyone is now focused on. Would you prefer to speak about it live or do it in the chat room?"

Jacob was speechless for a few seconds, trying to figure out how she had his number, and had known it was him online, even when he was using Quip's Brutus persona. He noticed that the inbound number identification was blocked.

"Yeah, I was hoping that you might help me with an issue that is nothing like what is in your chat room at present. I know you are probably still angry, but this is important and a bit out of my expertise, but totally aligned with yours. Can you help me out? I did, after all, go home as you had instructed."

He practically held his breath, waiting for what he hoped would be a positive response. She held too much interest for him, with her voice making his blood race through his veins.

Petra chuckled a bit. "Yes, you did, but the way I hear the tale, it took a whole different twist. Thought that was just rumor. Glad you made it home, and I hope you took additional precautions. You are actually well-known for many things by many people. What is the issue you are having?"

Jacob explained the code and his concern about the rootkit. He also explained its magical disappearing act that he'd witnessed. He ran through all the activities detailed in his log book. She asked a few questions regarding the order of his steps. He left out the part about his code via Buzz. She pointed him to a few areas but soon overran his knowledge.

"Hey, I was able to bring a portion of the code home on a thumb drive, and I am looking at it on an old PC not used for anything useful outside of testing stuff. I would send it to you, but I don't think you want this on your machine."

"No, transfer of this via the Internet would likely cause more problems than good. Can I come take a look at it? Where are you now?" she asked.

"I am at home in New York. Sure, if you can look at it that would be great. Are you still in town?"

"Yes, I am still working here but wrapping up soon, then back to Europe for a meeting if it can get set up. What is your address?"

He rattled off his address. She said she would be by in a while and asked him to have coffee ready.

"I will help you, Jacob, but at this hour caffeine is a must. See you shortly."

Less than an hour later, she knocked at his door. He answered with coffee in hand to which she smiled.

"Thanks." Taking the coffee, she waited for him to move then entered. "So where is the beastie?"

Jacob took her all in, realizing that his thoughts, now that he saw her, were hardly focused on code. She wore a well-fitted set of jeans and a sweater that hugged her curves, showing assets that had not registered before. She was a pretty lady, he thought, as he tried to untangle his brain and focus.

Half a beat later, he responded, "Wow, you got here fast. Come on in. Petra, I really am glad you could come over."

They both seemed to grin, recognizing an undercurrent of attraction. Jacob took her to his machine and began showing her portions of the code. The distraction for him was still there but diminished for the time being. They both poured over the code he had captured for a long time. She created some code to help open doors to parts he had not even seen. He was focused on her hands as they caressed the keyboard and highlighted areas on the screen. He noticed that she was frowning, and he wanted to reach out and wipe away those frowns. He forced himself to refocus on the project rather than the woman and to learn from what he was seeing.

Suddenly she let out a gasp and highlighted some code. "This portion of polymorphic code, right here, is my code. It was something I put into a bank in Germany two months ago. Only a small part, but I know my signatures. Someone is playing games here."

With that revelation, Jacob came clean. He told her about the code he had found that was his and related how he had created it and provided it to his buddy Buzz. He did not go into all his history with Buzz, but she frowned as he explained the situation. Jacob realized that she was incredibly easy to talk to and admonished himself for the desire to move it to a personal, deeper level. They continued in earnest to review the portion of the malicious code that he had captured. The search was on for the capabilities of this code.

"This code is a combination of several elements coming from different programmer sources. Like the portion I know is mine as well as the elements you provided Buzz. I am also seeing a decryption method I think was developed by someone I work with occasionally, meaning we are likely dealing with someone that can selectively steal, has insider access at multiple places, and knows how to put codes together in a rather menacing manner. The cloaking elements are very sophisticated, and I may have an idea of the creator, possibly in the APAC region. I have been seeing more ability from folks in China who are educated in part in the U.S. but on the payroll of the Chinese government. So, it is possible," Petra explained with growing concern.

"I can see that this is a very creative method of access and malicious code that can jump machines. Just from looking at how you are breaking this down, combined with what I saw on the bank's machine, I think there is more to this that we likely need to find. As far as our code goes, they do say the best form of flattery is imitation," Jacob stated. Suddenly he felt driven with an unfamiliar conviction to work this problem with her. Combined, he thought their talents could make it happen.

"We? Jacob that could prove interesting on many levels. However, unless I can see some of what you saw, we can't establish a method to neutralize and destroy it. This then becomes simply an academic effort. I do not appreciate use of my code without permission." She was visibly angered.

"What if I can get you authorized to see the systems at the bank? I have full authorization, and I can call my boss and the customer and get that pretty quick, since we have a better idea of the nature of this beastie, as you said earlier. Would you be willing to go with me now if I gain the approvals?"

"Yes, that's a good plan. I can do it tonight and through tomorrow as I am technically off my project until then and not expected. Try to arrange it now."

Jacob called Brian. He agreed that Jacob could add his resource as a temporary contractor based on Jacob remaining present at all times. Jacob mused that worked for him. He then called Larry Cornwall and advised him that he and his temporary contractor would be going back to the bank tonight. Larry had no issues and agreed to contact security and alert them.

For the next thirty minutes, Jacob and Petra worked their planned approach, and she created a bit of code to be used for containment and exposure of, hopefully, the whole code stream. Jacob copied the code to a separate, new thumb drive. They were ready to go.

"I'll call a cab. They usually take fifteen to twenty minutes. I'll fix a snack while we wait."

"No need for a cab. We can take my car. The snack to go would be nice." She grinned, knowing he had forgotten she had driven over.

"That works."

A few minutes later they got into her car. Jacob maneuvered to open her door. She showed a smile of appreciation with a bit of surprise.

"Hey, my mom taught me to be a gentleman."

Jacob provided clear directions, and they had some conversation. In the confines of the car he could look her over. Again, he was amazed at how much he noticed her as a woman. She wasted no movements and seemed focused, just like how she approached programming. He found that she was very easy to like and he appreciated her for not only her brains but her beauty as well. Likely that would not be an avenue that the efficient Petra would welcome. It was also not a path he was willing to vocalize until he had a clearer understanding of his feelings. This was too different from his normal approach to life situations. He couldn't quite wrap his brain around it.

They arrived at the bank and cleared security. No one, not even the third shift staff, was around in the data center so they set up and got to work. Jacob showed her the machine, and she confirmed that it was not connected to the network. The CPU utilization was still sky high as it continued to try to connect to another system. As she watched the processes and poked it herself, they saw the code morph again. Then it disappeared as if it hadn't existed.

"This is very clever, but not as bad as I thought," she assured him. "It is not something that you want in the bank. It could do some real damage, but it hasn't had enough time to morph far enough to destroy anything when you disconnected it. The reboot, however, did increase its ability to adapt. Your process is standard, contain and reboot. The code leverages that to complete its lifecycle adaptation process. Most techs, however, would not have initially taken the safeguard to isolate the machine from the network. It is good that you thought ten steps ahead."

Jacob grinned, "Okay, then let's see if it is anywhere else in the systems that are connected. I had left a trace program on the network earlier just to monitor activity. It looks clean to me."

Petra validated his claims and agreed. The rest of the systems were good. She then applied her code to kill the malicious code on the isolated system. Initially the program downloaded and seemed to be working, then stopped.

Jacob raised his eyebrows in question.

She smiled and said, "Wait. Watch what it does when this program gathers all the tendrils of the threat. It will tell me when it is done. This we can handle."

Thirty minutes later the program whirled to life, repeatedly grabbing then deleting code. It was like watching an exterminator killing rats, one right after another. He had to laugh as the screen suddenly created a message box that looked and sounded like a California valley girl. The screen presented the following in very bright colors, PROBLEM TOTALLY RESOLVED-FOR SURE.

"Now that is a fun program. Self-monitoring and speaks too. What does it say if it is partially resolved?"

"Of course, this would never occur with one of my programs these days, but it would say, TRY AGAIN PETRA, YOU TOTALLY FAILED. A little trick my papa taught me so that he could avoid saying critical comments. My programs run or fail on my efforts alone." She chuckled, recalling how much she had learned from her father.

They reran all the verification after they cleaned the machine and reinstalled everything. Once they were satisfied with the machine's behavior, they reconnected to the network. No other issues showed. They were both satisfied with their success.

Petra looked tired, "We're done here. I'm ready to go home and catch some sleep. You have things to do. Let me see your cell phone."

She grinned with her hand out. He provided his cell, and she quickly added an app and her cell number.

"Jacob, I want to give you my number to connect to me, but it is critical that this app run whenever you call. It's what you heard when I phoned you. This encryption method is important, Jacob; do not forget, please, if you call. I trust you," and she handed back his phone.

He took it and looked at what she had done.

Then he surprised himself and asked, "Perhaps we might get together over the weekend for a more pleasant activity like hiking or riding and getting to know each other. Would that be of interest to you?"

"I think that might be very fascinating, Jacob, and possible. I will contact you by Friday morning to see if time will permit. As I had said earlier, I am waiting for a confirmation on a meeting that will require my return to Europe. I would like to see you and get to know you better." She surprised him with a hug and a smile.

They walked to security and checked out. She dropped him at his home then left. Jacob was tired, but knew he had a report to write that documented the events, what was found, and the next steps. He also needed Larry and his team to find out who the insider was that had brought the malicious code in, as that was the only way it could have started. Dealing with Buzz and getting to the bottom of that betrayal was also on his list. As he organized all the notes and papers he needed to write the report, he noticed the envelope that had become caught in his notebook. As he grabbed it, he realized it was the one from Las Vegas, which he'd totally forgotten.

He removed the single page letter. The company name at the top said Ronnie, Ltd., with New York City underneath. No street address and no phone number. With a quick glance at the envelope, he began to read the letter,

Mr. Michaels,

Please accept my apologies for not being able to meet with you during DEFCON. I trust the event ticket was helpful. I was looking forward to meeting you. I hope you enjoyed the sessions and networked with all the top talent brought together at such an event. I will try to set up another attempt for discussion soon.

Sincerely, Otto

Okay, this was odd. He did not know an Otto from any of the customers he'd worked for. Plus, the mention of the ticket cleared up that mystery, but no mention of the t-shirt, hotel or airline ticket seemed inconsistent. He'd think about that later. He had a project to complete.

He worked through all the areas of the report and cross-referenced them with the program segments. He had left out the origin of the programs, and of course no mention of Petra's code being discovered was included. He would brief those details to Brian. Once he completed the report, he checked to see if Brian was online.

> Jacob: Brian, I know it's early but are you in the office? I would like to have you read my report before I provide to Larry and his team.
>
> Brian: I am on the way there.. Email it to me with your standard credential code. Are you finished up there as I think I want you here this morning for a new problem?
>
> Jacob: Yes sir. I can be there after a little sleep. Same type of issue, or is it different?
>
> Brian: No it's different. But a problem. We can get onsite early.
>
> Jacob: Sure. Sending now. Make necessary changes and send back so I can deliver.

While he waited for Brian to review the report, he checked his email.

Most of the requests were easily dealt with. Then he came upon something weird. He was so not in the mood for weird right now. The email was from Otto, with a formal apology repeated about missing the meeting at DEFCON due to an unexpected conflict. The note asked for another meeting on Wednesday in New York City close to the PT offices. Then Jacob's cell phone received an SMS text with a reminder confirmation and a repeat of the location almost as if on cue. He reread the email. He definitely didn't know an Otto, but he did want to meet and thank his DEFCON benefactor as well as possibly thank him for the t-shirt. The meeting time showed at noon for an hour and a half, so he replied with a C to confirm. He had this nagging feeling that things were traveling out of his control.

After a few hours of sleep Jacob made the minor changes Brian suggested and set up a review session with Larry. Jacob met with Larry in his office with his lead tech John close to noon. He pointed out the next steps necessary to find the actual perpetrator. The details of who wrote what portions of the code that were used were left off the report as confidential, though it would be something that Jacob planned to brief his team on, to a degree, to explain the exploitation of this code and the creator. After the briefing he went home, ate and crashed into a sleep disturbed with provocative images of Petra.

CHAPTER 11

The poison is also part of the antidote.

Jacob arrived to work early. He was surprised to see Julie open for business at this hour with her usually perky manner. He grinned at her infectious smile.

"Morning, Julie. May I please have a straight up coffee?"

"Sure thing. Too bad I saw you coming and started your tea but that's easily changed. Guess I should not overly anticipate my customers." She laughed as she handed him the coffee. "Rough weekend?"

"Actually, it was, but it turned out good. I'll get my second wind soon with this cup. Thanks." He paid her and moved to the elevators.

He arrived at his floor and dropped his stuff on his desk then immediately headed to Brian's office. Brian was in of course and looked up from his PC as Jacob entered.

"Hey Jacob, glad you're here early." Somberly he continued, "We have an issue brewing at World Bank, and after reading your report, I want you to go to site. I think the issue as I was briefed yesterday by Gorman is different, but it sounds like an inside breach. I think you are in the best position, with the other projects on the team's plate, to quickly address their issue."

"Can do, Brian. Should I head over now, or can I get a few things tidied up here?"

"They do not want you to arrive before seven-thirty so you have time. Short timeline too. They open at ten, if we resolve the issue. Keep me posted."

01010101001100

Jacob arrived at World Bank and was checked in with security. Gorman briefed him on some random denial of service attacks and a standard maintenance process that failed to finish. As he listened to the details and ran through the possibilities, he tended to agree with Brian's initial assessment. Gorman introduced the rest of the team of three, who all looked like they also had experienced a frustrating weekend.

Jacob was suspicious and asked how often the bank had experienced these DOS attacks. The techs told him a couple of times a week for the last month, but they were at random time intervals and of varying duration. One had occurred about five minutes ago, that one of the techs had watched but had located no proof in the logs. The techs all looked dreadfully weary. Jacob double checked the firewall log files and also couldn't find any evidence of the occurrence that had just happened. The team was rattled, tired and understaffed. One of the techs, Sammy, indicated that there was a mirror computer that could be turned on and perhaps the next attack could be properly recorded.

Sammy looked for validation as he suggested, "This was the next step we were going to take. We could not get the back up to restore or open this morning either, as per standard practice. We are set to open at ten. Anything you can help with would be welcomed at this point. We would all like to keep our jobs."

Jacob noticed from the firewall logs that the DOS packets didn't come through the firewall from the outside. However, during the time they indicated, a large file transfer occurred that was sent to a file share in the Bahamas. He checked to see who or what had sent that much data to an offshore account during a DOS attack and saw that the source IP address was a BOGON IP address internal to the bank. Again, Jacob questioned the team about this activity and began to piece the puzzle together by working backwards from the large file transfer during the DOS attack. At first no one took Jacob's theory that the DOS attack came from within the bank seriously.

Jacob recommended that during the next DOS attack they pull the plug on the server room and cut all external access to the Internet and to the bank's affiliates, including their Swiss parent company. The idea was too farfetched for anyone to get on board.

Jacob persisted, "Hey, if the attack really is from inside, then when access is cut the attacker would not be affected and we might have time to track the beginning and end points. If I'm wrong then when the network access is disabled, the attacks will stop."

While the logic was sound, no one wanted to take responsibility. Gorman was confident in Jacob but not completely convinced. Jacob volunteered to trip over the cables in a staged act of clumsiness to disconnect the server room, which was more like a server city, emphasized by the sign above the door as you exited, *You Are Now Leaving Gotham City.* Jacob argued so persuasively that they were willing to let him try. Gorman granted him five minutes. Gorman wasn't quite ready to deal with the department head who would probably 'blue screen' when he found out what had happened, but nodded his head in approval.

When the next DOS attack occurred, Jacob disconnected from the outside world, and they all watched the screens. Jacob saw the activity and quickly started the capture and IP address resolution. He then applied the current patches that should have been applied months ago. This was a newer server for this team, and they weren't performing all required due diligence. He oversaw as one of the techs updated the processes and procedures with the patching methodology that might have avoided part of the breach, but not all of it because it was likely from within.

Based on the IP address resolution, it was definitely an insider. Sammy tracked the address internally and located the user about twenty feet outside of Gotham City. The logs trapped all the instigated activity, and Gorman called for a security detail and HR support to apprehend the employee, identified as Nelson Delf.

Jacob provided a quick overview of what had occurred. "Your security patches were a bit dated. Honestly it is critical to stay current when using a VMware hosting server. It was undermined likely to support the nefarious bidding of a group outside. This virtual server host platform spawned a series of virtual servers, which launched a denial of service attack inside the environment. It generated just enough traffic hitting the firewalls to make it look like the attack was coming from the outside. During the chaos, the compromised VMware hosting server spawned a database server from a snapshot backup image that assumed the identity of the actual database server. This was why your restore failed to complete."

Really getting into his subject, he added, "The problem with this is that you can use VoIP, LAN, or Wi-Fi access. You only have to punch onto the network via an access point and provide a login and password as required. This makes peer-to-peer attacks easy because there is no access restriction. Presto, I have a conversation going and sniff the packets via both 'Man in the Middle' and 'Denial of Service' attacks. Then the compromise begins with sharing the secrets. Sort of an, I'll show you mine if you show me yours, deal."

Jacob explained additional details to the team and the other follow-on problems that were possible. A bright team, they asked good questions, and he clarified where needed.

The team restored the files under the maintenance process. Together they quickly checked the systems and logs. Everything checked out clean, and access to the outside was restored. Another review across the systems was completed. Jacob did his standard tests for security and declared they were in good shape to open a scant ten minutes before ten a.m. The techs departed to their normal work efforts after they thanked Jacob for quickly finding the problem. Jacob departed with a quick glance at the Gotham City sign and shook his head on the way out the door. As Gorman escorted him out, he again thanked Jacob for his efforts.

Jacob responded, "Glad to help. It is really a shame that your guy was the cause, but you know the right steps to put into place to avoid a future occurrence. The rest of your team is top notch. Call us if you need any help."

He continued out the door and decided to walk back to the office to take time to stretch out and recharge his batteries. He called Brian with an update that all was well.

It was odd though to have two significant issues with two of the bigger institutions targeted over the same weekend. He'd heard some talk with regards to a group of Russians called the Dteam. Their trademark, according to the chat rooms, was to disrupt financial institutions and capture funds for their own endeavors. The copied code from this World Bank problem was on his thumb drive for further analysis.

As he walked, he hummed to himself as he thought about meeting with Petra this weekend and getting her take on this incident. Maybe he would call her later after he analyzed this program.

CHAPTER 12

If you look where everyone does, you will miss that which is important.

Jacob returned to the office, briefed Brian and finished the formal report at his desk. He also had some thoughts on additional inserts to the International Bank report from the weekend and sent both to Brian. Shortly after he sent the report, Brian called a staff meeting and put Jacob on the agenda to discuss the two recent situations. The team listened and conveyed admiration at the results and methodology. They all wanted to read the detailed reports. Brian indicated they were already up on SharePoint.

Ready to call it a day, Jacob packed up to return home for dinner. He was really revved up. His thoughts drifted to Petra, although he brushed them aside. He thought perhaps he would call her later. He took off on his bike for the trek home, and just as he reached Central Park, he saw her sitting on a bench, feeding some pigeons and ducks, looking very relaxed. Funny, he just would not have imagined her there. He headed toward her, and as the birds took flight, she looked up and smiled.

"Well, hello there, long time no see. What brings you here, Jacob?"

He grinned and said, "I'm surprised to find you here. Me, I'm on my way home. May I join you?"

She was again dressed casually, but with everything hugging her petite shape. The bun was undone, providing his first view at how long and soft her hair looked. It was very feminine, with highlights of blonde, almost down to her waist. His interest, he delightfully recognized, was definitely not just her mind. He would just keep telling himself that the complications of a relationship were not yet in his plans.

"Of course, but only if you are serious about feeding these poor greedy birds." She encouraged his participation by passing him some bread then asked, "So how was your day? Did you catch up on your rest? I certainly did and spent most of the day relaxing. Fairly close to heaven in my life."

"Well, since you asked, it was an exciting morning with another customer having an insider security breach. In fact, it was a very interesting use of automatic virtual server spin up coupled with DOS attacks to mask data transport. Fortunately, it was fixed in time for the opening this morning. Though the guy was good, he obviously is working with another outside source for this to work. It reminded me of a group out of Russia that I had heard was working to infiltrate financial institutions."

"Ah, you must be referring to the Dteam. There was some discussion about them at DEFCON. I too have seen chat discussions about them increasing significantly over the last year. The goal of their efforts is funds extortion. I suspect they are very adept at targeting folks and swaying them to work for them. They aren't brilliant but definitely bothersome if they gain support from an insider. They are prone to using sex-oriented operators to manage their recruits, I've heard."

"There you have it. I try to avoid casual relationships, and now I know why. I'm waiting for my career to be fully established before I work on a serious relationship." He grinned but thought about how pretty her heart-shaped face and perfect mouth were.

"You mean you and your buddy Buzz don't hit the clubs? I am sure you would attract ladies without a problem. And Buzz, is he like you?"

"Buzz, he likes all the ladies. He always has, keeping several on a string. Patty, his latest, works at the local bar and grill and does some modeling and catering on the side to make ends meet. I still haven't spoken to him yet on what I found in that program we worked, but I will before the end of the week."

His anger over that started to escalate, so he tried for a subject change so he could spend more time talking with her. He picked up another piece of bread and absentmindedly broke off bits and tossed them to the greedy birds while he defused his anger.

"So, madam, what can you tell me about cryptography?"

Petra immediately brightened and became very animated, but a bit cautious. She had learned that people sometimes glaze over if she talked too long on this, her favorite topic. His interest kept her engaged in the discussion, though clearly she was afraid to take it too far. This was not exactly the discussion for a warm sunny day in the park, feeding feathered friends. She recognized that socializing was not her strength.

Jacob was enjoying her enthusiasm on the subject but sensed her withdrawal from the technical discussion. Being a pen-tester in the security world, Jacob was always looking to expand his knowledge, but he also found that he needed to impress her.

As she paused, he asked hopefully, "Have you ever worked with elliptical curve algorithms? You know, pen-testers don't get much exposure to encryption algorithms. If they do, it is usually just the linear equations rather than the advanced elliptical curve computations. Perhaps you can enlighten me?"

Petra quickly retrieved her enthusiasm, then sizing Jacob up, asked point blank, "How much do you know about elliptical curve cryptography?"

Jacob, seeing the enthusiastic light return to her eyes, confessed, "I don't really know that much, but I am willing to learn. I am a quick study, and you seem knowledgeable."

He was focused on learning how she thought and finding a common ground between them. He wouldn't mind feeling how soft her skin might be either, but he chided himself for the thought.

Petra was both pleased with the compliment and amused by Jacob at the same time. She wanted to know him better and understand how his mind worked. She found herself unable to refuse the invitation to teach someone who wanted to learn. Hopefully, he would be as fast as she suspected he was. She had the sensation that he would be good at everything he attempted.

Petra opened what could be a very technical discussion, "Okay, we need some working definitions before starting any security discussion. In layman's terms, a cryptographic system is secure if an adversary with specified capabilities is not able to break it, meaning that they are not able to solve the specified task in a reasonable amount of time with generally available technology.

"Most public key cryptosystems get their security from a one-way function or algorithm that cannot easily be inverted to obtain the original value inputs. Inverting a one-way function must be difficult for the adversary from an algebraic standpoint. Asymmetric cryptosystems work because the inverse operation, the decrypting portion, rapidly gets more difficult as key length increases. Key length that is specified gives some indication of the complexity and thus the amount of time that will be required for an adversary to break the code."

"That makes sense," Jacob acknowledged, totally focused on the discussion.

She continued on with the discussion in great detail because of Jacob's rapt attention. For him it was like being with a tutor, and she was in her element. Petra liked sharing her years of study and experience with someone as smart, and yes, as attractive as Jacob. He was attuned to the discussion. An outside observer would have considered likening them to two high speed end points exchanging data. She even provided a drawing and further detail on elliptical curves and how these were used.

Jacob said, "Okay, got it. Can you give me a real-world example that will help me cement this concept?"

Petra studied him for a second to consider a good example and then said, "You know how a telephone book works? All last names in a geographic area are alphabetized with a first name which creates a useful index for finding the person you want to call. Once you have found the name of the person you want to call, you run your finger across the page to their associated telephone number and make the call. Simple and easy for lookup and use. But if all I gave you was thousands of phone numbers and told you to find the people associated with those numbers, you would have no way to work backwards to the original telephone book alphabetic listing. This is an example of a one-way encryption algorithm. Does that help as an example?"

Jacob nodded and smiled. "This is complex but easier with your explanation. I can even see the use of quantum computing in this encryption process to improve the reliability and integrity of the security routine, right?"

"Yes, of course." She smiled with his understanding.

It was refreshing to find someone to discuss these topics with, and she basked in his silent approval during their rather lengthy discussion.

"I can see how leveraging this could be of great value. Ahead of the curve for stopping bad guys," he chuckled.

Jacob thoroughly enjoyed her delivery of what some would suggest was a complex casual discussion. He found himself even more drawn to her, and he was fascinated with her grasp of the information and delivery. Great mind, with a very nice wrapper.

"My research indicates that quantum computing is feasible and that it can be used to quickly generate the inverse of an elliptical curve discrete logarithm and read the cipher text as quickly as it is being generated. Much like what was done when Bletchley Park had decrypted the German enigma cipher machine at the outbreak of World War II," Petra added.

At that point, Petra stopped looking at him for understanding or acceptance, yet she was slightly embarrassed at being perceived as bragging.

"Okay, so I get this and did not realize these roots went back to the WWII cipher machines, though it makes sense. Humans build on information over time. Hmmm, I wonder what other complex discussions we might have." He smiled at her. "I think for right now, with my lack of sleep, I have heard all I can digest. However, I'd like to continue my education in this area at another time. You have a way of explaining that works. Thank you very much."

She beamed at the compliment but returned to a more serious expression, trying to keep him from seeing too much. She was finding him too attractive as well as too smart.

"Perhaps if the weekend works out, we can discuss further or cover other topics of mutual interest, Jacob?"

"Agreed. I need to head home and catch up on some things. Let me know about the weekend on Friday, or sooner. I think we'd have fun."

He felt her watch him as he mounted up and began the ride home.

Arriving home, he parked his bike and picked up his mail on the way inside. He found nothing of value in the mail but ads, which he added to the recycle pile. He connected his PC and did a small amount of clean up. Confronting Buzz was a good idea, but he simply wasn't in the mood. He replayed some of the conversation with Petra. The information shared was good, and he could apply it. He needed to get perhaps a sample program that leveraged the formulas and tested his ability to effectively apply them. Maybe she could grade him. However, he found his thoughts strayed to the visuals of her face, hair, graceful hands, and willowy frame. Admonishing himself, he decided sleep was in order.

CHAPTER 13

The good guys always wear white hats.

The Russian Cartel/Mafia, commonly referred to as the Dteam, had started off in the cyber space Black Hat Community as a small player at the bottom of the malware food chain. They had gained notoriety and some oblique visibility in some of the chat rooms for obtaining information. They had compromised a group of PCs with their drive-by downloads and had put together a collection of hundreds of machines to relay their spam email offerings. They were initially a small, indiscreet organization, content to pull in the easy money harvested through their spam business with operatives in Russia as well as the U.S.

All that changed when Grigory took over leadership from his New York City location. Grigory stood just under six feet, mid-forties, unruly dark hair, and eyes as black as sin that missed little, with a squared jawline and a voice that commanded obedience regardless of the volume. He radiated ruthlessness, emphasized by his wardrobe of black fitted clothing and trademark black leather coat. Under his direction, the pace of their business quickened, and the Dteam started moving up the cyber malware 'food chain'. They stopped wholesaling their commandeered machines and using other groups' mailing lists and started embarking on more ambitious endeavors.

Grigory divided the operators in order to optimize the focus and leveraged his number two enforcer, Sergei, for different special projects. Sergei was a loose cannon, but Grigory knew how to use him. One group specialized in generating targeted mailing lists, not using these, but selling them to others. Another group specialized in providing infrastructure so customers could rent the machines to send the spam out that would deliver malware and infect machines, scamming user IDs and passwords. The software coder group-built malware to a customer's request and expectation, which was then incorporated into the spam payload to infect the target machines. Each of these groups had loosely integrated relationships but were successful entities by themselves.

Lastly, there was the exploiter group who would bid on final lists of hapless victims who had been compromised to gain access to their identities and financial resources. Once into a person's bank account, the funds were drained and the money laundered without leaving a trail. These folks took the most risk and made the most profits for the Dteam. These were the folks that the sovereign enforcers wanted and created the best cases against when caught.

Grigory, after a few months, believed that more refinement was needed. He realigned the organization to extract greater profits and minimize the risk of disclosure. He had surmised that if the target victim was in on the scam then it would be easier to stay clear of the sovereign enforcers. He hit on the idea of selling identity thefts to people who wanted to get their money out of a financial institution in a particular country. His value was discretion for the prices he charged. The value to the customer was the significant in-country tax savings and frequent payouts by the customer's insurance carrier.

The concept was relatively straightforward. You hunted for wealthy individuals who are not quite legitimate or are looking to extract their money from one bank or country and move it to a bank or country with attitudes more sympathetic to the new customer. The Dteam would then stage an identity theft for the client and move all funds to the new destination, which could be the client's preference, but usually was the Dteam's preference. A percentage for the effort was extracted, leaving the client's money laundered and typically safe.

Originally the Dteam catered to Russian clientele, but the business expanded exponentially as the European Union financial system started to crumble under its own weight of debt. The opportunities significantly increased when European banks started limiting what their citizens could pull out of a bank and move elsewhere. Capital extraction became big business for people unwilling to let the government seize their money for bank failures. Clients started surfacing in North America as sovereign enforcers started pressing the high-income targets for more taxes. Individuals who tried to move their monies to off-shore banking that honored bank secrecy laws were accused of drug dealing and money laundering schemes to escape the tax burden.

Clients that leveraged the identity theft program offered by the Dteam paid ten percent on the transaction and set up an annuity to pay themselves back from a bank location that ignored extradition of exported monies. As an added bonus, the client could also write off the identity theft and its associated loss on their taxes, thus making back, in most cases, more than the ten percent fee in a very short time.

The routine worked quite well since the identity theft client helped to provide good evidence of the theft but poor or bogus clues as to the location or identity of the Dteam's agents. The key to the success of the operation was reliable information that could not be intercepted before the exercise was completed.

Those known as information mules provided this valuable service. The Dteam had higher reliability from these agents because they could not go into business for themselves as easily as they could when they were moving money or drugs. If the information was properly delivered to the correct destination, the mules received a wire transfer for their efforts. The information mules delivered content that had no outside commercial value since the media was encrypted and had to be delivered to receive payment. Tracking by the intelligence communities was far more difficult, and with a near zero success rate for prosecution.

Grigory had originally adopted simple USB drives to transport the identity theft data. This was quickly outdated when the intelligence community began to routinely intercept and decipher the data being transported. One of his minor mules in New York City was caught by the police with a USB drive. The day she was caught she had come to him with a new proposal for transport that piqued his interest, but she'd wanted too much money. After her arrest and a few weeks of letting her wallow in the New York City legal system, Grigory had lent a helping hand and got her out of trouble. In return she now worked in several areas for the Dteam, along with giving them the enhanced transport method.

This particular mule had hit on the idea of encoding the message into a tattoo on a person. She was able to create a canvas within the tattoo to store relevant information, with the mule and their tramp stamp going to the assigned destination. During the process of getting a tattoo, she had stumbled upon the idea of an embedded image. Her tattoo artist completed the message's holding area with a carefully constructed image.

At a high level, the information image was scanned onto a lightweight piece of nearly transparent paper, the skin was lightly coated with water proof adhesive, and the paper with the image was carefully placed so that the ink outline of the image was left on the skin. She'd experimented with this process until the information could be encrypted and laid down as an image that could be read by a smart phone code scanner application. The process to replace the image began with alcohol, which destroyed the existing information.

High end laser printers took the code scanner images and put them on the membrane tissue. The code scanner image was placed on the individual's skin almost as a membrane and then covered with a lacquer to protect the image from damage while in transit. With this method, the tramp stamp area was repeatedly reused with new information. It was particularly useful when moving through airport security, especially when a full body search was triggered. The tattooed message was simply not detectable. The tattoo artist had no visibility to the encrypted contents or the process to extract the data.

The points of failure in this new process of information transport was only if a mule died en route, which delayed but did not compromise the data. Grigory liked the new transport model so much that he incorporated it in his other operations.

Besides providing the enhanced transport method, the rescued operative had continued to prove valuable. She'd brought Grigory a decimal point rounding program. Grigory decided to make Sergei her routine contact as his attention was needed for other operation aspects. When she protested that Sergei bothered her, he reassured her that he controlled Sergei. The Dteam leveraged this program for their new off-shore accounts to generate the unclaimed income flow into the Dteam accounts.

Sergei did not like babysitting a mule or operative. He suggested to Grigory several times that she was a potential leak and should not be trusted. Grigory told Sergei to not rock the boat and to protect her as a valuable resource. At some point, Sergei advised, she would spill everything on their operations. Grigory firmly overrode the warning and had Sergei send her additional assignments to locate information on specific people. Patty was Grigory's new rising star, which rankled Sergei to no end.

CHAPTER 14

2 + 2 = 5
for very large values of 2.

Tuesday began with a call from Buzz. Jacob was quiet as Buzz rapidly and, sounding almost frightened, outlined the problems that his program was causing at his father's bank. The more he heard, the angrier he felt toward Buzz.

"Man, Father is so upset that the passwords now appear to be compromised, resulting in a company-wide reissue of passwords to folks, which is keeping the Help Desk way too busy and delaying work." The whiny tone in Buzz's voice was amplified by the phone. "I am asking PT to come out and take a look to see if there are any other problems around our information access security. Father asked me to call. So how soon can you be here?"

"Buzz, you know there is a process to engage with PT and it is through Brian, not me. I will be happy, since this is business, to alert Brian and ask to be assigned. Besides, I have a bone to pick with you on my code as well," Jacob conveyed in an even tone.

"A bone to pick? Get off it, man!" Buzz's tone changed. "I don't see why you would have an issue, since I have the egg on my face. I made the modifications you recommended, so no one knows where this came from. I just need help in repairing it, so I can still leverage it.

"You must have missed something, but I can't find it. I did what you said, very carefully. The only step I missed, and admitted to my father, is that I should have asked your team to double check it before putting it into production."

"That's not how I see it, but I will tell Brian of the need and get over there as quickly as I can. We will discuss it then or later, but I will get to the bottom of it, make no mistake, Buzz. I'll call you from the lobby so you can let me up."

Jacob went to Brian and outlined the problem at New York Finest Bank and Savings. No specifics about the code, but he emphasized a security breach with passwords and Buzz's request to have PT step in and assist. Though Brian frowned at the circumvented process, he agreed that Jacob should go at once and keep him posted.

Brian must have called Buzz, as he was waiting in the lobby when Jacob arrived. Jacob signed in and got his temporary badge. They proceeded toward the data center area.

Buzz summarized, "Thanks for coming. I really am not certain what happened. I just know that individual logins and passwords seem to be randomly sent to others via email. It started this morning with the higher ups and is cascading. It looks like it's only to internal addresses, but across all levels of personnel. The team immediately reset all passwords to all systems to force users to either complete a manual password change process or call for support. The phone lines have been going nuts. It appears to have started when the program I uploaded went into production at five this morning."

"Okay, so you are on lockdown now? And the program disabled?" Jacob asked.

"Yes, and resetting of all passwords across the board is in place," responded Buzz.

"Okay, point me to a machine, give me credentials with no restrictions and sit here to guide me on program locations. I want to get started, ASAP," Jacob said, with his professionalism intact.

For the next few hours they reviewed all the systems to make certain all was well. All security levels were intact and functioning correctly. Then Jacob started to review the program which was supposedly the culprit. He looked through it from one end to another. Buzz had in fact made all the correct changes per directions.

Jacob commented along the way, "Yes, this was corrected, you signed it here, you changed to main access here, fine."

Through all of the review, Buzz simply nodded a few times, saying, "See, I told you this was done as prescribed, Oh Great One." Clearly, he was seeking exoneration.

Jacob paused in one area near the bottom of the program and followed it to another area. A new executable was attached to the program. This executable was not a part of the original design.

Inspecting it more closely, the confusion cleared. "Buzz, see this right here. Where did this come from and why is it in here? Look, this portion is where the problems spring from. This was not what I provided to you, so when did you attach it?"

Looking closely at the area, Buzz softly spoke, "Honest, I have no idea. I do not even recognize this. I do not recall it being here when I last compiled it at the house, after I made your prescribed changes. I finished the changes, completed the retesting and zipped it up onto a clean thumb drive. I brought it to work yesterday to apply it onto the system. I was so proud of what it was doing and feeling so much better about myself, I didn't even tell the others on the team or get PT to perform final review. I simply applied it to the production box. It looks like removing that whole sequence will regain the program as designed. Right?"

"Yep, that is about it," Jacob agreed. "However, it is crucial that you figure out how this was added and who had access to your stuff, your system, and your passwords. I know you gave them to me, but you clearly made the changes. I could not have easily gotten into it, so who did? Who did you brag to, man?"

"No one, I swear. I didn't go on chat rooms, or tell anyone here. I was totally wrapped up at home making the changes. I deleted the original code after completing the revisions, just like you said. The only one around was Patty, hooked on watching movies while I was working and then focused on my pleasure," he said with all sincerity and continued, "I promise this was never part of our conversation. She can be quite the little distraction, if you get my drift."

"Alright man, I believe you," Jacob replied. "However, you need to know that a portion of my original code showed up in another bank that had a significant problem. My code was added to a very extensive routine that was designed to cause some significant problems. I can't figure this out. If you didn't share, how could that happen? Something is just not right. I think it was compromised. Maybe Patty?"

"No way. She was watching TV, cooking or we were playing in bed and in the shower. She never even asked what I was working on," Buzz said, shaking his head.

"Okay, well, let's finish this up, and you find out how your passwords were compromised here to get that code modification at the end of the program. Update me when you figure it out but make certain that no one has your information," berated Jacob.

0 1 0 1 0 1 0 1 0 0 1 1 0 0

Jacob returned to the PT offices and wrote up his report. In updating Brian, he was clear on what had occurred and even relayed how he had provided the program routine to Buzz for a portion. He admitted that he'd done it on his own, rather than billable through PT, and promised Brian that would not happen again.

Brian was actually very understanding. He indicated he too helped friends at times with programs. Brian knew Jacob's history with Buzz through school. That had been discussed upon employment and when the contract with New York's Finest was renewed. All was good between them, but the rogue code was highlighted in the report and the compromised security information noted.

Jacob checked his email and some other requests from the team that he had received while out of the office. In checking the schedule for the next day, he had a team meeting in the morning for project reviews and then the meeting with the unknown Otto. He alerted Brian to a longer lunch for the next day but left out the details of where and with whom. Something told him this was personal. He loaded up his stuff and went home.

CHAPTER 15

No one has to forgive you for your successes.

Finally feeling caught up on his rest, Jacob biked to work, admiring the clear warm morning. His dreams had actually been a lot of fun last night, if a bit too free-flowing with the pretty Petra. He knew he hoped to see her this weekend and see if any portion of his wayward dreams could be explored with her.

Reaching the front of the line at Starbucks, Julie flashed that megawatt smile, "Morning, Jacob, what is your pleasure this morning?"

"Morning, Julie, I think I will have my tea, please."

"Sure, one tea coming right up. Anything special on tap for your day?" she asked, trying to prolong the interaction.

"Nah, pretty much the same stuff, different day. At least that is my hope that nothing ends up burning out of control. I'm sure you can relate when the rushes hit," he conveyed, appreciating a bit of interaction for a change.

"Well, I will keep my fingers crossed that it all works in your favor. Here you go, and have a muffin on the house to insure your good day." She handed the goods over, then again smiled broadly.

"Thank you. Keep the change," he conveyed after passing her a five-dollar bill.

He went upstairs to his office. He settled in and gathered the information he needed to update the team for the meeting. The meeting went on until almost the lunch hour. Jacob's cell buzzed with his meeting reminder, and he received a text that the meeting was set to start at noon with directions repeated. Odd that it had an oblique sender number. Not surprising, he decided, as he headed over. It promised to be interesting, and he hoped enlightening.

He arrived at the Rothman building. It was not one of the more famous in New York, but older and established like a stately law firm. This was a building he had not ever seen from the inside. The offices he sought were on the 25th floor, the top floor of the building per the only name on the building directory, Ronnie, Ltd. He had never heard of them, but as he entered the elevator he tried doing a quick Internet search on his smart phone. No hits. He made a mental note to research later. He absentmindedly wondered if the rest of the building was empty.

The elevator opened to a tastefully decorated, plush suite that seemed to speak of European aristocracy. The suite was filled with rich leathers and tasteful oils of older homes that made him think of Germany or maybe Poland. All browns and burgundy with splashes of gold in the lighting, frames, and tones of the rich carpeting had him feeling he was entering a chateau rather than an office in the heart of Manhattan. Near the window, he spied a woman that looked up from what she was doing as he approached.

"Hello," he said. "My name is Jacob Michaels, and I have a meeting at noon with a gentleman named Otto." Then hesitantly, he added, "Can you tell me what your business does, madam?"

He noticed her expensive clothing, beautiful red hair done in a professionally contained way, minimal jewelry, enhancing make up, and gentle grey eyes. Up close she appeared in her fifties rather than her thirties, which was his first impression.

"Of course, Mr. Michaels. Welcome. My name is Haddy, Otto's Executive Assistant," she said with a welcoming smile. "He is expecting you, and lunch arrived a few minutes ago. Your timing is perfect. Let me escort you to his offices. Ronnie, Ltd., has been in business a long time. We handle discreet customer financial requests. We have been in this building for thirty or so years. I am sure Otto will answer all your questions."

She rose, conveying an air of aristocratic breeding. She reminded him of Granny, walking like a duchess. He followed her and took in the surroundings. They passed a couple of rooms, each one appointed in the same formal manner. For a few seconds, he was concerned about his casual slacks and shirt, but, hey, he had no idea what this was about when he dressed this morning. At the end of the hall, the door was open, and the most elegant area so far came into view.

Standing at the sideboard was a man Jacob presumed was Otto. Jacob did a rapid assessment of the man who stood almost to his height. He commanded respect, with a stock of full white hair and penetrating blue eyes. He was obviously older, not terribly fit, but not blatantly overweight. Age-wise he could easily be from sixty to eighty, yet nowhere near frail looking. The man emitted a sense of knowledge and power as he approached.

"Ah, Jacob. Welcome. Glad we could do this over lunch. Thank you, Haddy, that will be all for now."

He extended his hand and provided a firm hand shake. His accent was, to Jacob's ear, perhaps Polish or German, with a clear mastery of English. Otto's face conveyed little, but he seemed approachable.

"I hope that lunch is suitable. I am sure you have many questions as the young always do. You are, however, to be commended for coming here with so little background knowledge. Likely you are feeling a bit like a fish out of water. Come select your lunch, and we will talk. I have wanted to meet you face-to-face for some time." He gestured Jacob to the lunch spread and indicated his chair.

"Thank you, this looks good. I believe I owe you a thank you for my DEFCON ticket, hotel coverage, and airline ticket," Jacob indicated, filling his plate with food. Sitting down, he started, "So what, Mr. err. . ."

"Please call me Otto, all my friends do." Frowning slightly, he added, "You are certainly welcome for the ticket, but I cannot take credit for the hotel or airline ticket. Good idea. Wish I'd thought of it. I will mention it to Haddy."

"Okay, Otto, I am at a loss. How do we know each other, and what does Ronnie, Ltd., do? I do not recall any dealings with this firm."

Jacob struggled in his mind to place the old guy into a logical slot and yet schooled his face from revealing his uncertainty. Thanks Mom, he silently thought.

"We really have never met, Jacob. I and my associates, however, have been following your career since you entered MIT. You came to our attention with your academic success and, of course, the security program contribution to Open Source that you have done. I did send you the t-shirt which was voted on by committee. I had hoped to meet you at DEFCON, but something unexpected came up that changed my plans. I was pleased that you accepted the ticket and went to Las Vegas. Outside of not meeting you there, I myself was secretly glad I couldn't go. That is not my favorite place." Otto stated all of this, as if intuitively obvious.

"Fortunately for me, you and I work in the same vicinity so having the meeting here actually makes more sense, more relaxed and private. This first meeting, of what I hope will be many, will barely satisfy your curiosity. I can see all the questions racing through your mind. My suggestion is that you demonstrate your patience, which I know you have. I can tell you though, you have a bright future, my boy, whatever your choices. I am hoping that over time I can convince you to join our firm. I think you would be a good fit."

"You're right, sir. I have lots of questions," Jacob continued, his voice remaining even.

He also filed away for now the hotel and airline ticket issue. He would think about that later.

"I would like to know who you are and what is this company? Why me? How you got my identity information?"

"Those, of course, are the obvious questions. Let me provide some background that may help, though likely not enough for your bright mind." Otto chuckled, then continued.

"Ronnie, Ltd., is a part of a much larger organization that the original partners established near the close of World War II. This particular entity deals with our wealthier customers in the States for investments and financial endeavors. The headquarters of our larger organization is in Switzerland. With that country's financial discretion and neutrality, I suspect this doesn't surprise you. Different branches we have established in key markets include finance, investments trading, information and technology, and real estate practices. Our clients cover the whole realm of the higher, powerful echelon, as it were.

"We are, as I think you say here in the States, a family-controlled business. Our interests in you are primarily your abilities in technology, programming and security. Our business focuses on keeping our clients in balance."

Watching Jacob for a reaction and finding none, he continued. "Your abilities could fill a gap that I have noticed exists in our organization. Technology seems to be the way of the future.

Though I have personally had experience in information gathering and security layers, it is not at the level of someone younger, like you. Others in the organization have reviewed your profile and believe you may fit. We are a cautious, tight-knit group though, and require some levels of commitment before extending offers or fully opening the drapes."

As Otto provided that background, Jacob's mind was trying to categorize the organization. The broad-brush overview was interesting but very vague. Certainly not the details he needed for clear understanding, such as origin, charter, and competitors. He couldn't decide if this was a firm that would be valuable to his career, but the global reach mapped to his long-range goals. Without a doubt, this man would give nothing away unintended, but two could play at that game.

"Are you essentially saying that you are an investment firm for global customers? Or are you more nefarious in your objectives?" Jacob asked.

"Nefarious, as a whole, would not be our prime objective, but rather the other end of the spectrum. Our clients are sometimes part of the rich and spoiled ranks that need to be reminded of humanity in order to retain their wealth. Greed, we believe, is singularly undesirable. We offer a full range of investment management services. Does that help to clarify?"

Otto chuckled again with a sudden twinkle in his intense blue eyes. "Well, our meeting regrettably is drawing to an end. I am glad we have now met and are measuring ourselves against each other. I would like to meet next week at the same time. I will have some more things to show you, I can answer more questions which you will of course have lined up, and perhaps if you have interest, a bit of a testing exercise. How does that sound? Say, starting at noon for the entire afternoon if your schedule will permit." Otto rose and clapped Jacob on the back. He escorted him down the hallway.

"I will try to arrange my schedule for the entire afternoon next week. I'm sure I'll have questions after I think about our discussion. It was nice to meet you and thank you again for the ticket to DEFCON and the t-shirt. Sometime I will relate the odd experience of that trip. Perhaps you will have an opinion to share," Jacob stated, while clearly focusing on Otto's face for any hint of his knowledge of what had occurred.

"Sounds interesting. I look forward to it." Otto's comment revealed nothing.

As they approached Haddy's desk, he said, "Haddy, please block my calendar next Wednesday afternoon for another meeting with Jacob."

"Yes, sir. Nice meeting you, Jacob. Lunch will be similar unless you have other preferences?" she graciously asked.

"It was delicious and included all my favorites. You must know me fairly well," he said, trying to see if she revealed anything.

"I find that people enjoy good food that is not too filling during the work week. I am glad I chose well," Haddy said, without missing a beat. "Enjoy your week, sir."

After Otto saw Jacob disappear behind the elevator doors, he smiled at Haddy and placed a call on his cell phone while returning to his office.

Standing in front of the window overlooking New York, he said, "The meeting is over. He is an impressive young man, much better than his photographs. Continue your reconnaissance efforts. Just do not reveal your involvement. And don't let yourself get too personally involved. He is not in our fold yet," he gently warned.

"I know my job, Otto. I am a professional who has been a part of this team since I was born. If you do not trust me, then get someone else for this part. I like him and would not like to see him hurt," the person at the other end of the phone call rebuffed with mild irritation.

"Yes, my dear. I know that you do not mix business and personal, but he is a striking man, is he not?"

"It does not surprise me that you of all people would think that, Otto."

"You know me so well, my dear. Well then, I am meeting with him next week and will give him a bit of a test. I may need your help in crafting something that would prove interesting to him and yet give me some insight to how he thinks. Julianne seems to have done well by him, or perhaps it was more Adriana. Alert JAC that we may be ready to move to the next stage within a month. I am sure she will be grateful for a change of pace," he said, knowing no response was needed as he disconnected.

01010101001100

Meanwhile, Jacob headed back to the PT offices. He mulled over the conversation and considered the possibly high-end job offer. He would do some investigation on the firm and see what additional information he might gather. Being a family-owned business based in Europe, he doubted there would be much public information. Foreign entities revealed very little, and he sensed that this organization would be no different. Maybe he could ask Otto for a financial statement of some sort. Although in his mind, money was still not the primary goal. Good projects, interesting details and learning new skills were still his focus. He had enough money within his own investments to feel very secure.

CHAPTER 16

Odd! Everyone wants to play to win but no one wants to get hurt.

Midway through Friday morning, as Jacob worked on his projects, he was sadly reminded that Petra had not phoned. Pushing the thought to the back of his mind, he began his newest code review project assigned that morning. All the guys were busy working on projects both on and off site. Working through this latest test exercise, his mind drifted back to the two evenings he had spent trying to find more information on either Ronnie, Ltd., or its parent company. All avenues had pretty much been fruitless. He was not surprised, but he'd wanted to find out some additional details not provided by Otto. Odd man, Otto, though strangely Jacob had felt a sort of bonding with the man. He was looking forward to this second meeting, and he did have some questions ready.

As if on cue as the testing completed, his cell rang. "Hi, Jacob here," his voice was confident and professional when he saw no number in the display window.

"Hello, Jacob, it is me, Petra. I am wrapping up this project this afternoon so I can be free tomorrow if you still wanted to get together." Her voice was melodic in his ear.

"Well, I was beginning to wonder if you would call. Sure, tomorrow is good for me. What do you think about riding over to Long Island and hitting a few of the wineries? The scenery is pretty if you haven't been there." Coming right off the cuff, it sounded very nice as he said it.

"Hmmm. I had no idea that there were wineries anywhere close in New York. That sounds like fun. What time would you like to get started? I am an early riser most days, and if it is pretty, I will want to see it all." There was a softer quality to her voice, laced with excitement.

"How about we meet up at eight at Central Park where I saw you the other day then? Plan on the whole day, and you can see something very non-typical New York," he asked.

"Okay, eight it is then, but I will meet you at your house," she stated with certainty of agreement. "See you then."

"Okay, then," he replied to the already disconnected Petra.

Jacob finished up at work, though a bit later than he wanted, and went home. Rather than his usual Friday night perusal of the chat rooms and tracking down program bugs, he was busy cleaning up his bike and gear, adding some travel rations and funds to his fanny pack and extra water into the holders. They could easily reach their destination riding and by subway as needed. Spending time with Petra was his entire focus. He had some things he wanted to run by her in general, perhaps even Otto. But mostly he looked forward to learning more about her.

Waking up early, he shaved, showered, ate and dressed. He was sipping coffee and reading some periodicals when she knocked at the door. Right on time, he noted, looking at his watch. He did like people that were on time.

When he opened the door, he was a bit surprised at the head-to-toe leathers Petra was wearing. Not that they weren't flattering, hugging every inch of her body. However, the heat later in the day would require their removal, and the heavy clothing would be difficult to carry on the way home. It might be a bit chilly this morning, but the afternoon high was expected to reach the mid-80s, and she would be overwhelmingly warm. Her hair was in her tight bun with no hint of the long locks he'd seen before. Her face was radiant and smiling.

Petra likewise checked him head to toe as the door opened. The biking shorts and vented overtop displayed long muscular legs and a very manly physique. She caught her breath as she memorized every detail. His hair was thick and a bit wet as if he'd recently gotten out of the shower. She caught herself as her mind wandered. This was just a chance to get to know the real him.

It was a tie as they both said, "Hi and good morning."

He invited her in and offered her coffee, then suggested they sit and plan out their route. He outlined the roads and turns and asked about her tastes in wines so they could stop at a few wineries. Fortunately, she also seemed fond of Burgundies so he had an idea of the top three stops he would like to make. As he outlined some of the sights along the way, she seemed more than eager to see it all. He also planned to take her to the farmers market for lunch, deciding to save that as a surprise as time permitted. The wineries also offered food, as well as areas to sit and enjoy the surroundings. Now, he thought, how does one suggest a change of attire to a female?

"Jacob, I can see that we had different thoughts regarding this adventure today. I brought my Harley, and you appear dressed for your street racer. Granted it is only around eighty miles, less if we take advantage of a few of the trains." Frowning slightly, she said, "I don't have a street racer here, but I had shipped my Harley here as it is the only way I have found to get away some in the evening or weekends as time permits. Do you have a motor-cycle, or would you consider riding together?"

"We definitely had different thoughts. I sent my Harley for a tune up and haven't arranged to pick it up yet. The weather has been perfect for riding my street racer to work. Let me go change and grab my helmet since you offered that we could ride together. Are you a good driver?"

"I am. My papa taught me. Safety is the number one priority. I have to take extra care as I like the big bikes, but I do not have the strength of a man, like you," she said sweetly with a grin. "Go change and hurry. I am ready to see Long Island and all the scenery you promised."

When he returned in less than ten minutes in shirt, jeans, and boots, she couldn't help but admire his form as he added his leggings and vest on top and carried his helmet. He locked up and grabbed the waters and snacks from the bike. Walking down the steps, he admired the Harley parked to the side.

Ready to comment on the bike, but a bit concerned, he gently asked, "Petra, this is a nice ride, but have you ever driven with a rider bigger than you before? I probably easily have seventy pounds on you. The balance issue is really different, if you haven't experienced it."

At first, she wanted to be the typical strong, in-control girl, but he had asked in such a nice way without a hint of distrust that her logic won out when she responded, "Honestly, I have not carried any riders before. I was hoping that you had and that you would consider driving. I do not think you would be any less safe, not since you drive a bicycle in New York City during rush hours."

"I think that will work and then you can really enjoy the ride and see everything. I appreciate the confidence you are showing in me."

He outlined their now revised route and added a few points of interest that might be seen. They mounted up and took off.

Traffic was light as they easily made their way to the Island. It was still early, and most folks headed out of town either late on Friday evening or midday Saturday. Blue skies were dotted with random cotton ball clouds, making the winding roads and expansive farmlands breathtaking. They pulled over after an hour or so, he checked the fuel, they drank some water and he pulled off the leggings as the morning was heating up. He figured they would be at the first winery easily by ten when they were scheduled to open.

She tapped his shoulder and pointed at this and that along the way. The flowers, the farms, children playing, nothing seemed to escape her attention. The signs pointed them along the winery trail with distances from the entrances clearly marked. He pulled into the first one he had planned. As he removed his helmet, he noticed that she looked like a kid in a candy store, all full of energy and an ear-to-ear grin. Petra took off her leggings and stored them in the side bin. She also shed her jacket, revealing slim fitting jeans and sleeveless top. She re-secured her bun, which had dared to loosen when she'd removed her helmet.

"What a quaint place," she admitted. "Like wineries I have visited in California and even in South America. And you like this one, you said?"

"Yep, this is one of my favorites. Family-owned and established for some time. They specialize in vibrant reds. As Burgundies were at the top of your list, I think you'll enjoy these." He grinned at her exuberance.

They had a few samples and listened to the owner recount his latest wine competition victories. He was pleased with their attention, very entertaining and had some excellent wines. They each selected a favorite as a glass which they took to the outside patio area that overlooked the property. As they sat enjoying the quiet, Jacob wanted to find out more about this pretty lady.

"So, Petra, how does a lady as pretty and smart as you have such a big Harley that she obviously enjoys driving? It is not something most ladies in the States seem to embrace."

"Really, it was my papa that got me hooked when I was a teen. One of the goals of my parents was that their first child would have a variety of experiences. My education was all tutors; however, my folks were very involved as well. Mama is the cook, the creator of fun things, the painter, and homemaker, so I was required to learn all those skills.

"For work, Papa travels all over the world. Sometimes we would travel together and see the sights, other times he would travel alone and regale us with stories and adventures. Mama liked being at home with her charities and friends, so sometimes I would get to visit Papa alone.

"Once, when he had a four-month project in the southwestern United States, he flew me in to spend two weeks here. Papa promised it would be an adventure I would never forget, that I might even see cowboys. As a teen, almost eighteen, adventure was the right word to get me excited, especially if horses were in the mix. Even without the details, I knew it would be fun. He told me to pack light with only casual clothes, like for hiking.

"When I arrived in Dallas, Papa picked me up and said we were going shopping for our adventure. On the way to the store we chatted, and he asked me if I had ever seen a movie called *Easy Rider*. When I said I hadn't, he explained a bit about it being a wonderful trip on motorcycles, seeing the country-side and sleeping under the stars. He had noticed, with the two months he'd already been in Texas, that the stars were amazing, and he wanted to show me. Sounded great to me, especially since we had been riding dirt bikes and smaller motorcycles all over Europe for many years. I guess you could say I'm more of a tomboy."

"I can promise you certainly don't look like a tomboy," Jacob grinned as he took in her face, slightly flushed from the outdoors.

He wondered if he could coax a bit of a blush from her, but let it go for the present.

"We arrived at this totally amazing store like nothing I'd ever seen before. It was called Harley Davidson. They have outlets in Europe but I had never seen this type of store. He bought me a helmet, rain gear, and leather gloves. Then he had me look at all the motorcycles to see which one I would like. He had selected a Road King for himself but wanted me to get comfortable. The people were so nice and let me try several of them until I landed on a Softail. I was totally hooked. Arrangements were made to pick them up the next morning.

"I'm sorry, this is a really long story, and you probably aren't interested," she suggested, as her cheeks began blooming pink.

"You have me hooked now." Jacob was so enjoying her animated description, watching her every move.

Obviously her family love was strong, and this helped him understand who she was, at least in part. The last thing he wanted was for her to stop the story.

"It is so wrong to start a story and then stop before the end. You owe me the whole story, Petra. Plus, I think you like the telling. Your papa sounds like lots of fun."

"Papa is fun when he is not working and when he is showering me with attention, of course. He likes that his little girl has no fears and tackles everything." Beaming with pride, she continued.

"As we drove back to his hotel to get ready for the next day, he told me the rules for our travels. Papa is big on following the rules in all things, even holidays. The rules were no timetables, no grousing about weather whether hot, cold or wet. We would purchase food daily and use a camp stove, and we were going to stay at state parks in a tent. I was so excited all evening while we got our sleeping bags, a tent he had already purchased, and three changes of clothes all ready to go. I hardly slept.

"Have you ever been to Texas, Jacob?" She asked.

"Nope, but I think after this story that may change. You need to tell me what you saw and did on this trip. It is amazing that you looked forward to what many would consider the rough life," he responded, still interested in hearing the whole story and her animated way of telling it.

"We arrived to pick up the rented Harleys, and Papa had mapped out the whole route he wanted to take. We started out from Dallas to see and experience the Texas Hill Country. Texas has lots of pretty winery estates. They also have the most amazing tasting white peaches. On the way we saw a medieval castle built on a hillside over-look. We had to stop and knock on the door. My family is not the shy type, especially my papa. The owner, Mr. Winters, invited us in after Papa told him he was impressed with his castle home, as it reminded him of Europe."

"He actually answered the door and let you enter? Wow, no wonder you recall this trip." Jacob was duly impressed, hanging on her every word.

"Mr. Winters was, well is, a very nice man. In fact, Papa still works on security systems for him now and again. He called his hill country home Falkenstein Castle. It was actually based on plans that Mr. Winters had found in his travels of Europe. The castle had been built in Europe so he built a duplicate in Texas. It had turrets, of course, a wine cellar, two great rooms, five or six bedrooms that we saw, patios and gardens all around. The view was fantastic. We had so much fun visiting he actually asked us to stay for dinner and for the night. I had to laugh with Papa, later admitting it was a welcome delay from sleeping in the tent."

The rapt attention from Jacob and his encouraging nods and smiles told her to continue her story. That he was interested in something so simple made her heart beat a bit faster. He had gotten another glass of wine for each of them and indicated she could continue. The other wineries could wait.

"The next morning, after exchanging contact information with Mr. Winters, we continued south to Enchanted Rock. It was listed as a mystical destination for the Comanche Indians and was the site of one of the last big Indian and U.S. cavalry battles of the 1870's. Papa insisted from his research of the place, that we would only gain the true impact of Enchanted Rock by climbing it.

"Half way up, we met a lady, Bobby, and felt compelled to ask if she was resting or reflecting. After verifying that we were not park authorities, she said she was re-hydrating herself and wanted to know if we'd like a beer. We declined the beer, but it did not stop Papa from launching into his James Bond routine, saying he was a shaken not stirred kind of person. Once on top, we explored all the hidden areas and hidey holes.

"We stayed in Pedernales Falls State Park. This was my first view of the state parks in Texas, and I was impressed with the maintenance and care that was taken. Each camp site had water and electricity as well as a cooking barbeque. It actually made me a believer in camping and seeing the natural outdoors. Good exploring, hiking trails and sometimes lakes and nice people. Much of the U.S. has state park systems, and I try to take advantage if I'm staying for weeks or months in a location.

"Then we continued our drive the next day and unexpectedly ran into a rather unusual phenomenon just outside Boerne that continued for two days. Locals claimed it was the Butterfly Blizzard of Bandera County, saying it happened for a few days every couple of years. At first the modest butterflies felt whimsical, but they became a torrent, covering our windshields and helmet shields. We rapidly realized the out-and-out danger of driving through them. When I told Papa that I could hardly see to drive, we took refuge in the Lost Maples State Park. It took hours to clean the bikes and ourselves. We laughed for hours; still do to this day if the subject comes up."

Jacob laughed with her. Sounded like a great trip. He enjoyed watching her get so animated. He liked listening to her technical explanations, but this lighter side was so endearing. Take care, he told himself, you are falling for her, and you don't have time right now for this.

"Petra, let's head over to the next winery, and you can continue the story. This winery is worth seeing."

"Great."

They continued on their route through the wineries coming upon another estate set back from the road. The choices of wines were nice as well as some light fare to complement the wine. They settled into a shady area with colorful flowers and acres of grapevines everywhere they looked.

"What happened after the butterfly masses?" he encouraged.

"Well, Papa insisted we had to find a place called the Devil's Sink Hole and watch the bats fly at sundown. Swimming was also suggested. We found it alright," she said, getting tickled with the telling. "I do not know why he thought we could swim there, as the bottom could only be reached by rappelling forty-five meters straight down. The bats did fly at sundown, and the wave of them exiting this hole in the ground was unbelievable. The bats came swirling out of the hole like a silent black tornado.

"On the way back to our campsite it was dark. I am not much for driving a bike at night. We intercepted a group of vultures dining on a deer carcass at the side of the road. They were so into their feast that they waited too long to leave, even with me honking, that the last one that took flight missed me by inches as I was leading us down the road at seventy miles per hour.

Papa said later I was simply trying to play tag with the birds, like I did when I was little with the geese on our property at home."

Laughing with her, Jacob said, "Please tell me this story isn't over yet."

She laughed and continued, "Oh no, there is more. We wanted to go way south. I can tell you the terrain changed dramatically from the hills of Texas to the flat, desert-like area that you see in movies. Really hot. We hit a border patrol check point where no less than eight officers were standing on the hot pavement under an open metal shed. I figured we were in for some thorough searching and being sniffed by their dogs. But my Papa, always looking for a humorous opportunity, stopped first and said in amazingly perfect Texan, 'Whata all y'all doing out here in the heat?' Followed by, 'Is this where I kin git ma margaritas to go?' They simply waved us on through with hardy laughs and huge smiles."

"It all sounds like a great adventure. Perhaps you can show me sometime?" Jacob queried, knowing he was captivated by her all the more with this story.

"Maybe someday I can show you the pictures and fill in other details. I think you would be fun to take on a similar trip."

She feared that her smile and the heat she was feeling would get her too involved with this delightful man. That was not part of her plans at all.

"I think it is time that we head back. I would like to fix you dinner after such a great day and your story. Perhaps chicken pasta if you like," he said in a casual yet friendly manner.

"Sounds good to me, and it has been a nice day. Thank you for listening, Jacob. Now onto a nice dinner of your chicken pasta. I can fix salad."

As they mounted up for the ride home, Jacob said he wanted to take her on a scenic ride back so she could get the full effect of the area. Along the way they shared the different points of interest.

They arrived at the townhouse. Jacob showed her around and offered an area she could use to freshen up. He met her in the kitchen after a fast shower and a change of clothes. She made nice comments on the house and décor overall. The kitchen was large enough to divide their tasks. Soon the smell of garlic, onions, and Alfredo sauce filled the air. They took turns stealing glances at one another during the preparation. Smooth jazz played softly in the background, not too distracting to their playful comments. Jacob poured some wine they'd procured that day and placed the serving dishes on the table. The delicious meal and light conversation made for a perfect evening.

Once finished, Jacob suggested they retire with their wine to the living room. With dim lights and romantic music, the mood seemed to shift slightly, taking on a more tender quality.

"Petra, you are amazing, both intelligent and beautiful. Being here with you and wanting you was not my expectation." His eyes lowered to her perfectly formed mouth with thoughts about how soft her lips must be.

"I would have to agree. I find you very attractive, and I'm drawn to you like a missing piece of a puzzle. Would you think me bold if I..." and with that she leaned into him and tentatively kissed him.

Requiring no more permission, he pulled her into his arms and deepened the kiss, feeling every nuance as her mouth begged for more. The passion of the kiss cascaded heat surging through them. As they continued to explore, clothes magically disappeared. Nothing would stop the urgency they felt. He caressed her body, feeling her responsive quivers, hearing her soft moans that begged him to continue. He stroked the curves of her waist and cupped her ample breasts, then plied her nipples with his fingertips feeling them swell with desire.

She shifted to increase his access while stroking and touching every inch of exposed skin. His hands roamed further, causing increased moans, and her body arched toward his pleasing touches. His mouth covered her extended breast as his hands sought the pleasure point between her legs. Her reaction was immediate with responses that indicated her need for fulfillment. He entered her with a desperation to join and immediately sensed her approaching release. Urging her on with strong even strokes, they fell off the cliff together. They both hugged closer, willing time to suspend.

Once their breathing evened, they drew slightly apart.

Petra looked deep into his eyes with a bit of sadness, yet smoldering passion, "Oh Jacob, how could we have done this. This complicates everything."

"My beautiful Petra, I was powerless to stop. It's a complication, but one I willingly accept."

"I need to go. I need to think. This is not part of my plan. We were powerless, but we shouldn't do this." Quickly she extracted herself, dressed and slipped out the door, saying just before the door closed, "Give me time to think, my dear Jacob. I will call you."

With that she was gone, and he sat totally confused as he replayed their day. Oh, to get her into a bed and wake up with the sunlight across her body. Perhaps the couch had not the best choice, but one he vowed to rectify at the earliest opportunity.

CHAPTER 17

Without the event there is no recovery, maybe only slow death.

Jacob entered the PT building and paused to get a cup of coffee. His behavior was disconnected and robotic. He completely missed the vibrant Julie's smile-turned-frown as he walked away. Grateful for the mundane activity, he connected his machine and waited for all the programs to load while he reflected on the weekend.

He'd spent all day yesterday smiling at odd times as he thought of Petra, then tried to understand why she'd rushed out. He had begrudgingly honored her request for time and hadn't phoned. Relationships were hard to deal with, but the connection between them was not casual in his mind. The only bright spot was that he'd been distracted when he'd found a new Open Source posting that kept him busy.

After he'd worked at the changes for nearly 12 hours straight, Jacob had posted his recommendations. The confidence he felt when he'd added in some of the encryption tricks that Petra had so painstakingly shared was worth the time. He'd escaped most thoughts of her as a woman in his arms until he'd tried to sleep.

The dreams were relentless and caused him to wake up wanting her, and not for her terrific mind. Petra had captivated him. He feared he'd lost his heart to her.

The office was busy for the first part of the week. He had just finished a final deliverable when his phone received a text reminding him of his pending meeting with Otto at the top of the hour. After he bundled up his PC and secured his work area, he passed by Brian's desk and reminded him that he would be gone the rest of the day.

A short time later he arrived on the 25th floor of the Rothman building. Jacob was surprised to see Otto himself calmly waiting. Otto rose from his chair and met Jacob.

As he extended his hand, he said, "Welcome, I am glad you could make this meeting, my boy. We will be meeting in one of the workrooms rather than my office. Lunch first, then your current questions, and then the test, as it were."

"Sounds good to me, Otto," Jacob replied, actually looking forward to the test.

They re-entered the elevator and descended to the 21st floor, where they walked down the hallway to a door with a handprint security pad. Otto placed his hand to the pad, and the door opened to reveal a very impressive system set up. It was close to being a compact Data Center. The humming of the machines and flashing screens immediately comforted Jacob. Lunch was set up at the far end where they made their selections and were seated.

"Otto, as you are undoubtedly aware, my searching for background information on Ronnie, Ltd., came up nil. From our last discussion, you'd indicated the company formed during World War II. Can you discuss the beginnings and wartime opportunities you were able to capitalize on?" His face was level and focused on Otto's as he wanted to see every nuance of the response.

"Well, that is a good place to start I suppose," Otto said with a slight grin. "There were three of them, as I might have said earlier. For now their names are not important to you. I am the descendant of one of the men and was born after the end of the war."

His recall began, and the edge to his voice was sharpened with anger at certain points in the discussion. "I am not certain how knowledgeable you are on the European havoc that Hitler brought to my family's homeland of Poland. They were young and idealistic but focused on interfering with the Nazis' communications. In 1939 the Nazis were overrunning Poland and had successfully captured the government. However, they failed to capture the minds of these three.

"The Polish Secret Service captured the Enigma Machine and gave it to the Brits. However, one of the three young men was in the right place at the right time and was able to copy the Enigma Machine's plans and photographed it. If you aren't aware, the Enigma Machine was capable of encrypting and decrypting communications very quickly. It was very effective during its time, and the Brits modified the machine several times to keep pace with what the Germans were changing. You might be aware they used an evolved version to intercept the Desert Fox transmissions.

"These three knew that they might be able to take advantage of the Enigma Machine's plans in a different way. The war was going badly; their families were at extreme risk, especially with being recruited to serve as Hitler's minions."

Tears glistening in Otto's eyes as he continued. "These families were wealthy and had provided the young men with great educations. Their fathers could not bear losing their families, so arrangements were made for the three families to slip out of Poland and into Switzerland. The families' financial connections and influence worked in securing new identities shortly after arrival. Though not connected by blood, the three young men behaved like brothers. Sadly, they also were soon destined to become heads of the respective households. The war was very hard.

"In discussions about the copied plans, they determined that additional value could be leveraged in the financial world. With some modifications, of course. Securing information on financial matters was not only important to the elite Europeans but also to the Nazis as those thieving individuals stole and looted along their murderous path across Europe. The three immediately began the Enigma Machine's modifications. They were certain that it would be useful as they prayed for victory for the Allies.

"If you know some of this history, then you are aware that all conquered territories were looted of art, precious stones, currency, anything of value, even wine. Our families had not gone unscathed. But as the fortunes of war began to turn against the Axis powers in 1942, the Nazis began to move their treasure to safe havens. Much of the stolen loot was converted to liquid assets and parked in the neutral banks of Switzerland. With the modified Enigma device, these three Polish lads were able to recover and restore many of the looted items to the rightful owners. The Nazis were thieves, and our family group were Robin Hoods. For us, securing and maintaining information has become an art form."

"So then, Otto, from this beginning your business ventures evolved to the areas you outlined during our last meeting?"

"Exactly. And the changes in the needs of our clients, inroads in communications and technology, as well as the vision for where we need to secure information remains ahead of the curve. We effectively add to the organization as we find elements that align with our overall beliefs. As bad as the war was, these days the battles are often fought in cyber space, which is why I believe technology is the total key to managing the changes in human temperament, commerce, greed and information."

"So then, are you morally enabling good or evil?"

"I would have to answer you honestly, Jacob, that the end game is for humankind's good. However, sometimes our team has taken the low road or appeared evil until the end of a given engagement."

Otto smiled again, "Which is why you and I need to move onto the testing segment of our meeting. That is, if you are, in fact, still interested in considering our opportunity to secure information and to avoid evil from impacting our clients. I will tell you upfront that the test is designed to challenge and determine your logic flow as well as your abilities."

"Honestly Otto, I don't know if I am convinced or not that your firm is on the up and up. I am not ready to accept an offer as there are a lot of gaps which I am taking on face value as a part of your security measures. However, I don't like walking away from a challenge, and the possibility of taking the next step does interest me. So, let's go."

Otto led Jacob to the machines and their associated monitors. The test, as it was outlined, would be to manage the three machines and solve whatever issues appeared as accurately and quickly as possible. Two of the machines represented two financial institutions that sent and received transactions, with virtual servers configured. The third machine was for the customer or the financial institution's user access to the respective financial institutions. Transactions occurred automatically via programs. He was provided the administration logons and passwords for the servers within each financial institution. Standard system monitoring tools were enabled and appeared to be very sophisticated.

Jacob was allowed to power up his laptop in case he needed some of his standard tools and his thumb drives to solve the problems. He was not allowed to connect his PC to their network. Any programs he moved to their machines would face standard virus software scanning. Reaching out to the Internet from his laptop was not an option either.

With that, Otto said he would check back in a couple of hours. If Jacob needed anything he had only to speak loudly, and Otto would be notified.

As a final parting word Otto said, "You may not be able to address all of the issues. It is the approach that we are looking to understand."

Jacob spent time accessing the systems and determined where things were located. It was very consistent with the other financial institution configurations he'd worked. After a scant 15 minutes, one of the financial institutions began experiencing problems with customer access. He saw Help Tickets automatically opened from the respective service desks which appeared in pop-up windows. Jacob found the source of the immediate issues, took corrective actions and was almost finished when another problem was presented on the machine of the other financial institution.

For three solid hours, issue after issue flared, including DOS attacks, password compromising, attempts at funds diversion, and so forth. Jacob used every trick in his bag from best security practices through encryption routines to thwart the issues and bring them under control. He added various safeguards pro-grammatically to stop any similar situations. He documented the problems as he went to ensure that he was tracking the right issues to the right institutions. Ultimately, he covered 25 different issues, which would likely not occur in a single day at any given institution. As no new issues were presented, he then took the time to run other tests to see if anything could be proactively corrected. As these were identified, he again took steps to elimi-nate them as problems.

When Otto came through the door, Jacob glanced at his watch, surprised to see it was after seven.

"It seems, my boy, that you have things well in hand. This is good. You have been simply monitoring and looking for breach holes for the last half hour."

Grinning, Jacob offered, "Very interesting set up and issues faced by these firms. I have faced similar challenges in my role at PT, but these problems are seriously on steroids. Are there more surprises stacking up while we are visiting?"

"No, in monitoring your progress, I am pleased that you have completed this phase of our interview ahead of expectations. The team is in agreement with me, that you might be brought to the home office as a next step, after a final evaluation of your efforts is completed. I would offer dinner, but I do have a prior commitment so I would ask that you remind me I owe you one."

Otto's eyes had a look of amusement in them. "Let me escort you out, Jacob, and I will let you know definitively of the next step by Monday."

Jacob packed up his laptop and his notes and followed Otto to the elevators. They shook hands as the elevator arrived. Once outside, Jacob heaved a sigh of relief. He couldn't imagine working that fast and efficiently on a daily basis, but it had been rockin' fun. With a lighter step, he unlocked his bike and rode home. He was exhilarated but exhausted and knew he would be ready to sleep as soon as he'd eaten something. His last thoughts before drifting off were to share this crazy interview test with Petra, if she ever contacted him.

CHAPTER 18

We don't have to be right all the time, just more times than our competitors.

Friday afternoons were pretty quiet at PT, and Jacob had finished the last of his assignments.

Walking over to Brian's office, he asked, "Do you have anything else for me to work on? I'm all caught up until the testing for the two projects being worked on is done. The guys do not expect to have anything else for me to review until Monday."

Brian looked up and grinned, "Well, I guess your intuition is alive and well. I was about to ask your status. Sit down. I want to tell you about something new that is in the works. A new customer overseas is trying to work through the Ts and Cs of a contract for our services for system verification and expansion planning review of their information services for the next eighteen months. The timeline requested is one month on site and then periodic follow-up visits."

"It sounds interesting. Who is the customer? Short-term introductory on-site relationship building with long term contact is very cool. Can it be done remotely or are they insistent that their contractor be on-site? As you know, Brian, travel is not a problem for me," Jacob stated.

He was aware that most of the other guys had families and avoided travel. They believed long hours were acceptable as long as home was a viable goal at the end of the work day.

"I know you are always willing to help out and travel, which we all appreciate. As a matter of fact, in this case part of the slow down on the contract is specifically because you are named as the primary. The customer is Regal Financial Zürich. Though they have multiple locations across Europe, Zürich is their headquarters. Our Legal is trying to determine if this is a risk for us in case you have another customer that is a priority over this one due to their contracts. I don't expect the legal team to get done arguing before the end of next week. How do you feel about being the prime for a customer? I know you can do it, but it takes away a bit of your agility, which you have enjoyed and frankly so have I."

As he carefully responded, his mind immediately went to Otto. "Brian, that is in line with our services, but it is up to you to assign me as prime. I wonder why they would specifically name me. I haven't heard of them before."

"You know, Jacob, I wondered that myself. But over recent weeks with the customers that you have worked with, your name is likely being bantered about as the expert. I called Mr. Buswald at New York Finest to see if he had familiarity with this overseas institution, and he spoke highly of them. Apparently, they are one of the oldest multinational finance companies to interact with our U.S. financial institutions. They are known for being extremely discreet. Swiss banks have always been attractive for the wealthy, in or out of the United States. PT Legal will also do their checking. As you know, PT has not done too much offshore unless it is a branch of a North American based-institution. Mergers, acquisitions, economy and technology are continually affecting the size and reach of these institutions."

"That does make sense. Let me know how the legal guys progress. Happy to help, but I think unless you have something else, I will head home. My cell, of course, is on."

Once he arrived home, Jacob decided to catch up on some household chores first. He sent a text message to Buzz seeing if he wanted to get together over the weekend. Keeping busy was a part of not contacting Petra and being patient while he waited for her call. Once he was caught up with everything domestic, he verified his passport and even packed a suitcase just in case Brian notified him to travel. He settled into his work mode to prowl for problems in the chat rooms.

Finding a particular piece of Open Source worth exploration, Jacob spent close to 30 hours on and off over the weekend working the code to find the streamlining and encryption options. He'd offered some suggestions to the chat rooms and actually received some interesting feedback. But the screen was close to blinding him when he decided to rest for a while. The last two days had finally caught up with him. He felt he'd no sooner laid down and shut his eyes when his cell rang with the name display masked.

"Jacob here."

"Hello, Jacob." Petra softly spoke, "How are you?"

Fully alert now and definitely pleased to hear her voice, he responded, "Actually, glad to hear your voice. What's up?"

"My assignment here is at an end. I am headed back home. I was hoping that we might get together for dinner tonight if you have no other plans."

"That sounds great. Did you have a place in mind? I could meet you of course," he suggested as he specifically placed control in her court to avoid spooking her.

"There is a quaint little place on Fifth Avenue called Marvel's Gardens which has some discreet seating so we might talk as well as enjoy great fare. They begin dinner service at 4:30 to cater to the folks attending a show. Have you been there?"

"Nope, but I know where it is. What time is good for you? I am fairly flexible timewise, so you decide."

"Let's meet up at five-thirty. That way we can have time to relax and talk."

"I will see you then," Jacob said just prior to disconnecting.

There was time for a fast shower, and a shave and change of clothes were in order. He would have to hurry if he was to meet at her the appointed time. His early afternoon nap would have to wait. Jacob had just gotten into the taxi and indicated his destination, when his cell rang. It was Brian.

"Hey, Brian, what's up?"

"Wanted you to know the latest on the Regal Financial contract we discussed. The legal teams have come to an agreement, and the final contracts are expected back no later than tomorrow morning. They have still indicated you need to be the prime and expect you to be at their site in Zürich before the end of next week. There is also an additional area in the security review highlighting your opinion on protecting their Intellectual Property, which I equate to customer's information. I wanted to see if you were still good and if we should go ahead and book your travel for you unless you would rather? They have identified the Russmon Hotel, and they are covering that directly, as well as providing a driver for the duration of your stay. In looking at the hotel website, I think you'll be pleased."

"No problem, Brian. I located my passport and actually packed just in case. If you want to make the flight arrangements, I would appreciate it. Can you send me the contract or is Monday at the office soon enough to review it?"

"Monday is fine. We will talk then as well. I think your current assignments are finished so the overall timing is good. I added a caveat into the contract that you may do some work activity on other assignments if needed, while in Zürich. That way if we have another customer need you, I can reach out to you."

"Great, I will see you then. Thanks for the update, Brian."

After he arrived at the restaurant, Jacob paused inside the door as he spotted Petra. She looked stunning in a trendy short dress that showed off those great legs. Her long hair was left undone and shimmered in the candle-lit interior. As if sensing him, she turned with a smile that reached her eyes. Taking a deep breath he walked toward her. She gave him a slight hug and on tiptoe placed a soft kiss on his cheek.

"Ahhh, right on time, Jacob. So nice to see you." Her voice was soft and again melodic. "I am so glad we could arrange this."

He leaned in for a hug then rumbled in her ear. "Me too."

They ordered their drinks and perused the menu, commenting to each other on preferences. They provided their selections to the waitress and spent the next several minutes in silence as they observed each other. Jacob reached across the table, taking her hand gently in his and stroked her fingers. She did not pull back as she weaved her fingers through his.

Her eyes sparkled as she softly said, "Jacob, I have been doing a lot of thinking." Then she took an extra breath before what seemed like a rehearsed speech. "First, I am sorry that I ran out so fast. You are terrific. I was, and am, concerned about a relationship with you. We come from different worlds and have different goals. I like talking with you. I think our minds and logic flow work well together. Making love with you was a surprise but wonderful, and I want more. But I am going back home. Long distance is very difficult, especially when I feel so much better when you are in close proximity, like now."

Jacob looked into her eyes and gathered his thoughts. "Petra, I have no idea where you and I might go. You were not in my plans, but I want to explore the possibilities. As it turns out, on my way here I was told that I have a new assignment in Zürich and will be going next week. How far are you from Zürich?

Could we perhaps meet up on weekends? The trip might be a month long. You could show me your view of Europe, and I would enjoy showing you how important you are to me."

A flash of surprise and confusion flitted across her face before she composed herself. "Very interesting, and something I had not conceived of as a possibility. Who are you going to see in Zürich, and for what reason? I thought PT had only U.S. based clients," she said evenly.

As dinner was served, Jacob provided highlights of the customer needs without the name of the actual customer. The duration of the work activity was vague at this point. They discussed meeting up which Petra indicated she would try to arrange. She was leaving on the Monday evening flight home. He agreed to send her a message regarding his arrival information and hotel that would give her time to plan. The lightness in her voice and the smile on her face indicated that she was pleased with the possibilities. They continued with casual conversation through dessert until it was time to go.

As Jacob flagged a taxi for her, he impulsively took her in his arms and kissed her with passion and intensity. She immediately responded and clung tightly to him for a moment before letting go.

"That was very nice and hopefully to be continued when you arrive in Europe, Jacob." She chuckled a bit. "Not exactly what I meant earlier by taking it slowly, but I suspect that once you have your mind set that would be impossible. You are very tempting, but I need to do some thinking about us. See you soon."

"You travel safe. I will see you next weekend."

He memorized her features and kissed her one more time before he handed her into the taxi. He watched the taxi pull away and hailed another for himself. As he climbed in, he ran through the possibilities in his mind, and all of them started with her face and her smile. He knew he was in trouble and wanted more of her. He hoped her thinking would be in his favor.

01010101001100

The taxi arrived a short time later at Petra's hotel, barely giving her enough time to register the possible issues of Jacob in Zürich. As Petra entered her hotel room, she selected a number on her cell phone. The connection was almost immediate.

"Are you certain you are making the right move? It seems sudden to me. Why wasn't I advised?" She spoke without a proper greeting.

The person on the other side of the connection said in a placating manner, "You need some surprise in your life. A little passion wouldn't harm you either, if you want my opinion. Don't worry, Liebchen, all will work out. Get some rest and we will get together next week. I will see you at home. Safe travels."

This was the last she heard as the call disconnected. She mumbled about the manipulations of some people who thought they could control everything.

Petra replayed the lovely evening in her mind. She analyzed how she'd become so personally involved with Jacob. She feared that he would not like being surprised by the potential twists and turns in the weeks ahead. She hoped that keeping secrets, when he learned the truth, would not result in him pushing her away. She craved being wrapped in his arms and feeling like a woman protected and cared for. She wanted to maintain the balance and trust with Jacob. Annoyed with her meddlesome family, yet giddy with seeing Jacob soon, she finished her packing.

CHAPTER 19

Careful what you wish for, it might be more challenging than expected.

Jacob stopped for coffee on the way upstairs on Monday morning. Julie was in rare form with a stellar smile and extra bonus muffin. He could not get over how she was able to be so perky all the time, but she was sweet, wishing him a great day after his modest tip.

Upstairs he connected and reviewed the work items he'd been assigned. He started in on the list hoping to get them accomplished before the team meeting at 10:00. Each assignment was straightforward but also required some documentation and characterization attributes that needed to be conveyed to the customer. As his meeting reminder sounded, Brian leaned over his cube.

"Just a heads up, Jacob. I am announcing our new overseas customer and your role in our meeting. You and I will meet afterwards to work out the details and review the contract."

"Okay."

True to form, Brian reviewed the weekly project completions, handing out a little praise on a couple of deals that impacted this quarter's revenue numbers. He announced that he was looking to add a specialist in finance and analytics to the team. It was a growth move, and he asked that if they had any recommendations for the position to let him know. The team made comments back and forth about a new addition and where this individual could be used. New assignments were given, and team relationships were outlined for these projects. This brought about the background and discussion on their new customer in Zürich and Jacob's role in some initial activities beginning soon. Since all items had been covered, the meeting adjourned in time for lunch.

Brian and Jacob went into his office and closed the door. They reviewed the contract and talked about how updates would be securely completed, and specific items that Brian wanted included. They also worked out some signaling that would be used between them if there were any issues. Brian had a buddy in the region and provided contact information along with the airline tickets.

The flight was scheduled for Thursday morning, with Jacob expected on the customer site Monday morning. The work included traditional penetration-testing, review of security, protection of intellectual property, and providing other observations with recommendations. Monday he would meet with a yet-to-be-named gentlemen at the security desk just inside the building.

The early flight provided a couple of days for Jacob to acclimate himself and even see a bit of the region. He left his flight and hotel information on Petra's voicemail. Seeing her world was the icing on the cake for this assignment. Without a doubt she was the one he would fight to keep, no matter the distance. For the first time ever, he envisioned a new family beginning with her. Big jump, he thought. Quite different from his plans to wait. Guess that was what finding Miss Right was all about.

Flying First Class to Zürich provided Jacob time to reflect, not only on his new assignment but also on Petra. In his mind, he wove a life for them together. He realized that Petra was really his first true love. The food, beverage selection, movies, and Wi-Fi access provided the distraction he needed. He had all his contact information, both within Regal Financial Zürich and from Brian. He would end up with a couple of days with Petra if her schedule allowed.

After the plane landed and he deplaned, Jacob breezed through customs and collected his luggage. People seemed happy here, even at the airport. As he looked for the location of ground transportation, a gentleman approached him and called him by name.

"Mr. Michaels, welcome to Zürich. I trust your flight was uneventful. My name is Jacques Bruno, and I would like a few minutes of your time, please."

To guarantee Jacob's agreement to the meeting, he flashed his Interpol identity card. Jacob did not have time to more than register the identity before Bruno escorted him to a public area with no one around.

"Thank you, Mr. Michaels. Could you please explain your purpose in Zürich, as well as the planned length of your stay? I also wish to provide you with my contact information in case you require extra help while here or anywhere in Europe." He smiled slightly as he handed over a card that contained contact methods.

Jacob steeled his features so as to not give away his concern at being approached by a representative of the well-known agency. He doubted that American visitors all experienced this type of greeting. Something was up, but he was clueless.

"Mr. Bruno, it is nice, of course, to meet you, but I do wonder why. I would think that Interpol has better things to do than worry about a consultant, here to support Regal Financial Zürich in some technology and security reviews. My company, PT Inc., in New York City, was requested to conduct a technology review, and I was assigned the job. The duration will likely be several weeks, though that is open to change."

"Of course. I understand, Mr. Michaels, and applaud you for assisting with one of our finest institutions. Financial institutions in this country are an enormous source of pride for us and are front and center on our radar. My role is to introduce myself and provide you with contact information should you need assistance. We are very good at tracking people of interest. You are of interest, both for your capabilities and the organization sponsoring your visit." His body language was open and friendly with a hint of formidability behind it.

Jacob immediately bought that the guy was tough and not to be messed with. He certainly wasn't going to start an argument.

"I appreciate you going out of your way to provide introductions. I will keep your card handy and take you up on your offer of help if I need it."

Just then a tap on Jacob's shoulder as well as a familiar voice added to Jacob's odd arrival in Zürich.

"Jacob, welcome. I have the car out front. I did not see you exit and thought you might be confused regarding the pickup area."

Dressed in a conservative, off-white suit with delightfully fitted cropped jacket, Petra shyly smiled, but the caution in her eyes immediately put Jacob on alert.

"I apologize for delaying you. This gentleman stopped to chat for a moment. I am ready to leave. All my bags are with me."

Jacob was tongue-tied at this unfamiliar view of Petra. She was almost regal in her carriage and practiced composure.

"Hmm, Miss Petra Rancowski. What a surprise to see you here. How are your father and mother, still taking life easy? I've not seen them in some time. I had no idea you were meeting

Mr. Michaels," Bruno said, with a smile forming that could barely hide his surprise at her arrival.

He reached for Petra in typical European fashion and gave her a slight hug as if she was a family friend. Slightly taken aback, Jacob realized he had made love to and fanaticized about a woman without ever learning her last name. He mentally shook his head, not certain why he had not recognized that omission before. He also realized he had not even tried to Google her or her background and wondered why he had thrown so much of his normal caution to the wind when it came to her.

Returning the hug and looking every inch the aristocrat, Petra said, "Mr. Bruno. I am sorry I didn't immediately recognize you. Nice to see you again. Jacob and I met during my last shopping adventure in New York. I suggested he contact me if he was ever coming to the region. He said he had a few days before starting his work so I thought I would show him our local flavor. Is there a problem for Jacob that I might help with or shall I vouch for his character?" Her smile was formal and did not reach her eyes, like she was daring him to delay Jacob any further.

"Oh no, of course not, my dear. Nothing to worry your pretty head about. You and your young man go enjoy yourselves. Give my best to your parents."

Confused by the exchange, Jacob turned toward Bruno and extended his hand, saying, "Thank you again for the information, sir. I will of course keep it handy."

"Yes. Enjoy your stay. Be nice to Miss Petra Rancowski. Our families have been friends for a long time," Bruno said as he shook Jacob's hand, bowed slightly and turned away.

As they exited the terminal, Petra said under her breath, "That was interesting, and you played it very well. Almost instinctive I would say. He is a good family friend but still a bit nosey."

She looked up at him and smiled, using her hands to indicate her car.

CHAPTER 20

Life and love are best as a shared endeavor.

Just outside the airport property, Petra pulled over and stopped. Simultaneously, they reached for each other in an embrace that briefly suspended time.

"Jacob, I am so glad you arrived safely. I am sorry I wasn't there when you came through customs." She smiled with the statement and looked into his eyes for approval.

"I am glad you were here, even if I didn't believe I would see you so soon. Heck, I just learned your last name, I am embarrassed to admit."

Drinking all of her in, he added with a touch of reservation in his tone, "I'm having a hard time wrapping my head around your sophisticated presence, compared to the woman that sat in Central Park feeding the birds, or pulled up to my house on a Harley. Your connection to the guy from Interpol is odd. You are different here, maybe a bit out of my league," he said, not willing to admit that he was besotted with her.

Her features relaxed as she chuckled, "We just do things a bit differently in Europe. The expectations of people vary from those in the U.S. It is the same me, just another aspect. Bruno and my father have a long-time relationship.

"However, we, my dear Jacob, have lots to learn about each other, and I have been thinking about that a great deal. Let's go to your hotel, deposit your luggage and decide what you might enjoy seeing. You lucked out by staying at one of Zürich's West District Five-Star hotels. It is close to businesses, night life, and transportation. My plans are to stay for the weekend and be your tour guide."

"That, pretty lady, is more than I wished for. You can stay with me at the hotel. I understand I have excellent accommodations, set up by my customer." Pulling her close, he kissed her deeply again.

Breathless, she released him, smiling more with a flush appearing on all her exposed skin. "I was thinking of a separate room, but I can rethink that. Let's get going before the passing traffic gets more of an eyeful than they should. I may look sophisticated as you say. However, you, Jacob, scare me and excite me equally at the same time. Your aura of danger is intoxicating, and the layers of your complexity are disconcerting. It is me that should worry about you."

Shrugging with agreement as he looked at her, he did move more toward his side of the car. He decided the safest approach would be his most comfortable: observe and gather information before making a decision on his Petra. After a brief drive they arrived at Jacob's hotel. As he was checking in, the clerk greeted them.

"Mr. Michaels, welcome to the Russmon Hotel. We have you booked for a minimum of three weeks with a possible extension to that. You will notify us two days ahead of your departure date. Is that correct?"

"Yes, as far as I know right now. I will provide as much lead time as possible."

"Thank you, sir. The room is already paid for along with any room service used, so no credit card on file will be necessary. I will need to make a copy of your passport as we do with all our international guests. Your room has a king-sized bed, one of the hotel's best views, Wi-Fi, iPod docking station, tea and coffee-making area. You have full access to the Executive Lounge located on the 14th floor which also provides total business traveler services. Our steakhouse restaurant offers a wide range of inter-national cuisine and wines with no reservations needed for you. You might want to take advantage of the sauna, steam bath and solarium at these locations mapped from the book in your room. Anything within the hotel is covered for you, Mr. Michaels, with your signature and room number. I will also alert our concierge of your arrival so that any request might be handled for you."

Quickly glancing at the clerk's name tag, Jacob said, "That sounds great, Pierre. Thank you for being so thorough. It is my first trip to this fair city so I may have questions along the way."

"I appreciate that, sir. Er…does Mrs. Michaels also require a key, sir? The booking was only arranged for a single key, but I can easily add her."

Jacob grinned, saying, "No, umm I think Mrs. Michaels will be just fine using mine. She actually can only stay for a few days. We should have let you know in advance."

"No problem at all, sir." Pierre handed over the room key card with warmth in his eyes and a welcoming voice. "Please allow me, or any of the staff, to know if you require assistance. I have taken the liberty of already sending afternoon tea to your room, so you might relax before venturing out. It is something we provide to our most valued guests."

Taking their bags, the bellman showed them to their room via a walk through the lobby area and past the lounge. Jacob noted the décor was elegant yet modern. It appeared to be the ideal home away from home for the business traveler or those desiring rich surroundings with all the amenities of the well-to-do.

Opening the door, the bellman pointed out the tea service for two that was set on a table by the window that provided a gorgeous view. They both caught their breaths as they took in the beauty. Jacob pressed a tip into the bellman's hand against his protest. The bellman exited, closing the door softly behind him.

Jacob suggested Petra sit down to tea while he quickly stowed the contents from his bags. He locked his PC into the wall safe. His eyes strayed to her repeatedly, noting how pretty she was and how well she looked within the elegant surroundings. He noticed she'd slipped out of her shoes exposing her dainty feet with polished nails. Quite the lady, he thought. She likely came from a wealthy upbringing with her talk of tutors and travel. But watching her, he felt that she was perhaps at an even higher echelon. Compared to his upbringing, he questioned again his logic in wanting her. The hotel clerk, with his reference to Mrs. Michaels, only confused him more. He suddenly realized that was a possibility that he wanted desperately to come true.

Jacob joined Petra for tea, and together they admired the view. It did appear that this city would offer some variety and energy vastly different from New York City. As they were sipping and snacking, Petra decided to run through the list of possible sites to see, places to go, and things to do.

She looked so pretty and composed as she started down her list of suggestions. "There are several things that you might enjoy. The Zürich Zoo, Urania Observatory, Lindenhof Park, or perhaps the Swiss National Museum might be of interest. If you think any of those would be fun, we could list them in order of preference and plot our route. We both like parks so perhaps that would be a good first stop. The people watching is always fun in any park in my opinion." Catching his gaze and looking into his eyes, she softly smiled even as the blush began to rise up her neck. "What would you like to do?"

"Though all of your suggestions do sound interesting, as I watch you, none of them seem to compare with just looking at you. You are so lovely with the view behind you, the light catching your hair, framing your form. Perhaps I am a bit jet lagged, but right here, right now seems good."

His smile was sincere, and his eyes held hers, opening his soul for her to see. His silence extended. Jacob's mind suggested that he not deepen their involvement, but his blood was heating as thoughts drifted to how she might feel as he explored each and every inch of her. He remembered her quick flight after their first time so he reeled his emotions back into check. She would need to decide.

"Sorry. You decide, Petra. It all sounds worth exploring."

Petra felt the heat from his gaze and knew that if he was willing there would be no sightseeing for now. Somehow she had little doubt regarding his willingness for another suggestion. Their connection, though fragile, should be explored and was worth the risk. She had thought of little else since that evening with Jacob and wanted more. She wanted to see if it was just lust or if her soul had responded to his soul. But she was at a loss for how to approach a change of plans.

"The tea is lovely and this suite is fabulous. Nothing says we cannot simply visit and enjoy. I would like to get to know you better. What you like, your dreams. You know, the real you. We have had some intense technology discussions, and you listened to my stories about my papa and our trip to Texas. Tell me about your favorite memories." She smiled to encourage his response.

Not wanting to leave the suite and wanting to know her better, he recognized that he needed to open up for them to have any future.

"I'm really an open book. I like technology, as you know, and since my earliest days I have focused on finding my way in that world. I grew up with my granny and mom, both of whom were very technology focused. I think I would classify them as intense, methodical programmers who gained their experience in an extremely male-dominated field. The constant approval they felt was required rubbed off on how they trained me to approach the field. Consequently, they taught me process and methodology first. They also felt value in balance."

He thought the mundane might be turning her off, but she smiled again and encouraged him with a simple question.

"And did you have fun as a child? I told you how my parents wanted to make certain I was exposed to a variety of activities and places."

She shrugged out of her jacket and settled it on the chair behind her, then leaned forward, her face open with interest in him. Her sleeveless top glistened like an abalone shell as the light bounced off it, further brightening her creamy skin.

Distracted by the additional flash of skin and recalling some of what was underneath, he struggled to keep the conversation going. This was different, the talking about himself. Even when he attended college, no one really cared to hear about his pre-college life. But she was sitting there, seemingly wanted to know, so why not.

"When I was a kid, we did visit the zoo, go to the parks, and see all the historical sites in and around New York City. We never owned a car, so I learned all the ins and outs of public transportation. Granny and Mom both took a few trips with their jobs, but I always remained at home with one of them, doing the school thing and learning to be thrifty. I never considered the house rules difficult so really did not go through that rebellious stage some kids face. Lots of love, hard work, caring, and protecting of each other, I guess you could say, were the lessons learned. There were lots of disagreements between them but always compromise.

"For example, we spoke several languages at home, which really started when the two of them argued about which language I should learn with the greatest fluency. Since they both spoke several languages, they each had a strong opinion on their favorite. They also tried early on to do, what I suppose many parents do, which is spelling words, so the child is excluded from the conversation. When that stopped working, they shifted languages when they wanted me not to know what the conversation was about.

"The compromise came when they designated different days for different languages. It was sort of funny when I would pick up on some thread of discussion in a language before they thought I knew it. Found out my Christmas present in advance one year from Granny which frosted my mom. When they realized I knew what they were saying, they tried being more clever. Mom said years later it was because I was smarter than they realized. I always thought it was because they spoke a lot to each other, and I just picked up on it."

Restless, he got up and started to pace a bit.

"Granny passed away quite some time ago, so it was just Mom and me living in the house you visited. She had her job, and I had mine after college. Everything was fine until several months ago when she was killed by a hit and run driver that authorities never identified. I've never dated much, because I was focused on learning my craft."

He shrugged a bit, thinking that he had revealed a bit more than he'd intended, then added, "By comparison to your travels and background, I guess it sounds a bit dull."

Rising and moving toward him with tears glistening in her eyes, Petra sympathized, "Oh, Jacob, I am so sorry about your mom. And you are not dull. You are an accomplished genius who is here with me."

She wrapped her arms around his waist and pulled him close to her, laying her head on his chest, feeling his heartbeat thrumming. He was at a loss for words, feeling her heartbeat as she pressed into his body. His hands began stroking her back, pulling her closer. The scent of her hair and perfume were intoxicating. He ran his hands over her slight frame, feeling the curves and contours. Her hands were moving as well over his back and hips as she leaned further into him. His mouth sought hers as his fingers laced through her hair and brushed the back of her neck. A mewing sound came from her throat as she deepened the kiss further, her tongue seeking out his.

Breaking from the kiss but not letting her body move further away, he said, "Is this really what you want, Petra? Because you are undoing me."

He felt an intensity as never before and hoped she would not ask him to stop. He wanted to take time and enjoy every second if she agreed.

"Yes. Oh yes, Jacob, I want you. Every bit of you."

To emphasize her desires, she pulled his shirttail out of his slacks to reach under and feel his skin, his muscles. No further encouragement required, he found the zipper for the top she wore and slid it down with ease, revealing her back and waist. He ran his fingers over her delicate skin. He felt for the clasp on her bra and deftly unhooked it.

She in turn had pushed his body slightly away while their kiss continued to deepen, quickly unbuttoning his shirt and running her fingers across his chest and stomach. She pushed his shirt over his shoulders, desperate to remove it. As her hands pushed his shirt down his arms, her top fell forward, sliding off. Jacob looked at her and, with the intensity of his gaze increasing, pulled her closer needing to put their naked skin together. No words were needed to understand the desires they each felt.

He picked her up and carried her to the bed. She was so light, and with her kiss so demanding, he lay her down and continued his exploration of her peaked nipples and moved his kisses from her lips to the rest of her exposed skin. His hands worked toward her pants zipper, searching for more. Her slight figure allowed the silk lined pants to slide down her hips, revealing a lacy swatch of panty.

Her hands and fingers were also exploring as she responded with similar urgency. He wanted nothing more than to feel his hands on her. She wanted to discover more of him as well. She was able to remove his belt and get his zipper down. He helped remove his slacks so that she felt his entire body naked next to hers. They were both stroking and feeling as the passion increased with skin next to skin. Their breathing and heat intensified with each kiss, each touch. Each of them shifted to expose more areas as they sought and delivered pleasure, as each promised more. Both of them kissed whatever skin was exposed until he finally murmured in her ear to relax and let him please her.

Jacob continued to kiss her lips, her neck, her throat, while his fingers explored her hips and sought out her core. She spread her legs, willing his fingers to enter her and feel her gathering excitement. She pushed against his hands wanting even more. Moaning and sighing escaped her lips as he followed her direction, stroking her with his hands, feeling her needs. She was so hot and slick, her building excitement not escaping his touch. His mouth sought hers, and the kiss went deeper still as he felt her intensity building and her body straining against his as she reached an explosive release.

She pulled him into a wordless plea for more with her fingers wrapping around his core, shifting her body to pull him deeper. He entered her with a heavy slide that quickly reached to her very depth. The deeper he went with his steady stroking, the more she opened herself to him, further urging him on. She stroked her hands and fingers over his back, his shoulders, even his hair, wanting to feel every inch of him at the same time. Their bodies united as he continued to thrust into her slick wet heat, feeling her tighten and contract more intensely with each stroke, and her encouraging moans met each inward thrust. He wanted the feeling to go on forever, but he felt her pulling him closer and deeper. He felt her climax begin so deep within her as her entire core tightened around him, almost forbidding his stroking from continuing. A cry of pleasure from her as she grabbed him closer was enough to push him over the edge as well, releasing him with a rocketing intensity that seemed to go on and on.

They lay together, feeling the radiating sensations continue as their heartbeats slowed and normal breathing returned. Their moist skin cooling caused Jacob to reach over and pull the covers over them, keeping them within the cocoon of warmth. He wrapped his arms around her as he shifted them apart and yet not. No words were needed by either of them to discuss what was obviously right. They drifted together for a while in that lazy after-lovemaking haze. They randomly touched as if to make certain each was still there. A while later he felt her fidget, and he murmured for her to stay as she fit so nicely against him.

"I'll be right back," she whispered as she slipped from the covers toward the bathroom.

His eyes followed and admired the view of her walking away with her slim waist and gently rounded bottom, smooth and finely muscled with no sense of embarrassment. He smiled at the thought as he arranged the pillows and straightened the covers.

As she walked toward him with a washcloth in hand, he was equally fascinated with the view of her coming toward him. Her breasts gently swayed, and her hair was all undone and flowed with her movements. She pushed his hand away when he grabbed for the cloth. The moist heat as she cleaned him, along with the sight of her nakedness, resulted in an immediate stiffening of his manhood. His smoldering eyes clearly told her he wanted her again. The cloth was tossed to the floor as he easily pulled her underneath him and began kissing her again. Laughing gently, she matched him move for move as they continued exploring one another, giving and receiving pleasure.

As they cooled down again, in a lover's embrace, time stood still or drifted on without them. As their breathing returned to normal, a mutual sensation of completeness filled the room. He left first and returned to clean her before getting into bed and gathering her close, his arms gently resting over her breasts.

He broke the silence as he held her. "Petra, you may not have been in my plans; however, you are amazing, and I don't think I will ever want you too far away."

"I think we are matched. It is a complication, but I do not want you too far away either." As if gathering courage to speak further, she took a deep breath then said, "You are not dull, Jacob. You have opinions, a sharp mind, and grace about you. Our bodies fit so well together, like nothing I have ever known.

"When we had our wine tour on Long Island, you portrayed yourself as an honest forthright man. Not like other men who use looks like yours in a totally different way. You are somehow more real, more honest, an original."

Chuckling at her conclusion, he agreed. "Yes, we seem matched in many ways. I like the feel of you. I like making love to you. I am hooked, my dear. I especially like you walking to and from the bed and admiring your attributes. You have an impressive inventory, my love."

She grinned. "Yes, an original." Then, wanting to shift the discussion back to his childhood, she suddenly wanted to know if he had missed out. "I did not realize you did not grow up with your father. Was it tough for you? Your granny and mom sound like wonderful ladies. They obviously raised you well. They were in the pictures spread about your house, right?"

"No, not tough. We had some gentlemen neighbors that filled in some of the male perspectives of what boys need as they are growing. Getting fed by the fabulous food Granny or Mom cooked up was influence enough for them to make some time for me. And yep, they did take pictures. Many of them are in albums, in case you ever want to see them. They put all of them in chronological order and even added notations for something significant on some of them." He chuckled, thinking of some of those comments. "My young life story is much like the documentation of a complex program routine, now that I think of it."

"I think I would like to see them and have you tell me the stories behind them. My next trip to New York we need to set aside time for that. Now, I am hungry. A little-known fact, I do not like to be hungry for long, so let's find dinner."

Laughing, he said, "With your slight figure I didn't figure you for much of an eater. Do you wish to go out to eat, or I can order room service?"

The glint in his eye was a clear indication that the latter would include more than just a meal.

"You cannot travel to Zürich and be relegated to a hotel room, regardless of how much fun it is. Let's get dressed, and we will walk around. There are a couple of restaurants close by, and I will let you choose if you wish."

Smiling, she kissed his cheek and deftly slipped out of bed, escaping his hand as it reached to restrain her. Internally she was fighting the urge to reveal more. She simply could not stand the idea of ruining their time together with a history lesson.

Petra slipped into her clothes as he admired the view. He had no inkling of the turmoil of her thoughts. Turning again into the sophisticated woman that had met him at the airport, she was a mystery he wanted to continue to explore.

As she faced him, securely out of his reach and holding up his shirt as an example, she grinned and said, "Jacob, I am hungry and I am leaving to find food shortly. Put on your clothes and join me."

He slipped out of bed, retrieving his shirt from her and buttoning it up. Reaching for his socks then pants, he finished dressing and combed his hair.

"Okay, but you promised to stay for the weekend, right?"

"Absolutely!" she said with a smile as she twisted her hair into the formal bun.

He caught her around the waist and kissed her soundly, then whispered in her ear. "I love your hair down." Then he undid the clip, letting her hair cascade over her shoulders. "Show me the choices for food. I fear I've kept you waiting too long."

Hand in hand they walked from the hotel to explore the area. The city seemed friendly, and people smiled as they passed by. They agreed on a little restaurant with outside seating so that Jacob could people watch. They chatted about many things, laughed and ate a fine meal, then shared a lavish dessert. They agreed on the sites to see the following day and leisurely walked back to the hotel and locked themselves in his room to explore each other the rest of the night.

CHAPTER 21

The obvious is often missed, when it is hiding in plain sight.

Jacob arrived at the bank on time after a wonderful weekend of sightseeing and lovemaking. Petra returned to her home with a promise of visiting the next weekend, as well as a call or two during the week. Security checked him in and provided him with a badge that allowed access to everything needed to complete the work. Erich Watcowski, the head of the IT department, met him. Erich provided a brief tour of the bank, which was elegant and quiet, as well as displayed efficiency in each area. Jacob was introduced to several of the staff, though he was unsure if that was for his benefit or so that they might recognize him.

In the Regal Financial operations area a total review was provided of the systems, documentation to the programs, and available tools. Jacob was provided with a nice workspace, a phone, a connected PC and administrative credentials to begin his efforts. He categorized and analyzed the servers and associated program interactions. The support techs around him went about their assigned activities, though they provided help when requested. They were helpful yet reserved when they interacted with Jacob. Jacob documented his findings and cross-referenced them in his documentation. As the day ended he'd been through almost half of the systems, which he had found all in order.

Day two continued much the same way as he reviewed, documented and cross-referenced items. Erich provided some access information on the systems for the bank's pending acquisition, Baltika Bank, for inclusion in the report. At Jacob's request, Erich provided the remote access to some of those systems. Erich delivered another laptop for Jacob to access the Baltika Bank servers. The network access for that machine would be isolated from the Regal Financial systems to ensure that nothing was contaminated.

As Jacob established the connection to the first target server from the list provided, he went immediately to log files to get a flavor for what it was doing. According to the documentation provided, this was one of the main servers to the outside. As Jacob poked around and looked at the logs and programs outlined from his paper copy, the logs started rewriting themselves. Then his machine alerted him to a pending security download. Had he not been so experienced he might have accepted the download, but instead be broke the connection to the server, and the alert ceased.

That was weird, he thought to himself.

Jacob made a note and then opened a connection to another server on the list. The behavior from this server was fine while he validated the data back to his paper copy. He completed the review of several more servers before he decided it was time for lunch, and he needed to stretch his legs for a while. Closing down all the programs that had been running, he powered off the two machines he'd been using. He checked out with security, left the building and walked around.

"So how is the lad doing, Q?" Otto questioned as he walked into an area of Regal Financial operations center isolated from where Jacob worked. "He's been here for almost two days, and you've not provided me with any updates."

"I could suggest patience, but the truth of the matter is he is so quick, I am trying to stay up with him. Bottom line is, he is very good. Better than the test you gave him indicated. In addition to that, I think he has located the problem we were seeking, possibly even the source," Q replied, his eyes not leaving the four monitors surrounding him. "Erich and I have been reviewing all the captures we have been making of his screens, and his approach is incredible. It is almost as if he progresses on instinct first then experience second. Even the break he just took was due to wanting to think it through before the next step."

"Are you saying Baltika is a source? Interesting since they approached us." Otto furrowed his brow as he mentally connected some dots as well. Then chuckling, he added, "Perhaps our acquisition target is attractive to our friends in the Russian Mafia. How clever to try this approach. Futile, but clever."

Q's eyes never left the screens, darting between them as he concurred, "Yes sir, I think that is the case, but I want to see how Jacob approaches the sources. Nothing he does will affect any of our main systems. But it could save us an immense amount of time and resources if he discovered the source right out of the gate. He's good. We'd be lucky to have him. Is it a matter of overcoming the unknown?"

"It always works that way. Fortunately, that is my specialty." Otto moved to the door then turned back toward Q. "Let me know this afternoon, how it goes. Perhaps I will meet with him tonight and ask him again to consider joining our team."

He left without waiting for a response.

0101010101001100

After a lunch filled with more thinking through how to attack the server than eating, Jacob returned to Regal and signed back in with security. As he sat at his assigned desk and fired up the laptops again, he executed his plan of attack. He suspected he would find a similar problem to the one he and Petra had worked through in New York City. He also had her tracer code which he'd added to a thumb drive and plugged it into the Baltika accessible laptop. Access was established to the Baltika problem server. He had no sooner re-connected than the security update download alert started. He isolated the download to a separate area on the laptop and let it proceed.

Once it was complete, Jacob watched as it spun up another program and began the same behavior he and Petra had witnessed. After he neutralized the program, he returned to the server and hunted the source code. Finding it after several attempts, he was able to download the source and started to analyze it. All the same components were represented in the source code, including his code, Petra's code and some additional portions that reached to outside sources. He had the problem and the source identified. Jacob then applied changes to the server's source code and watched it fall apart on the server, making it inoperative. Essentially, he'd killed it.

Although it had only been four hours, he felt like he'd run a marathon and he wanted to document the activity.

He was now convinced that the systems from Baltika were designed to infiltrate Regal Financial if a standard acquisition approach had been used. He reviewed in summary with Erich, alerting him that a full report would be completed. He also advised that all the servers would require an isolated review before incorporation with their systems. The downside to this was that operations by Baltika customers might be affected.

Erich understood completely and indicated that a maintenance window would be established to minimize the customer impact. The activity would take place in the Baltika operations center in advance of any merging of the systems.

Jacob closed down all the laptops and returned to his hotel to complete the report.

01010101001100

Once Jacob had left the building, Q called Otto in his office upstairs for an update.

"Otto, he found it. Not only that, but he pulled the source. With some effort I think we can identify the originator. It looks like Grigory's bunch is up to no good, but I thought I saw something that reminds me of Po," Q said, while still watching the screens during their playback.

"He has returned to his hotel to write his report and probably check in with his boss. He is off the scale on interdependent program understanding. Erich and I both definitely want him."

"Understood," Otto affirmed. "I will see him tonight then to begin discussions. I suspect he will take some convincing. We don't want anyone else discovering his identity or skill levels."

With that, he returned to his office and placed a call from his cell phone. He started speaking as soon as his call was answered.

"Hello, my dear, Otto here. I wanted you to know that I am going to speak to him tonight. Is there anything I need to be aware of going into that discussion?"

"No. That is fine if you feel he is ready," she said with a resignation tone in her voice. "Leave me out of it, please."

He chuckled then said almost in a consolatory manner, "For now. You need to let me know the why for that sometime soon, my dear." Then he disconnected.

CHAPTER 22

Cleaning up loose ends can confuse things further.

When Jacob returned to his hotel room, the first order of business was to boot up his laptop and get it connected. After it was connected, he completed a secure connection back to PT, Inc., and connected with Brian over IM.

Jacob: Hey there, gotta sec?

Brian: Yeah, I'm good. How's it going?

Jacob: Good, but weird. More of the same kind of problems like in our other two bank friends

Brian: Really, you're sure?

Jacob: Yep. Only I have even more detail this time. I captured some additional details and successfully maimed the problem area. Working on the report now.

Brian: Wow. Ok when will the details be ready? I've had a team working on a corrector that we can distribute if you think that will help.

Jacob: Report draft in a couple of hours, I will forward. A corrector will help, but I would like to review.

> Brian: K, send it along and I will take a look at. Was planning on your finalizing the corrector routine period. Good job son.

Jacob worked on the report for a couple of hours and again reviewed the source code. He loaded up the report onto the drop box area at PT. He started coding a routine that would need to be added to the corrector routine with detailed instructions for where to insert it and uploaded that routine as well into a separate folder. He planned to finish the work later that night, but he needed a break. Grateful that the hotel offered 24-hour room service, he ordered a late supper and went to take a quick shower. He had just finished dressing when he heard the knock on the door.

Thinking he had marvelous timing, he opened the door. He was only mildly surprised to find Otto on the other side.

"Good evening, Jacob," Otto said with a smile. "Welcome to Zürich."

Jacob produced a wry smile. "I'm not surprised, Otto, to see you at my door. You are involved in Regal Financial, which I suspected but had no way of proving. Please, come in. I just ordered dinner, which should arrive soon."

Looking almost contrite, Otto grinned, "Yes, I know. I took the liberty of adding a little more to your order. I hope you don't mind."

Otto took the seat Jacob indicated. Jacob then positioned himself in the other seat near the window. Jacob looked out at the city lights, resigned to the fact that even if he had minded Otto showing up it wouldn't have mattered.

"To what do I owe this visit, Otto, more tests?"

"No, not at all. I think your tests are all completed. I am happy to report you passed them all with flying colors." He smiled broadly. "No, I wanted to speak to you about a few things and discuss some options with you."

Just then a knock sounded at the door with the standard phrase, "Room Service."

Jacob went to the door and motioned the waiter toward Otto. The waiter rolled the cart in and quickly set the service on the table between the men. He left after Jacob pressed a tip into his hand with a "thank you". Jacob then returned to the table where Otto had already helped himself to some of the food. He added selections to his plate as well. Otto poured a red wine into both their glasses.

Raising his glass toward Jacob, he said, "Prost!"

"Prost!" said Jacob, as he moved his glass toward Otto's to seal the ceremonial start to their meal.

They proceeded with the meal, with some casual queries by Otto on how Jacob liked Zürich and what had he seen since he'd arrived. Jacob commented on some of the sites, how delightful the accommodations were, and the good food. They were almost like old friends, catching up while each knowing that the more important discussion would wait until they'd finished eating.

Pouring the last of the wine into each of their glasses, Otto began. "When last we spoke, Jacob, I had filled you in on our organization's foundations at a high level. A bit more background at this point might also prove useful in resolving some of your unspoken questions.

"We fill a need-to-know role with many of the governments and intelligence communities around the world. The reason for this is partly a history lesson of the world order since the war, as well as shifts and changes in technology that have made the world closer, even though ideologies are still firmly apart. Much of this you can find in history books and recounts by various individuals that lived during and through the war, so I will make this as concise as possible and from our family's business perspective.

"You may or may not realize that Poland was crushed by the German Army in September 1939. The bastard Hitler postured to invade Czechoslovakia, but at the last minute British Prime Minister Chamberlain interceded. To appease Hitler, Czechoslovakia was handed over to the Germans. The Czech government split in two, and Eduard Benes headed up the Czech government in Britain, while Czech underground forces were forced to move to Poland. The Czechs warned the Polish officials that they would be next. Poland got treaty agreements from Britain and France that if invaded, Poland would be protected. The German Wehrmacht with their SS contingent overran the Polish defenses in thirty days. It was the SS who committed the atrocities in Poland.

"Our families were forced to flee south to Switzerland as the only choice. Our homeland was divided between the Germans and Soviets who had no hand in the fighting but received their agreed-to portion by promising not to interfere with the German subjugation of Poland. Poles were further disheartened by the Western European and the United States governments for recruiting and using ex-SS personnel for intelligence gathering at the end of World War II."

Taking a breath, he visibly gathered his composure, then continued, "After the war, many police and secret service groups of Western Europe were desperate for information and intelligence on the Russians and their satellite countries once Stalin's Iron Curtain came down and divided Europe. People like General Reinhard Gehlen put together Bundesnachrichtendienst or BND, the Soviet intelligence service in the days of the cold war, using ex-Nazis and ex-SS officers of Hitler's Third Reich. There was little difference between Hitler and his Nazis versus Stalin and his Soviets."

Looking at Jacob to make certain he still followed the history lesson, Otto added, "The world has come a long way since the end of World War II in 1945. Our family business's self-appointed mandate is not to let events go unchallenged that would take the world back to those dark times. To that end, we need new members willing to champion the overall cause. Finding people with the proper skillset and intelligence level, but also possessing a good sense of ethics and moral backbone has proven more difficult than originally imagined. Finding people with a proper balance of the necessary qualities has turned up a lot of almost candidates that we do not bring into the inner circle but use for specific contract efforts."

Trying to clarify if he understood correctly, Jacob asked, "Contracting efforts for what, or should I say whom?"

"A very astute question, Jacob. The whom is based on the information we want on new groups that are active in power struggles, those out for financial gains, or more these days, those trying to bastardize technology avenues to attack the masses. For example, we have a contract to help a group supported by the Chinese government, which we know is also working with persons associated with the Russian Mafia. We are watching where this association might be headed."

"Exactly how is helping those two groups of cyber criminals good for world order? You said contract so that means money in your direction. So, you don't care who you help as long as it is for your greater gains?" Jacob stated, clearly getting more incensed by the minute, his eyes not leaving Otto's face.

"Don't jump too quickly to conclusions, my boy." Otto leveled his gaze to Jacob. Emitting sincerity, he continued rather grimly, "We care that economic balance is maintained. Humans must feel they have control and power over their destiny. The option is there until the pros and cons of their choices reach a point to impact one or more societies in a significantly negative way.

"For example, China's move to alter the standards of U.S. currency used for international selling and buying of products and services is not acceptable. What is most interesting is how China decided to make that move, as well as their economic strategy. We monitor information and forward it to the appropriate intelligence communities to handle. Our ability to tap into and gather information far exceeds any of the existing services like the CIA, Interpol, or others in the alphabet soup, as you Americans say. We stay out of political relationships between the global neighborhoods as much as possible. We do have a fondness for freedom and as such embrace more of the Western beliefs over Eastern."

"So then, who monitors you?" Jacob calmly asked, hoping for a logical answer.

"A fair question again." Otto sensed a shift in Jacob. "We have internal checks and balances, and no single person makes the decision. A sort of committee makes the decision, though it is very small and made up of those who knew or are aware of the pain of the war and all that has followed. Our relationships with the intelligence communities are key as well. Although most of those entities are, to a degree, government-controlled, the individuals recognize the differences between actions and political agendas. We maintain relationships with these entities as well as those you would label as evil. It is the information and knowledge that is key. You must have some engagement with the enemies of humanity if you are to be effective. So yes, we deal with the Chinese cyber warfare college and the Russian Mafia because we operate from the high moral ground. Remember what Sun Tzu said in his book The Art of War; keep your friends close and your enemies closer."

"Okay then, so why me? How do you see me as a part of your plans?" Jacob asked. He was less confused but still wary of Otto's motives.

"You, Jacob, have a highly structured background, good education, and a proven record to right wrongs derived from information technologies. I believe your term is a White Hat, versus Black Hat." Otto grinned at this then continued, "We have watched your activity, when you know you are being watched as with your actions at Regal this week. We have also watched your activities in hunting for problems and the contributions you make to communities like Open Source.

"We would like to have you here in our operations team and show you even more details on our capabilities. Some will surely surprise you, and others your input could dramatically improve. I can assure you that your salary will be more than double that of your current PT wage."

Taking a breath at that statement but steeling his features to not show his pleased surprise, he said, "I need to think about what you have said. I have promised to finish my reporting for the probable acquisition of Baltika, which needs to proceed with great care. I have responsibilities and a life in New York City that I am not certain I am willing or ready to give up." Jacob spoke with thoughtfulness, but a hint of determination that he would not be ramrodded into a decision.

Otto solemnly suggested, "Thinking is good, of course. Do not delay too long in your decision, as time is not your friend right now. You have a name for yourself in the industry that too many people may want to control. It is late though. I've kept you from your work. Thank you for listening and for letting me join you for dinner. The food here is quite good."

Jacob escorted Otto to the door. They shook hands, then Jacob closed and locked the door. Glancing at the time, almost midnight, he figured he had a couple of hours in which to finish his report and forward it to Brian to be reviewed and responded to by first thing in the morning. He sent an email to Erich which stated he would arrive after lunch.

CHAPTER 23

Patience can be a great virtue or a profound evil.

China has changed a great deal in recent years and has become attuned to the global communities. China wants to be a force as a recognized world power.

Since 1997, which marked the end of the British 100-year lease on Hong Kong, the Chinese province of Guangdong and associated growth cities had focused on adding multinational corporate offices to promote growth and opportunity for the Chinese people. Most Chinese believed that the Chinese communists would nationalize their assets, so many sold their businesses or moved them to more suitable areas, and some just fled based on their party politics. What most people hadn't realized was that the old guard communist Chinese were quietly being moved out of power. A new breed of government officials with their new economic thought slowly replaced the old guard.

No one understood it at the time, but the 1997 government wanted Hong Kong, not to bring it into their communist way of thinking as much as to learn from this economically powerful city-state. The new economic minded communists downplayed the assimilation of Hong Kong in order to adapt the rest of their economy to the Hong Kong model. This was the presumed lynch pin to power Chinese economic growth. It was clear that the Chinese could not outspend the Western governments on military and weapons without having as powerful an economic infrastructure as the West.

The Chinese also watched with dismay the collapse and fragmentation of the U.S.S.R. as it had tried to play and lost that game with the West. The new thinkers and government officials in China correctly concluded that while they couldn't outspend the West, they should be able to out earn the West with their vast human resources. This included the belief in their ability to learn how to compete business-wise.

The Hong Kong learning laboratory was a good start for China's economic expansion. That growth also brought along a taste for Western entrepreneurial thinking, and some resented being under a centralized government that wasn't quite ready to drink all the Western Kool-Aid. Some of the experiments in Western business were deliberately set aside to avoid some perceived westernization adoption. The Chinese government wanted to dominate the Western economies but retain the power of a bureaucratic centralized state government. This was a hard lesson which had come to light with the Tiananmen Square uprising.

By the early 2000's the Chinese had retooled their economy to move forward. Much of the technology they wanted or needed was restricted from their consumption. The Western governments correctly observed, with some interest, the changes occurring in China. The Western export restrictions were for innovations in technology which would have provided faster and easier progress for the Chinese.

To circumvent the lack of technology which could be imported, the Chinese simply created an alternate way to gain the technology. They selectively invited the companies that had the advance technology that they needed to come partner with Chinese companies for exclusive marketing rights.

Once the selected Western companies moved in to China, their technical leadership was lost due to piracy and theft tactics. Other tactics in the Chinese standard business approach included reverse engineering, copying, and simply putting on another label over the original product or technology. The Chinese government never seemed to be willing to enforce patent or copyright laws of Western companies. Why protect intellectual property of the Western competitors that you were trying to crush? In fact, this was the beginning of the cyber warfare division of the Chinese army.

For many, many years, Lt. Colonel Ling Po had been the Chinese cyber warfare chief administrator and first chair of the curriculum board that decided what was important and what was taught in Chinese schools. She was a brilliant mathematician and had graduated at the top of her class in the United States.

The other students in her graduating class were all males who appreciated her 5'3", fine-boned, slight stature, with quick dark eyes, long straight black hair, and pretty face. She learned early how a female leveraged her assets versus a male. She valued her education in the West but had a total disdain for the cultural shortcomings. However, she picked up some Western habits, such as speaking her mind, which was still deemed unacceptable for traditional Chinese.

Her goal in life had included work on her country's space program and assistance in programming rocket launchers to deliver nuclear payloads. She was bitterly disappointed when the project was scrapped in favor of emulating the Western economic models and was very vocal in her criticism of the decision. She had annoyed enough people that she needed to be moved out.

As in all governments, when someone needs to be eliminated from making noise but are still presumed valuable, she was promoted.

The Chinese military promoted Ling Po to Lt. Colonel and transferred her to the computer awareness training facility in Guangzhou. Her detractors and political enemies were delighted when she was assigned to this back-water teaching facility, where they thought she would be forgotten to death. However, Ling Po had other thoughts on how she could help her China. There is an old proverb that says, 'sometimes you run into your destiny even after trying to take a road to avoid it'.

CHAPTER 24

Ask me no questions, I'll tell you no lies.

Otto's calendar was loaded with activities for the morning. Haddy had provided the updates on the current projects for review, and he'd been doing his own follow-up as needed. Additional assignments for existing customers were handed out to the team and were mostly quick remote jobs. Part of what he loved about his job was the busy interactions, but it was also part of the stress that had increased over recent years. Though he strived to transition relationships to others on the team, it was a slow process. Haddy had suggested more than once that he was part of the barrier. Perhaps she was right. He liked being in the thick of things.

Otto had reviewed his discussion with Jacob with his counterpart. They'd agreed that the lad was certainly astute enough and skilled in areas that would be suitable. However, they'd also agreed that he had some significant gaps in his family history that needed bridging. Filling in the gaps was certainly doable, but it was when it should be done that was unclear. How much or how little information he should reveal to gain Jacob's trust had been analyzed between the elder three of them. Unfortunately, the right approach to this dilemma had not been agreed to at this point.

The entire team knew that Jacob's education was impeccable. He had no other family ties, nor did he have any significant social life based on all that they had seen and reviewed. His progress had been monitored for most of his life but they had made very little contact. That had changed now, and with that change Otto felt they had to adapt and move forward quickly before he was recognized by others. Some of the seemingly random incidents that had recently occurred, Otto felt, drove home the need for a final push. Otto hoped that he and his counterparts could reach the decision on the approach this afternoon.

Otto continued to review some of the viable avenues that might be pursued for bringing Jacob on board when his cell phone rang. Based on the screen information he saw not only the original number that had been called, but also the number of jumps it had taken across their network as various encryption steps were automatically taken before reaching him. Otto had laughed when he was told how effective this could be in eliminating the ability for anyone to actually pinpoint his location, and darn if it hadn't proven itself time and again. He smiled at the brilliant contributions of the team. He also knew exactly who was on the other side of this call and schooled his thoughts on the best way to answer.

"This is Otto. To whom do I have the pleasure of speaking?"

"Good afternoon, Otto, this is Master Po. I am surprised you were not already aware it was me," Master Po said, with no hint of how much she needed his services.

"Master Po, what a welcome respite you are to an otherwise challenging work day. How are you and your innovative school doing these days? And likely more important, how might I be of service to you?" Otto asked, ever the professional.

He liked Master Po and understood the challenges she'd faced over the years. She was smart, innovative and honorable when treated with respect. He understood her background, trials as a female within China, and her dedication. She normally would not call unless she felt she had no other choice, but he would let it play out at her pace. That always worked well with her.

She chuckled, "It is always a pleasure to speak to you, Otto. Things are going well with me these days. I am pretty much ignored by the current powers which, as we both know, makes life easier. I am sure you realize that I am hardly a political animal, which seems to be more and more a requirement.

"Perhaps I simply want to catch up on new technologies and innovations that might be adopted over the next couple of years. We both seem to have limited time to just talk. And how are you, old friend? Still helping provide a second pair of eyes where it is called for? Your efforts are so quiet and discreet that I never hear much about new things your team is doing, though I suspect much."

"My team is working hard to make certain that clients have inroads to new methods of security and encryption while helping with wealth preservation. You know, Master Po, that I have simple needs and no desire to interfere in other's business activities. I, of course, do like to applaud the efforts of my brilliant friends, such as you. Are you doing some of the wonderful things you previously mentioned last time we actually had time to sit down together? You know how much I admire your skill and tenacity."

She could feel the blush rising in her cheeks at the welcome compliment. No one inside her own country could make her feel quite so good about her abilities and accomplishments. It was what made Otto both wonderful and dangerous. He had always helped her get a leg up, but what she didn't know was if that was because he respected her or because it somehow served his goals. Po hoped it was both since no one does anything for free. He had always been straightforward with her, and that was what she needed now.

Master Po asked in the most business-like tone, "Otto, I am working on something that could gain me some notoriety within Asia and perhaps beyond. Toward that end, I am looking for you to perhaps provide me with a second pair of eyes to do a review of what I have established. I would like to know of any gaps that might exist in my design and information flows. I also am hoping that you can provide some of the latest encryption routines to thwart unwanted access."

"I would be delighted to assist with such an effort and feel quite honored that you would call upon my team. Would it be possible to leverage this from a remote location, or do you require staff at your location?"

"Otto, you know I enjoy a good learning opportunity. I think that one of your team on site for a few days to complete the review and provide the appropriate encryption routine would be ideal. Follow-up information and the associated report can be done up to two weeks after. Two weeks on that delivery is your standard, correct?"

"Yes, your memory is superb as always, Master Po. We can still deliver that separate report either at an agreed neutral location or electronically, your choice. I believe that the resource that would be best for your described need is actually available if you wish to start immediately. I can confirm that, if that is the case, and get the travel plans made. Can you also house the resource at your location or recommend nearby accommodations?"

Master Po smiled at her good fortune. "How wonderful that our timing needs align. I can provide accommodations here for your resource with support staff as needed. I would treat your resource as an honored guest. Would it be possible to do the follow-up in Macau? I am already scheduled to take a vacation there in three weeks. Can we make that work?"

Otto agreed wholeheartedly, "Yes, that can work. Let me get back with you in an hour or so on the travel times that are possible and confirm my resource's availability. Can we discuss the fee?"

She laughed, "Of course. None of us work for free. Send me the quote for the project as outlined, with travel costs reimbursable. I will forward you my Macau schedule for the follow-up report. Password protect the information with lower case grasshopper as a single word, and I will do the same with what I am sending. We can use our standard email exchange unless you have had a change."

"That is perfect, madam. You are very kind and thorough as always. Thank you for the opportunity to service this request. I am deeply honored to hear from you directly. I also look forward to sharing a meal with you in the near future."

"Very good, sir. Let's proceed." Then she disconnected.

Otto smiled at the disconnected phone. What a nice time for this particular access and on location as well. He quickly confirmed that the resource was agreeable and outlined the additional items that could be pursued. Of course, there would be an additional briefing with others, but he was crystal clear on his goals. He rubbed his hands together in satisfaction as he conveyed the travel arrangements required to Haddy as her immediate priority. Some days things worked well. Perhaps the rest would get resolved as well.

CHAPTER 25

Reflections can be good or bad, based on the ripples across the surface.

Jacob awakened after a solid, dreamless sleep. He'd completed his report before crashing and sent it to Brian for review. He expected Brian to make any changes that were needed before he presented the preliminary to Erich along with the rest of Erich's team. He idly wondered if Otto would be in that meeting but suspected he would not. Without a doubt the man would still see the report.

He called room service for some breakfast while he logged into his laptop to check for messages from Brian. Fortunately, Brian had responded with some good comments and suggestions. He began applying Brian's changes in addition to spotting a couple of other minor changes that were also needed. He wanted to add the information to his thumb drive, but it wasn't in the laptop. He sighed with the knock at the door, as he had hoped he would complete the report before breakfast arrived. Now he had to locate his thumb drive. When he opened the door, he did not see breakfast.

"Am I disturbing you too early, Mr. Michaels?"

"Well, good morning, Mr. Bruno, this is a surprise." Jacob racked his brain wondering if Petra had perhaps complained to her family. Then grinning a bit, he decided that was not likely at all. "To what do I owe this visit?"

"May I please come in? This matter is a bit delicate, and hotel hallways always have ears in Zürich." Bruno's face was pleasant but serious.

"Of course, do come in." Jacob smiled and opened the door wider to accommodate Bruno.

He was not quite six feet tall, Jacob guessed, with neatly groomed dark hair, trimmed mustache, and an ill-fitting suit that did not disguise his thick girth.

"I thought you were the breakfast I ordered. I could call and ask them to add more if you want to join me."

"No, but thank you for the offer," Bruno said, as he took the seat by the window. "I ate some time ago, but we can talk while you eat."

Jacob sat down then asked, "And the reason you are here, is?"

"Yes, well let me think of how to begin." Bruno's face became featureless, the way a cop looks when testifying in court. "Early this morning we found a man murdered at the back of the hotel. We are investigating the circumstances. However, we came across some things that suggest you might be involved."

His thoughts immediately turning to Otto. Jacob said, "I'm sorry, Mr. Bruno, I do not understand. Who is this man? Do you have a name?"

"He has been identified as Nadir Imonstra, a known minion of the Russian Mafia. We knew he was in Zürich but had lost track of him two days ago. We are uncertain what he was doing at this hotel. I was hoping that you might tell me if he is familiar," Bruno said as he handed Jacob a photo.

Closing his eyes briefly and readying himself to see Otto, Jacob took the photo and opened his eyes.

Totally relieved, he said, "I can say with certainty, Mr. Bruno that I have never seen this man before. I had someone with the bank visit me last evening. We had supper here in my room and talked for quite some time. After he left, I worked for a while. I haven't left my room at all. I understand that the use of the door key is tracked by the front desk in their security system."

Looking Jacob straight in the eye, he solemnly related, "This is true, Mr. Michaels, and we have already checked with the desk which confirmed the key usage you described. However, that does not explain what we found with this man. We suspect you may have been robbed, not that you were involved with this man's demise."

"Robbed? How can I help you then?"

In the pause, a knock resonated from the door. The waiter entered, set up breakfast and offered to get something for the guest. Bruno declined the offer again. The waiter left quickly and closed the door behind him. Jacob poured coffee but only picked at the food based on Bruno's earlier statement.

"We found two items which we believe you may recognize. One is your passport which we have already verified is valid and the one you used at your customs entry to Switzerland." Bruno passed it to Jacob.

Jacob was shocked. He had glanced at it yesterday. He kept it in his backpack and had carried to everywhere with him in Zürich, just in case.

"May I have it back? I did not realize it was gone. I have been very careful about keeping it with me at all times."

"Yes, we have checked it for prints and discovered our murder victim's print. It is not critical to our solving his murder though."

Then Bruno handed a thumb drive to Jacob. "This is the other item that I believe may also be yours. Is there a way to verify that?"

"Okay, Mr. Bruno, now this is strange. I actually was looking for this just prior to your arrival."

Standing up and taking the thumb drive from Bruno, Jacob inserted it into his machine and entered the password he'd used. As he opened the drive, he clearly recognized the contents. The only thing on the thumb drive at this point was the draft of the report he'd sent to Brian. He'd removed the program which had permanent storage on the hard drive of his laptop.

"Yes, this is mine. It contains my findings for the bank in draft format. Since I am sure you already looked at it, I would appreciate your maintaining a level of bank confidentiality on the contents."

"Of course, sir. For us it is like it never existed, and I personally made certain there is no reference to it in our files. I did read it and can see why you are considered so valuable to the bank's effort. I also gained an extra sense of your integrity."

Jacob returned to the table but again he could only focus on Bruno's findings.

"Thank you, Mr. Bruno. So how else might I help with your efforts? How did the victim die?"

"Our investigation is ongoing, though we know he died of gunshot wounds. We also found some cocaine on him and near him. We suspect at this point it was a drug deal gone wrong. I also suspect, as I said originally, that he burglarized your room. His death was after midnight and he was found at five this morning by the incoming crew. Our medical examiner will determine the exact time hopefully during autopsy."

The seriousness of the situation did not escape Jacob.

"My visitor left and I worked until around two-thirty this morning. I was practically comatose when I fell into bed. I was quite tired after a long, long day. I would like to think I would have heard an intruder, but the bedroom door was closed, so I could have missed it."

"Thank you," Bruno said as he added the information to his notebook. "I would like to look around to see if I can determine the method used to gained entry to your room. I know that no room key was used."

"Please help yourself and look wherever you need to. If you do not mind though I need to finish up here, complete the report, and get ready to go to the bank," Jacob indicated. "I really appreciate the return of my passport and thumb drive."

"Please go on with your business. I will try not to disturb you. I can let myself out when I am finished." Bruno smiled his appreciation and shook hands with Jacob, indicating the conversation was finished.

Jacob put the final touches on the report and placed the updated version onto the drop box at PT. After he encrypted it, he then copied it to the thumb drive, which replaced the encrypted draft version. It also took an hour or so, but he completed the presentation he would use at the bank to discuss the findings and the recommended approach for the information systems and data integrations, should the acquisition go forward. He left a message for Erich that the review call could be scheduled for late afternoon and that he would be in shortly.

After leaving the message for Erich, Jacob rocked back in his chair to try and make sense of the recent events. First the hardcore press from Otto to join his company. The late-night hours from working on his report left him so tired he didn't even hear the intruder who robbed him. The police quickly find the thief who got himself whacked before he got away with Jacob's passport in what sounded like a drug deal gone wrong. Conveniently the police promptly returned the most important stolen items before Jacob even realizes they are gone. No wonder he had no appetite for breakfast.

CHAPTER 26

Like odds, statistics can be altered to meet the theory.

Jacob finished getting showered and dressed for the meeting. He secured his passport and laptop into the backpack. He decided he would reach out to Petra and relate the morning interview with Bruno. Running her secure program on his cell, he dialed her number.

She surprised him by answering on the first ring. "Jacob?"

"Hello, Petra, do you have a few minutes to talk?"

"I do. How is it going with your review? Are you making progress?" She asked sweetly, then added, "I am hoping that we will get together this weekend for more sightseeing."

Grinning, he replied, "I would like that a lot. I am actually presenting my findings to their team this afternoon. There was some weirdness though in connecting to the target company servers that was much like what you and I discovered in the New York City bank. Thanks to your little program, along with some modifications I provided, I was able to neutralize it rather quickly."

Her tone changed from the possible fun to all seriousness when she responded, "Really? That is not a good sign. Thank you for letting me know." Then after a long pause, she asked, "Is it in your report?"

"Yes, but not with any details of the origin of the code. There was a different slant to this one, however, that does concern me. It had further modifications over the one we reviewed. I also located the source and eliminated it. I don't know if there are copies floating around, but it had a recent complete stamp date and changes that were timed as very recent. I am hoping that it was a testing exercise before another copy was made and shared. You and I both know that sometimes people are lazy about making backups until they are certain. This target machine is in Moscow, and historically their programmers play fast and loose. They also have a reputation for code stealing, which might explain the inclusion of our pieces of code." He'd thought about it a lot. Saying it out loud helped him see the clarity in his conclusions.

"You are right, and I have known a few of them. They steal and what they cannot steal they buy. Sounds like you have it in hand. Thank you." Her voice was back to serene with a hint of smile again.

"There is something else I would like to tell you. Can you wait to get mad though?" he teased her.

"Sure, I will wait to get angry."

"Do you recall Mr. Bruno from the airport? The man from Interpol that knows your family."

"Yes, of course. A very serious man that loves his job," she responded.

"He paid me a visit this morning with regards to a man killed outside the hotel. Someone connected with the Russian Mafia is how he termed it."

"Really, so what does that have to do with you?" Concern was evident in her voice but not anger.

Hesitantly, Jacob added, "It seems that the man may have broken into my room. He had my passport and my thumb drive on him when he was found. Bruno returned them to me."

"Oh, Jacob." Concern was clearly in her voice with a hint of anger rising. "What was on the drive? Did he get my program?"

"No, I had removed it before I went to bed. My laptop had not been touched. Plus Bruno said the guy appeared to have been involved in a drug deal."

"Okay, that is good. Glad you were careful. Are you finished with the project? Perhaps it is time you returned home. Maybe it is no longer safe for you if he had friends."

"My darling Petra, and miss seeing you this weekend? Not a chance," he said, lowering his voice seductively.

"Jacob, someone is watching you. Plus, my work may prohibit it. Let me see how it goes, and we can speak on Friday or sooner." Her tone indicated she was now distracted and annoyed.

"Okay, I need to give my presentation. We will talk soon. Wish me luck. I miss you."

Softly she said, "Good. I miss you too. I want you safe though. Goodbye." Then she disconnected.

Frowning at the cell, he gathered his stuff and headed off to the bank and his meeting. He felt good about the review and his findings. However, he knew something else was in play and he felt uncomfortable about his circumstances.

CHAPTER 27

You can't be in two places at once when you're nowhere at all.

Jacob roused himself up from sleep and pulled on fresh clothes after a quick shower. After arriving home late last evening, he had practically fallen into bed after a quick check of the mailbox. There was nothing that he was going to even look at until later. Even the contents of the package were of no interest. The last 24 hours were a blur. The report findings he delivered had gone well. Erich and his team were very pleased.

Erich had handed him an airline ticket for a Saturday departure. He indicated Regal would convey glowing comments to PT on Jacob's thoroughness and professionalism, but that this segment of the effort was completed. Jacob had thanked the team for their help and support and had returned to his hotel. He felt let down that the assignment had ended so quickly. It meant less time to be with Petra.

A message from Petra indicated her work would prevent her from coming for the weekend and that she would call him during the week. He stuck to the hotel, enjoyed the food and did some remote work for PT. When it was time, Erich transported him to the airport.

All the way home, he mulled over the events of the trip. Not able to classify everything, he'd think it through like always.

He loaded up his backpack, locked up the house and took off on his bike to work. He needed to go by Buzz's and drop off the search and destroy code for the failed program Buzz had done with Jacob's section. This was Jacob's insurance policy to make sure his code and Petra's code remained cloaked. Like always he had started the day early before the crush of traffic. His phone chimed for his scheduled dentist appointment at eight. Good. He'd forgotten about the appointment, but he'd make it after going to see Buzz.

He knew that he would reach Buzz's before he would be totally awake, but that was what you did to friends. Jacob knocked and rang for close to 10 minutes until a drowsy Buzz opened the door.

"Hey there, morning, Buzz. Brought you the code as requested. Sorry it took me a while, but I've been busy. In my defense, you did say you weren't in a hurry."

Rubbing his eyes, Buzz looked like he was still asleep. "What are you doing here, man? Or am I still dreaming?" Buzz croaked, still trying to fully focus.

"Wow, you must have had a really long night. It's nearly seven, and you usually arrive at work at seven-thirty. Did you have a sleep over with Patty and I interrupted...?" Jacob grinned.

"Man, after you sent me the email three days ago that you were going to take the remote job with that fancy customer, I sure didn't count on seeing you for months. Glad you got my request. What happened, did they get smart and send you home? Come on in. I think I have some coffee I can start, and you're right, I need to get ready for work. Tell Buzz all," Buzz said, as he moved toward the kitchen for coffee.

Jacob entered, trying to digest his friend's comments getting a bit concerned and annoyed. "I didn't send you any email. What are you talking about?" Jacob thought Buzz was just being Buzz.

"Yeah, you sent me an email saying you were committed and that you would reach out with new contact information in a few weeks or so. What is the new job and obviously what happened?"

"Look Buzz, I don't have time to talk about this right now. I need to get to my dentist appointment. I've got a lot happening in my life right now, but I didn't send you an email. How 'bout we catch up later tonight? I have been away from work here and know that catch up will be hellacious today.

"Load this code onto your program, and it will erase any trace of me or you in the program as well as fix the problem permanently for the bank. And by the way, do not use my code in that way again, buddy. Later."

Jacob left feeling rushed to get to his appointment yet growing more concerned about Buzz's comments. He wanted to look at his email on his phone, but not in front of Buzz. Jacob mounted up and headed toward the dentist. He figured that this way he would be a little early for his appointment and could check email from the dentist's office. He was not inclined to forget what he did and did not send via email. He parked his bike and realized the office was not yet open.

Leaning against the wall, he opened up his email and scrolled through all the outgoing mail. Nothing to Buzz for over a week. Clearly, his buddy was confused and needed to stop drinking. But Jacob had that unsettled feeling again.

A car pulled up, and someone who looked like a tech or receptionist got out. She looked at him oddly and with a bit of fear as she opened the door.

"Hey, can I help you, sir?" she asked. "We are not actually open to patients today."

"Of course you are. My appointment is at eight with Dr. Kent for my overdue annual checkup. I made the appointment some time ago, and this was the earliest I could get at the time." Jacob smiled, trying to put her at ease.

She said, "Well, come on in, but I am positive that we have no appointments, and Dr. Mitchell has taken over for Dr. Kent. Dr. Kent had a great opportunity to do some teaching out of town, which he accepted. Who are you again?"

"Jacob, Jacob Michaels is my name, and Dr. Kent has been seeing me for years. I am sure it is a simple scheduling error," Jacob said with great certainty.

"I do not recall seeing that name when I reviewed the pending patients for this month, but I'm sure we can get it sorted out," she said without conviction as she booted up her computer.

It seemed to take forever, and Jacob was getting a prickle on the back of his neck. "I am sure you will find your mistake, and we can set up a new appointment," Jacob said, still extending her a smile.

She focused on her screen as she made several queries into her database, but she was frowning.

"Okay, spell that again, please. It must be an odd name."

"No, it is fairly traditional. J A C O B ...." He said with a bit of doubt creeping into his mind.

Typing as he was spelling, she looked at him, saying, "Are you sure you are at the right dentist office? I have no record of anyone by the name of Jacob Michaels being a Dr. Kent or Mitchell patient ever. All these brownstone professional buildings in this area look the same, so I could understand your confusion."

"I'm not certain if you are simply incompetent or what, but trust me. My Mom, Julianne Michaels, and I have been coming here since I was a toddler, so you better look again. Or I will be happy to come around there and show you how a computer works," he said, with annoyance rising.

This was so not the way today was to start, not on top of all the other peculiar events he'd recently encountered. Maybe he should consider drinking a bit more with Buzz to get a better perspective on the alternate reality.

"Look, sir," she stated firmly, including her own hint of annoyance, "I am perfectly capable of working this system. I am telling you, no one with your last name has ever been a patient here. My files are all electronic and include all patients over the last forty years since the original practice was opened. The back-ups are done routinely and have a program in them to validate that all files are complete. So, you can go back and check your information," she finished as she reached for the phone.

Jacob moved his hands with palms open, signaling peace between them. "Alright, alright, no need to panic. I am angry, but not at you. Nor am I the violent type. It just makes no sense to me, and I am fairly certain this is the correct practice and Dr. Kent is the man. Perhaps you can give me a phone number where he is located, and I will contact him directly. I would like to stay with someone that I know and that knows me. I am sure you can appreciate that." He smiled, trying to remove the rising concern from his voice.

"No way, Mr. Michaels, would I give you any information. You could be some sort of kook, for all I know. Now, you aren't a patient, and I want you to leave this office or I will call the police," she said as she held the handset on her ear with fingers poised to dial.

"Come on, there is no need for that, Miss…ummm…Carol," he said as he glanced at the name tag on the desk. "Is the Office Manager going to be here so that perhaps the paper patient folders could be looked at?"

He did know they used a color banded system that really did not correlate to patient names but some other number they associated with his as a way to protect his health information.

Just then the door opened, and a lady walked in like she owned the place. "Carol, I thought we had agreed today was a cleanup day and no patients? Is there anything going on that you need to tell me about?"

The woman looked at Jacob intently, and he noticed her hand was in her purse, as if she was reaching for a weapon, or possibly pepper spray.

Jacob quickly recapped the situation from his perspective, tossing no blame on Miss Carol. Without a word, Mrs. Peters, as she introduced herself, stepped around the desk to retry the search.

"Nope, you are not in here, and frankly I do not recognize your face, but then I have been here for just a year. Without finding you in our system, there is really no way to begin to search for you in our paper files. We have had over 25,000 patients here over the length of this practice. Those files more than three years old are located in offsite storage. I am sorry, but we cannot help you, Mr. Michaels." She smiled like a true professional but clearly indicated there was no more to discuss.

CHAPTER 28

Coming and going, very subjective points of view.

The incident at the dentist office had left him in a disoriented state. How could they not have a record of me or my mom after all these years? he puzzled. Troubling as it was, he was late for work and needed to get moving.

Once at the office building, he noticed there was a line to get through security. When it was his turn, his badge turned the light red, and the guard came over, obviously annoyed at the situation and indirectly at Jacob; however, this was always expected from the guard everyone called 'Hostile Hank'.

Hank asked, "Let me see the badge, and I'll log you in manually. Boy, what a day! Our security system has been down since last night. It's given me nothing but problems all morning."

The uneasy feeling from the dentist office encounter began again.

"Can't you just look me up in the computer? I know I'm in there after all these years."

That sounded so much like the exchange with the dentist receptionist that the uneasiness made him a little short of breath.

"Nah, I'll have the new guy do it. I recognize you, and it's time for my coffee break anyway." Hank waved Jacob on through.

The doors to the PT's offices upstairs were propped open.

When Jacob saw them that way, he asked Ted, who was walking by, "What's wrong with the office security system?"

This system had been installed as a separate system from the building's general security system so that the company wouldn't be vulnerable if the building security went off-line. 'Best laid plans are no match for Murphy's Law.' Jacob mused.

"I'm not certain. It was like that when I arrived. Most of the guys have moved into one of the conference rooms with a locked door to work. At least the elevator seems to use the floor access code, so unannounced visitors are not likely."

"Okay, cool. Thanks," Jacob said with a grin to his coworker.

Jacob went to his cubicle and tried to login to the corporate network, but all attempts to login failed. He even took out an Ethernet patch cord thinking that the wireless access point was acting up again. There was no connection and no successful login attempt. Just then Brian came around the corner and was somewhat taken aback when he spotted Jacob.

Brian questioned, "Hey, what are you doing here? After I got your email and told you I didn't need your two weeks' notice, I presumed you'd be long gone."

Jacob struggled to stay focused and replied, "What two-week notice? I'm here to work, and if I could get into the network and my email, I can prove that I didn't send a resignation letter. Why would I do that when I am under an employment contract to this firm? Is that why you disabled my login account?"

"Actually, I didn't authorize your login to be disabled as I was hoping to talk you into staying to finish out the bank contract. Those guys raved about your work. Let's go to my office so I can use my system admin ID to re-enable your login."

While Brian worked, Jacob checked his cell phone to see if any email had shown up on his corporate account. He also looked again for the Buzz email and now the one Brian had mentioned. Not finding them, he walked into Brian's office. Jacob muttered under his breath "Why is everyone getting email I didn't send?"

"Brian, this is odd. My smart phone doesn't seem to be syncing with corporate email. In fact, I don't have any bars indicating service." Trying for a bit of humor, he added, "I guess that's what I get for buying a high-tech communication device named after a fruit."

Brian chuckled, then turned serious. "Well, I went to re-enable your account, but it's not there. Who the hell would wipe out your account? The only reason we ever disable logins is for audit purposes, but we leave the account history there. Jacob, your account is gone along with your network file directory. It looks like the missing files include all the work you've done for the last couple of years. All those forensic reports." With his concern growing, Brian continued, "This is crap. Let me check the on-line DVD backup system that should have all your material archived there." In a low, stunned voice Brian indicated, "All the archives on Jacob are gone too. What is going on here?"

"I don't know, Brian," Jacob replied, panicked, "But I can tell you it feels like I am being erased." He related the experience at the dentist then said, "I think I am going home. Perhaps I will wake up later from this nightmare and begin anew."

CHAPTER 29

You can only be re-born after being destroyed.

Jacob grumbled under his breath, "Just great, not only did I not send an email stating my resignation, but my complete work history at this company has vanished because of an email I didn't send! Since there is no evidence that I ever worked here they can't even give me my final check!"

Absentmindedly, he went in to his favorite coffee shop to order a bold brew.

Julie was there and did a slight double-take upon seeing Jacob. "What are you doing here, Jacob? I thought you were out of the country."

Jacob hardly heard her comments as he looked at the menu and then ordered, "I'd like an Espresso Venti, please." He handed over his registered reward card.

Julie couldn't make it work and handed it back to him, "No worries. My treat."

The day wasn't adding up, and Jacob's disorientation was mounting. He finished his coffee and went to get his bike from its familiar chained location. Thankfully it was there due to the fact that he only used analog chain bike locks. He wasn't particularly careful during his ride home. He was too busy pouring over the morning's events in his mind and unfortunately pulled out in front of a police car while still in the parking lot. The officer jumped out and pulled him aside to issue a warning. Jacob was sullen and distracted but tried to remain pleasant while the officer took his ID to run it through the system.

The officer came back much more formal and tense. "Okay, kid, who are you and where did you get this bogus ID?"

Jacob was having trouble comprehending the officer's accusation. "What are you talking about? That is a state-issued ID I got from you guys," he said, almost shouting.

The officer suggested, "Stop shouting, or I'll take you in and book you. There is no one with that name in the system with that ID number so this license is not valid. I think you're coming with me," he said, as he reached for Jacob.

At that moment, car tires screeched, and two cars collided extremely close to Jacob and the officer. Jacob's back had been to the crash. "I guess it's your lucky day. Beat it, Jacob, or whoever you are, for now," he said while he walked toward the wreck and called over his radio.

Not one to look a gift horse in the mouth, Jacob grabbed the bike and beat a hasty exit, taking several side streets in a winding fashion to shake any would-be pursuer. After such a thoroughly bad day of unresolved issues, all Jacob wanted was to go home and think things over. He unlocked the door and stepped inside, which should have made him feel better, but the hallway light didn't come on. Great! I probably don't have a spare bulb for it either, he thought. After he stumbled around in the dark for a few more minutes and tried other light switches, the reality of the situation sank in. There was no power to the house.

The sick feeling that had dogged him all day now threatened to empty the contents of his stomach, and only some yoga stress release exercises helped him keep things under control. The mail that he hadn't looked at this morning had gotten knocked to the floor during his search for a working light switch and now threatened to become a hazard walking in the dark. He grabbed a flashlight out of the drawer and turned it on while gathering up the mail. He lit several candles which provided some comfort.

When he replaced the flashlight in the drawer, he noticed the package on the hallway desk. While it was not very big, it seemed compelling because of how little it had in the way of addressing on it. It seemed as though it hadn't come through the mail system or any other package delivery service.

He opened it and read the printed note inside. Sorry about your cell phone service, but use this burner phone for the time being and check the text message on it after you login to it. He powered up the phone only to realize he didn't know the password to the device. This was maddening! Who sent this burner phone, and how did they know his cell phone service was gone? Why did Brian think that he had resigned? Why didn't he remember an email to Buzz? His state-issued ID now appeared to be bogus, and how did Julie at the coffee shop know he was out of the country? What was happening?

CHAPTER 30

It is important not to fall into the trap of paralysis by analysis.

Petra looked at Otto and asked, "Are you sure we're taking the right approach? Are you sure he won't wig out when all this comes down? People have been known to go insane when they step through the erasing of their identities."

Otto confirmed, "Yes, I am aware of the famous incident. The young lady who leaves her sick mother in the apartment to go to the pharmacy for something to help with the fever only to return to an empty apartment. Everyone in the building insisted there was no mother, and no one admitted she had ever even existed. The young woman had to be institutionalized and never learned that everyone had to be in on the deception. Her mother had cholera and had been taken away so the rest of the building wouldn't become infected. She died not knowing the truth, but that's not going to happen here. Has JAC made contact yet?"

Petra questioned, "I know that JAC is one of our best, but is it a good idea to move in this manner? I mean he only sort of accepted your offer a couple of days ago, just before boarding his flight. We didn't get a chance to discuss how this would go down. Perhaps a little space would have been prudent before the cyber assassin went to work on erasing his identity. He was hit psychologically with an awful lot."

Otto nodded in agreement. "All the more reason to send in someone he already knows but really doesn't. JAC is experienced in this bridging process to get Jacob to our working playground. We need some personal turmoil swirling around in his head with no area of comfort to retreat to in order to get him to continue to move forward.

"I've seen before when we didn't clean the recruit's identity. They always fall back to their old lives and become emotional cripples, incapable of our kind of work. If a person has their old identity to run back to, they will. That's why it has to be erased in front of their eyes so they believe it and will accept the fact that they need to move on.

The hit attempt, which fortunately missed, in Zürich proves that Jacob has been targeted. For his sake he must move on. The timeliness and the proper handling of the individual by the cyber assassin is key at this stage. The formula works, and JAC is a master at leveraging it to everyone's advantage."

Petra asked, "Assuming JAC is on target timewise with Jacob, what is our start date?"

"I will firm up the time, date and place this evening after speaking with JAC and let you know," he said, patting her arm for reassurance. "It seems you care for him more than just as a professional team member."

Without responding, she turned and walked away, closing the door behind her.

CHAPTER 31

A new day isn't necessarily the answer, but rather the question.

Light peeked in through the window, and it had a familiar and comforting effect on Jacob. The events from yesterday had a surreal feeling to them, like it had all been a bad dream from which he could awaken. He even tried to persuade himself that yesterday had never happened.

To help cement the thought, he said aloud, "Okay, self, no more hallucinogenic days induced by double espresso lattes! Let's start over by rewinding our life and re-recording yesterday's events."

However, the lights were still off which meant no power and no shower since the water heater was electric. The smart phone still had no bars and almost no power since he couldn't plug it in to charge. He stared at the burner phone that had no password with which to login.

"Nothing like fast forwarding through your nightmare to the next sequence of horrible events. Yep, I'm having a real good time," he said to no one but himself.

His wallowing in self-pity, like Buzz would have done, would have to wait because someone knocked at the front door. Julie greeted him with the same dazzling smile she used at the coffee shop.

"Hi," she offered, like she was there to pick him up for a date. "May I come in? We need to talk."

"I guess, sure. Come in and have a seat," he said, as he tried to figure out why she was there. "I would offer you some coffee, but I am having power problems this morning."

Sitting and still smiling at him, she said, "No problem. I came prepared and with a muffin too. On the house to thank you for taking me out of the barista role. I brought you something," she added as she pulled out his coffee perks card and handed it to him. "I took the card and asked our people what had happened to it, and they couldn't figure it out easily so they just issued a new card. I thought I would bring it to you since it looked like you were having a bad day."

Jacob took the coffee and the card, not really comprehending anything she said. Why was she at his home? That was the question.

"So how did you find where I live? And thinking about it, how did you know I would be out of the country on assignment for a couple of weeks? I'm fairly sure I never told you either of those pieces of information." His suspicion was growing.

Julie giggled. "Your address is on your ID that I found on the ground outside the coffee shop. As for the other, I overheard two of your co-workers talking about you while they were getting coffee a couple weeks back. As a barista, I watch and listen."

She paused for a minute to really look at Jacob, smiled even brighter, then continued, "Anyway, I am sorry about the electricity being cut off and the lack of hot water. Do you need a place to clean up?"

Jacob practically stormed at her, "Alright, so what's the password for the burner phone? You seem to know everything else!"

Julie looked hurt for a moment, then answered, "The password for the burner phone is the serial number on the back entered right to left. It also has a program on it that you can launch before making a call to ensure encryption routines. A similar program needs to be added to your laptop to further mask your location. All your contact numbers have been migrated to this phone just in case you require them." She handed him a thumb drive. "This contains the program for your laptop."

Then her facial features dropped the sweet female routine, and she became the thorough professional.

"I am better known as JAC, which is a twist on my name and role. I work for some mutual friends, sometimes referred to as the R-Group, as a cyber assassin. You are a very important person to this organization. I am assigned to remove your identity history as well as avenues to gain DNA on you. Essentially, you are now a person with a completely cloaked identity.

"All traces of who you were need to be erased, so our adversaries cannot hunt you down. All trails directly to you are to be eliminated. Anyone you know that could be leveraged against you becomes a ghost. Folks have been trying to get closer to you as they did in Zürich. They almost had you yesterday with that bogus cop. But a quickly improvised diversion, like a loud car crash only feet away, allowed you time to make good on your escape. By the way, if you look at the ID closely you should notice that it's not the same one he tried to take from you."

Jacob looked but couldn't see any changes. He was obviously confused and tried to make sense out of her statement.

"What's different?"

Smiling again at him, JAC explained, "It has to be good enough to pass inspection. There is a small pressure sensitive switch behind the picture that, when pressed, will rotate to the proper areas a different name and address which also matches the bar code strip on the back. I left your original identity in there. There are four other bogus identities that will cycle through the display areas each time you push the pressure switch behind your picture. I shouldn't have to tell you, but don't use your real name and address anymore."

"Okay," Jacob said in a resigned manner. "What other changes are coming? Just for the record, this seems a bit over the top." He didn't add that he was confused as to why. He wished he'd spoken to Petra. He'd left a message but had received no response.

Looking a bit contrite, JAC said, "This is the first step toward protecting you. I'm sorry about having to empty your bank account, but we needed to close it with no forwarding information. Your investment funds were also liquidated. Your Harley was sold, for a great price I might add. All your funds were put into this highly useful credit and debit card that is programmed to mimic your state-issued ID card. You will find the return on your funds more lucrative than any of the investment vehicles you have ever used. I also wanted to congratulate you on how well you hid your funds. I found it challenging to locate and access them. When you change the state-issued card identity to one of the four other IDs, the new credit card, using near field communications, will alter itself to mirror the selected ID."

She handed him the new credit card. It looked like any other to Jacob.

JAC continued, "Now, I assume you want to keep your existing home for your family memories?"

At this point he only nodded since he now felt incapable of speech. The magnitude of changes Julie – or JAC – indicated was overwhelming.

"This is a little more challenging than keeping you mobile or getting a new location for you. I like doing the difficult, and I think that angle is covered. A courier should be by sometime today with papers for you to sign that will transfer the owner-ship of the property to a dummy corporation that we use from time to time. The dummy corporation will lose track of Jacob, and the money will end up moving through several anonymizing checkpoints and end up on that credit card.

"The sold sign should be up sometime today, so all your casual acquaintances will see the property as sold and deduce that you have moved. For the really nosey people, they will see in the property ledgers that the house did in fact change hands. Oh, and since you are leasing from yourself, make sure to give yourself a good rate. I can arrange for monthly housekeeping if you wish," JAC said, then winked at him.

"Okay, that is better than leaving it abandoned and neglected. Thank you," he sadly responded.

"We had to eliminate your work history. Yes, you resigned from PT, but we did put your severance pay and a modest hiring bonus into the funds on the credit card. Brian will receive an apology note shortly regarding your recent conversation with confirmation of your resignation. Buzz is also going to receive another email that says you moved to a new job and will contact him when you get settled. We assume you will still want to remain in contact with your close friend. I would advise that you only contact him through a limited chat room you will be provided or when you come back to New York for work. That is their most likely attack vector."

Although he was not thrilled with her making decisions in what he perceived as a vacuum that did not include his input, she had clarified some of the incidents. There were some things though he was compelled to request.

Jacob firmly stated, "The reports and studies that I did while at PT need to be provided to Brian. He cannot pass an audit without them. Can you fix that?"

Then Jacob slowly looked down at the card and showed some concern for what was on the card. All his money was there in his hand.

JAC said, "Okay, I can fix the reports, but your name will not be on them." Then she noticed his concern when looking at the card and added, "Don't worry. I know what you're thinking. What if this is stolen or lost? Well, it is biometrically linked to you, so even if it is lost or stolen no one but you can use it. A replacement can get to you anywhere in the world in twenty-four hours or less."

Jacob questioned, "It needs my fingerprints?"

JAC explained, "Mostly, but if there is any ambiguity, hold it up close to your eye so it can do a retina scan. We haven't been able to miniaturize the other biometrics possibilities so that's what we use for now. Your college, doctors, hospitals, dentist and the places you've worked sure had a lot of biometric info on you that was very helpful in establishing a new identity. Of course, it all had to be removed so no one could follow behind and figure out how your mind works, your DNA. Fortunately, you are basically a loner. You have your friend Buzz and of course Brian, but no one else really knows you. You don't have a girlfriend to worry about being included in your changes."

Jacob swallowed hard at that but kept his counsel and did not mention Petra. He did not know exactly how she might fit into this, but he hoped she did someplace.

JAC continued, "I need a little more time with your new passport for international travel which will have to have special treatment and a separate credit card. As soon as it's ready, it'll show up here with your airplane tickets. Sorry in advance, but the itinerary will take you through several airports and airlines as well. Say goodbye to direct flights as they make it too easy to trace a person's movements. Just play the American tourist. Even with your languages your accent will place you as American. No frequent flyer programs. You do, with the identities that correspond to the IDs, have access to any airline clubs. Just make them look you up by name."

Jacob suddenly noticed that his mouth was extremely dry, which was due to the fact that it had been open all through JAC's tour of the cyber assassination. She gently reached over and helped him lift his chin up to close his mouth. Her slight giggle underscored the fact that she was still attracted to him. That much was genuine about her.

"This all seems extreme. Why is it so necessary to essentially reinvent me? People know my name. I can't stop that."

"There are a few other details that are still a work in progress. The point is to remove your location, your style of programming and documentation, your friends, and your DNA from a probing from the likes of the CIA, Interpol, or the Russian Mafia. I would recommend that you keep clear of your friends, Buzz and his lady Patty, since you will need time to practice using your new identity changes. Stay clear of your old employer too. True, they know your name, but outside of that they will have no way to find you or tell anyone where you are located."

Jacob asked, "What if I need to buy something? What is the limit on this credit card?"

JAC replied, with a bemused look on her face, "I once had to do cyber cleansing for a person, and I needed to get them to a remote, quiet place of their liking. I looked for something in the South Pacific. I found a nice little island with a landing strip long enough to accommodate a good-sized, long-distance corporate jet. We thought it prudent to buy the island and two jets in case repairs grounded one of them or to use one for spare parts if the need happened. As it turned out the card could buy the island but only one jet. Spare parts and provisions for a year were no problem."

"Okay, good to know. If I get tired of this insanity, I can buy an island." He grinned with the lunacy of his statement. "What else do I need to be ready for Julie…umm I mean JAC?"

"That is pretty much it for now. You might want to pack light for your pending travel. If you don't have something, you can easily afford it wherever you go. Any important memorabilia could be moved to your safe. I have the combo now too," she responded with confidence.

Shaking his head as if nothing else would surprise him at this point, he stood. JAC rose to leave and gave him an impulsive hug, then quickly went toward the door. He followed and held it open for her.

She called over her shoulder as she went out the door, "I may not see you again anytime soon. If there is a problem, I will work it from my side. Don't get too frustrated when things are different than you expect. It will be easy for you to adapt to the changes. You're a smart guy." Providing one final dazzling smile that he would never forget, she walked away.

He closed the door and returned to the couch to try to digest the brief encounter with JAC. Unlocking the phone, he verified all the numbers were present. The program looked similar to what Petra had provided for secure conversations. He booted up his laptop and downloaded the program off the thumb drive. He launched it before performing a simple Google search and was pleased that no performance degradation occurred.

Finishing his coffee and muffin, he reviewed the conversation with JAC a couple of times. Obviously, he was running with a totally different crowd. He played with the ID card and was impressed by the technology. A bit unnerving, but he was actually looking forward to the next surprise.

Packing seemed like the next activity while waiting for the courier with the papers for the house. He packed photos of Mom and Granny to help him remember. Not knowing where he was headed, though he expected back to Zürich, he ended up packing two suitcases with clothes. Regardless of the no limit card, spending money unnecessarily was not his style.

The courier arrived and waited while Jacob signed the papers. The sold sign was placed in the yard, which made it rather final in his mind. At least JAC had assured him it would be maintained.

He placed a call to Petra with the program running and left a message that he was traveling soon and not certain where. Glad he'd memorized her number; he did not leave her a detailed message only the phone number to his burner phone. He would try to contact her again as he received more information on his travel. He really wished he had reached her. Jacob would have liked her thoughts on the events of the last few days.

A short time later the phone rang. Hoping it was Petra, but knowing he would not be seeing any numbers on the display, he answered "Hello."

"Hi, it's JAC. Your passports and travel documents will be arriving within the hour along with a limo for your ride to the airport. Are you packed yet?"

"An hour is fine. I am almost ready. Yes, I signed the papers and the sign is in the yard."

"Great! It'll all be good, Jacob. See you around."

"Yeah, see you," he said to the already disconnected phone.

CHAPTER 32

A word to the wise: live and love safely.

Buzz and Patty were always together but never seemed to be really committed to a standard relationship. Buzz didn't grasp the concept of next steps or solidifying their relationship, but for the near future he was happy with just the here and now. Patty wasn't interested in moving their relationship forward but wanted a level of control over Buzz. To those that knew them, they just seemed to be a couple of corks in a bottle, together but separate.

Buzz was too self-absorbed and self-centered to be close to anyone. Patty wasn't one to embrace a male dominating her thinking or her life. Neither of them seemed to be cursed with self-awareness, which was clear in extended conversations with them. No way did anyone drop into Buzz's unannounced anymore, because you could be stepping into something quite unusual.

People used to show up at Buzz's now and again unexpectedly, before Patty became a part of his life. After Buzz hooked up with Patty, friends who showed up at Buzz's place usually found Buzz answering the door naked and with Patty yelling to come on in and join them in whatever activity they were involved. After that, most friends would only meet them at their favorite local bar unless prior arrangements were in place or it was really early in the morning, shortly before work. Some things one simply cannot un-see.

While neither Buzz nor Patty were wealthy, they never seemed to be short of money. Buzz's family was well off; however, Daddy kept him on a short leash so he had to work for a living. Even though he worked for the family bank, he supplemented his income with contract software jobs that might be construed as somewhat shady if he'd listened too closely to Jacob. Buzz didn't mind veering off the straight and narrow for a fast buck. He was aware that he seemed to have more opportunities since Patty came into his life.

Patty never had a regular job but lots of contract work that seemed to include modeling, exotic dancing, waitressing, and adult toy and lingerie introduction parties. She was a looker and knew how to play with the boys without giving too much away. Over time she had included Buzz in more of her off-hour's activities. Buzz liked helping with the adult toy and lingerie parties, starting with modeling the products for men. Everyone usually had a good time at these parties, drank often and purchased a lot. Over the course of a couple of months, he started modeling some of the female items. Modeling is, after all, modeling and the attendees ate it up. It always made Patty hot and she became a wildcat in bed those evenings that sales soared.

Eroticism was what drew and kept Buzz and Patty together. Great sex was their common ground. All you had to do was show up unannounced to see for yourself. It was not unusual to be asked to join in the fun. Even if you had been asked a couple of times, but neither Buzz nor Patty took offense at their embarrassed or quick retreat. In that regard Buzz hadn't changed much from college.

Patty said she had a catering business which was true but not quite accurate. She got started with catering while throwing lingerie introduction parties. Toward the end of the evening, when everyone had slugged down enough adult beverage of choice, she added the adult toys, oils and leather items. Catering to the attendees' knowledge levels of how to use the devices and where the most pleasure could be obtained became great selling techniques. Being able to demonstrate on Buzz was eroticism incarnate. For those folks who needed more privacy and more instruction, Patty had established the game room. Not everyone needed more game room instruction, but it soon evolved into full demonstrations that earned extra fees from the requestor.

Patty also noticed that gays, both male and female, started attending her parties out of curiosity, and soon she was catering to special parties based on attendee's sexual orientation. The game room had to be reserved in advance, since demonstrations of adult toys now included the proper use of leather harnesses and restraining devices. Patty showed the proper use of all the erotica based on the individual's tastes for pleasure or pain. Buzz was now fulfilling several roles in Patty's catering business and loved every minute of it.

Tattoos were introduced into their offering when Patty introduced Buzz to her associate Joshua, the gentleman tattoo genius. Once or twice a month, Joshua would setup at the catering event offering to draw and discuss appropriate tattoos for the guests. Discreet tattooing and piercings were his specialty. He had a steady stream of clients and referrals from Patty's catering business. She also routinely provided him specific contract work.

It got to be a regular routine for people flowing through the parties to ask to be shown into the game room for an erotic exchange or demo. The game room was equipped with sound proofing and electronic sweeping gear so the patrons would feel more secure in their personal discussions. While Buzz wasn't exactly jealous, he started noticing the regular clientele with some interest.

One patron came in one day and was promptly admitted into the game room with Patty. He was something of an oily individual with a foreign accent, but Buzz let it pass since Patty exhibited no undue concern. Plus, nothing slowed Patty's interest in Buzz and his erotic interests. They both thrived on experimentation.

After the door was closed, the male patron grabbed her arm roughly and asked, "Do you remember that assignment I asked you to take on about a certain individual?"

"Let go of me," she said fiercely, holding her own for the moment. "Yeah. I'm still looking for a good approach vector and need to go back at him. I haven't forgotten." She glared at him as she rubbed her arm, "I don't think your boss really wants me hurt, do you?"

The oily individual smirked and pulled out his smart phone. He showed her the photo of a real estate sign planted on Jacob's property with the sold letters on it and asked, "Did you know about this?"

Patty's comment summed up her thoughts with just two words. "Damn it."

"Now fix it or else," he demanded and then left.

Buzz noticed when Patty returned that she looked white as a ghost. He put his arm around her and said, "Everything okay, babe?"

"Yeah, I think so. Sergei is being difficult. Nothing new there." Regaining a bit of her color, she added, "Let's change the subject. How are you doing?" She pulled him close and kissed him with lots of tongue. "Do you think your buddy Jacob would like to come to one of our parties?"

Reaching around to bring her hips tight against his groin, he laughed. "I don't think so. Plus, he has moved to some place unknown. I received an email from him earlier. I was just glad he gave me the program changes I requested before splitting town."

"Really! Do you have any idea where? He is your friend after all," she said, masking the panic in her voice.

"Nope, not a clue. He's been more distant lately. He probably wants to give us our space. I love it when your nipples get hard enough for me to feel without you being naked. What time is this party over? I have some new ideas I'd like to try out." He gave her a heated look and crushed their lips together again.

"Soon, lover, soon. I have to take care of a few things first. Why don't you walk around and try to push a few more items on these people before we close up here for the night?"

"Okay, but don't take too long. I want you naked and in my bed." He patted her fanny as she took off.

They finished with the party and everyone left by eleven. They showered and continued their playtime in bed. Buzz indeed had some innovations to show her, which she thoroughly enjoyed. After they finished playing, he fell into an exhausted sleep. Once she was certain he was out for the night, she went to his laptop and downloaded a copy of the programs recently uploaded. She also emailed them off to her handler with a note that the next transmission would be a while. Then she returned to bed and snuggled up under Buzz's arm, as if seeking protection.

CHAPTER 33

Our approach to work
is a mixture of Zen Buddhism
and currency arbitrage.

Jacob felt like he had been run over by a truck. It took him forever to make the trip what with the airport layovers, changing airlines, and fighting with his luggage. He should have taken JAC's advice and packed a simple carry-on bag, which would have been infinitely more convenient. But since he was leaving his old life behind, it made him feel better bringing his stuff. Now if he could just find the hotel, he could rest and clean up for his first day at the new job with Otto.

He'd had clear instructions on choosing his hotel in the paperwork received with the travel itineraries. Nothing at the high end or highly computerized chains. No frequent guest accounts. But something above the no-tell motels or owner-operated bed and breakfast inns where they would remember his face and thus leave a potential traceable footprint. A low-profile hotel that was comfortable was harder to find than he originally thought. He now wished JAC had arranged his hotel, but he suspected that this was part of his maiden voyage as the new Jacob, or Edward as the identity cards and passport reflected. Another test of sorts.

JAC had said that he probably would never be able to blend in as a local and that his best camouflage would be to pretend to be himself on a tourist adventure. He was a little indignant at the accusation and felt that his language skills would help disguise his nationality. However, no matter what he said or how he said it, the listener would suddenly interrupt him and ask him to simply speak English. United States English, in fact, with the New York dialect. JAC had been correct in her assessment of his language skills.

Finally, he arrived at the Hotel Ruston and checked in with his current ID. It was nice and contained a bar and restaurant. His room was nothing elegant, but the bed was a king which looked inviting. He retrieved his gear for the night and a change of clothes. A quick shower later he fell into a much needed but dreamless sleep.

Morning arrived. Jacob felt well rested and ready to take on anything. He quickly repacked and took his bags with him. After checking out of the room, he enjoyed a delicious breakfast. Lingering a bit over his coffee, he suddenly felt very nostalgic for home, and very lonesome. It occurred to him that he would never see Julie in the mornings anymore for coffee and that weighed heavily on him. Strange how some things seemed so important when looking back, but at the time he clearly hadn't noticed.

He found a cab and provided the address to the driver. Driving a car himself would have been challenging at best. The driver wasn't familiar with the specific location, but his onboard GPS provided coordinates. The view of the countryside out the windows went from city bustle to quiet housing and then digressed to sparse industrial. After driving through undeveloped areas with road surfaces that likely hadn't been repaired since the last war, they arrived at a very large, non-descript building. No manicured lawns or welcoming signs. It was certainly not what Jacob expected, based on his memories of Otto's offices.

The driver pulled Jacob from his confused thoughts. "Are you sure this is where you want me to drop you off?"

Though Jacob wasn't sure at all, he wasn't about to admit it. The grimy, uncared-for building exterior was not inviting. There was a door close to the road, and the driver stopped there. So far nothing was as Jacob had expected in this endeavor.

"Yes, this is good. Thank you." He paid the driver and added a modest tip. He gathered his bags and exited.

The driver rolled down the window and said, "Hey, I'll wait a minute and make certain you can get in. It could be hours if you have to call for another car to pick you up."

Jacob waved acknowledgement as he walked toward the building door. He wasn't sure that it was an entrance. As he moved closer, what he had taken for overgrown vegetation turned out to be high tech video cameras. They seemed to be motion-activated and had a slight hum as they tracked his movement.

He finally heard a hushed monotone voice that said, "Go back and send the cab driver away. If he persists, tell him you have a romantic rendezvous with a married lady and that you don't want her reputation at risk or to be observed. Don't forget to wink and give him another tip."

Jacob followed the instructions, and the driver smiled knowingly and started turning slowly to drive off.

"The more outrageous the story the easier it is to sell," said the voice when he returned to the entrance.

The door opened. Surprised and delighted at seeing her, he knew everything would work out. Petra pulled him into her for a magnificent kiss, hug and fast grab on his bottom.

"There. Perhaps that will lessen the nostalgia of home and let you forget JAC a little sooner. I am so glad you are here. We have much to discuss." She smiled and touched his hand.

"Good to know. I have been calling," he agreed, as his fingers stroked her hand. "Things are a bit odder than expected, especially seeing you here."

"I know. Sorry things have been busy. We will talk soon, I promise. You need to accept some things for now at face value," she conveyed with a concerned glance.

As they walked to a main area, Jacob tried to add some levity. "Agreed. However, I'm thinking of changing my name to Mr. Cellophane since I'm so transparent," he said with a note of disgust in himself, yet a grin on his face.

He was surprised that he'd actually got a corresponding grin out of Petra.

Otto met them. "Good cover, Petra. With that driver watching, it was quick thinking to give him a smooch, the hug and pat his fanny." In a lower tone, but still loud enough for Jacob to hear, he added, "Uh, don't forget the high definition cameras parked everywhere."

Petra blushed uncontrollably, and the old coot even grinned a little and winked at her.

"Jacob, I know this is very confusing for you, but hopefully it will become quite clear over time," Otto said, with a slight smile. "We are all quite glad you are here. There is a great deal to tell and show you. Come, we begin."

CHAPTER 34

Truth or lies can be based on omissions or additions.

While Buzz wasn't the brightest bulb in the string of Christmas lights, he figured Patty wasn't just moving lingerie or modeling or waitressing. It was actually Jacob who had made him suspicious when the code showed up somewhere else. He'd been watching her. After the Sergei character had shown up at the last lingerie show and was so not the sex toy type, plus Patty's nervousness, he was on alert. He ended up catching her pulling programs off his laptop. They'd had a serious argument but resolved it like all their arguments with hot sex. In the end he told her he wanted the whole story.

Patty weighed how much he really needed to know as she explained her activities. Her catering and lingerie businesses gave her good income and were fun. She admitted that she also did some information brokering for special clients, like Sergei. As she'd evolved her catering and lingerie businesses, it turned out that these provided good cover. It also made good cover for those clients. Funny enough, some of them had even used the other services.

In telling her history to Buzz, she began, "In the beginning I correctly deduced that the best method of moving digital information was to use an analog vehicle, something non-digital. I had originally tried to move information by encrypting it and then placing it into a digital image known as steganography. But this amateurish approach was quickly caught, I got arrested, and I almost did time for it. This was way before I met you," she hedged. "Then I hit on the idea of encoding information in a barcode-like image. This can then be used by someone on the other end of the transaction to decrypt the actual information. It's worked successfully for about six months."

Buzz listened, then replied, "Okay, but why didn't you just ask me? I thought we made a pretty good team. You knew I was technical."

"Yes, you are totally amazing." She caressed him in just the right way to distract him. "But honestly, I really didn't want to you mix you up in my messy deals or create a problem for your family," she said with the right level of concern and sadness in her eyes.

Buzz softened with her concern for his well-being. It was exactly what his ego wanted to hear.

"I appreciate that, but you did steal my code and shared it with someone."

"I did, and I am sorry. I didn't ask. I figured it was mostly Jacob's code so you would be in the clear if anything ever came out. I'm so sorry. Please don't be mad at me," Patty said with tears glistening in her eyes.

Laying it on thick, she almost purred trying to convince him it was for his own good. And he bought it.

"Then what happened with your initial arrest? Do you need help? Did you already go to court?" He asked as he drew her closer.

She decided to milk it for all she could. "I got out on bail. A friend gave me a hook up to an attorney. I don't understand the

mumbo jumbo legalese stuff. The case was postponed, and then
the attorney said it was dismissed. Since I couldn't afford the
legal fees, I agreed to a trade to take on information gathering
assignments. I felt I owed them for keeping me out of jail. No
sex though."

Buzz smiled at that. "Good. So, is that how this guy Sergei
got connected with you?"

"Yep, though most of my initial agreements were with his
boss. Sometimes the requests are program type stuff, though that
is rare. Other times it is just observing and relating information
about people, times, and places."

Her mind drifted from the active discussion with Buzz to her
involvement with the Mafia. The Russian Mafia, to be specific,
had many interests and was always working on acquiring new
assets to further their activities.

During her initial meeting with her Mafia handler, when
her case had been dismissed, he'd told her, "Last decade was the
decade of the money mules. Before that were the drug mules.
This decade is the decade of the information mules. We need
people to move information for us. We also need people who
can orchestrate that information movement for us and keep it
confidential. I want you for that person, as you already know
what to avoid.

"I will be in contact in two days and provide you with your
cover business, our time schedule, and your deliverables. This is
how you pay for your freedom."

She remembered feeling gratitude for avoiding jail time. She
thought she'd gained a second chance. She became a little scared
when she started to give him her cell phone number and address,
and he'd interrupted.

"I know this information. Don't let anyone else know of our
discussions, not even a lover. I own you for now, but I think you
will like the profits."

Anyone else would have been alarmed at the fact that they already knew everything about her, but somehow it made her even more determined.

Patty asked, "Can I still use a lover if it is to my advantage? I have a target named Buzz that could prove very useful. I am in the process of convincing him we are well-suited to each other. Will you protect me?"

The handler smiled in a way that clearly indicated he had ice water in his veins as he responded, "Yes, use him, of course. You are safe as long as you deliver what is asked. We'll talk more about your expanded operation soon. Oh, and in the meantime keep an eye on Buzz's friend, Jacob. I need to know more about him."

She shivered slightly as she recalled that meeting. Buzz tightened his embrace, bringing her back to the present.

Buzz demanded, "I want to know the details. I will help you."

Patty hugged him back. "I can tell you some of it, but, baby, I don't want you at risk. You are too important to me."

He smiled, then let her show him again how good it was to be with her.

CHAPTER 35

Clarity is a by-product of knowledge.

As Otto led the way through the labyrinthine interior of the building, Petra leaned close and whispered, "Jacob, there is a lot you will learn. Try to trust me that it will be okay."

He briefly glanced at her, accepted her comment with a nod, but focused on Otto.

"My boy, there are several different areas within this building, each serving a very specific purpose. You will learn them all over time." At several points, Otto completed a security sequence at the door, each varying in approach. "As part of your indoctrination, you will be provided with access as needed."

The fourth doorway opened into a well-lit room rather than a continuing hallway. The room contained the steady hum of servers running, bright wall screens, and a central command area with a single male who looked vaguely familiar from behind.

As the man rose and turned, Otto interjected, "Meet your new project manager."

Jacob was taken aback when he recognized Quip. "Should I bother to ask how or why you are here, or will I just get some flippant story?"

Jacob remembered bumping into Quip in a chat room just before some security conference and had asked if he was going to attend the event. Quip, never one to give a straight answer, indicated that he wouldn't be able to attend. Jacob couldn't resist asking why.

Quip had responded, "Not this one, JAM. It's my turn to escort my church's nuns on their annual retreat. This year the nuns asked to be taken to the Royal Gorge in Colorado so they can do bungee-jumping from the 1,000-foot suspension bridge. They need help securing their habits so when they hit the end of the jump, their habits won't fall over their heads and immodestly expose them."

Playing along with the absurd scenario, Jacob had wished him all the best and as a parting gesture asked Quip to send him a memento from the location. A few weeks later, a shot glass with the logo of the Royal Gorge suspension bridge arrived in the mail with no return address. Jacob was never really sure one way or the other as to how it had arrived at his home. It had been the beginning of increased personal security on his part. Then there was the DEFCON scenario with Quip's explanation of his limp.

Quip stepped forward, hugged Petra, and then shook Jacob's hand. "Welcome. I am going to ignore your wounding comments for the time being as we've too much to cover. Presuming you're ready to go to work, I'm going to start you off as my 'reckie-pilot' and work you through all the phases of an operation."

"Okay. Not certain if that is a step up or step down. Let's go."

Jacob struggled to assimilate all this, as well as mentally outline his questions. Quip here with Otto and Petra in an operations center for what? What was the relationship between Quip and Petra? How much was this leap of faith decision to join this business going to cost him? And how fast could he put the pieces together? And what was with this title, reckie-pilot?

As if reading the last of Jacob's thoughts, Quip stated, "Reckie-pilot is an old Air Force term, short for reconnaissance pilot. Field recon is the most important step in any project. We must know the target thoroughly and be able to map out their entire environment before considering which attack vector to use. We don't want to use our best technology on a low value effort nor, conversely, send in a basic technology for a complex initiative."

He added with a grin, "That would be like showing up at a tank battle carrying only a Bowie knife. Intel-field recon is as much of an art as our other areas of responsibility. I need to see how good you are and what else you need to learn. Intel-recon is about quietly, carefully, and discreetly mapping out the resources so we can then map out the attack, and we don't want to get famous in the process. If the target knows it's being scanned and mapped, then our follow-on activity is that much harder or maybe even out of the question. I know you are good. I've been tracking you a while from lots of different angles."

He indicated a space for Jacob to sit that had a PC labeled JACOB's Rec Vehicle. "This is a new viewpoint for you. Let's see whatcha got, kid. Tell me all you can about this site."

Quip returned to the chair at the adjacent PC labeled Commander. Jacob sat down at the assigned workstation and pulled a couple of items from his backpack. He loaded up a Virtual Machine to be his rec vehicle, put in his trusty USB drive, and started setting the environmental variables to disguise his electronic identity. He then masked as anonymous to cover his probing efforts and launched an intelligence gathering program called Pscan, which started capturing information to a file.

The program recorded computer processor types, operating systems and versions, services available, and then applications that were running along with the associated firewall ports. Pretty standard stuff, he thought. Then Jacob's keyboard froze on the last data record entry, and the workstation became unresponsive.

Quip showed only concern that something was wrong. "Hey, this wasn't supposed to happen. Let me remotely drive a minute to see what's going on."

Quip then pointed to the process viewer for his local PC that showed his machine was being scanned for relevant information.

In disbelief, Quip added, "Something is wrong! How are we being scanned? It looks like they are returning the scanning activity! How is that possible?"

Jacob clarified, "You tripped over a poisoned honeypot! They've retraced our steps and are scanning us for our identity. Unless I'm mistaken, they are about to deliver a logic bomb in return! Quick, link to my USB drive and launch the program there called Nosferatu. As soon as it comes up, give the command Stake, wait five seconds, kill the VM instance, and pull the cable to the router out of the network!"

Quip parroted in an attempt at levity, "Type in S-T-E-A-K? What, didn't you get any breakfast this morning?"

Jacob spelled out, "S-T-A-K-E, not sirloin of beef, Quip."

Fingers flying across the keyboard, not missing a beat, Quip responded, "Oh, STAKE as in kill the vampire! I get it!"

With the final action completed by yanking out the physical line connection, Quip ceased the frantic activity.

Jacob queried, "So how did I do with the practice session on the dummy server across the room?"

Quip studied him a minute, taking his measure, then responded, "So you spotted that, eh? Good lad! We might be able to use you yet."

As Jacob started to respond, Petra interrupted. "Q, I think you've made your point. We both know his value, now show him the rest."

Turning specifically to Jacob, she said, "Otto and I have something to take care of. I will see you in the morning."

"I think I will be busy for a while, so that works. We will talk soon," Jacob said as he squeezed her hand and gently kissed her cheek.

CHAPTER 36

The mark of wisdom is doing fewer things for the first time and more things for the last time.

Quip said, "Okay, Macabre, let's move into the playroom and get started with your education."

Jacob responded, rising to the jab, "Now you know my name is Jacob, not Macabre. You are also aware that I am fairly well-acquainted with pen-testing and data security. So why yank my chain?"

As they approached the door, Quip grinned at him in a way that made Jacob not only suspicious but just a little scared of what he might find on the other side of the secured door. Handing Jacob the access token to get in, Quip took the cell phone from his belt. Before using it to gain access to the next room, he offered the following explanation.

"This phone is equipped with a special Programmable Identity Processor or PIP that leverages near field communications. It allows us to sync with the security system for access. Watch!"

Quip moved the cell phone over the wall-mounted reader panel for the audible squeak. Then, with an almost comic and melodramatic flare, including a toothy grin like the Cheshire Cat, he said, "See, Jacob. This door was opened by a PIP-Squeak."

Quip then looked into the retina scanner to complete the door opening sequence. Jacob mimicked the efforts, and the door opened.

"Two-form factor authentication. Something you have and something you are. Fairly standard access protocol that you have seen in most places."

After they moved through the door, Quip abruptly stopped on a large unobvious tile and enthusiastically started clapping his hands and singing the words 'it's just a jump to the left...then a step to the righhhhhht....put your hands on your hips....then bring your knees in tight' while deftly executing a dance sequence he had learned from a musical when he was growing up. Jacob was dumbfounded by the exercise, his mouth twitching at the comical performance.

Quip abruptly stopped the activity and calmly returned to his standard character and said, "However, here at the R-Group we use three-factor authentications. Something you have, something are, and something you can do. The same thing is required in reverse to get out. Now it's your turn to complete, unless you want security procedure Omega to be launched. Your burner phone had the PIP chip installed before JAC gave it to you.

"You should know that whatever dance or footwork sequence you want to use will be recorded, and you can have multiple expressions so don't feel limited to just one. Petra has a nice pirouette she does quite well, and Otto has several dance sequences that are right out of a Fred Astaire movie. Quite impressive, actually."

Jacob quickly recovered from his visual. He smiled, then asked, "Do I need to provide some air guitar work as well?"

Quip only grinned. However, undeterred, Jacob mimicked the motion of the security sequence but used a dance sequence he had seen in a Broadway musical he and his mom had gone to. He also really hoped he was around when Otto and Petra had to enter. Some things one just had to see.

Once they were through the security checkpoint, Jacob asked, "So what's security procedure Omega?"

Quip laughed and then looked very serious. "Have you ever watched those Wile E. Coyote and Roadrunner cartoons where the Coyote gets hit by something heavy? I'll leave it at that."

The room was unlike any data center Jacob had seen. Jacob had worked in some of the most technologically advanced server rooms for in the world. This center was impressive to say the least. Sort of a cross between a sensor-round iMAX theater and the Star Trek Enterprise Bridge from the *Next Generation* TV series.

Quip chuckled under his breath when Jacob stated with mock authority, "Mr. Worf, warp factor nine. Engage."

Quip was obviously quite proud of his 3-D virtual graphic playroom. He took great pleasure as he shared not only the operational nature of the playroom but also as he explained its origin.

"Not what you expected, is it, Jacob? You probably want to know where all the server, router, and storage gear is located. In here everything is wireless and motion-activated. I keep the keyboard and mouse around for some tasks, but mostly for nostalgic reasons. The traditional data center design is not conducive to real collaborative work such as ours. This is the Immersive Collaborative Associative Binary Override Deterministic system, or ICABOD for short. We work with speech, touch, motion, and intention gestures, and let the ICABOD build the target vector in a 3-D modeling fabric from our intelligence gathering activities."

Quip continued, following a pause for Jacob to look around, "A couple of years ago we had a subcontract with the U.S. Army to help program battlefield training scenarios in their 3-D system called MOSES. In that system you had a 3-D canvas, if you will, in which to put weapons, transport vehicles, obstacles, and soldiers into near real-world scenarios that would then function

223

like real life. Trainees would come in, take the identity of one of the Avatars and, almost like a video game, play out the script.

"The MOSES grid was built on open source code, downloaded from opensimulator.org. With some gaming and programming knowledge, one can customize it to build a near-life battlefield for training. It occurred to me that I could build any virtual-world environment imaginable. After MOSES concluded, I pitched my idea to build ICABOD as our launch platform."

"This sounds like an Artificial Intelligence attack platform based on what you have described so far, Quip."

"Well yes, though not really," beamed Quip. "Let's work through a modest attack vector, shall we? ICABOD, load the primary bank attack routine, and let's target the Iranian bank X."

"Should I get the bank's location and gateway address?" Jacob queried.

"Nope. Let the program hunt for it. ICABOD will find it. There, see? It shows the external IP addresses as well as the admin ports for vendor support. Machine-to-machine communications is far faster than trying to look it up and then key it in yourself.

"Watch this interaction between ICABOD and me, only using speech."

Quip addressed the system. "ICABOD, paint the gateway equipment learned so far."

Immediately, three-dimensional servers with the manufacturer logos on the front and firewall devices appeared in the foreground on the central screen.

"I know that piece of firewall gear, ICABOD. See what level of patching it is at and match that to all known vulnerabilities."

ICABOD displayed the information in a text balloon suspended over the appropriate 3-D image. It showed two known vulnerabilities and what the current patch level should be as well as the dependencies to each server. The firewall had not been patched in six months.

"Now, ICABOD, display what is in the bank's DMZ. Discover and map the DMZ up to the internal firewalls, please, and paint them too."

Jacob was impressed with the responsiveness between the request and the displays. Quip then suggested that Jacob make requests of ICABOD, leveraging his knowledge of how bank data centers were laid out. What would have taken a person weeks of reconnaissance, sleuthing, and running digital interrogation tools to complete was built in a few hours by ICABOD. All the defensive infrastructure, application servers, and all relevant digital vulnerabilities were mapped out in a 3-D map visible from the Captain's Chair. ICABOD included the printers and the new high-tech soda machine since these were connected to the corporate backbone network.

"Very slick," commended Jacob.

Quip said, "This has been a good exercise for you. Now let's talk about how to save and store this work. I typically use five different cloud service providers for each of our projects. I run a fragmentation program against the data you see in the image, break it into five data streams, and encrypt each separate data stream before depositing it in our cloud workspace. Petra essentially invented this technique. It uses a parity bit with each data stream so that if we lose any one cloud storage service, we can rebuild the one lost data source using the other four data sources. Sort of RAID data-striping, but in the cloud."

Quip and Jacob continued to explore the existing programs and implemented agreed changes over many days that stretched into weeks. Petra and Otto contributed on some days but were also working on other client projects. More than once Jacob caught himself mentally pausing to gaze in awe at where he was and the gravity of what they could do. He felt like he had arrived at White Hat nirvana.

CHAPTER 37

Show business
is not for amateurs.

Jacob had spent many nights in a private suite in the building. The security process was just using the two-form factors for identification for his bedroom. Thankfully no footwork required. He mentally reviewed the activities and filed away the new information. He'd been disappointed not to speak privately with Petra and was conflicted with his personal interest in her, yet he figured since he now knew they were on the same team, they would cross paths soon. The facility seemed to have everything one would want or need for an extended stay. The food was delicious, and learning the access to the different areas was increasingly easier. This was definitely a well-designed, technical, yet utilitarian facility.

After breakfast, Otto met with the project team of Quip, Jacob, and Petra with an obviously atypical U.S. government official in tow. They were all able to spot him a mile away.

Otto initiated the introductions. "Team, this is our client contract officer. It is important, as a reminder, that people's actual names are not used in our discussions. If you wish, you can choose an alias for your analog Avatar persona which can be used in our non-digital communications. As such, this is Mr. Monty."

Before Quip could say anything, Mr. Monty opened, "I already know who you are, Quip," with a little disdain mixed with some respect.

It was evident to Jacob that there was a story somewhere there. He casually thought about what he'd have to go through to get it from Quip. Mr. Monty appeared serious, of average height, average build, hazel eyes, well-fitted but inexpensive suit, and zero facial expression. Most definitely U.S. government, non-military.

Petra introduced herself as Sasha. Odd, thought Jacob, that Petra had an Avatar alias while Quip was just Quip. That made him want the full tale of Quip explained.

Jacob, put on the spot for naming his analog Avatar, said, "Hi, I'm Raja."

Otto suggested they adjourn through the security doors into the operations area using the PIP-Squeak technology, which caused Quip to giggle a bit. Once in the meeting/operations area, Otto set the stage for the discussion.

"Mr. Monty is hoping to get a demo of the ICABOD system, if time permits. This assignment is an amendment to our ongoing contract that has been in place for several projects that we have completed and some not yet delivered. I am not going to cover the T&C's here, but suffice it to say that the compensation meets expectations, and your cooperation is required. Mr. Monty, will you proceed with the briefing and our deliverables, please?"

Without leaving his chair, Mr. Monty stated in a dry, monotone voice, "We need a full but discreet mapping and everything you can unearth about the Chinese cyber warfare capability. We have our own cyber warfare group, but any missteps that they might make could lead to our exposure. That could lead to serious repercussions on the world stage of politics and potentially international finance."

Verifying that he held their attention, he continued. "We are quite satisfied with the contract work that the R-Group has done for us in the past, as well as the additional reach you seem to have. I want to convey, of particular note, how helpful the collaborative effort you delivered was with our allies, the Israelis, in derailing the Iranian uranium-enriching project with the Stuxnet virus.

"I want to state that we know it wasn't your group that leaked the ownership of the Stuxnet virus, but it was traced to the Russian Mafia identified as the Dteam. They blackmailed an insider who knew the origin of the project but not where it came from, so our arrangement is not at risk. That lead has been closed. But let's be clear. We are NOT asking for anything other than reconnaissance of the Chinese cyber warfare group and its capabilities. Clearly, we do not want to alter anything in their environment at this time. No traces of your efforts should be detected nor traced back to my government. Have I made this requirement clear, lady, gentlemen and Quip?"

It seemed to give Quip pleasure that he had and continued to annoy Mr. Monty. Maybe the story would be worth the bullshit, thought Jacob.

For his clarity, Raja asked, "What can you tell us about the target vector or anything that might help us to get started? You must have some intelligence data for us. Also, what has prompted your concern enough to extend a contract for this project?"

Otto grinned at the obvious way Jacob broached the elephant in the room without being offensive. A positive difference from Quip's standard approach. He loved Quip and appreciated his talent and commitment to the business, but at times his people skills lacked finesse. Jacob clearly added that missing dimension, plus Petra approved of him. With any luck, Jacob would provide many more advantages.

Inclining his head to show he appreciated the questions, Mr. Monty explained, "Raja, it is a reasonably complex puzzle as the Chinese are very inscrutable. For over 25 years, in an effort to catch up to the rest of the world's economy, they have lured Western companies into business arrangements based on low-cost labor and business-friendly laws. The fence they straddle is to minimize exposure of their citizens to perceived Western cultural evils and to train their human resources on leveraging technology for financial freedom. Basically, they looked the other way so companies would come, set up shop, and bring their technology. The technology pirated from these naïve companies is often re-branded as Chinese innovation. The Chinese extraction machine makes grand overtures to many Western companies.

"Like the telecommunications companies, intellectual property has been systematically pirated for at least ten years for China. The property buys in the U.S. and financial investments seem like long-range plans to hold individuals and companies hostage. We have evidence that they repeatedly took the intellectual property and funneled it into so-called private companies run by Red Army personnel. This appears to be the case with the Chinese telecom company, as it is now competing globally for business. The U.S. is the only government to date that said NO to permitting them to sell directly or to U.S. subcontractors. This was emphasized with contract inclusions that stated if Chinese telecom gear was in your network then the U.S. government wouldn't do business with the company."

Sasha shook her head slightly then asked, "If this is such a threat to national security, then why are the European governments lined up to buy their gear? I just saw where the UK government bragged about how much they saved on the Chinese telecom gear. Why the divergence of opinions?"

Mr. Monty said, "We are confident that there is something wrong with the Chinese products, but proof has been elusive. Besides, the Brits didn't put that tainted Chinese gear in their military, communications infrastructure, and high value financial networks. They have a cloaked second communications network like we do, and they put the Chinese gear on the low value consumer network where they can watch it.

"We don't want to have to go fix even the low value networks based on what it would cost. The Brits, as well as the other Europeans, however, have to make those purchases to keep investment monies coming into their economies from China. The Chinese know how to squeeze trading partners by placing equipment-buying requirements into loans and investments being requested."

Raja countered, "But don't the Chinese have a lot of leverage over the U.S. government what with them being the biggest U.S. Treasury note holder of all countries?"

Mr. Monty smirked. "It's actually the other way around, Raja. It is we who have the leverage because they have so much invested in U.S. Treasury notes. They love to hate us, but they hate loving our Treasury notes because they are secure and profitable. Every month, like clockwork, they get an interest payment. So long as everything remains status quo, they can't go anywhere. All they can do is complain about their dependency on the U.S. We are fairly confident that is about to change. This is part of what we are hoping your team will uncover."

Quip interjected smugly, "What change, StandartenfÜhrer Monty?"

Quip was obviously referring to an earlier exchange between the two. Mr. Monty glared at Quip.

"I am not, nor have I ever been, a Colonel in the Waffen SS. Don't call me that again, Quip," Mr. Monty said with an undertone of dangerous anger. "It is even low for you," he added.

He resumed his stoic appearance then continued in monotone. "The Chinese were trying to move a lot of their U.S. Treasury holdings into Euros. However, as the EU started to buckle under their monetary and fiscal problems, the Chinese stopped, or they would have lost a fortune in the currency exchange. We liked that, as we didn't have to do a thing. The EU poisoned the whole thing for us without being pressured.

"The problem is much different now. Our analysts are now modeling a theory that if the Chinese can take control of our power grid infrastructure, our water and waste-water treatment facilities, communications infrastructure, financial sector, pretty much everything that depends upon moving ones and zeros, our civilization would come to a halt."

Raja was disturbed by the scenarios that popped to mind but was unconvinced. "I've heard these doomsday scenarios before, and frankly they make terrific movies. Are you really suggesting they could turn off everything, and the U.S. population would sit in the dark with no flushing toilets?"

Mr. Monty, schooling his features, responded, "Raja, you're starting to sound like Quip. No, I'm talking about ransoming our lifestyle back from the Chinese. Basically, the think-tank scenario suggests that the infrastructure is invaded, and nothing moves without their say so. Military logistics and transport ceases to function correctly, if at all, so no armed response can be coordinated, and since proof is all electronic and under their control, two-thirds of the country is paralyzed. Imports/exports stop and all financial transactions revert to barter.

"They then could dictate terms to restore normalcy and lend us our own dollars to rebuild at an inflated rate. The first order of business would be to dismantle the U.S. military and confiscate the weapons. They buy the most valuable assets of the country at a huge discount because of the chaos they've inflicted. Since they can afford to buy and wait, infrastructures and industries change ownership overnight. Copyrights and patents simply become their property, and all future innovations become theirs. I don't mind telling you that we really don't want this scenario to have a chance in hell of coming true. Which is why we are here today."

Quip said without rankle, "Okay, point made. Can you at least tell us where to start looking?"

"In the Guangdong province in and around Guangzhou, Macau, and Hong Kong, we have noted increased electronic technologies more prevalent than should be present. In areas of dense populations with multinational corporations, Chinese nationals, and electronic dependent operations, the potential is created for a great place to hide government-sponsored activities simply because of the electronic noise centralized there. All of the multinational corporations doing business there admit to loss of intellectual property ranging from leakage to outright theft and chalk it up to the cost of doing business there. One of our operators in that area believes the province holds the cyber weapons school of the Chinese Red Army."

Quip smiled knowingly and suggested, "Now you're talking about the Advanced Analytics and Reconnaissance of Digital Video & Audio Research for Kinetics. You're talking about AARDVARK!"

Mr. Monty actually grinned at capturing Quip's interest. "Precisely. We think there is a four-story building there that houses the research facility, the training labs, and the administration that governs all their cyber-weapon research and testing. Rumors have it that a Lt. Colonel Ling Po runs the facility but that she goes by the handle Master Po. These are all unconfirmed rumors. There are also rumors that projects she supports range from nuclear involvement to cyber terrorism.

"That is the primary goal of your contract. Now, how about a demo of ICABOD? Quip, did you dream up yet another screwy acronym?"

Quip replied, undeterred, "Right this way, Mr. Monty. You won't be sorry to see this."

He led them to the far end of the conference room. Jacob hadn't discussed the remote access to ICABOD with Quip, so this was enlightening for him.

Quip loaded up the program quickly. He stated with genuine enthusiasm, "Watch!"

Otto, under his breath, whispered, "I think I'm about to be sorry."

A 3-D Avatar looking similar to Quip marched up into the forefront of the viewing area and winked. It promptly turned an about face, unfastened its britches, and proceeded to moon Mr. Monty.

Then Quip asked, "ICABOD, what can you tell us about the guest?"

The bubble above the Avatar painted the text, You showed me yours; it's only fair if I show you mine. It was then quickly replaced with, This is the full Monty.

Petra struggled unsuccessfully, as did Jacob, to suppress the snickers of mirth. Mr. Monty shot daggers at Quip. Otto simply closed his eyes hoping all this was just a bad dream. Quip smiled, then proceeded to go through a basic identification of a data center, scaled down from the review with Jacob.

"Quip, you are a pain in the ass to work with. But if this will work for what we need, then get going. You have a very short timeline, funny boy, so suck it up."

With that, Mr. Monty rose, and Otto escorted him out. The three took one look at each other after the door sealed and burst into laughter. Quip knew he was in for a lashing by Otto, but it was so worth it.

CHAPTER 38

The finest diamonds emerge from ugly lumps of carbon.

When Lt. Colonel Ling Po first saw the grubby little four-story building that held the computer awareness training facility in Guangzhou, she fought hard to hold back the resentment and tears. She had sacrificed everything for her country and this is how they treated her. She was shown to her quarters which completed her feelings of despair and remorse. She had done prisoner interrogations in nicer facilities. Her stoicism would not let her quit or ask to be reassigned. Ling Po would try. After all she had beaten the odds before and actually excelled under similar circumstances.

Her sarcastic wit flared up as she said to no one in particular, "All it needs is some wallpaper, some plants, a few throw pillows, and a phosphorus grenade to make it a wonderful little bungalow."

The next day she was given a tour of the facilities by her new assistant, Quan Chun. The facilities were so run down and antiquated that she faltered briefly in her resolve to keep a professional outlook about the assignment. She requested to see the budget and asked how soon the computer equipment could be upgraded.

Chun hesitated and quietly informed Ling Po, "We have no budget, and what we get is cast-off equipment from people who feel sorry for us or those we repay with favors."

Lt. Colonel Po frowned. "Okay. Let's see exactly what we have here and create an inventory. What kind of telecommunications capabilities do we have? Do we have modem and dial-up access? How much bandwidth do we have?"

Again, Chun hesitated. "Lt. Colonel Po, we have none of the things you enjoyed at the physical weapons lab. People who are sent here to study are being punished for some infraction. Those sent here to run the facility are sent here because they are of no further use to those in power."

Lt. Colonel Po studied the assistant and then stated, "That is changing, as of now. Contact the telephony service today and schedule twelve new circuits to be installed tomorrow. From now on, people only get to come here if they are the best of the best in computers and cyber warfare. We are changing the name of the facility to the Advanced Analytics and Reconnaissance of Digital Video & Audio Research for Kinetics. It will no longer be punishment to come here and learn, but a privilege."

Chun was astonished but respectful. "It takes six months to get even one circuit, and you asked for twelve, and you already know that we have no budget to pay for it even if they did give us circuits. What magic shall I use to accomplish this feat, Lt. Colonel Po?"

Lt. Colonel Po smiled slightly as she handed him a slip of paper with the number to call. "This is our magic. Indicate that you are calling on behalf of the director of the Cyber Weapons College of the Chinese military. Add that unless he and his immediate family wish to be relocated to a re-education facility, he will complete this exercise in the allotted time frame. Oh yes, from now on I am to be addressed as Master Po. Understood?"

Chun, smiling ever so slightly, then asked, "Then, Master Po, how do we pay for circuits when we have no budget?"

"Grasshopper, your loyalty will be to me as we travel this road. We will go to work finding funding wherever that might be. We will work as a powerful team."

"I am not given to easy loyalties, but I sense that you are the person to be the master. My intuition tells me to follow your course. You should know I will not challenge that, Master Po. I have hope for the first time in years." Chun scurried away to complete the first assignment.

CHAPTER 39

Often the old and the new are both essential.

The team was assembled in the command center to work the assignment for Mr. Monty. Jacob, Petra, and Quip were checking out various elements that were required to begin the covert probe. Otto was present for questions and just to watch the team interaction.

"Otto, we are going to have to have that high-speed circuit looked at. It's been giving us some trouble. You know, dropped packets and lots of retransmissions. Before we crank up this project, I'd like to have it examined. Any objections?" asked Quip, while completing a round of testing.

"None at all. By all means, call it in and ask for Andrew to be assigned. We need a thorough person to review our telecommunications. He is the best."

Quip whined. "I was afraid you'd say that. Can't we go with someone else for a change? He grates on me and you know how he talks." He mimicked a very thick southern drawl.

Otto stared expressionlessly at Quip until Quip acquiesced. "Alright, alright, I'll put the call in, but have the tranquilizer dart gun charged up just in case I have to be calmed down again."

Jacob looked quizzically at Otto, Petra and then at Quip, searching for contextual clues as to what the issue was. After Quip left the room to contact Andrew, Otto provided a little history on the subject.

"Andrew came over from Augusta, Georgia, in the late 1960's as part of the U.S. military police group on a rotation to Europe. Andrew is a large lad, and by that I mean he has to stoop down and turn sideways to get through a standard doorway. I am told that he had to pull the webbing out of his helmet so he could actually fit it on his head.

"The story is told that a large spool of insulated copper communications cable about 400 to 500 kilos rolled off the mezzanine floor of this building, down the stairs, and right through the plate glass doors heading towards some foreign dignitaries. It would have crushed them against their bomb and bullet-proofed car if Andrew hadn't jumped in front of it to slow it down. He actually stopped it. The Swiss government was most grateful for his selfless act. Andrew was injured in the process and could not return to his former duties as a military police officer when he was discharged from the hospital a few months later.

"Andrew asked to be trained in signals/communications based on his near-death experience with the large spool of cable. When his tour of duty was up, the Swiss found a telecom position for him to reinforce their gratitude. Andrew has worked on everything from Morse code teletype devices to the fiber optic Dense Wave Division Multiplexer commonly called DWDM communications used at the super collider facility in Cern. Andrew has worked on everything and anything that moves ones and zeros from one location to another location. We also like him because he is very discreet when it comes to supporting our efforts here."

In the other room Quip was on the phone with Andrew. Quip swallowed hard trying to calm himself in preparation for the discussion.

Quip asked, "Hello, Andrew. Do you have time to help me troubleshoot that last circuit we got from you guys? I'm seeing a lot of retransmits and dropped packets with regular activities. I have a big job coming up that will depend on fewer errors on that circuit."

Andy responded, "Well, if it ain't the Quipster callin' in with a problem. Howdy, young feller! I thought we agreed yer supposed to call me Andy. What kind of favor do ya need this time?"

Quip tried to maintain an even tone but failed as he practically spit out, "I just told you I need you to look at the last circuit we had installed, Andy."

Andy harrumphed, "Oh, that's right. I'm supposed to remember everyone's circuit ID's or be able to read their minds over the phone. How 'bout let's start with y'all giving me the circuit ID and then we'll do some troubleshootin' on that bad boy."

"Just a minute. Let me go get the circuit ID off the wall jack." Quip was annoyed with himself for not having the presence of mind to get it before the call.

He returned quickly and relayed, "Okay, the circuit ID reads 457 – Alpha – Papa – Jack – Indigo – Golf – November – Tango – Zulu – 9834578," in a very deliberate manner to Andy.

Quip then prepared for impact.

"Okay, let me read this back to you, young feller. I have 457 – A as in Apple – P as Pig on the barbeque grill – J as in Jack Daniels – I as in don't forget the Ice for the Jack Daniels – G as in Gator – N as in No-Tell-Motel – T as in Trailer Trash – Z as in cream-filled Zinger – 9834578. Is that right, young feller?"

Quip was on the verge of a heart attack. Quip stuttered, "You know I hate it when you do that! Stop it. Stop it. Stop it!

I just want to have the circuit looked at for the errors that are occurring. I need the circuit to run error free. Can you set up a 24-hour monitoring flag on this circuit so we can see what needs to be done?"

Andy chuckled and lengthened his words to emphasize his drawl. "Well, I kin do that. But I can also come down there and put my T-bird on the circuit, and we can do some real analysis if ya want, young feller. I always like visitin' with all y'all, so I can make the time if ya want."

"Yeah, the last time you did that we spent most of the day listening to your 'good old days' stories. If we can keep this short, how about this afternoon?"

"You buyin' lunch? All that circuit readin' activity makes me hungry. If memory serves, y'all feed your vendors pretty well. I do have a hankerin' for some barbeque."

Otto, standing behind Quip all this time, said over his shoulder, "Andy, this is Otto. We'd be honored to have you join us for lunch before we start troubleshooting. It so happens that barbeque is on the menu for today, including all the sides."

Haddy insured that any menu requested could be accomplished in short order by the staff. Andy showed up in time to sit down for lunch. He claimed it was just like home. As the others sipped iced tea, Andy couldn't help but relay yet another cable-pulling story.

"One time I got sent over to rig up a new telephone system on a customer's premises. I ran into this real surly, uppity union cable crew manager. I was there to do the cross connects and needed a vertical cable run down the elevator shaft from the twelfth floor down to the fifth floor. They had this real heavy grade cable on a spool, and I was going to help them, but this cable crew manager said to me, 'We'll handle it. You're not union so you can't help. Just sit over there out of the way with your non-union helper.' I said okay.

"Me and my helper go sit down and wait for the show. They hafta feed this heavy cable down the elevator shaft from twelfth floor and fish it out on the fifth floor, and we hafta watch. Well, those good 'ol boys get the cable unrolled from the spool and fed down the shaft seven stories. All that's holdin' it in place is this huge staple through the cable into the big wooden spool. My helper started to suggest something helpful like 'Better secure the cable on this end before pulling the staple out,' but I motioned to him to be quiet.

"I motioned to my helper two more times 'cause the uppity union cable manager wasn't seeing what we knew was gonna happen. Sure 'nuff that manager, with his clip board, ordered the staple to be pulled out. You could hear the cable go 'ZZZZZZZing' right down the elevator shaft all the way to the bottom. It sounded like they had hooked a big game tuna fish with one of them big deep sea fishin' rods."

Andy made the same ZZZZZZZing sound again.

"Naturally the union cable crew manager took it out on the crew once he got over the shock. It put us behind on the project which was okay since me and my helper laughed the rest of the afternoon saying ZZZZZZZing! Har!"

Quip caught himself as he laughed at Andy's story along with the rest of the team. The guy could tell a story. The rest of the afternoon, the team's troubleshooting efforts found the problem, and Andy fixed it himself.

CHAPTER 40

It pays to advertise.

L t. Colonel Po always liked a strong cup of tea before her class instruction started. She smiled when she remembered the early days of the computer school that she had been sentenced to run that was now the Cyber Warfare College of China. People now considered it an honor to get to attend and even more prestigious if you got to learn from Master Po. If a person got into the school, which was difficult in and of itself, they then had to demonstrate their abilities to the regular instructors. Only the top 2% of the advanced students got the privilege of being in Master Po's advanced classes.

The curriculum was not just programming but included advanced mathematics, telecommunications, encryption algorithms, virus construction, social engineering techniques, English, and of course advanced hacking techniques and approaches. Lt. Colonel Po didn't segregate these topics but instead flooded the course with all of these simultaneously while teaching. Her favorite phrase used before almost every class was, "Knowing how your opponent thinks is the first step in defeating them."

It was an extremely difficult course offering, and not everyone who got into the class completed it successfully. It was a black mark against a regular instructor to allow a student into Po's class if they couldn't take the demands of the advanced course. All of her instruction was in English and all of her attack vectors and example hacking techniques were designed to exploit Western thinking. Most of the regular graduates went on to work for Western-based companies that soon discovered that they could get quality programmers, that spoke English well, and at a discount. The school brokered their graduates to these companies for a fee which was used to fund the school's operations.

In fact, almost from day one, when Lt. Colonel Po took over as the senior administrator, the school hadn't had to request funding from the central government. Soon after she arrived at the facility, Lt. Colonel Po had established her method of creating a budget. She obtained funding from some Soviet acquaintances, also known as the Dteam, who were now laundering money using identity theft. She had proposed her plan for the school and its potential benefits to a then up-and-coming player named Grigory. The school would, in fact, gain his team some specialized programming training. He made an initial investment which allowed her operations to get off the ground.

She then assembled a small but dedicated team of cyber bank robbers who were tasked with procuring the necessary funds to keep the Cyber Warfare College functioning with no government funding. Hers was the only Chinese government division that didn't need or get monies from the Chinese government. In fact, as the Cyber Warfare College evolved, it contributed the excess monies it received to the Chinese Treasury.

The funding mechanism of the college was so successful that she was questioned often about its success. One of the first and last higher-up Chinese government officials to try and squeeze not only an explanation but also an on-going percentage of this income stream was Khan. Khan was not very well liked, but because of his boldness he had reached a level of power that few could touch.

He approached Lt. Colonel Po and suggested that it would be wise of her to explain the funding mechanism to him, and in return for his discretion he would take seven percent of the income stream funneled to an off-shore facility that he named. Part of the agreement included her guarantee not to raid his off-shore account as a professional courtesy. Conventional wisdom was that no one ever refused his requests. She shivered to think that he could have insisted on sexual favors as well.

Khan did not get very far before things started to unwind by something that took on a life of its own. Before his next visit with Lt. Colonel Po, news reports started coming in that Khan was now leading a Chinese Human Rights movement. The first group Deputy Khan wanted to champion was the socially outcast gays and lesbians in his community. Khan had seemingly asked the newspapers to print ads soliciting people of these persuasions to join him in a Human Rights march on Beijing at the first of the month.

In a press statement that went global overnight, Khan had supposedly stated he felt justified in leading this effort, with him and his Afro-American lover being the poster children for the movement. The press release detailed his complaint of government interference, as well as official objection to Khan, a sixty-plus-year-old man, and his 13-year-old Afro-American lover. He denounced this kind of government repression and claimed he had come out of the closet and so should those who were also of a like mind. The ads were carefully but apparently paid for with funds from his off-shore banking account, which surfaced rather quickly upon a hasty secret police investigation. Deputy Khan's personal computer had surrendered the final incriminating evidence in the form of sexually explicit photos of Khan and his stable of male admirers.

Khan vanished rather abruptly and was never talked about again, except as a corollary to a conversation when someone asked how the Cyber Warfare College was able to fund all of its own needs as well as contribute to the state Treasury. It was simply referred to as the 'Khan Incident'. Any time someone in high government circles had to be reminded of what their role was in the scheme of things, the phrase 'Khan Incident' was invoked and was sufficient to intercept behavior that was considered too ambitious.

The only one who really knew what had happened to Khan was his new cell mate, Char Chun. Char Chun had once been the director of the Chinese space program and had been responsible for Ling Po's removal from the program. Lt. Colonel Po may have looked like an easy person to bully, but she always extracted her revenge. Her adversaries never recovered.

CHAPTER 41

And all the world is a stage.

Quip began, "Okay, people, it's time to launch project OCELET."

Jacob questioned, "OCELET?" with some reluctance mixed with dread.

"Yep!" clarified Quip. "Optically Clear Evaluation of Linear Electronic Telephony systems. OCELET. Let's get started. Shall we?"

Petra mumbled, "And another B-grade movie gets under way."

Quip clapped his hands together and motioned to Petra and Jacob as though he commanded a group of kindergarten children.

"Okay, team members, time for the show. After all, we are in show business here. Let's proceed. Hmmmm?"

Jacob asked, "What do you know about show business?"

He immediately regretted voicing the question. Quip hardly needed encouragement to be offbeat.

Quip flat toned the response. "Only there's no business like it, no business I know…"

Then he chortled and clearly would have broken into a rendition of Ethel Merman's version of the song if Otto hadn't perfectly timed his entrance.

Otto had heard Quip's comment and hastily interjected,

"Please don't, Quip. Let's keep in mind our contract and the requirements for our customer. Our charter is mapping and reconnaissance only. If, however, we leave behind some sleeper code on their internal printers, where it's harder to find, then that will be good. We don't know when we may need additional information, but having our code in place would obviously be to our advantage in the future. I am familiar with the head of this program, and she is the master of unscrupulous. Understood?"

"Oui, mon Capitan!" responded Quip with a French Foreign Legion flare.

The next three hours were consumed by voice commands, kinetic hand gestures, and uniquely-coded programs uploaded for use during the collaborative effort. ICABOD took all requests, gestures, and uploads in parallel mode so no one had to wait to talk with the master program. The more that ICABOD interacted with the team the faster it could assemble the mapping exercise. From the casual onlooker it looked like pandemonium although solid information was being gathered and catalogued.

Everything worked according to script for a few hours, when suddenly ICABOD flashed a warning signal that was hard to miss or ignore. The entire 3-D image started pulsing orange, indicating that the target had discovered them. ICABOD immediately required a response from the team.

Quip cursed, "Oh, poop!" and then quickly stated to the team, "I'm sorry you had to hear that, my apologies."

Quip launched a rapid evaluation scenario that confirmed his suspicions.

"We've been spotted. ICABOD, launch Octopus Ink and get us out of there!"

Petra probed, "Octopus Ink? I hesitate to ask Quip, but what the hell is that?"

"Young lady, I am going to have to ask you to watch your language. There are gentlemen present, one I believe you are rather fond of, and I don't want to have to explain your vulgarities to them."

Petra reddened and couldn't raise her eyes to Jacob or Otto. She contemplated various ways to get even with the jokester later.

Quip explained primarily to Jacob, "We have several ION-cannons parked around the world that can deliver Transmission Control Protocol-sync attacks on our failed reconnaissance efforts to the host. This permits us to extradite ourselves from sites with minimum identification risk, much like an octopus dispensing ink in an effort to evade an attacker."

Jacob was impressed with the process as well as the fact that such a complex system was already in place as a part of the operation. He also understood the tongue in cheek demonstration for Mr. Monty. His respect for the technology capabilities of this organization continued to grow. Their extraction efforts were sufficiently cloaked, and they were not electronically followed as their gateway hops were terminated one by one. The results of the actions pleased Quip.

"Okay, let's wrap up the program, put the signature file on it, and print it for delivery to the client," said Quip.

"Petra, while I'm saving this to our cloud storage, can you please generate the signature file?"

Jacob looked puzzled trying to comprehend the reference.

Finally, he queried Petra. "What signature file? What exactly is the reference used?"

Like everyone with a hobby they are passionate about, Petra seemed eager to discuss the concept of signature file.

"Jacob, what do you know about poetry? As in the creation of, the rules for building a poem, word selection, the circular thought structure, and the mathematical attributes which are a part of its construct?"

"I'm certainly familiar with the humanistic values and some of the subtleties within some poetry. I confess that I'm not likely seeing this from your perspective, so fill me in on the details. Especially the part about the mathematical attributes of poetry?"

"While in my advanced mathematics courses I also took, as an elective, a class called Interpretive Poetry. That's where I found the advanced circular logic, the subtle word choices that completely alter the interpretation of a stanza, as well as the hidden or allegorical meanings. The best poetry examples show a helical mathematic parallel to elliptical algorithms that are used in advanced encryption examples. In other words, excellent poetry provides three-dimensional thinking, not just two-dimensional. Thus, it can be used to represent an encryption algorithm.

"The additional benefit is that the encryption/decryption process can be spoken as well as written to lock or unlock a program or file. The extra touch is to use steganography to hide the poetry in the 3-D program that we are about to print out on the 3-D printer sitting over there. The poetry key is embedded in the program in plain sight but unusable unless you know where to look and what you are looking at. Without the key you can't open the program," Petra finished.

"This is the signature file Quip requested from you?"

"Correct."

Jacob followed the process as Quip took the poem key feeds into the component entrance tray of the 3-D printer and finished the print job. Out popped a 3-D image of the target site with poetic phrases scattered here and there on the image making them almost invisible.

"We put the poem through a security code randomizer before printing just to make it a little more difficult to open the program," Quip added. "With the mathematics built into the poem, unless you recite it correctly the program dissolves. Thus security is maintained."

Jacob wanted additional clarity. "Why would you do that if ICABOD is the only machine that can run the program? What's the point of a Poetry Key to unlock the program?"

Quip sighed, "Kid, there was a movie I saw one time where this one country builds the world's biggest, fastest, most advanced computer. The humans were so proud of themselves with their achievement until the electronic monolith meets its electronic peer in cyber space, and they start teaching each other at machine speeds. The humans cannot disconnect the two machines. The machine pair began dictating what the humans should do. The egotistical people never expected to have another machine come online, let alone the two machines pool their collective processing power. I don't believe that we are the only ones capable of building a system as sophisticated as ICABOD, so I put in fail safes and back doors to defeat the unexpected."

Jacob acknowledged the logic of the statement then looked at Petra. "So perhaps you can teach me this poetry encryption technique you have developed? I'd love to learn more."

Quip interjected, "Hey, buddy, no hitting on team members during work hours!"

Jacob retorted, "Quip, in your case I'm quite sure that will never be a problem."

Petra handed him a small piece of paper with five lines written on it.

She chuckled and said, "I thought you might want to learn, so here is your first assignment. Break the code! If you can."

Otto laughed out loud. "You two are something else. Quip, is everything buttoned up here and transmission completed? I would like to alert your favorite, Mr. Monty, that the project is complete."

"We are done here. The files are shipped to the secured point. We can wrap up the final details' tomorrow. I think it is time to show Jacob some of the finer accommodations we have at our disposal."

"Agreed. Jacob, as much as I am certain you like the room here in the facility, we do have a chateau close by. It belongs to one within our inner circle, and you need to meet him. To be honest, Petra and I have been sleeping there since your arrival. We have all agreed that you deserve to learn a bit more about our roots and meet another key player."

Intrigued, Jacob nodded. "I would like that, sir. I think that this operation is impressive at the very least. While I cannot pretend to understand all the layers and underlying business ventures, I believe I would like to learn as much as possible and really begin contributing to the efforts. I do have some ideas, but not until I see a little more to make certain I am thinking far enough out on the potentials."

In the many weeks since Jacob had arrived, it had been solid 15-hour days, with no weekends off. He hadn't had one minute alone with Petra to discuss anything. He'd been good at masking his frustration. True, the technology operations were extensive, but he'd learned a great deal. The programs he'd modified had been reviewed but immediately placed into operations. Each day, Petra and Otto both had arrived for breakfast and stayed until the call by Quip for lights out. The passing touch of hands with Petra only made him fantasize in his dreams. Now he would be seeing a different side of the operation and meeting yet another key player. He was both excited and apprehensive about passing yet another test.

"Sounds good, my boy. I will call Haddy and have her bring the limo to take us all."

CHAPTER 42

As a hunter, beware of the feeling of being hunted.

Master Po walked in the classroom and asked the instructor, "What happened? I got the alerts on my machine. Did we have a breach, or was someone careless?"

"No one was careless, Master Po," said Jinny Lin. "I handed out the class assignments as usual. The students loaded up mirrored systems, per standard operating procedure, and they began their reconnaissance exercise. I was watching individual progress when I noticed that someone or something was mapping the interior of the classroom, but at a speed I've never seen before. It was so fast that I almost didn't notice it at first, and then it stopped like it knew I was observing its activities.

"None of the students noticed the activity since they were focused on the assignment. I began interrogating equipment in other areas of the academy and noticed only fleeting reconnaissance activity which was also very fast. I went to the security appliances and firewalls, and they all without exception showed no intrusion activity. That's when I launched the WEASEL program which tripped the cyber intruder alarm. WEASEL got as far as the Internet gateway before the systems were inundated with a SYN-Flood attack, and WEASEL was terminated.

"I could affect no reverse tracing of the cyber intruder. Additionally, no telemetry information was captured by the mirror system, so the cyber intruder either erased it, presuming he knew of its existence, or it was never observed by the mirror system. Up to this point, I would have stated that would be impossible. The mirror system always sees every electronic pulse of activity inside the academy."

Master Po was convinced that Lin was not hiding anything and said, "I agree. I will do some checking as well. Contact me immediately if any other activity is noticed. Perhaps it is nothing more than a power surge."

0 1 0 1 0 1 0 1 0 0 1 1 0 0

Master Po returned to her desk for her afternoon tea and reflected how different her life had turned out from where she started. Things were always so cat and mouse in this world now, but so different from 20 years ago.

Ling Po had become emotionally involved with a career military man in her early 20's, Captain Win Lom. He had been dashing, engaging, funny, and hopelessly infatuated with her. They had not only a deeply romantic relationship but a very sensual one as well. Sometimes he would pick her up, and they would go to a seedy bar in civilian clothes and consume just enough fermented grain alcohol to release their inhibitions. She might remove her panties while at the table and hand them to him before scooting a little closer in their booth. She had learned to use her hands and mouth to stimulate and arouse him, and the more public the tease the more he was pleased.

Sometimes their early evening trysts in the bars got them caught, and they were asked to leave. She would smile prettily, and they would rise to leave. At times, almost as an act of defiance, she would make sure on their way out that she deliberately fumbled with buttoning her dress so she could show her breasts to those paying attention and would stop short of the door to put her panties back on. She and Win Lom laughed about it later.

On an outing one time he had borrowed a car to take them to the countryside. While he was trying to put fuel in the vehicle, she had pulled her dress top open to show off her breasts and was slowly and erotically rubbing her crotch. Finally, she had pulled her skirt up past her hips and called to him, asking him to hurry please. The erotic visuals she provided caused him to let slip the gas hose used to dispense the fuel, which ended up discharging gasoline all over the car and on the ground. They never made it to the countryside that day, for their activities in the car were far too fascinating.

Ling Po had a married older sister who understood her younger sister's appetite for sensual pleasures and frequently sought her out and asked for guidance on sexual techniques.

One time her older sister, blushing and stammering, asked, "What should I do when I have collected a mouthful of essence of man? I mean, uh, can I spit it out? Will he be offended? Or must I, uh, swallow the essence of man?"

Ling Po grinned from ear to ear, partly because her older sister was asking for guidance, for something she obviously did not care for, but also because she herself liked the taste of essence of man.

She suggested, "If you do not care for it, then keep a small towel handy and discreetly transfer it to the towel so he does not notice."

Ling Po's mischievousness surfaced at this point, and she offered, "If you need me to provide a tutorial session for you, I can."

They both dissolved into laughter at the dynamics of the conversation.

One day, Ling Po and her military man's passions had over-run their good judgment. As the phrase goes, they didn't love safely. At that time, the Chinese government was giving incentives for childless marriages, and since they were both government employees the arrangements were made for an early termination of her pregnancy. She agreed that early termination was the right thing to do, but she couldn't stop thinking about how things might have been if she had declined the State's generous offer.

While Win Lom was supportive of the decision they made together, the relationship suffered. While she was already talking how they might keep the next offspring, he threw himself into his military career and slowly drifted out of her life. He told her he was not ready and that perhaps they could revisit this issue of starting a family in a couple of years. He took an assignment in Western China to help further his career, but she suspected that he wanted the distance.

They agreed to still see each other, but she could feel the door closing between them. She wanted a family, and he wanted his military career. Six weeks later he was killed in a massive earth-quake. So many had lost their lives that the site was turned into a mass grave with a solid fence surrounding it. No bodies were to be exhumed or additional questions asked.

Ling Po focused on her work in the Aerospace Industry of China as no man held any interest for her after his death. The male colleagues in the defense industry referred to her as Ice Po. It was rumored she was untutored in bedroom skills which was why she was never seen with a male. How wrong they were. But, as with all skills requiring hand, eye, and mouth coordination, without practice the skill fades away, and so it was with Ling Po.

CHAPTER 43

Life is like an onion with many layers to peel back to reach its heart.

Haddy arrived with the limousine. She gave Jacob a quick hug of welcome as she entered the operations center to collect the team.

Jacob grinned, "Nice to see you again, Haddy. I can honestly say that I am not surprised you are here as well."

"The car is out front and warm as toast. I have our chef preparing us a fabulous meal that will expand your palates and help ease the day away. Wolfgang is waiting in the study ready to have before-dinner drinks. Are you finished for the evening?"

Otto took Haddy's hand and kissed it. "You, my dear, are simply priceless. Everything covered as always. We are ready to go, and Jacob packed a few items as well. I did not think we wanted to waste time tonight moving him over, but perhaps tomorrow."

"I can help take care of that tomorrow." She smiled at him. "Let's go then."

The road to the chateau was not the one that Jacob originally came in on, but on the back side of the building and well-camouflaged. The road wound through a heavily wooded area, and a few nocturnal creatures appeared curious at the visitors' passing. Jacob noted deer and foxes and was certain there were more critters that he'd missed. After twenty or so minutes, they arrived at a double gate which stood open, as if awaiting their arrival. After a short drive up a tree-lined road, the chateau appeared with enough light on the outside to hint at its size. Haddy deftly parked near the steps leading up to the front door.

As they exited the car, Jacob noticed that Haddy took Otto's hand as a partner might. He had to smile. He hadn't seen that one coming. Quip sauntered up the steps in a surprisingly dignified manner. Petra bumped his shoulder, smiled reassuringly and stayed by his side as they walked up the steps.

"Tonight you will get some answers, and we can talk privately later. Stay open-minded, please," she whispered.

He leaned close to her ear and whispered, "I hope we can do more than talk privately, Petra."

The door was opened by a butler that greeted each of the arrivals and took their coats and bags.

Petra introduced Jacob. "Bowen, I would like to introduce you to Jacob Michaels. He will be staying for some time and might need your guidance."

Bowen studied Jacob for a moment and then said, "Master Jacob, a pleasure to meet you, sir. Please let me know if you require anything. I hope you will be comfortable, and please check out all the amenities the chateau has to offer during the daylight. Miss Petra can show you to the study where Master Wolfgang is pacing while awaiting your arrival."

Petra escorted him toward the study. The furnishings were rich and tasteful with the older European style, similar to the offices where he had met Otto in New York City. There were several rooms that were open, but not really lit for use. Stairs in the center indicated a floor above which Jacob suspected were bedrooms or perhaps servants' quarters. The rugs, wall hangings, paintings and furniture in general were well cared for but obviously mostly antiques. He suspected the history of the chateau would be charming. Making a turn they arrived in the study, which was a great room scattered with loosely grouped chairs and couches. A fire was burning in a very large fireplace, and the lighting was warm and inviting.

As they entered, the conversation ceased, and a tall, dignified looking man with grey hair turned toward them. His angular face was lit up with a smile upon seeing Jacob. The blueness of his eyes was even more startling as he closed the distance and extended his hand.

"And you, son, must be Jacob. I have heard so much about you. Welcome to my home."

He extended his hand and shook Jacob's with his other hand covering the two as if to make certain Jacob was real. The twinkle in his eye and his smile were contagious.

"Thank you, sir. It is nice to meet you. Your home is lovely. However, you have me at a bit of a disadvantage as I only heard of you a short time ago. This is a need-to-know group, it seems." He smiled, finding something almost familiar in the man. "But I would like to learn more about you. You seem familiar for some reason."

"Please, call me Wolfgang, everyone does. You will learn a great deal about me, and I hope you will not be too disappointed. We are serving drinks here and will visit for a bit, unless you wish to see your room first and freshen up. Quip selected the refresh option and will be back shortly."

He then leaned over and gave Petra a fatherly-like embrace. "Glad you are back, Petra. Did you wish to go refresh too?"

"Yes, I think so, Wolfgang. Just to change out of these clothes would be nice before dinner. I can show Jacob his room, if you like."

"Yes, my dear. That would be helpful." His eyes twinkled, and he grinned some more. "You two run along, but return soon. Petra, your usual? Jacob, what would you like to drink, and I will have it ready upon your return?"

"Yes, my usual, please." She smiled with her whole face relaxing as if being in this home was very comforting.

"Wolfgang, a dry white wine would be great if you have it," Jacob requested.

Petra and Jacob left the study and at the stairs began the climb up.

She took his hand and said, "Our rooms are next to each other. I know right where you will be. Each of these rooms is a suite with its own bathroom and most have small fireplaces as well. Some of the rooms on the back also have balconies, but ours do not. Quip's usual room has a balcony, so he is on the other side. I gather you were not aware that Haddy and Otto are married. They share one of the larger suites, also with a balcony. Each room has a phone which connects to the staff in case you need anything at all."

As they reached midway down the hallway, she indicated the door to her room, and as promised she opened the next door reaffirming it was his room. The rich, dark burgundy drapes blended with the rug and the spread, though it was not oppressively dark. The bed was huge and set to the back of the room with a small sitting area by the fireplace. The drapes were opened and a mixture of moonlight and outside lights shone through the windows.

She had just closed the door when he spun her around and took her into his arms, kissing her and feeling her passion back tenfold. They held each other and kissed until their breathing grew irregular, and the rest of the world drifted far away.

"This is what I missed. You, right here in my arms, kissing me, like you want me." He rumbled in her ear, pulling her closer.

Hugging him closer and listening to his heart pounding, Petra replied, "Of course I want you and missed you terribly. We need to get changed though and return. It would be too rude to dally here right now."

"I will hold you to that promise later. I want you here with me all night, Petra."

"Yes," she said as she scrambled out of his grasp. "I will meet you in the hallway in ten." She closed the door as she left with a wink and a grin.

He checked out the bathroom, finding both a tub and a shower and a full assortment of toiletry items. He washed his face and then opened the closet to hang up his duffle. There was a nice assortment of clothes, and thumbing through them he noticed that they appeared new and in his size. He grinned as he located slacks, shirt, a light sweater, and loafers to change into for dinner. All in all, this would be comfortable, he mused as he went to the hallway. Petra was very pretty in a flowing dress that hugged all the right curves.

"You are beautiful and make it very difficult to want to go back downstairs."

She hugged him and sighed. "You look way too good yourself, so let's behave and go have our drinks and dinner. I am starving."

They arrived at the study to find everyone accounted for. Wolfgang handed their drinks to them and asked Jacob if his room was adequate.

"Yes sir, more than adequate. I really appreciate the extra clothes since the rest of my belongings are at the facility."

"Call me Wolfgang, please. No problem. Haddy arranged for the wardrobe. She takes care of all of us. So, tell me what you have been doing, and your thoughts on our little operation so far."

They talked for a while. Jacob conveyed a lot of his impressions and thoughts. The conversation continued during dinner with Jacob at Wolfgang's right during service. The four-course meal was delicious and varied with several wines to complement each course. Jacob declined dessert. After the rest finished theirs, Wolfgang suggested that he and Jacob return to the study. He suggested the others go to the game room, while promising to meet them there after a while.

Once Wolfgang and Jacob were seated in the study near the fire, each with a glass of cognac warming in their hands, he took an envelope from his pocket and seemed to debate briefly with himself.

"Jacob, I have a letter here for you. Before I give it to you, I want you to know that I am so very glad you are here. The team has enjoyed working with you and want you to become a real part of the operation if that is your final decision. I know that you coming here was a rushed commitment, and if you really want to not accept being a part of it, I will help you make other arrangements. I want you to be happy. Now I will leave you to read this for a bit and then return to answer any questions you might have."

"Wolfgang, I am not certain I understand, but thank you for your support," Jacob said as he took possession of the letter.

As he opened the letter, dated eight months prior, he caught sight of a very familiar handwriting that gripped his heart.

My Darling Son,
If you are reading this letter, then I was unable to take you to Europe as I had planned. This was only to give to you as a contingency that I thought I would never need. I actually laughed when Father suggested it.
With any luck the man that handed you this was in fact Wolfgang, rather than someone else. Wolfgang is my father and he is your grandfather. He and Granny were

married, but she refused to let me come to the U.S. alone to raise you. Her travels to Europe now and again were to see her husband.

By now you have some exposure to the family operations but how much of the history behind it I wouldn't know. I want to give you some background which will also help answer many of your childhood queries.

The family business started during the war with the confiscation of a copy of the Enigma machine. It was used by the three founders, your grandfather, and his friends Tavius and Ferdek. I suspect you've met Otto, the son of Tavius, and Petra is his daughter. You may have met Quip and his brother Erich already. They are descendants of Ferdek's son, who died with his wife in a car accident.

The family business, as we have always called it, is one that tries to right wrongs and keep guard to prevent the atrocities again as were a part of war. I have over the years added some components for the communications side and created some very bleeding edge elements. Quip can go chapter and verse if needed as he is the holder of all the contributions made over many, many years.

Every descendant who was able and willing to contribute was taught an element. Each descendant was given a choice to join the business or not. Jacob, I wanted you well educated and strong enough, that you could make the wisest choice for yourself. Sometimes our family operation deals with some really bad individuals that need to be avoided. Our success rate is actually very good. Sadly, I must have missed a step to not be there with you.

Your father was a high-ranking military man who died in battle before knowing you were conceived. That was when I took myself to New York to begin a new life

with you, not full of sadness with my old friends and
memories at every turn.

Please know that I loved you from the moment you
were conceived and wanted you safe more than anything.
Whether you decide to join the family operation or not,
I will be proud of you and find comfort knowing you are
trained well and very brilliant. Father will add all the
details you might want, just ask him.

Love Mother

Jacob was stunned and reread the letter over and over. It was unbelievable and the revelation that this was his family completely dwarfed everything in his life up to now. The unexpected answers created a tsunami of emotions in his being.

CHAPTER 44

Which is more important, things you can see or things that you sense?

Master Po reviewed all of the data surrounding the afternoon's interruption. She could not find anything that suggested a breach had occurred. However, with her years of experience, her second sense suggested otherwise. After a discussion with Lin again over the incident and her subsequent review, she decided the best course of action would be to add another layer of defense, just in case.

She programmed the changes that were required and asked Jinny Lin to review them before activating it. Master Po knew it was perfect, but Lin needed to be a part of the process. It was possible the changes might spark some additional defense maneuvers from Jinny Lin.

The relationship between Master Po and Grigory was one of respect and mutual obligation. She provided training support, and he provided information. In the back of her mind she wondered if the incident today was Grigory's team testing their knowledge and trying to attack the teacher. That would simply not be tolerated.

Knowing the volatility of the Russian, she decided to call him to determine if she might sense something from a conversation. Other methods of escalation were certainly available; however, if they were not necessary, she did not want to go to the additional effort. Very few individuals outside of China had any idea what her institution was actually capable of doing. Only she knew all the pieces of the operation and their interdependencies. She placed a secure call to Grigory.

He answered immediately. "Hello, Master Po, what an unexpected surprise to hear from you."

"Always a pleasure to speak to you as well, Grigory. Do you have a few minutes so that we might speak?"

"Of course. I can always make time to help a comrade."

"Thank you. The last round of training for your team touched on some new areas, including cloaking for information retrieval. Has that proven valuable in practice for you yet? The reason I ask is I am outlining a special training segment and wonder how much review will be required."

"That team has been doing some cloaking with some of our financial targets. Though not totally effective yet, they do seem to understand the application of it well. A special session by you is deeply appreciated, but for what cost?"

She chuckled, "Grigory, we have worked together too long to lack understanding of each other's requirements. This is not a cost session, but more of a quid pro quo. It has come to me through an unreliable channel that someone may have an interest in my operations here. I am not in a position to easily validate that, so I thought perhaps your resources might be able to gather some discreet information."

"I have heard nothing but am happy to research this request. Your efforts have been staying under the radar, and I suspect someone is toying with your fears."

Immediately agitated, Master Po emphatically stated, "Make no mistake, Grigory. I have no fears. I do know how to deal with those who might try to harm me or my training facility." More calmly she added, "It is likely nothing but chatter, but I thought you might like to see what your team could find. Consider it a fishing expedition using their newly acquired skills. Regardless, the special course will be ready at the end of the month. I will send your team the times and connection method."

"I will make it so and get back with you soon with any news."

After he disconnected, Master Po reviewed the conversation and was convinced Grigory's team had not been testing their skills in her environment. It was likely nothing, but she still activated the additional defense program. It couldn't hurt.

CHAPTER 45

In the list of priorities for life, family should always come first.

Wolfgang returned to the study to find Jacob staring at the fire. He wasn't sure how to approach him and wanted to let Jacob begin the exchange. The pain that Jacob must be feeling was likely similar to the pain that he had felt when he had learned of Julianne's death. Not saying a word, he walked toward the fire and took the vacant chair. After a short time Jacob finally spoke.

"Wolfgang, thank you for the letter. It means a great deal to me though I guess I am feeling a combination of surprise and uncertainty. I am delighted to learn that I have family but sad that I had no way of reaching out to them. We have, it seems, missed a great deal of time."

"Yes, Jacob, I would agree. I was kept informed about you over the years. Obviously more than you were. I have letters from the years outlining each of your milestones and many pictures. In many ways I feel like I know you very well. I want you to feel free to ask me anything. If it is something that I know, I will tell you."

For the next hour they discussed things that Jacob wanted to know. Everything from what Jacob should really call his grandfather to how Wolfgang felt about the family business. The exchange between the two men clarified several questions for Jacob. He understood what the scope of his final commitment to the R-Group would mean. It would set the path for the rest of his life.

"Wolfgang, I do have one question that I hope that you know the answer to. In the letter, Mom indicated that there were bad people that she may have crossed. That said, was the hit and run an accident or on purpose? The police said it was questionable, but that they had no leads."

"To be honest, Jacob, I have my suspicions. She and I had spoken that evening before she went home. I don't think it was an accident, but we are still trying to find out who may have done this and why. When I know something certain, I will let you know."

"Alright. Thank you for the information and again for the letter. I am going to need to think about this. I will likely come back with more questions. Would it be alright with you if we join the others? I'd like to see the game room. This home of yours is impressive."

"Of course. Let me show you the way. I am sure the others are anxious to see that you are alright. They had an idea about our discussion but were not made privy to any of the details."

Jacob and Wolfgang entered the game room to catch Quip and Petra in a game of billiards. Apparently, she was about to win as she called the shot with the eight ball to the side pocket. Under Quip's protests that she was somehow cheating, she sunk the shot with precision.

"Quip, I win again. I keep telling you it is all about geometry. I know you did not like the subject, and well, it shows. Perhaps Jacob will play a game with you now that he has arrived." She walked over to him and gave him a fast hug, then pulled him toward the table.

"Sure, Quip, I'd like to play you a game, though I doubt I'll be at the same level as Petra."

"Bring it on. By the way, Erich Watcowski is my younger brother. I actually did a name change during my youth to the last name of Waters, trying to escape being Watcowski III. It was too much family for me to live up to at the time. Erich thinks you rock. Just so you know, we all have a stake in this business. That takes some getting used to. If you have questions, just ask."

"Right now the only question I have is, after you rack 'em, can I break?"

The laughter at that comment was echoed by the room. They played a couple of games with Jacob and Quip each winning one. Petra begged off playing any more tonight. They told a couple of funny stories of earlier days at this chateau, which brought comments from Otto and Wolfgang and lots of laughter. Otto brought the evening to a close, as he reminded them of more work to do in the morning. Each retired to their assigned room.

01010101001100

Jacob had just started to soap up in the shower when he felt a slight draft and heard some rustling. He grinned as Petra entered the shower. Her hair was tied up, and she was breathtaking as she stood beside him with the water coursing down her shoulders and over her breasts.

"You knew about my relationship with the family?" He asked almost as an accusation.

"Yes. Quip and I were to help gain insight into your capabilities. I never thought I would be so attracted to you. It was what scared me so badly after our lovely day in Long Island. It was not in the assignment. I am sorry I could not tell you. I also really haven't told any of them how I feel about you. I know my father, Otto, has surmised our relationship and is championing it wherever he can."

He kissed her and let the warm water dance over them both. The shower was absolutely delightful.

Pulling her closer and feeling her pressed up against him, he stopped the kiss and rumbled in her ear. "As long as you tell me the truth from here on, that's all I need. I want you."

"Yes. I promise. I want to explore us and what we can be."

With that he pulled her closer and kissed her with such passion she immediately heated up. Every response to a kiss or a touch by her drove him to please her. Using his hand while he held her, he pushed her to a climax. She had barely stopped trembling from her release when he picked her up and firmly place her over his erection and drove into her, thrusting with urgency and bringing them both to climax.

He held her and then finished washing while she scrubbed his back. They rinsed, dried and then retired to play in the enormous bed. As dawn arrived, they woke and came together again, then wrapped themselves in each other's embrace. A gentle knock at the door, followed by a call to breakfast in half an hour, ended their fun for the time being.

"Ah, another day. Let's get going, or I would be tempted to stay here all day."

She laughed and said, "Oh, no. That would get Quip in here faster than ICABOD can map a system, if for no other reason than to catch us and then embarrass us." She kissed him then continued, "Let's avoid that for the time being. I want you all to myself."

"Alright. But just so you understand my preferences."

With that he kissed her soundly, knowing her body was responding as was his. He rose in all his glory and tossed her robe over.

"Get going, my dear Petra, while the getting is possible. I will see you at the bottom of the stairs."

In a flash she was gone. He dressed with a smile on his face. As he headed downstairs he was whistling some tune he couldn't name. Bowen was at the foot of the stairs.

"Sir, breakfast is this way," he said as he walked away.

CHAPTER 46

Better the devil you know than the one you don't.

G rigory conveyed a portion of his conversation with Master Po to Sergei. He requested that Sergei do a little digging through some of his informants. If there was any reconnaissance activity going on, it was likely from some Western government. Grigory had many connections and a nice little business of information for sale on lots of interesting folks he liked to refer to as 'persons of interest'. Sergei also tapped into this resource. Sergei could not refuse any request as he owed his life to Grigory.

Sergei had grown up on the streets of Moscow and had lived in poverty as a child. His mother had been divorced numerous times and had at least four other children. She was more of a whore than a nurturing mother. She had thrown him out of the house when he was nine years old for selling marijuana, not for smoking it, but for refusing to provide her a cut of the proceeds. He had one silver tooth in his mouth to replace the tooth he had lost when she had punched him during one of her fits. The silver tooth was acquired with profits from his dealing and was a constant reminder to him of what he had achieved.

Grigory took Sergei in because he felt sorry for the kid. He provided him with regular food, training in martial arts, and some education. Sergei grew into a substantially sized young man who was nearly as brutal as Grigory. Sergei was hardheaded by comparison and often overreacted when he misunderstood a comment from others. Sergei had suggested he could provide value with some of his small unsanctioned businesses. By the time Sergei was 13, he had grown his personal business to include fencing stolen goods. He was permitted this small business, with Grigory as an umbrella for protection.

Grigory was a large, brutal, and cruel man, but usually had others do the heavy lifting when things needed to be straightened out. Early on he'd made an example of Sergei that helped to underscore a person's status in Grigory's organization. Sergei tried crossing Grigory one time, which resulted in a lasting limp. The cane Sergei used was no longer necessary for walking, but it gave him an excuse to hide a long, thin sword for insurance and protection. It was said that Sergei had offered lifelong service to Grigory in exchange for sparing his life. After his hospitalization and rehabilitation, Sergei had been a trusted model henchman, which is not to say Grigory strictly trusted him. There was always someone with Sergei to watch and report his comings and goings. Grigory made Sergei an example of what the perfect employee should be like by adding the element of fear for his life. This was often cited to newcomers or those that crossed him.

Grigory also had a white female tiger he had acquired as a kitten. The white tiger had been confiscated from a Las Vegas show personality who didn't make timely payments for goods provided. The tiger weighed in at 157 kilos, and she loved to wrestle with Grigory. Grigory frequently pointed out to Sergei her unfailing loyalty.

The tiger's name was Nikkei, but Grigory's associates called her the Interrogator. If someone wouldn't cooperate and tell Grigory what he wanted to know, they were placed in very close quarters with Nikkei. Nikkei always got them to talk; her emerald green eyes were so hypnotic, malevolent, and most certainly the tiger's greatest weapon to invoke fear in her victims.

Nikkei was the only real female in Grigory's life. He spoiled her just as any mob boss would do, right down to the jewelry one would lavish on a lady. Nikkei wore a magnificent gold and diamond-studded collar Grigory had commissioned for her. He figured the collar would be his liquid assets if everything crashed down on him and it was perfectly safe from theft. Who in their right mind would try and steal a collar from the neck of a white tiger?

Grigory sent word through Sergei to Patty to start looking for information from their U.S. Government sources about a cyber covert operation that might be directed at a premier Asian Government operation.

Patty received the request from Sergei but wanted clarification. Plus, Sergei had threatened her again on her lack of performance. She called Grigory for more information on what she was supposed to look for and the real timeframe. It irked Sergei that she contacted Grigory for additional information and annoyed Grigory.

Grigory snapped, "Just hunt quietly. This one is dangerous and has lots of money and favors attached to it. If you find a good source, there is extra in it for you. We must get information within the next few days."

Patty knew that tone and didn't press further. As she disconnected, she grumbled, "Go find me something in a haystack, and I'll tell you if it's a needle. Asshole."

She wouldn't bother Buzz with this assignment. She knew Buzz would do anything for her, but he was too focused on trying to find coins that had fallen out of someone's pocket into the couch cushions of the sofa. She had sources within her clientele that she could quietly interrogate.

Patty was hoping to get enough to get out and start over someplace else. The information gig had been fun at first, but now it seemed claustrophobic. She wanted the big score to get away from Sergei, and even Grigory. She knew the identity business well enough to leave completely but needed one good paycheck. Maybe Grigory was giving her the right payday at last if she could convince him her information was valid. Timing would be essential in order to collect and run.

01010101001100

Patty disconnected from the last call with her third contact in frustrated anger. "Great," she groused out loud, "No one knows anything and no one can do anything! All they care about is seeing some sex toy demo that will net me dozens of dollars while I'm looking to broker information for thousands. One big score and I can start fresh somewhere else where I'm calling the shots."

About that time Buzz came through the front door. He never quite understood the value of putting things away so others didn't trip over what you had just dropped on the floor. Buzz treated the place like it was his apartment, but she always saw it as her place of business. The collision between attitudes was eminent.

After dropping his workout clothes into a pile on the floor Buzz said, "Hey babe, how about you and me go out tonight? If we go out early, we can come back and play." He wiggled his eyebrows to convey his amorous intentions.

Patty, frustrated with everything, lost it. "Oh, go to hell! You really tick me off with your low-rent attitude and shit manners towards me! So, NO!" she screamed as she stormed off.

Buzz was not what you would call a man oozing with wit and charm, but even he had some concept of romance. After she left it occurred to him that she had been somewhat moody of late and perhaps a little charm might help his case. His brainstorm of an idea for demonstrating his charm was really no more than a modest, light drizzle, but Buzz was completely absorbed in how it should be perceived. After all, it was all about getting laid later tonight, wasn't it? He quickly resolved to send a bouquet of flowers on his way to the office. No snitching from the cemetery this go-round, and he would purchase a nice bottle of wine. That should do the trick, he said to himself as he took off.

CHAPTER 47

Now you see them, now you don't.

Petra, Jacob and Quip arrived back at the operations center right after breakfast. The focus was to review the monitoring that had occurred in China overnight and any changes that might have been implemented. The systems were going well, but there had been a program layer added overnight. Not a problem per se, but additional changes were made to the program by Jacob for an extra encryption element. Petra verified receipt of the report to Mr. Monty. Otto entered the operations center about an hour after the others had arrived, just in time to see some activity from ICABOD that looked wrong.

"Quip, is that sloppy monitoring on our art or the last element of our second phase?" Otto asked with a hint of annoyance in his voice.

Quip responded quickly, "It was as you requested, my Lord." This title always annoyed Otto. He felt it was a bit disrespectful.

"Quip, please make sure the self-detonation and the homing code fragments are installed properly. We are hunting for the food chain here, not just a single player. They have their agenda, and we have ours. We sold the analysis of the Chinese capability to our Western client and now we it's time to offer our services to the Chinese to strengthen their defenses. In this way no one falls behind, and no one becomes too powerful in the cyber arms race. This is a lot like the ebb and flow of the tides. You need to gather when the tides are low and sell when the tides are high."

"Jacob and I are both monitoring it. Things are working as prescribed so far."

Otto suggested, mostly to himself, "It's time then to reach out to Lt. Colonel Ling Po and offer our services again."

"I would agree, sir. The activity they are tracking is totally confusing them, and they cannot track it back to the source. It is a perfect play on our part."

Otto moved into his office for a quiet, encrypted phone conversation with Lt. Colonel Ling Po.

"Master Po, it's been a while since we've spoken. I hope this call finds you well."

Master Po said, "Good morning, Otto. How nice to hear from you again. Yes, all is well here, thank you for asking. Is this a social call, Otto, or something else? Are you following up on our last piece of business to see if I'm a happy customer?"

Otto, a master at buttering up clients, gently presented, "I wish that time permitted me to check in with you more routinely, but alas I am busy as usual. I thought I would contact you to see if you might want some consulting services from my team. Two of our premier customers engaged with us recently, and we resolved their infiltration issues in quick order. The chat rooms this morning suggested that your organization recently experienced a possible breach into your operations. If that is true, I thought there may be some services we could provide you, allowing you to benefit from perhaps what we are seeing as newer techniques to access systems."

Po was taken aback at the swiftness of chatter and sent a quick IM to Lin to ask about chat room activity. She had no tolerance for loose lips from her instructors or any of the students. She also knew that the higher levels within China, especially the Chairman, did not like her success and hoped to catch a misstep by her or her team.

Leveling her response, she stated, "I haven't been apprised of a problem, but I will check with my team. Are you suggesting remote consulting services? For the usual sum per engagement we've done in the past?"

Otto responded kindly, "The rates have gone up recently but based on our long association with you, Master Po, I feel compelled to maintain your usual rate. I would not wish to disrupt our long-standing relationship by quibbling over price increases I failed to alert you to some months ago. I trust you'd find that acceptable for any engagement within the next thirty days? I know you have struggled to make your operation world class."

Lt. Colonel Po, almost offended, said, "So you feel sorry for me and my organization, so much so that you offer a discount, thinking it would be pleasantly received. You don't think I can match what my competition pays for your services? Don't be rude, young man."

Otto laughed, "Young man? I like the sound of that, Master Po. As you wish. Please allow me to increase the rate by ten percent so as not to offend you. That will take it to our current standard rate."

Po paused for a bit, then queried, "If you raise the old fee by 20%, can I have all the information that the regular rate doesn't provide? I am confident that you usually withhold the juicy pieces for sale later and not necessarily to the original customer. So, I want all the information to begin with and a sixty-day moratorium on using it with any other customer."

Otto grinned, then stated, "Madam, you wound me! You have always been very astute, which is why I continue to look out for your interests. If I made it a thirty percent premium, that would entitle you to all the detailed information findings and the source identity. Is that more satisfactory to your fear of deceit, Lt. Colonel Po?"

Master Po responded with the appropriate hurt tone in her voice. "And now you wound me by addressing me with my rank. After all this time you should feel comfortable with straight business discussions. And no, you do not deceive me in our dealings. I have noticed that you are faster than I originally envisioned. Shall we use the usual banking institution?"

Otto agreed, "Yes, please. We will commence this afternoon which should be after your normal classes. And what information drop point do you require this time?"

Master Po grinned. "Macau is always pretty this time of year, so how about there?"

"As you wish. I would expect you would prefer the usual courier, JAC?"

"Of course. I like her thoroughness and directness in our dealings. She also provides the female vantage point, which honestly you fail miserably at. I will be there on Friday."

"That sounds perfect. She will be at the same resort as last time. Thank you, Master Po, and take care." Otto smiled as he disconnected and routed a note to Quip for the team to proceed.

CHAPTER 48

You can buy them books and buy them books but they still eat the glue.

Grigory had just received information from Patty along with her demand for extra payment for her effort. After her rude comment as their last phone call ended, it was the final straw. He didn't trust the information she provided in the slightest.

He had really worked himself into a foul mood by the time he'd sent word for Sergei. Sergei could tell something was up by the way he was summoned.

"Get your ass over here now," Grigory briskly demanded.

When Sergei arrived, Grigory was playing with Nikkei. She always seemed to have a calming effect on him.

"Yes, Grigory? You wanted to see me about something?" queried Sergei, hoping the storm was past.

Without turning his head to look Sergei in the eyes as he played with Nikkei, he said, "I have a situation with someone who seems to have lost their respect for me. I should like very much for you to reestablish that respect so that we never have to have this type of communication lapse again. You should understand that this loss of trust in an associate of our organization is very bad for business. My disappointment in this individual is most grievous. I want you to convey my displeasure to this person. Perhaps she will see the proper path to address this unfortunate turn of events. Do you understand, Sergei?"

Sergei could tell that Grigory was seething with anger and highly irritated, based on his choice of words. He would be happy to take care of this associate. More than anything he wanted the respect and confidence of Grigory.

Sergei agreed, "Yes, sir. I understand."

Sergei was always jealous of Nikkei and the affection that Grigory lavished on her. In many ways, Sergei and Nikkei were exactly alike. Both of them worshipped Grigory and always did his bidding no matter what he asked. Both had a malevolent streak that could turn them into the consummate predator in a heartbeat. But the one main difference was that Nikkei could be playful, cute. and so endearing no matter how thick the air was with Grigory's anger. She could get him to calm down with her playfulness and purring when he scratched her neck and ears. Sergei recognized he would never be cute and funny.

Sergei had always been emotionally retarded because of his dreadful childhood. His near-death experience at the hands of Grigory had exacerbated his ailment into a full-blown psycho-logical disease. He had a refined appetite for cruelty and pain, both delivering and receiving it. He actually enjoyed random incidents of getting his ears boxed by Grigory, since it was the only type of human contact that he found pleasurable. Unfortunately for others, he also found that dispensing pain was a source of enjoyment and pleasure.

Physically he qualified as male, but it would be unfair to all other males to classify him with this gender. He had no regular friends, male or female, because of his crippling mental disability. Pain was an addiction for him. Most of the time when he engaged in a pain for pleasure scenario, he had trouble pulling out of its grip. It was what made him an ideal enforcer for Grigory.

Usually when a man was so emotionally crippled, they resorted to paid companionship. The professional ladies who provided these services typically overlooked deficiencies of a client, whether it be a birth defect, or amputee, war wound, or obesity, but for a premium price. However, all the professional ladies who overlooked these shortcomings wouldn't take Sergei's money. Even the bitch Patty and her game room were closed to him. They all knew his appetite for pain, and none willingly accommodated his excessive tastes.

Patty found Sergei on the other side of her door when she opened it.

"Hi, Sergei. I didn't expect to see you here. What's up?"

CHAPTER 49

Sometimes slight misunderstandings can have colossal results.

The police were all over the building looking for clues when Buzz returned. After he'd argued that he lived there to get past the officer posted at the door to the building, he found the crime scene tape that blocked entry to his apartment.

Buzz yelled at the officer posted at the door, trying to also muscle his way through. "Hey, what's going on? This is my place and you have no right to be in here."

"Detective, this guy is saying this is his apartment. Do you want to speak to him?" The officer stated over his shoulder.

"Thanks, Joe. Yeah, I'll take care of him. Come on in, buddy. Who are you and do you ID?" said Detective Sloan.

"My name is Nathanial Buswald II. Here is my ID. Now, what are you guys doing in my apartment?" protested Buzz.

"Are you also known as Buzz? The one who signed the card for the flowers that said, 'Hope you like the flowers?'"

Buzz assented. "Yeah, but what's going on? Why are the police here?"

"I'll ask the questions; you just answer. Understood?"

Buzz nodded his head. None of this made any sense to him, but he felt scared.

Sloan knew he had the suspect's attention now, so he eased up a bit. "We received a call on a domestic disturbance, and we arrived almost an hour ago. Now, you say you live here so can you tell me where have you been?"

Buzz started to sweat and fidget, and then asked, "Where is Patty? I want to talk to her. You guys are creeping me out."

The detective signaled to Joe and stated, "Take him downtown. I want him in for questioning, and I don't want to do it here."

Joe muscled a set of cuffs on Buzz amidst loud protests and demands for his lawyer. They placed him into the back seat of the patrol car for a ride downtown. He repeatedly asked for answers, but no one responded. His imagination was running wild, and he was terrified.

Sloan walked deliberately and slowly back into the crime scene. The way the evidence looked so far was that the guy who had just been taken downtown was in this up to his eyeballs. The female victim, Patty he supposed, and this Buzz had had a fight, judging from the mess. Sex toys and broken glass were strewn all over the floor. The guy had probably gone out to buy some flowers to make amends. Then they probably got into it again, with no turning back from what was obviously rage based on the scene.

Sloan recalled how he and his ex-wife used to get into it. But even in their worst fights, he'd never conceived what he was seeing had happened to this woman. Of course, his ex-wife would never have used nor understood half the stuff in here. Sloan surmised that this couple were really into hardcore sex games, judging from the paraphernalia and the amount of wear it appeared to have. A little too far over the top for his tastes.

Chaining your partner upside down with her legs spread wide was not the worst thing he'd seen in homicides over the years. The heavy stripe markings all over her flesh, obviously from a serious whip, and even the choke collar, which totally distorted her facial features, was not original. But the additional twist here, which elevated it to the most disturbing thing he'd ever seen, was seeing her turned into a human vase to display all the flowers, with the card signed from Buzz shoved into her mouth. 'Hope you like the flowers, Love Buzz.' That really got to Sloan. How could someone do this to another human being? He needed the coroner to give him the time and precise cause of death.

As vile as the scene was, he continued to move his gaze over the grizzly scene. He'd taken several photos since he was trying to sequence the events. He restarted his scan of the room from the backside rather than the doorway, trying to identify the order of the escalation of this argument. He realized that everything on the floor appeared placed rather than randomly scattered. When he and his ex-wife got into a throwing match nothing was evenly spaced across the floor. Quite the contrary, stuff would collect in corners or, if it was broken, then things were in clumps. This place looked staged. Everything was too well laid out for a real fight. What had really happened?

There was blood spattered on the walls and ceiling but not so much on the stuff scattered on the floor. There was no item present that suggested it made the heavy striped markings either. Oh well, he thought. When the crime scene investigators arrived they would take prints and connect all the dots. He'd get their take on it and match it to his thoughts. He needed to get downtown and have a serious discussion with the suspect in custody.

CHAPTER 50

Bad habits are hard to break.

Chairman Lo Chang had specifically asked Lt. Colonel Po to attend the conference. She'd been maneuvered out of the Chinese Aerospace Program and given the Computer Training School as a way to humiliate her. In turn she had built it into a powerful tool for cyber warfare. The school had become so good at repurposing western financial resources that her school was self-funded and had a revenue stream paid to the Chinese Government Treasury. No one questioned her loyalty to the Chinese régime, and some cheered her resourcefulness; however, she was totally unsuitable for standard backroom political deals. No one was quite sure how to approach her. She was lord and master in the Cyber Warfare College but an incompetent in the complex world of Chinese politics, as were most females.

The Chairman had pulled her aside before the conference had begun and said, "I am pleased to have you here at this conference. We value your ability to analyze situations and provide insightful recommendations that might have gone unexplored. Your perceptivity and candor allows for meaningful dialog on these complex subjects. We don't want to face them without your deductive reasoning and capacity for parallel thinking."

Lt. Colonel Po replied, "I see. That is interesting. I thought it was just the excess funds my school donates to the Chinese Treasury."

The Chairman, caught in his excessive flattery, added, "That is the other reason we appreciate you so much."

With a slight smile he acknowledged the tolerance the group had for Lt. Colonel Po. Recognizing that Po was not going to allow him to shine her on, the Chairman resigned himself to the fact that the conference might be a bit more adversarial than he would prefer. Then again, he had not risen to this position by being timid when dealing with others.

The night before the conference was an art form to many. Prominent men renewed old acquaintances, forged new alliances, and traded favors for each other's agenda items. Everyone wanted to know how to deal with each other, and a lot of posturing was done to further those goals. Attendees who did not have good bargaining chips or could not successfully negotiate a weak position upwards were soon replaced by more capable individuals. The exception was Lt. Colonel Po. She didn't need anything from these people and refused to participate in political posturing.

The conference began the next day as the Chairman set the stage for the order of discussions. He quickly went through the domestic issues at a pace that clearly showed he was focused on a specific agenda item. Standard Chinese politics were such that the people at these conferences had earned the right to be heard. That was the protocol; however, just because one got to be heard didn't mean they could blather on and on. The Chairman pushed the domestic agenda items through almost too fast. The main agenda item was international finance and the Chinese dissatisfaction with the status quo.

The Chairman began, "I want to open up for discussion the Chinese position on international finance. I find it intolerable that we have let our country become dependent upon the interest income of U.S. Treasury notes, currency, and bonds to the detriment of our own Yuan.

"The first real reserve currency was minted by the Roman Empire. All commerce goods and power flowed through Rome. For centuries she dictated all financial issues, until her collapse. Another great power, Great Britain, saw the value of being a country with their currency as a reserve currency. At the end of World War II, Great Britain lost that reserve currency status, and the U.S. inherited that all powerful role. I see a trend for ownership of the reserve currency stewardship migrating ever westward across the globe. I ask all of you, why not China? Our civilization has as much history and evolution as any western country, but we are not taken seriously when we say it's time for a new global reserve currency based on our currency, the Yuan.

"You all came here for one thing, money. Money to run your projects and to make China great. I applaud your efforts to strengthen our country, but it is only an illusion because whatever we build, buy, invest in, or save is based on U.S. currency. The U.S. Treasury notes we own are not paid in Yuan but U.S. dollars. We have become dependent upon that income flow, and all world trade is dominated by it. We have been a good customer of these U.S. Treasury notes, but you know how the Westerners show their contempt for our support? They print more money to support their lack of fiscal discipline and use it to pay the interest. As long as the U.S. has the reserve currency status, all global trade is dictated in that currency. China must comply if we have any hope of selling our goods on the world market. We are being held fiscal hostages by this reserve currency status, and our destiny will not be our own as long as that is the status quo."

A conference attendee stood and stated, "So why don't we send a message and sell off the U.S. Treasury notes?"

The Chairman shook his head then detailed, "We have bought too heavily into what the Westerners call the Kool-Aid. You don't seem to understand. The action would be self-destructive and only provide amusement to the issuers since it is denominated in their currency, not ours. If we dump these Treasury notes, we would drive the resale value down. Then our original investment value would suffer."

Another attendee questioned, "How did we get into this one-way street? We kept our currency restricted, but you are saying that we have all these U.S. Treasury notes. Why did we get them in the first place?"

The Chairman patiently educated, "In order to trade goods and services globally you need U.S. currency, or at least the equivalent, like U.S. Treasury notes. We kept our currency closed to keep our goods and services underpriced against other global suppliers. Their currency flows in for goods and services, but we don't buy anything with the Yuan but instead use Western currency since other nations have stabilized their currency on a market-driven value. The U.S. currency flows are based on our below market valuation. We have not made our currency a globally valued one. Simply stated, theirs is liquid, and ours is not. Oil, raw materials, technology, even lending to other countries can't be done unless we have this reserve currency that everyone will accept. We need a way to make this change."

A somber mood descended on the conference. They all now understood that their fast growth exercise, through underpriced goods and services, had them boxed into a corner. While they had become a powerful economy, they could not sit at the table with other nation states as equals. They had schemed their way into dominate trading-partner status, yet still wanted to bend the rules one more time in their favor.

Lt. Colonel Po, after letting the gravity of the drama set in, requested to speak. "Gentlemen and attendees, I submit that this line of thought has no useful destination for our China. We have not come this far by playing by their rules but letting them play by Western rules while we exploit the flaws in their system. I maintain that if you don't like the results of the game, then we must change the rules.

"The Chinese may have been the first to print and issue money for convenience of transaction, but it must be admitted that success in the global trade economy evolved elsewhere. We should not try to fight with them about their currency, but instead we absolutely must deliver an alternative to their currency dominance. The only way to defeat the current circumstances is to put forth an alternative to paper currency; that is, offer up a digital currency."

One of the major player attendees, Kuan-Chun, looked at her incredulously. He was barely able to keep the contempt for her out of his voice when he asked, "What possible value could an idea like that have for our country? You seem to be seriously suggesting that we issue digital currency rather than use our own printed money or someone else's. Is that what you are saying? For China to rely on a string of ones and zeros to build our domestic and international economies? At least when you have printed paper money you have a tangible souvenir if it drops to nothing.

"Furthermore, how would anyone conduct business if they don't have a PC and a bank account with electronic access? As far as anyone can tell, currency counterfeiting has always been a sovereign problem ever since the invention of laser printers. Now you want to open up currency issuance to any hacker in the world. I can't help but feel astonished at such a naïve offering, Lt. Colonel."

Lt. Colonel Po, undisturbed by the tirade, calmly asserted, "My esteemed colleague, my apologies for my having tested your limited understanding with regards to digital encryption as a way to secure electronic transmissions."

Several members of the conference had to suppress their laughter.

She continued, "All things changed when the Internet came of age and provided electronic pathways for information to flow. Mobility instruments such as tablets and smart phones now access remote bank accounts using secure transactions from both parties. In many cases, two-form factor authentications are required before the ones and zeros are exchanged. My esteemed colleague, how do you think banks move money around between themselves and to off-shore accounts? They absolutely use electronic transmissions. Highly encrypted electronic transmissions are initiated to move vast sums of money in the form of debits and credits, and they do it daily. Electronic transmissions to move currency from one location to another anywhere in the world is infinitely more economical than having FedEx show up to move it for you. It may have escaped your extensive powers of observation, but electronic transmission of funds has been a standard practice in banking for decades."

Again, her comments drew more giggling and suppressed laughter from the attendees. Waiting patiently, Lt. Colonel Po continued after the mirth subsided.

"I expected a discussion like this at some point. We have already explored the possibilities of digital currency as an alternative to sovereign currency. The Secure Electronic Currency or SECcoin is our alternative. The acronym itself instills confidence. It has been on the Internet since 2009 and has received some positive attention. Originally it started as a proof of concept, but it gained far greater traction than we expected.

"The primary reason was that young people easily adopted it as it complemented their need for immediate gratification. Its social attributes are very persuasive and augmented many of their lifestyles. The SECcoin traded globally, but the bulk of the electronic currency is handled by a highly motivated associate of the Chinese government here in Asia. To add to the mystique of the SECcoin, the origin of the programmer is cloaked in secrecy, and the currency is self-limited to a predetermined amount of 120 million U.S. dollars.

"We actually got quite a boost of acceptance for our SECcoin when the island of Cypress locked down the banking infrastructure and froze the flow of Euros in and out of the country. One of our resourceful associates suggested that the Cypriots might be agreeable to an alternative form of currency. For a while the SECcoin soared on the modest little exchange setup. As a proof of concept, we have been quite pleased with the results and are ready to move it to the next stage. And by the way, even though the SECcoin is traded on the open market, it is fully under our control."

Kuan-Chun sneered as he belittled the obvious accomplishment. "We are just to set out our digital sign post that offers digital currency for sale alongside offers for male performance enhancement drugs?"

The attendees enjoyed the barbed comments from the two adversaries in this lively exchange. Most of the attendees were not supportive of Lt. Colonel Po.

Lt. Colonel Po, thoroughly engaged in the verbal combat, gibed, "Why sir, I had no idea you were a purveyor of male performance enhancement drugs. If you like I can put you in contact with a fringe group of aftermarket products. Perhaps they can recommend a reliable organization that can give you a personality transplant as well. It is well known that having an erection is not the same as having a personality."

Kuan-Chun fumed, "I did not come here to be insulted by the likes of you!"

Lt. Colonel Po was obviously amused and unrestrained at this point. "Honored sir, I believe you. Perhaps you should confine yourself to those places where you normally go to be insulted."

The laughter became more sustained to the point where Chairman Lo Chang felt it was enough.

"The attendees will curb their remarks and end this verbal combat of wits."

Lt. Colonel Po, casting her fates to the wind, couldn't let it go without one more comment, though she added a bow of deference. "Yes, of course, Chairman Lo Chang. It would not be appropriate to continue this battle of wits as it is much like swatting flies with your official limousine."

The attendees now could not be restrained in their laughter. Even Chairman Lo Chang had enjoyed her quick wit. Before the enraged Kuan-Chun could say anything, his nearby associate leaned over and reminded him quietly.

"Remember the Khan Incident, my friend."

At that point Kuan-Chun swallowed hard, composed himself and disengaged from the verbal combat with a bow to both the Chairman and Lt. Colonel Po. Lt. Colonel Po bowed ever so slightly to end the duel for now. Order was restored quickly by the Chairman.

He turned to Lt. Colonel Po and pointedly asked, "Why have we not heard about this proof of concept for your SECcoin prior to this conference? This is quite interesting, but a new currency being launched without discussion? Currency, whether paper or digital, is under the purview of the government so that it can be administered for the good of China. May we know how you intended to transfer it to the state if it is deemed acceptable? If it is judged to be too much of an alternative to our existing Yuan, then the SECcoin needs to be disassembled. If it can be used like the Wall Street derivatives that have been labeled as financial weapons of mass destruction, then we need to understand how that can be leveraged and the project then assigned to an appropriate group."

Lt. Colonel Po, dismayed at the direction the dialog had taken, responded, "The proof of concept was launched to test the viability of digital currency. The intention was that our group would handle the operations once the value was established. The program is filled with unique trap-doors should the test take an unintended direction from our collective wishes. My team absolutely must be able to continue our stewardship of this project before a final decision can be reached as to how we should proceed. I firmly believe that digital currency can prevail over conventional paper currency. If our project is allowed to run to completion, we categorically believe that we can dominate the global trade rules and have ownership of the world's reserve currency, but in digital form. The SECcoin project was not envisioned to be a hoax with just a kidding punch line sometime in the future. China absolutely must change the rules if we are to obtain our goal of being the global reserve currency."

Chairman Lo Chang cautiously suggested to the attendees, "I propose that we evaluate the excellent work that Lt. Colonel Po has created. At our next quarterly conference, we need additional information regarding global acceptance projections, potential negative ramifications, and recommendations as to how the group feels it is best to proceed. Does anyone have any serious objections to this course of action? Lt. Colonel Po, are you prepared to facilitate this evaluation and give a presentation at our next conference?"

Lt. Colonel Po, sensing political maneuvering at her hard-liner position, acquiesced to the will of the committee with a resigned nod.

Chairman Lo Chang looked to the Minister of Finance. "I would insist upon your close personal involvement in this evaluation, Kuan-Chun. Please provide all possible assistance to Lt. Colonel Po. I expect you to co-author the report and presentation we all will see at our next meeting."

Lt. Colonel Po now wished she hadn't engaged in the verbal combat with the abusive Minister of Finance. She had come too far to let some pencil neck bureaucrat usurp her work. For the time being, she had to make nice with him until he could be disposed of. They nodded to each other across the room, but everyone could already see the bad blood between them. The next meeting promised to be as highly entertaining as had just been demonstrated.

Kuan-Chun was always looking to acquire juicy projects, but not everything went to the State. He considered this opportunity with Po as a bump in the road. She sensed an oily back-stabber who could smile pleasantly at you while he slowly backed his car over your legs. She smiled as insincerely as he did. Yes, this was definitely going to be an interesting time.

CHAPTER 51

Some people are prone to snatch defeat from the jaws of victory.

Grigory caught a glance of Sergei coming in the door and said, "Oh good, there you are. Let's load up and go talk with Patty. She's probably still mad from the last conversation and your visit to explain respect and not answering my calls. What I need are fewer temperamental people on the payroll around here."

Sergei blanched and was unable to speak or swallow for several minutes. Finally, with extreme effort under the scrutiny of a puzzled Grigory, he regained his voice.

"Um, uh," Sergei coughed. "Well, I have fixed at least one of your issues. You do in fact have fewer temperamental people on the payroll around here. So why did you need to speak with uh…Patty? What do we need her for?"

The insolent questions gained Grigory's full attention. He immediately grilled "What did you do?" while running through the possibilities in his head.

Sergei began sweating, then stammered, "I um…got her respect back for you just like you told me. I admit I might have been a bit heavy-handed, but you were right. She needed to be taught a lesson. I can guarantee she now has proper respect, Grigory."

Grigory, in a tone that was unmistakably used to help keep his anger in check, said, "I've landed an important job from our Chinese contacts that requires my best cyber warrior on the case ASAP. Now I can't seem to get a hold of her after you pay her a visit. So why can't I get in contact with her? You need to tell me what you don't want to tell me before I lose my patience!"

Sergei slumped to the floor, then sobbed while he begged, "I didn't mean to let things go so far, but she just wouldn't cooperate. Every time I reached for her she would move away. I didn't mean to get so mad, but she wouldn't tell me what I wanted to hear. She wouldn't even let me touch her." Sergei sobbed harder and added between uneven breaths, "She gave me that look, like I was some kind of animal. The more she resisted and tried to get away from me, the angrier I got. She wouldn't listen. She just wouldn't listen."

Grigory, with his emotions barely under control, decided, "Alright, alright. So which hospital did they take her to? Maybe we can get past this episode and still take on this Chinese job. Take me to the hospital. I'm sure I can straighten this mess out, but the costs will come out of your wages."

Sergei cowered at Grigory's feet. "...I don't know which hospital. After things got out of hand, I ran and didn't look back."

Grigory, showing a little more control, said, "Okay, then I'll call my detective contact in the area to see if he can shed some light on this."

Grigory made the call, and Sergei tried to move away, but Grigory gave him a chilling smile and motioned for Sergei to stay put. Not much was being said on his side of the call, but Grigory obviously listened intently to what was being said on the other end. Slowly he put his phone away after the call concluded.

"Well, you are in luck. It seems that Patty is in the hospital and recovering nicely. A few bumps and bruises with a couple of missing patches of hair, but she seems to be her normal feisty self. One of the neighbors heard loud noises and called 911. Shall we go pay a sympathy visit, Sergei?"

Sergei could not believe his good fortune. He had no desire to be on the wrong side of Grigory.

Sergei agreed, "Yes, yes. I would like to see her and say I'm sorry. I didn't mean to be so hard on her. She really is a nice person, at least to others. I would like her to like me, Grigory."

Sergei scampered up off the floor and ran to get in the car like an obedient pet. Grigory slowly headed to the door behind Sergei. He stopped long enough to motion to another one of his associates, and a very short conversation ensued. Grigory got in the back of the car and requested Sergei ride in front. They were joined by the associate who took the seat behind Sergei, and the car rolled off.

Grigory directed the driver, "Let's take the scenic route, the one over the bridge with that nice view of the water."

01010101001100

An hour or so later, the car arrived at the precinct. Grigory secured the release of Buzz much in the same way he had done previously for Patty. Buzz was bewildered by the transaction. Grigory sensed Buzz's frail mental state and offered him a lift. Buzz absentmindedly accepted the ride.

Grigory suggested, "There are only the three of us so you take the front seat."

Buzz nodded and got in where Sergei had been earlier.

Grigory proposed, "Your apartment is not available to you right now. I'm going to take you to a nice hotel where you can recover from this ordeal. I will have Alex pick up some clothes and toiletries and bring them to you. I will take care of the expenses for this, so not to worry. I seem to be a bit short-staffed these days, and well, I could use someone of your wit and gender on my team. Let's talk tomorrow, shall we?"

CHAPTER 52

Do it and do it until you get it right.

O tto interrupted solemnly, "Okay, team, we have a client with a somewhat unusual request concerning our services. It seems that a blood feud has erupted between two factions in China. We are being engaged to take sides in a conflict that we shouldn't participate in but in reality can't turn down."

Quip, excited at the prospect, asked, "Is this going to be like the time we fed all our findings to that U.S. Senate committee about the trap-door code found throughout the Huawei telecom gear? I don't see how they sell their technology with that Swiss cheese code to any serious organization. It's like trying to sell slightly defective condoms and telling people to disregard the small holes in the end. Boy, what a firestorm that committee meeting was! When can we start?"

Otto looked over the top of his glasses, somewhat irritated. "Thank you, Quip, for that tour down memory lane. This one involves rivals within the same government, and that means a power struggle between warring factions. If this is done incorrectly, then we will be pulled into the vortex with no one to come to our rescue. They must be thoroughly convinced that their enemy is their rival, otherwise they take out their hostility on us. Remember what I told you about dealing with governments? They consider themselves above the law and can order retaliation with no fear of retribution."

Each of them understood the seriousness of such an effort. Even Quip lost his grin.

To lighten the mood and get them to relax a little bit, Otto uncharacteristically interjected, "And to quote our esteemed colleague, Quip, 'let's do this one ah la Teflon!'"

The glib remark had the desired calming effect on them all. He then took out his notepad which contained his roughly outlined plan.

"Now for the operating parameters. For phase I, we need a target mapping exercise on the Chinese Finance Minister, Kuan-Chun. A full profile on his personal digital persona as well as his professional role as the Finance Minister. He is known for being discreet, so you will need to cross-check several sources, I suspect, to get the full picture. Once we have that mapping exercise done, we then move into phase II. In this phase we make certain we have our files on the Cyber Warfare College of China, run by Lt. Colonel Po, up to date.

"The game sequence is 'cat and mouse' tactics with very subtle clumsiness from each of the players so as to barely be noticed by the victim. You've all seen the drill. Small indiscretions from each player on the other with an upward progression of hostility. Each must believe that the other is responsible for the transgression, so very modest electronic breadcrumbs need to be left behind for the target to find.

"I am uncertain if Kuan-Chun is astute enough in his electronic forensics to catch them, so that needs to be monitored. Po, on the other hand, is different, and I have no doubts about her abilities. I recommend we start simple, such as leaving digital fingerprints, copying some files along with obscure data breaches. Then escalate the tactics to digitally defacing one another and then finally electronic poisoning, along with complete data wipes as the final assault against themselves. We have only ninety days to complete the exercise, and I'm going to say that we need to be done in forty-five to fifty days. Any questions?"

Jacob probed, "I don't understand. Are we being engaged by both of these groups to hose-off each other? I mean, wow! What a dangerous game you've taken on. One slip up and they will target us."

Otto illuminated, "Actually we haven't been engaged by either of these two. Chinese Chairman Lo Chang has staged this fateful party. The request is for neither party to survive the pending slaughter. While he did not provide details to me of his end game, we can surmise the desired results from experience. Usually when we see this type of commission, both parties have become political liabilities but cannot be dealt with openly because of their connections or backroom power base. In those scenarios the only way to render them harmless is to terminate their power, which usually means terminate them."

Petra nodded then stated, "So if we are successful, then Chairman Lo Chang keeps his hands clean. If we fail, he points his problem children at us. They come after us, and he still keeps his hands clean. Probably then goes looking for another organization to tap into to help them self-destruct. Plus, we are still doing Master Po's request. Is that an adequate summary?"

"Petra, I think that all that terse encryption code you have learned to write over the years has made you a little too direct in your phraseology. Not that I would ever expect you to sugarcoat anything."

Quip chimed in. "Well, at least Chairman Lo Chang had the good sense to come to us for this type of work. There isn't another group that could pull this off in the timeframe given."

Otto grumbled, "Actually we weren't Chairman Lo Chang's first choice, as he made certain I was aware. Our Russian friends from the Dteam were in the contact queue as his first choice. Seems as though the Dteam had a personnel change that precluded them from starting right away, which we need to look at as well to update our profiles on them. Anyway, let's begin, shall we?"

The wheels for the project were quickly put into motion. With Jacob now a part of the team, he worked with Petra on phase I, while Quip would handle phase II. They compared the information profiles and began the slow burn.

CHAPTER 53

You can often get farther offering sugar rather than vinegar.

Grigory could demonstrate himself as a charming host, if required by a given situation. This was clearly revealed by his fawning over Buzz in an effort to get him to work for him. His underlings watched the display with disgust.

One whispered to the other, "When is he going to fluff his pillow and offer a breath mint?"

They struggled to suppress their laughter, as they didn't want Grigory to know he was being watched or made fun of.

Buzz couldn't quite come to terms with Patty's demise and was really not listening to Grigory's monolog about what was on the table and what was at stake. Grigory needed a technical lead for the data breach into the Chinese Cyber Warfare College before the window of opportunity was lost. Finally, Grigory sensed he was not getting through to Buzz and abruptly dropped the conversation.

He decided to let Nikkei, his white tiger, into the room for their playtime as if Buzz was not even there. Buzz's attention was immediately captured as the two of them played, and he was mesmerized by the white tiger. As if on cue, Nikkei wandered over to inspect the new attendee. Buzz started to reach out to Nikkei when Grigory intercepted him with a friendly smile and the shake of his head.

"I'm never sure about letting someone try to pet her. Since she has never met you, I wanted to be on the safe side. Sorry."

Buzz nodded his head and collected his thoughts in an attempt to pull himself together. He stood up and reached out to shake hands.

"I want to thank you, Grigory, for the hospitality you have shown me. I feel disoriented regarding everything. I just need a little time to digest everything that has gone on. I miss Patty. Forgive me, but I just don't feel like talking business. I just want to go home."

Grigory nodded understandingly then said, "Yes, of course. However, where is home for you now? The apartment you and Patty shared is still listed as a crime scene. No one is permitted back in, so the apartment and all the contents are restricted. I can have my people drop you somewhere if you like. Perhaps back to the hotel you stayed at last night?"

Buzz, as usual, hadn't considered all the ramifications of Patty's demise and sat back down.

Grigory picked the right moment to add, "Besides, I figured you would want to work this opportunity I've been trying to explain to you. This opportunity puts us at cross purposes with the R-Group. We believe the R-Group is the organization responsible for Patty's assassination and the brutal handling of her corpse. They are a stealthy group that has a broad reach."

Grigory played his hand so well that he even had a twinge of regret himself over Patty's demise. The effect on Buzz was fairly dramatic. His eyes brightened and then narrowed their focus on Grigory, much like Nikkei did from time to time. He tightened his fists and bristled all over.

Buzz recovered. "Suddenly I feel like talking business. How do we proceed?"

Grigory smiled, his hook securely in Buzz. The conversation proceeded with details that were embellished as needed.

CHAPTER 54

Round and round and round we go, where we stop nobody knows.

Kuan-Chun was doing everything he could to get Master Po to warm up to him, even addressing her by that title. She was barely civil. She was convinced that the Finance Minister was behind the firewall and data breaches that Jinny Lin had been seeing. There was still no proof. She had been ordered by Chairman Lo Chang to cooperate with this person and be prepared to do a show and tell in less than 60 days.

For Master Po, the spurious activities were more frequent and more disruptive each week. All of them were seemingly focused on the SECcoin project. Those attacks could not reach the location of the inner workings of the SECcoin project since she had taken the precaution of air-gapping it from access. She was certain it was Kuan-Chun, since she would only discuss the features and functional attributes of the SECcoin project, but not the internal workings of the code. However, she was surprised at his electronic snooping and occasional theft of digital information. It was fairly sophisticated and did demonstrate a high proficiency for someone who dragged his knuckles on the ground when he walked.

Kuan-Chun argued, "So when are you going to show me the inner workings of the SECcoin programs? We have our instructions, and it doesn't appear that you are on board. Are you unwilling to cooperate?"

Lt. Colonel Po responded, "And are you willing to admit that you have been electronically snooping around in my Cyber Warfare College?"

"Would it do any good to deny it again? I don't believe that trust is part of your nature. What about you nosing around in the Finance Ministry? Trying to hack into my personal computer system? You are just using this bogus intrusion incident to cover your hacking attempts on me! You are fairly transparent in your discrediting tactics, Master Po. Do not continue to provoke me. I can be a formidable adversary!"

"Do not use that tone with me in my domain, Finance Minister! Your expensive tastes are quite well known, and the people of China unwittingly finance your appetites. I do not intend to give you the keys to the kingdom and have you set up your own payroll with the SECcoin project. I have also seen the dossiers you keep on your enemies, and I am quite pleased to be at the top of the list!"

"Ah-ha! I thought you said you weren't snooping on my system! Well, if that's the case then you should know I found electronic souvenirs of the people you've ruined throughout your career. Wait until my secondary report hits the committee!"

Their raised voices brought Lt. Colonel Po's faithful assistant, affectionately known as 'Grasshopper', into the raging argument.

Chun asked, "Master Po, what's wrong? We can hear you both all the way down the hall through your heavy wooden door! Are you alright, madam?"

Kuan-Chun sneered, "Oh, do come along! We are busy here discussing State business, and you are interfering with that discussion. If we need tea we will ring for you, but for right now get out!"

Kuan-Chun gave Chun a good shove to help send him on his way. Instead of backing down Chun deftly stepped behind his master's adversary and twisted his neck until a sickening crack could be heard several meters away. Kuan-Chun's lifeless body dropped to the floor as Lt. Colonel Po stared at the scene, shocked.

With tears welling up in her eyes, she cried, "Grasshopper, what did you do? My beloved Grasshopper, what did you do?"

Grasshopper calmly replied, "I could not let anyone take out their hostility on you. You have cared for me and given me purpose here at the school. I will, of course, take responsibility for my actions here today, so you needn't concern yourself with my destiny anymore. But, my Master, I will miss you."

Crying, Master Po mourned, "No! No. It will not end this way, Grasshopper. I promise you it will not end this way. You were there for me during our early days when this place had no value, and no one wanted us. Many times it was your loyalty and confidence that helped me keep my head. No one but you believed in me, and at times I bordered on complete despair.

"I cannot give you up to them and I cannot bear to go forward without you. This school is everything I have left. It was because of you and your quiet confidence that we are here today. I don't want to go on without you in my life."

Grasshopper nodded then asked, "So what can we do, Master? I will not let you be implicated in this, so that is not an option. They will not believe you broke his neck. I will take the blame, and you will be free."

"I must think of something before this is discovered," she said while she quickly reviewed options.

"There is no other answer. You cannot take the blame for my indiscretion, and there is no honor in trying to blame someone else. You must go on without me, my Master," stated Grasshopper calmly.

Master Po took a deep breath of resignation, then added, "Well, let us at least have the afternoon tea before we do anything else. This will be our last afternoon tea together, my Grasshopper, so please use that special dark tea I have marked for the 'Master Only.' Then we can decide how to proceed."

Grasshopper smiled weakly, then bowed, "Yes, Master, as you wish."

Master Po immediately picked up her cell and dialed the number she had hoped she would never use. Though she had a few minutes while Grasshopper prepared the tea, she hoped her call would be answered rather than having to leave a voicemail. She decided that if her call was answered, that meant the Gods too were supportive of this decision. She held her breath until the call connected.

"Master Po, to what do I owe the distinct pleasure of your call?" A deep male voice asked.

"Things have abruptly changed. Is your offer still good for the option we discussed, and can you act on it immediately?" Her voice was strong and determined.

"Yes, I can have people in place. Are you sure this is what you want? You must take nothing with you, as we discussed."

Master Po responded in a resigned tone, "I am certain, and I will take nothing. I do need you to cover me and my assistant, Chun."

The man waited for a moment, then clarified, "Is this your assistant you often refer to as Grasshopper? That is not a part of our agreement, if you recall."

"That is now the agreement, or you get nothing. Grasshopper and me. We will be ready for the emergency medical team in thirty minutes. The rest is as we outlined before. Grasshopper will know nothing of the details."

The man agreed, "Alright, but if Chun messes anything up, I will shoot him myself."

"Thank you. There will be no call for that, I assure you." She disconnected and gathered their identity papers, placing them in her inside pocket.

When Grasshopper returned with the tea, Master Po insisted that she pour and serve their final tea together. As per manners steeped in tradition, Grasshopper let Master Po pour. Taking time to ensure that all tradition was followed, she poured for them both and indicated it was time to speak final words and drink. Grasshopper picked up the tea and waited.

Master Po smiled a strange, fatalistic smile, then said, "As we drink this tea, may we be intertwined on the other side. Nothing will ever be the same. Let us drink."

They both drank and bowed slightly to each other.

"Do you remember that first week I was here? I was so despondent and depressed that I bought this tea for myself because I felt I was at the end of my career and out of options. The vendor promised me that it would keep for years, and it would do the trick with little discomfort."

Grasshopper's eyes widened and, with a sense of impending dread, said, "Master Po! What have you done? What is this tea you had me bring you?"

Master Po struggled but explained, "The tea is called Dreamless Destiny, and this is my chosen solution. You won't let me take the blame, and I can't give you to them, so I cannot stay in this world.

"When the Chairman said 'you two must work together to bring us this solution,' I never understood what he meant until just now. Kuan-Chun and I were both doomed. I wasn't astute enough to know it. Goodbye, my Grasshopper. We will be reborn."

Grasshopper, with tears running down his face, whispered, "No. No, Master. Please no."

The emergency medical team arrived a few minutes later with Dr. Kim Lee in charge. He made his assessment, and then the team loaded both bodies into their ambulance. He called for another vehicle to pick up Kuan-Chun who was located in the other room. This afternoon he would inform Chairman Lo Chang of the fatal results at Cyber Warfare College.

CHAPTER 55

The end justifies the means.

Well done, team," offered Otto. "The scenario is completed, Chairman Lo Chang has his desired outcome, and this chapter is closed. I hope he can live with the results he achieved. I will miss periodic updates from Master Po, but not the drama. We do, however, have a few loose ends to tie up."

Jacob piped in, "So what else remains to be done? Just collect the fee, right?"

Otto chided, "You're so young! Come on, kids, what's the rule around here? Chairman Lo Chang owes us big time. You might as well know that he owes no one for long. We are now in the cross-hairs of someone who really can't afford to have us running around loose. You are not done until you get away. We have not gotten away yet. Knowing that, what is our exit strategy?"

Quip responded first, "I know, pin this on someone else! And I know just who might fit the bill. Our friends from Russia, the Dteam. After all, they were given rights of first refusal on the job, so how easy would it be to let everyone believe they did it?"

Otto smiled like a proud papa. "Right! Now let's discuss how we do that and also how to breach the air-gapped defense system put into place by Master Po. We need to copy the SECcoin technology, poison it, and ensure that Chairman Lo Chang believes that the Russians double-crossed him. To get his wrath vectored on them, he needs to believe they got there first."

Petra offered, "This might be easier to blame on the Dteam, if they had the SECcoin code, don't you think? What if we say that we were scooped by the Dteam by demonstrating they came in as a shadow ops group? Further, that they grabbed the SECcoin code and materials before we could intercede? After all, we can simply say we were trying to figure out how to bridge the air-gap when they came in with some of their heavies and copied it off. They, of course, will deny it, but when it surfaces inside their organization the cross-hairs will be moved from us to them. Of course, Chairman Lo Chang will discover this information through a series of lucky breaks. Do we know anything about the Dteam's lead info tech?"

Otto indicated, "Their lead info tech was permanently retired through an unfortunate misunderstanding and miscommunication. I understand that her boyfriend has picked up where she left off. I believe you know the person, Jacob. It is Buzz."

Jacob looked dumbfounded as he tried to assimilate Otto's words. Petra and Quip both knew that Buzz had been a longtime friend of Jacob's.

Jacob was appalled. "Buzz works for the Dteam? And Patty, is she dead? When did this happen?"

CHAPTER 56

Friends and enemies, who to keep closer?

Chairman Lo Chang was feeling most gratified with the recent results. He had ordered the events that precipitated the chain reaction that eliminated his most politically dangerous opponent, the Finance Minister, and his most technically astute but unmalleable personality, the late Lt. Colonel Po. Best of all, it appeared to everyone that they had taken each other out, with nothing pointed toward him.

Now all he had to do was to commandeer the SECcoin project for the State and let time eradicate the memory of his two late opponents. He chuckled to himself and felt this excellent play warranted opening that bottle of Johnnie Walker Red he'd saved for a special occasion such as this. There were the follow-on details that needed cleaning up just to keep things tidy, but those were trivial compared to what he had just pulled off.

He thought perhaps he would pay a call on the late Kuan-Chun's mistress to express his condolences. Kuan-Chun had always had a nice stable of ladies, and his current one shouldn't be allowed to go to waste. Of course, one should express regrets and give comfort for their loss. He needed to take care and not approach her too soon. Ah, the spoils to the victor; Kuan-Chun's mistress and Lt. Colonel Po's magical digital currency!

Looking at the bottle of Johnnie Walker Red, he broke into a big grin. He had always enjoyed word games, and it occurred to him that with a little label change he could make the drink JOHNNIE WALKER – A RED'S DRINK or even JOHNNIE WALKER – RED CHINESE DRINK. Ah well, enough of this. It was time to attend to the follow-on details to close out this event.

He summoned his lieutenant and had him arrange for the team to descend on Lt. Colonel Po's school for securing the SECcoin application and its support infrastructure. He instructed that it be taken to the Finance Ministry where it could be properly administered with his oversight. Now that Kuan-Chun was out of the way, his technical team would be more agreeable to what needed to be done. Working there would give him the opportunity to bump into the late Finance Minister's mistress. Things seemed to be falling into place rather nicely for a change.

It's too bad Kuan-Chun and Lt. Colonel Po didn't finish the report before their exit from this world, he thought. He could just have read the results and known all the attributes and possibilities in one nice, concise report. Their demise necessitated he do his own homework to understand all the details. He didn't dare have anyone else do that, at this point, for fear of being put into the same disadvantage he had been with Lt. Colonel Po. No, this was too important to be entrusted to anyone but himself.

When the Chairman and his team got to the Cyber Warfare College, they were not admitted through the front door. Jinny Lin escorted them to a more discreet entrance that would allow for privacy when it came time to remove equipment. The local police guarded the front door of the crime scene while his team removed important technology out the back. That reminded him that he needed to review the police report prior to its publishing.

Chairman Lo Chang had about sized things up in what appeared to be the inner server room when the police captain entered.

"May I know your business here?" requested the police captain.

The Chairman moved out of the server room to continue the discussion and to provide identification. Once identities had been established, the tension evaporated.

The police captain said, "Ah, Chairman Lo Chang, good day to you, sir. I am sorry I failed to recognize you. I did not expect your people back so soon. Your people said it might take a couple of trips, but I didn't expect you to come too. Well, I'll leave you to it."

Chairman Lo Chang queried, "What do you mean, back so soon? Who has been here already? When did people come here and what did they say?"

The police captain recalled, "Why two days ago, and they produced identification that showed them to be from your organization. It matched what we had in our database so we left them to their devices. They were gone in four hours. Is there a problem, sir?"

The Chairman's insides began to churn, and a sick feeling moved through him. Then one of his people quickly sought him out and pulled him aside.

"Chairman, all the drive bays in the target room you told us to confiscate are empty. The computer drives are all gone! Someone got here before us!"

The Chairman slumped into the closest chair and announced to no one in particular, "Sometimes this job just sucks!"

He quickly regained his resolve and looked at the lieutenant and the police captain and said with a voice steeped in anger, "Find me those drives! Now!"

CHAPTER 57

Remember the store sign: you break it you buy it.

G rigory found Buzz with a perplexed look on his face when he came into the server room in the Dteam operations center. It was not state of the art as it lacked many technical attributes of western data centers.

"Buzz, what's wrong? This is just your serious face while extracting the data from the Cyber Warfare College machines, right? Reassure me that there are no issues."

Buzz did not look up from the screen as he explained, "This is not what I expected. I expected encrypted files, numbers instead of names for directories, data-striping across all the drives, and password challenges at each step while going through the drives. Grigory, I'm not finding any of that."

Grigory looked puzzled too. "Okay, so what are you finding? Something that looks like your grandmother's PC with step-by-step procedures for cookie recipes?"

Buzz looked up from his machine and clarified in detail. "I don't get that far. Out of the 20 drives we removed, I have tried to load up and read two of them. Each of these has done the same thing. And before you ask, I have worked on these types of servers before.

"The drives should be spinning up to 7800 RPM's, but they don't stop there. They just keep accelerating way past that designated speed. Then I hear this high-pitched screeching sound that is the servos lowering the read/write heads all the way down to the platters until it shears the oxide media off the aluminum platters. As the oxide material goes, so goes the data.

"I opened the first one up hoping to save the platters and maybe even move them to another drive or perform some other high-end recovery activity, but the platters had been cleaned of all the magnetic media so that became a non-starter. I assumed that it was a fluke, and the other drives could be used to rebuild the lost drive using RAID, a Redundant Array of Independent Disks architecture. The second drive did the exact same thing. That's when I stopped. I'm pretty sure all the other drives will do the same thing."

Grigory couldn't quite grasp the situation from what Buzz was telling him. He hoped for a solution and asked, "Okay. So we take apart all the other drives and put the platters into like encasements. Then power them up to read the drives. How long would that take?"

Buzz agreed, "That's what I'm doing now, but frankly it should be done in a computer clean room so no particulates or dirt gets into the drives, which would also ruin the platters. I wanted to see if my theory is correct or not."

Grigory smiled, "Good lad! How much longer before we can try?"

Buzz cautioned, "I want you to know that the same thing is probably going to happen, and we will have three ruined drives. I really want this to work, but I have a sick feeling. Are you sure you want me to try this again?"

Grigory was starting to get not just annoyed, but panicked. "Yes, yes, of course! We have to get those programs off the drives!"

Buzz said, "Okay, hold on to your tuckus, starting now."

The drives started to spin up and did not stop, just like before. Then, just like before, they both heard the high-pitched screeching of read/write heads scraping off the oxide media along with all the ones and zeroes. When they pulled the drives apart, the results were the same; every platter had been cleaned of its magnetic media.

Buzz explained, "I'm sorry, Grigory, but it is as I suspected. Each drive has some special instructions imbedded on it that tells the spindle motors to accelerate past their normal velocity and then tells the servo motors to drop the heads down on the disk to clean the media off. Moving the platters to another drive won't help us since the poison is on the drive itself. Any image we might be able to get off of the data we want will include the poison. Whoever did this really know their trade. I can't think of a way to extract anything from drives like this so long as they have this kind of defense mechanism, and I don't want to practice on our remaining drives, so we are stuck. What are you going to tell the client?"

Grigory stared off into space, trying to think of a way to salvage the situation. He had wondered why the Chairman was eager to work with him, and now this screw-up made him think that he was being manipulated by the old fox. The Chairman must have known something was wrong with the drives since he wanted Grigory's group to pick them up and extract the data. If he thought he could get everything off himself then why bother with subcontracting. Why incur the additional cost? Speaking of costs, Grigory had run up quite a few costs on this exercise, and with nothing to show for it. Now, there was no motivation for the Chairman to pay for the effort, but there might be a way to extract something from this mess.

Grigory said in a resigned manner, "Buzz, thanks for your efforts, but it looks like no paycheck. Sadly, we are no closer to the R-Group than when we started. Why don't you go ahead and go? I'll deal with the client and try to get out of giving their deposit back. I'm just sorry that we can't get you any closer to Patty's killers."

The ploy on Buzz had exactly the effect he wanted. Grigory could almost see the wheels as they turned in Buzz's head.

Buzz paused, gathering his thoughts, then insisted, "Nope. I started on this hunt with you, and I'll finish on this hunt with you. Besides, they don't know the drives are poisoned. What if we say that we have already extracted the data from the first three drives as our insurance policy and are ready to let him have the other seventeen drives per our bargain?

"You ask for the balance of payment, and we give him all the drives as a show of good faith. Then we state that we will deliver the contents of the first three drives once we are put in contact with the R-Group. I bet the client's people think they can leverage data-striping to rebuild the missing drives. They will run into the same issue we did. When they ask, you say their guys must have messed up. The old adage applies, admit nothing, deny everything and make counter accusations."

Grigory nodded and added a wicked smile. "I like the way you think. But let's replace the first three drives with three blank drives that aren't ruined so that when they start toasting drives the way we did; we just say we got the info off and simply erased the first three as our insurance. It will appear that their people are incompetent. They won't be able to use the drives they ruin. Then we could insist that their guys ruined those sequential data-striped drives and now all the data is useless, even with our three drives that are in fact no good either. They kill their data geeks but only growl at us. We get away, and what's more important, we get our money."

"Even better. But remember, I want our lead to the R-Group. I have unfinished business with them."

"Patience. Patience. One step at a time. We'll get to the R-Group and get even."

CHAPTER 58

The most important thing in life is not money.

For many weeks now the chateau had been home base for Jacob and the others, based on work assignments. With all of the work that the team had completed during this time, the great food and company seemed to bring all of them closer together. Jacob was feeling much more comfortable about the directives the R-Group worked under.

Petra and he spent most nights together talking and making love. It was something Jacob had never experienced. She had to be on site for a couple of customers, but these trips were only for a few days. He had learned a great deal since he'd arrived. Now he was to the point where he challenged Quip and Petra as much as they challenged him. He'd also focused a couple of hours each evening getting to know Wolfgang. Typically, this was over a game of chess.

During one of their games, Wolfgang observed, "I see you have been studying up on defensive maneuvers. I guess you didn't like the outcome of our last game?"

Jacob laughed with mock sadness. "Nor the outcome of the thirty games before that! While I've never seen one in action,

I believe I understand what it is like to be an unlatched screen door in a hurricane. Bang, you're dead! Bang, you're dead! Bang, you're dead! I studied up on defense strategies in preparation for our game tonight."

Wolfgang agreed, "An excellent approach to a known problem!"

However, in three moves Jacob was checkmated. He stared in disbelief as he had been led to believe that his defense was appropriate. Wolfgang was a master, and Jacob was thwarted with each attempt.

"Where did you learn your defensive chess moves? Stalingrad?" queried Wolfgang.

"Uh, Stalingrad? There is a defensive chess scenario called Stalingrad?"

"Yes, of course. That is where you launch an all-out attack against your opponent. Then, while you are obsessed with capturing the city, you are hopelessly surrounded and systematically destroyed. Until the end, you continue to believe there is help coming from the air and the outside. Trouble is, those rescue forces are also being destroyed during the height of the Russian winter. Do you realize that out of the quarter of a million troops caught in this Stalingrad defense, only five thousand made it out and home alive?"

This was a subject close to Wolfgang's heart. He had been surrounded with endless discussions of various battles of the war his entire life. Jacob let him continue since he knew there would be a point made in the end.

"Whether in chess, finance, security of data systems, or in the animal kingdom, destiny favors the offensive player. The success in our ventures around the world is based on this premise. We are only interested in continually evolving our offensive strategies and tactics. That is our constant goal. A defensive strategy is not a strategy. That approach only makes us a target with no hope of success."

"An offensive position is not always the right answer. Offensive positions don't always profit or win. Besides, the German Wehrmacht was winning with their offensive strokes at Stalingrad before the weather turned against them," Jacob pointed out as he disagreed.

"That is correct. But once they changed from an offensive posture, when they were told to hold and not take a step back, they were caught in a defensive mindset. That was their undoing. Once their position was correctly identified as a death trap, they should have leveraged their offensive strength and broken out to the southwest as was recommended to Friedrich von Paulus by people who were far better at commanding an army.

"Anyway, I said evolve. You are thinking statically. If the assumption is that everything on both sides is evolving, then the prey will become faster, more camouflaged, as well as more alert. To continue to compete, the predator must become faster still, or stealthier, or even change their hunting tactics in order to survive. The evolution of the offensive attack must and does evolve faster than defensive strategies.

"That is why putting your trust in defensive security tools always places one at a disadvantage to cyber hacking. The defensive security tools are always behind offensive strategic thinking in the cyber arms race. In our organization, there is no room for defensive security thinking, because as soon as you do, you have lost. Oh, and based on your defensive chess strategies, you have another nine defense scenarios to practice before you play me again and think about what we just discussed. So, same time tomorrow, my boy?"

Without waiting for a response, Wolfgang rose and left. Jacob thought about what he had suggested. It made sense. He wanted to discuss the perspective with Petra as well and get her take.

CHAPTER 59

Cat and mouse is such an interesting game of patience.

Chairman Lo Chang postured, "I'm so pleased you called, Grigory. Where are we on this project? Did you have any issues retrieving the drives and extracting the contents? I am ready to discuss our next steps and, of course, erase your trail so my people don't find out what's going on. We are on an encrypted channel, so please expound on all details."

Grigory was noticeably angered. "Uh, wait a minute. We were only supposed to get the drives for you and deliver them to a place you chose, not decrypt these stupid things. I don't have the talent or resources to pull that off. I haven't received the funds transfer we talked about so my motivation on this project is fairly low."

"You expect me to believe you haven't tried to extract the information from the drives even though you've had those two days longer than the original scheduled time? I know you have the talent, so don't lie to me. How far did you get with the decryption?"

"My talent for this type of effort is no longer in this world. I haven't replaced the staff yet. So, no, I have not gotten anything off the drives. Where do you want the package delivered, and when can I have my fee?"

"You haven't tried to get the information off the drives, or you haven't gotten very far in getting information off the drives? Which is it, Grigory? You seem to be in a hurry to get the drives to me which is out of character for you. You always make copies of what you steal so you can use it later. You forget our history. I hardly think you care for my well-being or desires."

"Our agreement is to deliver the drives, and I want my fee. We did pull information off of three of the drives to verify it was possible. I don't have the resources, but you of course do. This is under the category of 'not my problem'. Now where is the delivery point?"

Grigory felt comfortable that he'd indicated they had pulled information off of the three drives, which was true. No need to convey that the method used rendered a stack of bare aluminum platters and a handful of oxide dust. It was the honesty of the answer that pleased him. He liked giving misleading answers that were based on true facts.

Chairman Lo Chang offered, "I'll double your fee if you will complete the decryption process and reestablish the operation of the programs on the servers. Since your team has already completed the activity on three, it makes the most sense. My cyber team is being reorganized, so no one is available to take this on. I think our organizations might partner on this effort. Once your team completes the decryption, I believe you will agree, the lucrative potential is there for both our teams."

Grigory countered, "I just told you my resource for this died, and additionally I want to confirm the identity of the slayer. I believe it is the work of the elusive R-Group. Perhaps you will offer some insight on this as well. Look, I have already invested too much work with the temporary replacement just to get the data verified. My primary business focus is not on this new scam. Repurposing IDs is my number one priority, which you already know. I will deliver the drives to you for the agreed fee, immediately. Besides, I've heard what happens to your associates when they outlive their usefulness. So, no thanks, on sharing in this new thing. You can have it whatever it is."

"Grigory, how can you say that after all the work we have done together? You have so little faith in our relationship. Your lack of trust wounds my sensibilities, sir. Very well, let's preserve what trust our relationship has left. Return my drives to where you picked them up. I will restart the operation at the Cyber Warfare College since they have the equipment anyway. I will complete the transaction at the exchange point once I see the drives for myself. As far as the R-Group is concerned, I can do some snooping. What was the name of your associate? May I know who you will be sending to make the delivery and verify the funds transfer?"

Grigory breathed easier, sensing the fee was within his grasp. "Patty Springs was my associate that was killed. I will send my new young pup, Buzz, whom she worked with. He will make the delivery and accept my fee in U.S. dollars. I'll make sure he is fully briefed before he arrives."

"No. There will be no cash at this meeting, so don't tell him to stand there with his hand out. Once we have the drives installed in the bays and everything comes up, I will direct my people to make the bank transfer to your usual account. He can watch the transfer being placed. Understood?"

Grigory acquiesced, "Yes, of course, Chairman. As you wish. When can you meet Buzz? You will be there and not some designate, correct? I don't want to mishandle a transaction as important as this."

"Agreed. I will send the meeting particulars to you in an encrypted email as usual. Look for that in the next two hours. Good day, Grigory. We need to maintain our relationship to our mutual advantage. Let this be the first step toward that."

"We will see."

Once the call was disconnected, Grigory studied Buzz to see if there was any reaction to the call, which he had heard.

"Buzz, are you clear on what's to be done? If you screw up, it will be a one-way trip, and I will forget your name 20 minutes after your untimely end. You understand that, right?"

Buzz said in a voice dripping with sarcasm, "Thank you, Mr. Warmth! I understand. I deliver the drives. They will want to install and boot them up. The first three we swapped out for newly formatted drives will come up, but the other seventeen will probably clean off the media like the ones did for us. I will look innocent and simply state that we didn't have that problem with the ones we extracted information from.

"I then accuse their process because the servers they were mounted in initiated a clean-the-drive program that was loaded into the boot ROM of the boxes. When that happens, he will want to take it out on me and not pay your fee. Now that I am saying this out loud, perhaps it isn't such a good plan. If all seventeen drives are cleaned of magnetic media, then your Chairman has nothing. Therefore, he has no reason to pay you or keep me alive. Hmmm, let's rethink this plan so I can make it out alive."

Grigory reminded, "A plan that gets me paid is what I want. What do we do, Mr. Brainiac?"

Buzz thought for a few minutes, then suggested, "How about I only let them spin up one drive. If the drive gets smoked then I say, well I was afraid of that and not let them spin any more up. I tell them I got the info off the first three drives by doing a mirror sector copy of the drives just in case they were poisoned, and it sure looks like they were. Then I can say that they can rebuild the fried drive with parity information from the other drives. Once we have that conversation he should be satisfied that he has his goods, we have our leverage, and then he should affect the funds transfer."

Grigory approved, "Sounds like a plan, my boy! You leave immediately upon receipt of that email from him. Let me get you the account routing numbers I want the funds transferred to. When you get back, we'll celebrate. What kind of beer do you like?"

CHAPTER 60

When looking for a needle in a haystack, always start with the right haystack.

The team relaxed in the study of the chateau with drinks before dinner. It was evident that the comfort level between all of them had bloomed after weeks of work together. Otto and Wolfgang watched the interactions with approval. They had had a private conversation earlier in the week, and both felt that these youngsters of theirs were being well-positioned to assume control at some point. The final key was if Jacob fully embraced the business. Wolfgang was confident, but Otto still had some reservations. It was also clear that something was happening between Petra and Jacob, though nothing had been said. Bowen had discreetly mentioned that they were sleeping together and that he liked the lad a lot. He said he was reminded of Wolfgang when he was a lad and even a bit of Miss Julianne.

"Petra," Jacob asked, with a bit of a glint in his eye. "How about another story of you and your father's travels. Since he is present, he might add some flavor as well."

Slightly worried, Otto asked, "Oh, no, my darling daughter, you are not telling him of our adventures, are you? You know how you always exaggerate when you do that."

Petra grinned, then said, "Now, Father, I never embellish. That is you and Wolfgang that embellish. I'll share a fun memory where you both were involved. Then you can both comment."

Otto and Wolfgang both groaned then smiled. Who knew which adventure she would decide to spring on the group?

Petra started, "One morning, Father announced at breakfast that it was our destiny to see the Russian Steppes from horseback, riding with members in the Triad and waving a sword just like the Mongol hoards had done in a dream he said he had the night before. We agreed on a compromise that we could see Russia from the comforts of a boat cruise if giving up the horseback riding wouldn't put him in extensive therapy. He relented after discovering that none of the people we invited, including Haddy and Wolfgang, would consent to being in a Mongol Triad. We tried to get Quip and Erich to go, but they both declined."

Quip jumped in, "No kidding. These folks are wild when they travel. Erich and I were scared of the prospect. Not to mention quite busy working on a project."

Petra continued, "Yes, but you can never say you weren't invited. So, we started out with a tour of Moscow before getting on our cruise that would take seven or eight days to reach St. Petersburg. Father, of course, did a bit of business on the side as the emerging Dteam was also becoming a factor. He always tries to mix business with pleasure.

"The Russians were eager to show us their city and some of the highlights that were only available to the public in state-sanctioned photos from the cold war. The most impressive sights were the view of Red Square and inside the Kremlin walls. Father claimed loudly he could see Stalin waving from the wall."

Wolfgang laughed. "I recall that and the horrified look on our tour guide. I thought that Haddy and Petra were going to try to crawl under the stones in the square."

Petra giggled, "We tried. Our tour guide recovered and showed us several buildings inside the Kremlin grounds including the building of royal baptism, the palace of royal weddings and coronations, and the royal mausoleum. Father, of course, complained that he would never remember these building names, so he suggested the guide consider renaming them to Hatched, Matched, and Dispatched, as he pointed to each of them. Uncle Wolfgang soothed our guide, telling him Father was in therapy and to ignore him. He also remembered why he had not traveled with Father often on his adventures.

"We'd of course been on trips where we moved constantly and couldn't unpack or settle into a room. The idea of being parked for a week on the Tolstoy ship with 400 of our closest friends and being able to unpack had great appeal for us. Excess space in our stateroom was not a problem. Haddy, Father and I had shared a room before. Confined in a tiny living space with a parent who wants to dress up like James Bond at the Bacharach gaming tables can test even the patience of Haddy."

Haddy exclaimed, "And your father certainly knows how to play a role to any audience."

Petra continued with interspersed giggles, "Of course there were no Bacharach tables on the ship, smoking was not allowed inside, there was no one under the age of fifty except me, so Father's James Bond activities were limited. The old joke about having to go out into the hall to change your mind must have originated on this cruise ship, and after a while even the ship wasn't big enough for my dangerously unbalanced parent.

"You can't really appreciate the term forest in the Russian context until you see it day after day while on the Volga. Oh yes, and did you know that to get to the Volga River, the Russians had actually dug a series of canals and installed several locks to get their ships into the Moscow area? It was interesting to learn the canals were first dug by Russian slave labor, then it was German slave labor, and finally finished by captured spy slave labor."

Otto remarked, "Yes, nothing much has changed in the region."

Petra added, "Jacob, I do not believe you have traveled to Russia from earlier talks we have had. Roads like the ones in the U.S. don't really exist in Russia, so ninety-five percent of all their goods are moved via waterways or rail. This is why their forests run virtually unbroken across huge tracks of land. In the story of Peter and the Wolf the reference to the forest takes on a whole new meaning because of its vastness.

"Even though it was May, we actually started seeing ice flows along the canal, and by the time we reached Lake Onega we were seeing pack ice. So much ice in fact that we couldn't go to our northern most destination and were forced to wait for an ice breaker. Father, of course, insisted that he had seen polar bears wandering over the pack ice in search of seals. After the second seal sighting, the ship's Captain asked Wolfgang if Father had mixed his medications with too much wine. After eight hours of waiting in the ice, with Father making jokes about us becoming popsicles, the Captain came on the loud speaker and told us the ice breaker had arrived, and we would be moving on soon. He then asked the passengers if they had seen the fur seals hauled up on the ice by the polar bears. You never did admit paying the Captain for that comment, Father."

"Nope, and I never will. He did that on his own."

"Now, Petra," Wolfgang added, "You must admit there was never a dull moment or that your father didn't add color to the trip."

Petra agreed, "True enough. Father was most insufferable for the next few days, particularly when we hit more ice at Lake Ladoga and had to have another ice breaker to get through to the river Neva which leads to St. Petersburg. He, of course made additional claims of seals, polar bears, and this time arctic foxes. Haddy and I had secretly hoped that after Father raced from one side of the ship to the other looking for more seals, he would be calm for the rest of the trip. We then had the ship's crew label the vodka tasting function as the Cossack Incident."

"Petra, let's skip that part," said Otto.

"But it was memorable," she said with a grin.

Just then Wolfgang's cell phone rang. Saved by the bell as it were, Otto breathed a sigh of relief. Though after watching the change in Wolfgang's features, his concern mounted. All eyes were on Wolfgang, listening to the limited side of the conversation, which told them nothing. His face looked angry, sad, and then resolved by the time he hung up the call. He walked over without saying a word and poured himself another drink. No one wanted to break the silence, but finally Otto could not stand not knowing.

Otto asked, "So who was that on the phone? Is there a problem?"

After a bit, Wolfgang looked at each of them, but his eyes rested on Jacob. The gambit of emotions ran across his face. He was gathering his thoughts, they all knew, before he spoke.

Wolfgang sadly related, with his eyes still on Jacob, "Of course. That was JAC. Earlier we had received some information with regards to a man with a silver tooth pulled from the river in New York. The description was reminiscent a member of the Dteam, so I asked JAC to look into it and get some information. The identity of the man was matched positively as the assailant to your friend Buzz's girlfriend Patty. She was a known Dteam Info Tech. We also know that Buzz was involved in some of her nefarious activities."

Jacob said, "Well, that's good. At least Buzz is off the hook for her murder if the police know that. The rest is up to him. I tried to help him with good advice."

"Not your role to change a person's nature. Sometimes people forget who their friends are. But that's not all. We have sources that provided some information ahead of the police. JAC went over to his last known location and did some extra investigation. She found his car in a rented garage and took pictures of the obvious damage and what turned out to be a sample of blood from the bumper. The bastard hadn't even had it cleaned."

Jacob asked, "Okay. What does that mean?"

Wolfgang sadly related. "What it means, son, is that the blood found was your mother's. He was the one that killed her."

With tears in his eyes he hugged Jacob, feeling the grief of them both. The others in the room were grief-stricken as well. Tears were welling up in all their eyes and, in Petra's case, overflowed down her cheeks. Nothing else was said for several minutes until Jacob pulled away and wiped at his eyes.

He whispered, "I hope that bastard rots in hell."

CHAPTER 61

When some things go wrong, it can be for the right reason.

Buzz was uneasy about the meeting with Chairman Lo Chang. Not only did he feel out of his league, he was scared. He had told Grigory that with a simple statement the Chairman would accept the inventory of drives, make arrangements to wire the money to Grigory's account, and then he would be able to leave. He would request the information on finding the R-Group as well so he could track down Patty's killers.

Buzz suspected it was not likely to play out that way. He was sure that the Chairman was going to want the low-level sector copy program that was referenced and have Buzz use it on the remainder of the drives. If he couldn't produce that program, and have it do as claimed, then things were going to get ugly. Buzz knew that Grigory was setting him up and leaving him hanging out all by himself. But he had to go through with it if he was going to make any progress on finding the R-Group.

Chairman Lo Chang formally said, "Welcome, young envoy. On behalf of the Chinese government and myself, I am pleased to make your acquaintance. Do you require some refreshments after your long trip? Tell me, what news do you have from the West and my esteemed associate, Grigory?"

Buzz ignored this traditional Asian introduction. "Can we drop the formalities and get down to business? I brought your drives, and I've been instructed to have payment wired to this account."

Buzz handed him the piece of paper with the routing numbers on it.

The Chairman frowned, "Quite the American, I see. You are all so predictable and time schedule-driven with no attention paid to social formalities that we take very seriously here in China. I had hoped that Grigory would have sent someone a little more polished for a meeting such as this. Usually he sends more than one."

Then, with a slightly repressed smile suggesting he knew something that Buzz didn't, the Chairman asked, "You mean that Grigory didn't send his regular lieutenant Sergei to make sure that the transaction is completed properly? Grigory must have a great deal of trust in you."

Buzz began to feel uneasy with this line of questioning and tried to change the subject. He hadn't been briefed on the usual sequence of events for this sort of meeting.

Buzz stated, "I would rather focus on delivering our part of the bargain so Grigory can have his wire transfer."

"And nothing for you? I'm impressed by such selfless dedication to our mutual friend, Buzz. It is not the normal activity that I have experienced with his team. Perhaps you are the way of the future."

"Actually, I need a favor from you, sir, no remuneration. I need to get into contact with the R-Group. I'm told you know how to contact them, and I would very much like that information from you, sir."

Chairman Lo Chang, obviously amused at Buzz's clumsy naiveté, said, "Ah! You see, if we had established a good working relationship, you could have asked for such a favor. I would be far more inclined to help with your request if we had completed simple pleasantries. But rather than the subtle posturing of protocol for a Chinese meeting, you just blurted out what you want. I'll tell you what I'm going to do. You will assist my people with installing the drives in their bays and bring up the program and its database so I can see that we have what was contracted. Facilitate all that, and then we'll see about the wire transfer."

Buzz frowned, "What about my request, sir?"

Chairman Lo Chang scolded, "Just showing up with the drives and sticking your hand out is not very conducive for generating favors. I sense reluctance on your part to assist with seeing this project to its conclusion. Therefore, I am assigning two of my people to see that I get what I want and to assist you. They don't speak English so you may have to draw some pictures to get your needs across to them. In other words, you don't leave until I get what I want. You are on Chinese time here. Time is now of the essence, just the opposite of the American approach to business. I'll be back tomorrow to see the progress on your delivery."

The following day, the Chairman returned to the Cyber Warfare College. He found Buzz had been fairly well-worked over, sporting several cuts and bruises, and moving very slowly.

Not really surprised, he asked, "What happened? You didn't try to leave the premises unauthorized, did you? I know my associates' work, and it looks like you bear their signature. Yes?"

Buzz had a little trouble speaking clearly but managed, "Well, I did as you recommended and drew some pictures to create some flash cards to help bridge our communications barrier. I didn't know how long I would be here, so here are the flash cards I used with them."

The Chairman looked at the cards with distaste. "I see these are fairly good at depicting your requested needs. Here is one for food, one for drink, and one for going to the toilet. This last one seems a bit obscure, but it looks like you requested them to sodomize each other. Is that what this is supposed to be for?"

Buzz said with some difficulty, "After having put up with them pushing me around for several hours, I wanted to tell them to go screw themselves!"

The Chairman, obviously amused at the ink drawings and the concept they were to convey, interjected, "Well, so other than that, how was your day? Are my drives up and happy? Can we begin decrypting the data?"

Buzz struggled to speak through badly swollen lips.

The technical lead approached and informed him, "Chairman, we are having difficulties with the drives. We followed the recommendations that Mr. Buzzard gave us in spinning up the drives, and so we loaded the fourth one first and only that one. Before we knew what was going on, the servo motors lowered the heads down on the platters and removed all the magnetic media, which means number four drive is gone out of the array.

"We have been unable to get anything useful out of Mr. Buzzard since then. We tried having your two associates talk to him, but they lost their patience with him as you can see."

Chairman Lo Chang said with disgust, "His name is just Buzz. He deserves no other label, especially not Mr."

Turning to Buzz, he asked, "So do you feel well enough to comment about accessing the information on the drives?"

The Chairman summoned the two associates and requested some ice for Buzz.

Feeling a little better, Buzz related, "Okay. Here is the straight story. We didn't suspect that the drives were poisoned and when we spun up the first drive the same thing happened to us. I ruined two drives in succession, and Grigory insisted on trying a third in his presence. He wanted his fee, so we cooked up this story that we used a low-level sector copy program, copied everything off the three drives, and substituted three newly formatted drives to make our story believable. I was to deliver the drives and recommend you only bring up the fourth drive.

"Once it was ruined, I was to suggest that your people could rebuild the lost drive with the parity bits from the other drives, but that you would have to perform the same low-level sector copy of the other drives before you could do that. Meantime, I was to indicate that unless you transferred the money and let me go, Grigory wouldn't give you the other three drives. With those missing, your project would be dead in the water. The bottom line is that you don't have anything that can be done to get the information on those drives. I can't maintain the deception anymore just to get Grigory's money."

Chairman Lo Chang thought about this. If this was indeed true, then the SECcoin was lost to him and to China. He had to be certain, and he also had to think of another way to recover the project to meet the end objective that Po had outlined. He considered all sides for a few minutes.

Chairman Lo Chang questioned, "So neither of us has the info on the drives? How can I be sure that you didn't just copy everything off and put the poison routine on the drives? How can I be certain Grigory won't try to sell the programs back to me later?"

Buzz considered the question, then suggested, "Look, if we had gotten everything off the drives and the information is as valuable as it sounds, then why bother to sell it back to you? Why not harvest the information for ourselves by selling it to your competitors? Besides, I have the receipt for the three new drives with me. Didn't your people notice that the serial numbers of the first three drives didn't match the sequence of the last seventeen when they checked them in? Boy, you must have some real green beans working in your data extraction group."

The Chairman looked at the receipt, then queried, "Okay, I actually do understand all of this. Grigory is not the most honest associate, but this business lends itself to that. What I don't understand is you. You might have been able to pull off the deception and then leave. Why tell me the truth?"

Buzz looked like a whipped puppy. "Like I asked you when we met and failed the social niceties, I am hunting the R-Group. I need someone to tell me how to find them. Grigory told me you knew how to contact them so I hooked up with him to get to you. I hoped to convince you to tell me how to get in touch with them. Will you tell me how to get a hold of them? I have done the Chinese thing and established a good social relationship with you by telling you the truth and preventing you from giving Grigory money he didn't earn."

Chairman Lo Chang was amazed at the request. "What's so important about contacting the R-Group? I mean, looking at you, one could easily deduce you are not a conventional assassin and are equally unskilled in the area of self-defense. What are your intentions with such contact information?"

Buzz asserted, "Grigory told me the R-Group killed my lady, Patty. I'm going to get justice! The police first thought it was me, but the detective let me go while they were working on other leads. They wouldn't give me any more information, so I decided I would work the case from my side."

The pause that ensued as the information was digested allowed Buzz to catch his breath and further assess his injuries. He didn't think any bones were broken, but he was sore everywhere. It was worth the pain to avenge Patty.

"Indeed. Well, Buzz, that's an interesting tale, but I'm still left with a problem. My information isn't just inaccessible from the drives. I've now just learned that an associate I had some minimal trust in is now untrustworthy. I usually have all the loose ends dealt with and then move on to other projects.

"In this case, however, I believe that I will retain you and your services for a new project you might be better suited for. When I buy wines, I typically put them in storage on the shelf so that they can age and mature, delivering better flavor when opened. I have the same intention here with you. I will allow you to age a bit more so that you can provide more value to me and my organization. So, to be clear, as of now, you work for me. My two associates will insure your loyalty to me."

Buzz thought for a second, then asked, "What does that mean for me? I get that I'm being spared, but for what purpose? I still want the R-Group lead in any event. And after working with your two associates, I'm not anxious to be in close proximity to them."

The Chairman clarified, "In my line of work, identity protection is valuable. I know Grigory had a very extensive identity theft and protection operation. Because of his deceit I now want that operation to work for me. After all, you did work with Grigory as his lead identity operative, right? I'm sure there is much we can discuss along these lines for our new mutual business venture."

Buzz was angered and bewildered, "What are you talking about? Patty was Grigory's lead techno geek. Sure, I did heavy lifting when she needed some code written. But no one knew that. I know she didn't tell Sergei or Grigory. How could you know about my involvement? And I'm supposed to work for you now too? You know I'm really getting tired of being the birdie in this badminton game. I guess when I finally get into contact with the R-Group, they'll have a job waiting for me there too!"

"Buzz, I am not without resources and informants. I had you checked out before you arrived and got more information after we met. Your theatrics do not impress me. And in answer to your question, yes, you work for me as your wellbeing is of great concern to me."

Buzz looked at the Chairman in amazement. "My wellbeing? Your goons worked me over, and that's how you worry about my wellbeing?"

The Chairman began to lose his patience with Buzz and said in a very restrained voice, "They just lost their tempers, and your drawings didn't help. Your wellbeing is based on me not losing my temper. So that is your only concern. Do you understand, or do you need some more loss of wellbeing?"

Buzz throttled back on his barbed comments after peering into the Chairman's eyes and simply nodded. He understood only too clearly.

The Chairman relaxed his gaze and said, "Good. You leave right away."

Buzz looked confused, but still asked, "I'm leaving for where? To do what? You still haven't told me how to get into contact with the R-Group. I'm leaving until I have a way to uncover Patty's killer. You owe me that much because without it there is no deal."

Chairman Lo Chang decided to add some clarity and solidify Buzz as his ally. "I can see you are passionate about this matter. Here are your answers. I am not paying the money to Grigory's account, and that makes you expendable to his organization. You are going back to New York City to take over Grigory's identity laundering business and groom it to my needs, which will put you at further odds with Grigory and his associates. Not a good place to be. The R-Group does not have a website or email address for you to simply reach out to them to identify Patty's assassin."

He handed Buzz a sheet of paper.

"Here is the chat room that they monitor along with every other underground organization. I would recommend that you not ask a blatantly foolish question like you are intending because every secret organization in the world will be down your throat. On top of that, you are looking in the wrong place."

Buzz's eyes narrowed. "What do you mean, I am looking in the wrong place? Grigory said it was the R-Group that did this."

Chairman Lo Chang was amused at the stupidity of youth. "Grigory is not someone who takes the loss of an associate lightly. Nor is he given to simply having some new young pup go on an avenging vendetta that will bring in law enforcement. And finally, Grigory's long-term associate, Sergei, is clearly missing in action. So, my question to you is, did you meet Sergei while you were at Grigory's? Was there any mention of Sergei while you were there, and why is he not part of your meeting with me?"

Buzz was quite uncomfortable with the information but hell bent on getting to the end game of avenging Patty.

"I didn't hear anything about Sergei, and no, he wasn't there at Grigory's. I figured he was doing something else."

"The more likely scenario is that the hothead Sergei accidently killed Patty. He was well known for unpredictable behavior. Grigory probably uncovered the fact that Sergei killed her when the contract between us for the drives was made. Knowing Grigory the way that I do, he probably killed Sergei, thus completing his threat to Sergei from years ago. Grigory needed you to help him now that Patty was gone. The only way to do that was to give you a false lead on her killer. The fact is the R-Group doesn't kill people, but Grigory does. What I just told you is the more plausible end to Patty.

"To summarize so that you understand completely, she was killed by Sergei. Sergei was probably killed by Grigory. And unless you do what I need done and you take my protection, you will be next. Do we have a deal or not?"

Buzz swallowed hard, seeing the truth in what was just said. "Even if what you say is true about Sergei and Grigory, how am I supposed to go back to Grigory without any funds transferred? How can I confront him about those two murders? If what you say is true, I don't have a prayer!"

Chairman Lo Chang added a slight grin to his steeled features. "Grigory won't be happy about the non-payment. I will inform him that the payment is deferred until the decryption process is completed. You came back to get some of Patty's cyber tools to help with that process. That protects you from Grigory since it will look like a work in progress. You'll be able to start work on converting the identity business, which Patty had built, to my purposes. Also, while you are there, you can start poking around for what happened to Sergei. We are going to need that information in order to take Grigory out of the organizational structure. Don't worry about getting in touch with me. I'll get in touch with you. My men will also be close at all times."

CHAPTER 62

The fun never ends until the end.

Well, here I am again," Buzz said to no one at all. "Except that now I am in a police interrogation room. I'm tired of being picked up, then put back down to do someone's bidding. Now I know how a yo-yo feels."

However, there was something uncomfortable about being compared to a yo-yo. While it might have been a hilarious analogy about someone else, it felt desperately tragic because he was living these events.

Detective Sloan returned with water for Buzz and sat across from him.

"Well, did you give some thought to what I asked? Did you recognize the man in the picture?"

Buzz responded, "How the hell would I know who that is? It could be a dead tuna that washed up on shore. I mean, look at how bloated and soggy that thing in the picture is. Sheeze Louise! Why don't you just dust for fingerprints like they do on TV?"

Buzz knew how stupid the comment sounded, but he was past caring.

Sloan responded, trying to think of a way to get some cooperation, "I can see you are not cursed with self-awareness. We found this guy downstream from a bridge that usually serves as a jump-off point for the distraught and suicidal of our population; however, we almost never find despondent people with the ability to wrap themselves in heavy chains and weight themselves down with cement blocks before jumping in the water.

"He might still have been there if some rich yacht owner hadn't hooked his anchor into the deceased and inadvertently hauled him up. Absolutely ruined the mood on board for those pretty guests. I'll bet it takes a week to clean up the deck the way their party girls were emptying their stomachs. The only thing he was concerned about was that his wife didn't find out about the guests he was entertaining. Turns out, it's her yacht and she was out of town. I guess when you get to be rich the first thing you do is trade your mundane problems for some that are more innovative and exciting. Thankfully, you and I don't have that issue."

Buzz almost smiled, "Okay, funny guy. Like I said, what does this have to do with me? I can't tell anything from the photo, and based on my delicate constitution, I am not about to go down to the morgue with you to see this thing up close and personal, because I too would be emptying my stomach. Why am I even here?"

Sloan admonished, "You're here mostly because I told you not to leave town or to try to cross the crime scene. In fact, you did both. Then you tell me that you don't know this guy, but we found traces of this guy's DNA from the scene at your place, and there was no sign of forced entry. Patty must have known who this guy was, so I have reason to believe that you do as well."

Buzz looked again, trying to see something he recognized. It was a gross sight, period.

"I'm telling you I don't recognize this person. Look, I want to find her killer too, but I can't help you with this picture or identify who it is. I was at the apartment because I needed some things to start my life over again. All my clothes are there, and I wanted to get cleaned up. If you have crime scene evidence, why don't you just match up the two?"

"Our forensics group is struggling to find a match for Mr. Tuna's identity. His DNA is not in our database. The only other positive item is his silver tooth, which is not showing in this picture. We are trying to track it from dental records, but so far nothing."

Buzz blanched, "Silver tooth? As in front tooth?"

The detective sensed that the comment had finally registered. "Yes. The corpse had a set of big front teeth, one silver, and multiple remodeled broken bones which suggests he had a rough life. The coroner estimates this guy was dumped at approximately the same time as a crime boss in these parts lost his prime lieutenant. The crime boss, however, didn't report his lieutenant's disappearance. We have some links between Patty and this crime boss as well, but nothing linking you to him."

Buzz shifted in the chair, found it difficult to swallow, but managed to squeak out his request in a broken voice. "A crime boss is missing his prime lieutenant? Do you have a name for this crime boss and what Patty's association with him was?"

Detective Sloan was growing impatient but sensed that the questioning was headed in the right direction. Buzz knew something, he felt it in his bones.

"You knew that Patty Springs had a rap sheet, right? She had been charged with information trafficking and some other stuff, and the crime boss, known only as Grigory, bailed her out. We have some surveillance photos of Grigory and Patty, if that will help jog your memory."

Buzz struggled to keep focused.

He asked, "So, why don't you just ask this Grigory guy? If this is who you think it is, he should be able to identify him. I'm telling you I don't recognize Mr. Tuna here!"

Sloan collected himself, then confided, "Actually we did just that. We asked Grigory to identify the body and help us fill out a missing person's report. Grigory just smiled and said that he couldn't help us. So kid, if you can't help us, fine.

"I wouldn't hang out with Grigory if I were you. He is bad news. If you do, you will inevitably fall out of favor. The rumors around this guy indicate that he becomes very friendly with folks he wants to off. He then creates some pretext for a road trip and always asks the victim to ride up front. Invariably the course of the trip takes the car over that specific bridge and yet another despondent person will take their own life."

Buzz blurted out, "So Mr. Tuna must be the guy called Sergei. I don't have any idea of his last name, but Patty feared him. Are you saying Grigory killed him or had him killed?"

Buzz blanched recalling his recent ride in the front seat of Grigory's car.

Sloan smiled, "So why do you think it is Sergei?"

"The tooth. The guy was a hard ass, with the tooth showing when he sneered, which was the case on the two occasions I saw him."

"Okay. We will work with Interpol to see if they have any DNA from this guy and match it up. There is nothing to pin this on Grigory, but our snitches indicated it was his practice. Mr. Tuna's DNA matched some items taken from the apartment and on Patty. We suspect Grigory had Sergei killed after he discovered the details around Patty's murder. All we have is circumstantial evidence, no reported missing persons, and no real proof. Your information might help, but it is doubtful we'll have enough for a conviction.

"Now I can detain you for leaving the state when I told you not to and for crossing into a crime scene. I would rather have you work with us to help catch the murderer of a murderer. Which would you prefer; helping to resolve this, or jail time?"

Buzz smiled slightly at the irony of the situation. He was now being forcibly recruited for his third unwanted job that might also get him killed. Buzz was quite sure that this turn of events would be hysterical if it happened to someone else.

Buzz shrugged, now resigned. "With the tooth, yes, Mr. Tuna is Sergei. Sergei would also try to sulk in unnoticed and stick to the shadows, which should have made it harder to notice him if he had been better at it. The silver tooth and those ruthless eyes always made Patty and me uncomfortable. I never said anything because Patty always treated it like business, and they never let me stay in the same room while they talked. But I had gone out that night for more stuff to help get past our minor argument that evening.

"I did not see Sergei come in or even lurking outside like he sometimes did. I sent the flowers and card for her to find. I hoped when I returned we could make up from the fight. Unfortunately, I stopped by my favorite bar on the way home from work which I told you before and you confirmed with my friends. I wish I hadn't done that. If I had come home right after work, I might have been able to stop him. She might still be alive."

Buzz started to tear up but fought to command his emotions.

Sloan sympathized, "I understand, kid. I truly do. So please help us bring these people down. You owe it to her and yourself."

"Okay. What do you want me to do?"

CHAPTER 63

Loose ends
can be so hard to re-tie.

After the confirmation from JAC via Wolfgang, Quip had monitored the chatter for the last couple of days. Both the Russian and Chinese dark angels seemed to be changing their tactics. Otto and Wolfgang both continued to fuel these fires. Jacob and Petra were helping with some minor assignments and not directly involved with watching what was unfolding with the changes. Quip was reasonably certain that Buzz was a lost cause, but during their last discussion on this, Jacob had disagreed. Jacob had admitted Buzz was dense at times but not a crook.

Later that evening, everyone was again together in the study waiting for dinner to be served. The discussion had gone from upcoming projects, to all the points being monitored, and then travel schedules. Several jokes had been told when Bowen entered and indicated that dinner would be ready soon. Otto took the opportunity with the conversation interruption to make a suggestion.

"Jacob, with the information we have gathered on your friend Buzz, and knowing your thoughts on him, I would submit that it is time you made a visit to him. Have you had any contact with him since you arrived here?"

"Otto, I haven't had any contact. I admit I have mixed feelings on Buzz. I know that Quip doesn't trust him in the least. Petra told me she thinks he is simply an immature leach."

Quip nodded and Petra blushed as Jacob fell silent.

"Jacob, my boy, we are all supportive of you. I think as well that you are the only one that can really determine if he is salvageable. At the very least, it is time to initiate contact. That alone may give you the answers you need. One of us can travel with you, if you like."

Jacob gave it some consideration. He could feel the support of this new family of his.

"No, I can reach out myself and travel if that makes sense. I will begin that process tomorrow and let you all know the results."

"I took the liberty of Haddy booking a trip for you. You travel in the morning, and she has all your arrangements in the envelope that is on the dresser in your room. Wolfgang and I both felt this was the right course of action, so please accept our meddling.

"Also, in the vein of full disclosure, it seems the airfare and hotel for your trip to Las Vegas was a ploy by the Dteam to get you into a compromising position so that they might control you. That information was a part of the social engineering that Patty worked on Buzz among the other items, like the programs she took off his PC. Petra was right to insist you leave the event. We just wanted you to know everything, Jacob."

"Petra, you're right. Sometimes he does overstep, doesn't he?" Jacob smiled. "Alright, I will leave in the morning per your request."

"Good. JAC will pick you up at the airport and provide you with some additional support, should you need it. Let's go to dinner. I want to see you finally beat Wolfgang at chess tonight. Quip and I have a gentleman's bet on it."

Quip laughed, "I am no gentleman, Otto, but we do have a bet."

CHAPTER 64

Those who long for the good old days did not wake up today.

Buzz was frantically trying to find Jacob online. Since Jacob had apparently sold his house and vanished, Buzz hadn't been able to contact him. At first it had been no big deal as Buzz had plenty of running buddies and frankly, he was getting tired of Jacob lecturing to him whenever they got together. Everything had changed when the police brought him in for questioning the night Patty had been killed. It had been a continual nightmare since then.

"What I wouldn't give to have Jacob nagging at me to do better and play it straight," Buzz said to his computer screen. "Hell, I might even use his advice this time. Anything has to be better than working for all these clowns that have their hooks in me. If only I could talk to Jacob, maybe he could help me figure a way out of this mess!"

Then 'ding' went the computer indicating an IM was waiting for a response. When he saw the window, he could hardly believe his eyes.

JAM: Ping?

Buzz: Hey man! Finally, there you are! I've been trying to catch up with you for weeks. Where did you go? No word, no good-bye, nothing!

JAM: Ah that's sweet! You missed me. ....or you want something.....

Buzz: Hey! I need some help here and no it doesn't have anything to do with coding.....

JAM: Dude no need to go off on me, I was just yanking your chain. Ok so what's wrong?

Buzz: I can't go in to it in this IM session. Where can we meet and talk mano-a-mano?

JAM: Wow! You do sound wrapped. I'm actually back in town for a little while and then heading out again so how about tonight and the usual watering hole? You still owe me a drink.

Buzz: Buddy I don't have any money. What I have are lots of problems. Anyway I would rather owe you that drink the rest of your life than ever cheat you out of it. 😊

JAM: Ah that's the old Buzz. I'll buy since I failed to say goodbye. So what time?

Buzz: I'll see you there at 7:30

Buzz waited in a booth, trying hard to just sip his beer, when Jacob slid in across from him. Buzz felt a wave of emotion flow over him as he looked over at Jacob, and he struggled to restrain the tears. Buzz couldn't even say hello for fear that his voice would crack, and he would not be able to control himself. He knew that he looked like shit. Sleep had evaded him for days.

Jacob dropped the usual frat-boy greetings and took in all the unspoken emotional and physical strain that was apparent in his buddy. He ordered a beer from the waitress and, after she left, decided to open the conversation.

"Buddy, what's wrong? I don't think I've ever seen you like this before, and we have been through some difficult stuff. Come on, this is Jacob. You can tell me. Whatever it is, I'm sure we can get through it. You look like I felt when my mother died, and you talked me back in off the ledge. I haven't forgotten how you helped me, and now I would like to help you with your obvious upheaval. I know how difficult it can be when the zoo animals are let out. Hey, where's Patty? Is there some reason she isn't here to help work through whatever it is that is upsetting you?"

Buzz lowered his head to gain control of his emotions. He simply stared into his beer. He wouldn't look Jacob in the eye.

Buzz whispered, "Patty's dead. She was murdered."

Now it was Jacob who couldn't say anything. Even though he already knew the answer, seeing what it was doing to Buzz was painful. He knew that his old friend was in there somewhere. He realized he had to try to help him.

Jacob said with true sympathy, "Oh, Buzz, I am so sorry! What happened? This is awful!"

Buzz started talking and let everything flow out in one giant run-on sentence.

"It's been awful. The police took me in as a suspect but couldn't prove that it was me. Then a jerk Russian business associate of Patty's springs me from jail but said that I had to help him with some computer stuff. Turns out the damn drives are programmed to self-destruct, and I end up ruining three of 20 drives, and the Jerk blames me for it. Then he makes me his errand boy, and I have to take the drives to some Chinese mucky-muck in order to get the finders' fee that's been promised. I only go along with it because the jerk tells me that Patty's assassins do business with this guy. If I do the errand then I can ask how to get a hold of the assassins.

"But the Chinese guy tells me that the most likely killer is the henchmen of the Jerk, and since the three drives are ruined, he is not going to pay the fee. The topper is that the Chinese mucky-muck says I now work for him and that he wants to take over the identity protection business of the Jerk. He has his two goons work me over to make his point. They drag me back here to start work taking over the identity business that Patty was apparently running for the Jerk.

"Then the police take me in again and insist that I now work for them since I had left the city when told not to. And I crossed a crime scene tape to get into my apartment to try to restart the Jerk's identity business for the Chinese mucky-muck. Detective Sloan is pretty sure that they found Patty's murderer that worked for the Jerk. Problem is this suspect is now Mr. Tuna after spending most of his time at the bottom of the river, desperately holding on to more chain and concrete than he could swim with. So that's where I'm at."

Stunned, Jacob's mouth moved but nothing came out. Compared to Buzz's horror story, his venture down the rabbit hole was downright pleasant. He wondered briefly if Buzz was exaggerating, but he already knew much of the story. No wonder Quip had his reservations.

Finally, Jacob gained his voice and said, "You're right, Buzz, this is definitely bad. I don't know where we should start. I mean, it sounds like you have two underworld groups ready to take you out, as well as the police who want to use you as a target while they try to solve the murder of Patty, who was perhaps more involved in criminal activity than I ever suspected. Probably more than you suspected as well."

Buzz shook his head, then complained, "I thought about trying to run, but I'm pretty sure that with these people, I'll just die tired. Besides, I've got nowhere to run to or any place to hide."

Buzz was despondent. That was clearly obvious. He looked beaten and disheveled.

Buzz looked up and pleaded, "Jacob, you have to help me! What am I going to do?"

Jacob countered, "Hey, wait a minute! I'm not buying it that I have to help you. From what you've just said, you are involved in two murders, a mobster from Russia and a mobster from China that both think they own you, and police swirling all around you. You think now I should get involved in this mess? Get serious, Buzz. What exactly do you think I can do to help you?

"How much of this did you cause by not thinking things through? All those programs you had my support with probably played right into this, which just makes me sick. I know, I can call in an air strike! Or use my satellite-based lasers to melt them from low earth orbit! Perhaps you want me to fabricate evidence for the police and hack their database to get you off the hook? You didn't even give me any real names to work with, and for all I know you made all this up!"

Buzz studied Jacob's face for a few minutes. He really wasn't sure if he could count on help from Jacob. But he had nowhere else to turn, so he tried to plead his case though he had resigned himself to the idea that this was a lost cause.

"I can see where you might think that this fantastic account is just a story. It's all so surreal that I'm not completely sure it's all fact-based either. I mean, me meeting with Grigory, the Jerk Russian thug, and seeing him play with his white tiger before being shipped off to meet the Chinese Chairman to deliver drives to what was supposed to be the Chinese Cyber Warfare College. And then finding out that Patty was running an identity protection racket for that Jerk Russian. Yeah, I can see why you think this is all made up and I've lost it. Never mind, Jacob."

Buzz then perked up and laughed, "Hey man, I was just messing with you! I haven't seen you in a while, and I wanted to yank your chain so you wouldn't forget my antics. Cheers!"

Jacob grinned, "Prost!"

Jacob and Buzz ate and visited a bit more. Jacob indicated
he had been working with a new company and doing a lot of
different types of programs. He was very vague about who for and
where, other than he was currently based in Europe. He never even
mentioned Petra either. He needed to make a recommendation,
and he would.

CHAPTER 65

Friends help you move, while real friends help you move bodies.

When he awakened in the morning, he wasn't sure where he was or whether he was in the midst of another drama or not. He was grateful that he wasn't naked or finding someone else in bed. Trying to sort out who he was working for at this moment, he recalled perhaps telling someone. Between his depression and the beers with Jacob last night, things were pretty fuzzy. He seriously wondered if he could even survive. His eyes wandered a bit and landed on a sofa. He recognized it but just couldn't place it.

Last night was totally fragmented. Jacob, damn him, had picked up the bar tab, which he knew only because he was broke. Then the man had allowed him to drink himself into oblivion. He thought he had asked for help and been refused. He wasn't sure where he was, but he wasn't terrified like when he'd been in China. The only thing for certain was that he'd made a mess of his life. There was nothing he could do but avoid getting killed. Then he recalled he was supposed to start moving the identity protection business to the Chinese hard ass.

He turned on the computer that Patty had used and realized he was shocked to find it on the table. He sort of recognized the table and the sofa he was on, but not really. His head was throbbing, and his hands shook. Plus, he could hardly focus his eyes on the flashing computer screen. He randomly thought he'd get a cup of coffee later or perhaps eat, but he didn't know where. Nothing was in focus. Then he started hearing this soft pounding in his head. He got up to get an aspirin and realized the pounding was actually someone knocking on the door.

Looking down to make certain he still was dressed, he walked toward the door. He debated if the smart move was to answer it. Yep, it could be another asshole with an agenda for him. He looked out the peephole but couldn't focus. He decided what the hell. He opened the door and was surprised at the beautiful girl standing there smiling. He had no clue as to who she was but had no doubt that she was pretty.

Buzz said, "Howdy, stranger. How can I help you?"

JAC just smiled and said, "Come on, Buzz, time to get moving. There is lots to do." She moved past him into Jacob's house like she knew it cold.

Buzz, talking to where she once stood, said, "Well, yes of course, come on in."

JAC then detailed, "Okay, this is what I want you to do. Take this burner phone and text his people that you can't move on the identity business that Patty set up until Grigory is out of the picture. Oh, and tell him that to square the deal with him, you'll give him five million dollars in diamonds but only if Grigory is eliminated from your threat vector."

Buzz looked so pathetically confused. "Who's people?"

JAC said with confidence, "Why, Chairman Lo Chang, of course. You know, the one you delivered the useless hard drives to. The same guy that wants the identity business that Patty built for Grigory. Does any of this ring a bell?"

Buzz was still having trouble processing the fast-moving information delivered by JAC. He was a bit distracted because his brain was still fuzzy, and she was pretty cute. On a normal day he would have said she had a great smile.

Finally, he questioned, "Uh, five million? Did I understand that you have five million dollars that you are going to give me so I can get away from these jerks? Inquiring minds need to know."

JAC clucked her tongue and sized up his condition. Yep, she needed to slow down with him.

She advised, "Okay, right now you are as sharp as a bowling ball. I'll use one syllable words so you can keep up your end of the conversation.

"Step one, this is a disposable cell phone.

"Step two, all the numbers you need are already programmed into it.

"Step three, text Chairman Lo Chang that you will not provide the identity protection business that Patty set up for Grigory, until Grigory is out of the way. Chairman Lo Chang will be furious with you.

"Step four, you tell him that you want out of the arrangement that was foisted on you. For that you are prepared to guide him or his flunkies to five million dollars in diamonds.

"Step five, when he won't take the offer, tell him you will sweeten it with something he cannot resist. A white tiger.

"Now was that slow enough?"

Buzz was confused. He questioned, "I do not have a white tiger, and I don't think Grigory will give me his. And my, you are very pretty."

She ignored the compliment and smiled as she continued, "Don't worry, it is covered in each step.

"Now. Step six, I know he will turn down the five million dollars, but his ego cannot resist the white tiger. Don't be in too much of a hurry to throw that into the bargain. When he agrees, then you are free and clear of his demands of you moving forward on the identity protection business.

"Step seven, once he agrees, he will ask how you'll deliver these remarkable items. You are to say that it is his team's responsibility to acquire the items, not yours. You will only tell him where to find these items. You must hold firm on this point, or you will never be free. Got that?"

Buzz was trying to track this step-by-step outline. He thought she might be onto something. She also had an eye-catching body that he admired. His brain was less fuzzy so he nodded.

"Step eight, tell him he must text you back that the transaction is completed when they have obtained the goods.

"This is how you get out. Do you understand?"

Buzz kept up but was again distracted by one thing.

JAC followed his eyes and admonished, "And stop staring at the girls, Buzz. Look me in the eyes so we can have a useful conversation, because if you don't I'm going to give your big Jim and the twins a short but eventful trip."

JAC stepped into a martial arts stance to drive home her ability to follow through on the threat. Buzz knew he was busted, so he quickly averted his gaze from her chest to other parts of the room. He then focused on her eyes and face. This woman had a fairly good sounding lifeline for him to grab onto.

Buzz said contritely, "I'm sorry. I did not mean to offend. Where is this five million dollars that I am to offer to him?"

JAC grinned, "Oh good, he can be taught. The white tiger has five million dollars in diamonds around its neck. Chairman Lo Chang cannot resist its value nor the prestige of having a white tiger in his possession. This is your ticket out of his clutches."

Buzz was a bit worried when he related, "Grigory loves that white tiger. I've seen them play together and how much affection they have for each other. The tiger will never bond with Chairman Lo Chang. She is not a trophy to be coveted without the bond. You'd have to kill Grigory before you could take Nikkei. I doubt she'd go quietly either."

JAC agreed with a grin. "Precisely. That is why you are giving Chairman Lo Chang that responsibility. He or his thugs will eliminate Grigory, they will take the white tiger and collect the five million dollars in diamonds from her collar as payment. Then you have left two of your three problems behind. Are you beginning to understand?"

Buzz was focused on her plan much better than before. However, Buzz wasn't sure if it was the logic that JAC communicated or her threat. But he liked the possibility. Buzz reflected on the conversation, then turned his eyes to hers as previously instructed.

He nodded he understood and said, "I get it, and it sounds good. But what about my third problem? The one with Detective Sloan thinking I'm involved in Patty's murder. Which, by the way, I did not do."

JAC stated, "That one you can't run from, but with no evidence, what are they going to do? Besides, they already really suspect Grigory waxed Sergei. Cops hate the unsolved stuff so they typically find what they are looking for to confirm and wrap up their theories. I shouldn't be surprised if that one is resolved all on its own. I think we are done here."

Buzz, feeling more relieved by the minute, responded, "Almost. But who are you and why are you helping me? I mean, even my best friend walked out on me yesterday when I begged for help. But here you are telling me what to do and how to play a dangerous hand. I don't even know your name. At least answer that for me, please."

JAC smiled, then said, "You're not stupid, Buzz. Perhaps you already know the answer. You need to think before reacting in the future and do the right thing. Lock the front door as you leave, after you clean up. I hope you will fare well."

JAC left without any further conversation. Buzz watched her go then shut the door after a while. He couldn't help but smile at the luck of her visit. He went inside, made the texts and smiled at the outcome. All steps in order. He showered, dressed, and picked up the computer stuff to get ready to leave. Reaching into the pocket of the slacks, he found several hundred dollars and smiled. As he locked the front door, he looked around and recognized finally that he was in the house that Jacob had sold.

CHAPTER 66

Is all well that ends well?

Otto asked Jacob, "So, are the wheels set in motion for your friend Buzz? Did Chairman Lo Chang's henchmen sedate the white tiger long enough to enhance Nikkei's collar so she would attack and maul Grigory?"

Jacob answered, "Yes. The white tiger was extremely agitated by the electrical impulses delivered by the collar. She was angry enough to turn on Grigory. The police investigated and declared that the animal killed him. When the police suggested the animal be terminated, the Chinese government used diplomatic immunity to get the animal out of the country on a private plane. Nikkei is safe and destined to be spoiled for a very long time. The current rumor is that the Chairman reads to her each morning and hand feeds her, trying to force a bond with her. Apparently, he tried a bit too quickly to force her bonding and had to have a few stitches as his reward.

"With the diamond collar and the white tiger in Chairman Lo Chang's possession, he is agreeable to letting Buzz go. The identity programs were turned over to him. Quip and I have been watching its overall progress. Because of the concern for wider spread identity thefts, Petra is gaining additional subcontract work as more businesses adopt better encryption. She is happy as can be.

"The extra seeding of evidence, where Grigory is shown to have murdered Sergei, made Detective Sloan back off of Buzz and close both cases as solved. He is going to receive commendation from the Mayor at the end of the month. Buzz is off the hook. All he has to do now is to go live a quiet life working for his father. We can only hope."

Otto grinned, "Yes, of course. Come. Time for our next meeting."

Jacob moved with Otto into the next meeting with the R-Group senior members. Everyone was present. It was funny that Petra, Quip and he were on one side of the table and Wolfgang and Otto on the other side with Haddy at the middle on the end. Erich, Quip's brother, and their grandfather, Ferdek Watcowski, were joining remotely. Ferdek had a great mind as well as a good sense of humor but was unable to travel. He and Wolfgang were the last living members of the original R-Group refugees. He still asked the tough questions and helped determine the long-term business direction.

Quip started the discussion. "So, what do we do with the SECcoin program we lifted from Lt. Colonel Po's Cyber Warfare College? Petra and I have been analyzing it, and it does look solid. Of course, Petra wants to improve the encryption algorithms, but other than that, we are ready to rebrand and relaunch it using our own digital currency. Erich believes it might be something the banks in EMEA could sponsor."

Wolfgang asked, "How do you see us handling the SECcoin property? Do we auction it off to the highest bidder or manage it ourselves?"

Otto concurred, "Yes, what should be done with this new property? Let's analyze our options from all angles."

Jacob, encouraged with the open discussion, remarked, "Well, our fastest time to money is to sell it. However, now that I think about it, sell it for what? I mean, if we sell it to someone for Euros or Dollars and they launch the SECcoin digital currency, we could be handling worthless paper in no time at all."

Quip nodded, pleased that this came up. "The magic beans syndrome."

They all looked at him, hoping that he would elaborate. He sensed everyone looking and interjected with a grin.

"You know, from Jack and the Beanstalk. Jack is sent to town to sell the milk cow, and he gets swindled for a few magic beans."

The analogy satisfied his audience without someone having to ask if he had missed taking his meds that morning.

Petra ignored Quip altogether and said, "So we sell it to someone who has a vested interest in keeping it off the market. That way our currency doesn't lose its value, and they get to retain their economic status. But what price would be enough for such economic power?"

Jacob questioned, "Can we be certain that the purchaser would keep the SECcoin technology completely secret? Or that they not release it for their own ends? I mean, what would there be to prevent them from buying SECcoin and positioning themselves to launch it to create their own economic supremacy? That's what Chairman Lo Chang was all teed up to do when we grabbed the code. We would have to do the same thing all over again, and we might not be so successful with another adversary."

Quip suggested, "What has been stolen once can be stolen again. Nothing is beyond possibility as long as we know where it is and continue to stay ahead with our offense evolution. Admittedly it would be more difficult the second time. Anyone we sold it to would recognize the value and potential, so I could see them guarding it most jealously. I propose that before selling it, we install backdoors and logic bombs in the code in case we need to re-invade the program."

Ferdek asked, "How can we ever be sure that the SECcoin will be used wisely? Let me give you some history on the Enigma machine. After we gave the British the one we had appropriated in Poland, we assumed that they would break the cipher code and start reading encrypted German transmissions to anticipate and prepare for the next acts of aggression. The British did break the code, and they did indeed start reading the encrypted German transmissions.

"However, what should have been used to help them stop the German bombing of their towns was misused. They intercepted a German communication that a massive raid was scheduled for Coventry, just north of London. Rather than intercept the bombers on the way in or alert the population, they chose to keep the attack classified. The reason? They were afraid that the Germans would deduce the fact that the Enigma cipher machine was compromised, and the advantage would be lost. They wrongly assumed that if the Germans suspected their Enigma cipher machine was compromised, then a new device or methodology would be used and the British would have to start again. The decision was made to let the raid occur as if no one in England was the wiser.

"My question to you all is a rhetorical one. What benefit is there to information when a government won't use it to help people or protect them? We gave that government a tool to help protect their citizens and country. They let the air raid be carried out on those poor people when they could have done something. What is the point if information is not used to defend and protect, I ask? What would you have done?"

Quip responded with some conviction, "Grandpapa, I believe they made the right choice. The British needed to leverage the secret as long as possible because they couldn't know how much longer they would get to use the intercepted transmissions. Don't forget, they also needed that information gathering for the other theaters of war."

Petra disagreed with some indignation. "No! You are wrong, Quip. They should have sent up every plane to fight the attackers and tried to evacuate people to minimize loss of life. Even if the Germans suspected that their cipher machine had been compromised, what step would they have taken? The machine could be broken. Later in the war the Germans got suspicious anyway and did in fact add in another rotor to increase the complexity of the cipher code. The British broke that code as well. They should have used the advantage of their knowledge to save those people because the cyber warfare cat and mouse game had already begun. A cyber defense was built and then the other side defeated it, only to have the process continue."

Jacob processed his thoughts while Quip and Petra were on opposite sides of the argument. He looked up and said, "So it occurs to me that if such a gift cannot be used wisely, then why give it? Perhaps there was no real value in having given the Enigma cipher machine to the British in the first place. They didn't use the information to protect their people, and when they tried to give advanced warning to Stalin and the Soviets of Operation Barbarossa the British were not believed. What was the point of all of it?"

Otto looked at Wolfgang, then back at Jacob, then said, "Ferdek, join in here when I finish. I believe, Jacob, you have answered the question most astutely. We are not re-launching the digital currency. It's too dangerous and too disruptive to the sovereigns and to the global economy. We confiscated it not to re-market it, but to keep it out of the hands of the foolish. The planet is not ready for digital currency...yet. We will wait for the right time."

Quip was astonished and almost indignant. His face radiating anger, he said, "Uh, excuse me. We busted our chops to get that code. The two people who were fighting over it are dead. There is a very high probability that Chairman Lo Chang is on the hunt for it as we speak. You mean to tell me we are just going to do nothing with it?"

Wolfgang said with a grin, "That is precisely what we are going to do with it. Nothing. That code would shift established wealth structures overnight, disrupt all social norms, and launch a chaotic fist-fight with everyone against everyone to control the new digital currency or launch their own. All commerce would halt until the clear winner emerged, but that wouldn't happen overnight. No, we don't want to see that scenario played out, not under our watch when we can prevent it."

Wolfgang's finality ended that particular discussion point. Otto went through a few other details and also had the younger members help prioritize the items and the direction that they needed to move toward. The discussion was solid and the contributions done with information and specific data points to back up the conclusions. Quip, Erich, Petra and Jacob were making fine progress, which Wolfgang and Ferdek had agreed with the evening before. Completing his agenda, Otto gave the floor to the team.

No one commented, so Jacob interjected, "I presume that is all the business items for discussion today."

All heads nodded, and Otto responded, "Yes, that is it for today, Jacob. Unless you have something."

"Actually, I do. Petra and I spoke last evening, and we decided that all work and no play is not a lifetime vocation. That said, unless there is an objection, we are out of here, starting Monday, for a couple of weeks or so in Mexico. Virtual work is possible, but not as the first order of business."

There were nods from around the table and applause from the remote team that had been conferenced into the discussion.

"I think that is a great idea. Haddy, will you please help with travel arrangements for these two, please?"

Haddy beamed at both of them. "Yes, of course."

Specialized Terms
and Informational References

http://en.wikipedia.org/wiki/Wikipedia

Wikipedia (wɪkiˈ pi: diə / *WIK-i-PEE-dee-ə*) is a collaboratively
edited, multilingual, free Internet encyclopedia supported
by the non-profit Wikimedia Foundation. Wikipedia's 30
million articles in 287 languages, including over 4.3 million in
the English Wikipedia, are written collaboratively by volunteers around the world. This is a great quick reference source
to better understand terms.

Air-gapping – An **air gap** or **air wall** is a network security
measure that consists of ensuring that a secure computer
network is physically isolated from insecure networks, such as
the public Internet or an insecure local area network. It is often
taken for computers and networks that must be extraordinarily
secure. Frequently the air gap is not completely literal, such
as via the use of dedicated cryptographic devices that can
tunnel packets over untrusted networks while avoiding packet
rate or size variation. Even in this case, there is no ability for
computers on opposite sides of the air gap to communicate.

APAC - **Asia-Pacific** or **Asia Pacific** (abbreviated as **Asia-Pac, AsPac, APAC, APJ, JAPA** or **JAPAC**) is the part of the world in or near the Western Pacific Ocean. The region varies in size depending on context, but it typically includes much of East Asia, Southeast Asia, and Oceania.

Bitcoin - **Bitcoin** (sign: ฿; code: **BTC** or **XBT**) is a cryptocurrency where the creation and transfer of bitcoins is based on an open-source cryptographic protocol that is independent of any central authority. Bitcoins can be transferred through a computer or smartphone without an intermediate financial institution. The concept was introduced in a 2008 paper by a pseudonymous developer known only as "Satoshi Nakamoto," who called it a peer-to-peer electronic cash system

DEFCON - **DEFCON** (also written as **DEF CON** or **Defcon**) is one of the world's largest annual conventions, held every year in Las Vegas, Nevada. The first DEFCON took place in June 1993.
Many of the attendees at DEFCON include computer security professionals, journalists, lawyers, federal government employees, security researchers, and hackers with a general interest in software, computer architecture, phone phreaking, hardware modification, and anything else that can be "hacked." The event consists of several tracks of speakers about computer- and hacking-related subjects, as well as social events and contests

EMEA – **Europe, the Middle East and Africa,** usually abbreviated to **EMEA**, is a regional designation used for government, marketing and business purposes. It is particularly common amongst North American companies. The region is generally accepted to include all European nations, all African nations, and extends east to Iran, but also includes Russia. Typically this does not include independent overseas territories whose mainland is in this region such as French Guyana (part of France)

Enigma Machine - An **Enigma machine** was any of a family of related electro-mechanical rotor cipher machines used in the twentieth century for enciphering and deciphering secret messages. Enigma was invented by the German engineer Arthur Scherbius at the end of World War I. Early models were used commercially from the early 1920s, and adopted by military and government services of several countries — most notably by Nazi Germany before and during World War II. Several different Enigma models were produced, but the German military models are the most commonly discussed.

German military texts enciphered on the Enigma machine were first broken by the Polish Cipher Bureau, beginning in December 1932. This success was a result of efforts by three Polish cryptologists, working for Polish military intelligence. Rejewski "reverse-engineered" the device, using theoretical mathematics and material supplied by French military intelligence. Subsequently the three mathematicians designed mechanical devices for breaking Enigma ciphers, including the cryptologic bomb. This work was an essential foundation to further work on decrypting ciphers from repeatedly modernized Enigma machines, first in Poland and after the outbreak of war in France and the UK.

Though Enigma had some cryptographic weaknesses, in practice it was German procedural flaws, operator mistakes, laziness, failure to systematically introduce changes in encipherment procedures, and Allied capture of key tables and hardware that, during the war, enabled Allied cryptologists to succeed.

Encryption – In cryptography, encryption is the process of encoding messages (or information) in such a way that eavesdroppers or hackers cannot read it, but that authorized parties can. In an **encryption scheme,** the message or information (referred to as plaintext) is encrypted using an encryption algorithm, turning it into an unreadable ciphertext (ibid.). This is usually done with the use of an encryption key, which specifies how the message is to be encoded. Any adversary that can see the ciphertext should not be able to determine anything about the original message. An authorized party, however, is able to decode the ciphertext using a **decryption** algorithm that usually requires a secret decryption key that adversaries do not have access to. For technical reasons, an encryption scheme usually needs a key-generation algorithm to randomly produce keys

Hackers and Crackers - Hacker is a term that has been used to mean a variety of different things in computing. Depending on the context, the term could refer to a person in any one of the several distinct (but not completely disjointed) communities and subcultures. A **Cracker**, or **Hacker** (computer security), is a person who exploits weaknesses in a computer or network. This term is used to describe people committed to circumvention of computer security. This primarily concerns unauthorized remote computer break-ins via a communication networks such as the Internet (Black Hats), but also includes those who debug or fix security problems (White Hats), and the morally ambiguous Grey Hats.

Malware - Malware, short for **malicious software,** is software used or programmed by attackers to disrupt computer operation, gather sensitive information, or gain access to private computer systems. It can appear in the form of code, scripts, active content, and other software. Malware is a general term used to refer to a variety of forms of hostile or intrusive software.

Near Field Communications - Near Field Communication (NFC) is a set of standards for smartphones and similar devices to establish radio communication with each other by touching them together or bringing them into close proximity, usually no more than a few inches. Present and anticipated applications include contactless transactions, data exchange, and simplified setup of more complex communications such as Wi-Fi.

Open Source - In production and development, **open source** as a development model promotes a) universal access via free license to a product's design or blueprint, and b) universal redistribution of that design or blueprint, including subsequent improvements to it by anyone. Before the phrase open source became widely adopted, developers and producers used a variety of terms for the concept; open source gained hold with the rise of the Internet, and the attendant need for massive retooling of the computing source code. Opening the source code enabled a self-enhancing diversity of production models, communication paths, and interactive communities. The open source software movement arose to clarify the environment that the new copyright, licensing domain, and consumer issues created.

Pen-testing – Penetration-testing is one of the oldest methods for assessing the security of a computer system. In the early 1970s, the Department of Defense used this method to demonstrate the security weaknesses in computer systems and to initiate the development of programs to create more secure systems. Penetration-testing is increasingly used by organizations to assure the security of information systems and services, so that security weaknesses can be fixed before they get exposed

Rootkits - A rootkit is a stealthy type of software, often malicious, designed to hide the existence of certain processes or programs from normal methods of detection and enable continued privileged access to a computer. The term rootkit is a concatenation of "root" (the traditional name of the privileged account on Unix operating systems) and the word "kit" (which refers to the software components that implement the tool). The term "rootkit" has negative connotations through its association with malware.

Steganography - is the art and science of writing hidden messages in such a way that no one, apart from the sender and intended recipient, suspects the existence of the message, a form of security through obscurity. The word **steganography** is of Greek origin and means "concealed writing" from the Greek words *steganos* (στεγανός) meaning "covered or protected", and *graphei* (γραφή) meaning "writing". The first recorded use of the term was in 1499 by Johannes Trithemius in his Steganographia, a treatise on cryptography and steganography disguised as a book on magic. Generally, messages will appear to be something else: images, articles, shopping lists, or some other *covertext* and, classically, the hidden message may be in invisible ink between the visible lines of a private letter.

Stuxnet - is a computer worm discovered in June 2010 that is believed to have been created by the United States and Israel to attack Iran's nuclear facilities. **Stuxnet** initially spreads via Microsoft Windows, and targets Siemens industrial control systems. While it is not the first time that hackers have targeted industrial systems, it is the first discovered malware that spies on and subverts industrial systems, and the first to include a programmable logic controller rootkit.

Two-form factor authentication – Two-factor authentication is a 'strong authentication' method as it adds another layer of security to the password reset process. In most cases this consists of Preference Based Authentication plus a second form of physical authentication (using something the user possesses - i.e. Smartcards, USB tokens, etc.). One popular method is through SMS and email. Advanced SSPR software requires the user to provide a mobile phone number or personal e-mail address during set-up. In the event of a password reset a PIN code will be sent to the user's phone or email and they will need to enter this code during the password reset process.

Read a snippet from the second book in the series…

the
Enigma
Rising

BOOK 2: Award Winning Techno Thriller Series

Breakfield and Burkey

Advice, like medicine, needs to be the right dose

Thiago stared at his most recent picture of his beautiful daughter Lara as if that alone would bring her back. Her long almost auburn hair, slightly wavy like his, big chocolate eyes with lashes that needed little cosmetic enhancement, generous mouth with perfect teeth smiling like she had a secret. Lara was around 1.7 meters, trim, with a well-proportioned figure he feared too many males would notice when she went away to university. Her grace when she walked and her lilting laughter, to say nothing of his wealth, made her a very sought after heiress, whom he'd overprotected her entire life. He missed that laughter in their home. The four months that his daughter had been gone had felt closer to a year.

Lara was brilliant in her subjects, fluent in English, Portuguese, and Spanish, with a stubborn streak that matched his own. Hard headed when it came to her dreams of modeling and being an actress. As if he'd allow his daughter to ever pursue a career like that. Maybe if her mother had lived, these pursuits would have been nipped in the bud and channeled into her legacy. Thiago knew she was more than capable of stepping into his shoes one day and taking over his interests in his iron, steel, and petroleum business. She knew a great deal about the business, the social requirements, and many of his associates. She simply didn't want it like she had when she was younger. Most likely because he wanted her to do it, along with the influences of college.

He hoped his meeting with Otto today for lunch would provide a new option for locating Lara. As wealthy and powerful as Thiago Bernardes was in Brazil and throughout Latin America for that matter, he hadn't been able to find his daughter Lara. He'd been able to keep the fact that she was missing from the press and friends with the contrived story of her vacationing at a spa. How much longer that would work was an open question. Oscar, the head of his security team, had done some digging and tracking, discreetly of course, but had no real leads.

Otto was visiting for an update on the financial investments that his firm provided to Bernardes Ltd. They'd been friends for many years, and Otto had advised him well for investments. Thiago knew, however, that Otto had many inroads to information sources. As Thiago entered the restaurant, he was delighted to see that Otto was already seated. Otto stood to shake hands as he approached.

"Thiago, my friend, so happy you could meet with me today. The cuisine smells amazing, and I hope you have a recommendation," Otto said as he shook hands with his old friend.

Thiago responded with a slight smile, "It is very nice to see you again. We get together in person too rarely, my friend. Yes, of course I have my favorites which I will recommend."

They sat down and glanced at the menus briefly while giving the waiter their drink orders. The waiter provided a list of the specials and indicated he would be back with their drinks and to take their orders.

"Business, by all reports, appears to be good here in Brazil and throughout South America. Your investments, I am happy to report, are doing quite well, and I have a few items for your consideration. But, before all of that boring discussion takes place, tell me about yourself and of course your lovely daughter, Lara. I thought perhaps she might be joining us today." Otto smiled, pleased to be there with his old friend.

A shadow crossed Thiago's face, deepening the lines of stress. "Business is very good, Otto. Lara however is a different matter. I was thinking of confiding in you and seeking your counsel. I require your utmost discretion, however, if we continue with that discussion. But let's order lunch first, shall we, and discuss the weather and such."

"Of course. I have never broken a confidence of yours. Problem with Lara? From all you have told me over the years, I find that difficult to believe."

The waiter interrupted when he returned with their drinks. They both chose from the specials offered, with the waiter indicating they would be most pleased with their choices. When the waiter left, they toasted their meeting and discussed the weather and such as they waited for their meals. Though Thiago looked less robust than previously, Otto strived to keep the conversation light. Their luncheon was served, and they were left in peace to their corner of the restaurant.

"Thiago, this salmon is excellent. How is your swordfish?"

"Very nice. To be honest I have yet to have a poor meal here. Consistently delicious though a bit pricey on some dishes. I find these days my appetite is not what it once was, so this always tempts me to eat more."

"Ah, so how is your progress on overcoming your health challenges? You look a bit tired, but I would attribute that to worry from what you indicated before lunch."

"The doctors were not encouraged at my visit last week. Some recommendations have been made, but I fear that the end is closer than they are willing to admit. That is another of the reasons I would like to discuss Lara with you and see if you have any options I might explore."

"Your health is critical so of course you must either seek other medical opinions or adhere to their recommendations."

"I have consulted with two other doctors, and they are all aligned in the treatment methods. They all indicate I can overcome this issue, but I need to reduce my stress, exercise, take their silly pills, and rest more. I am doing my best to adhere to their guidance and am scheduled for some additional procedures in a few weeks.

"Otto, Lara is missing. She has been for months. So far all my efforts haven't resulted in any leads on her whereabouts. Due to my health problems and lack of finding Lara, I have also redone my will naming you as the executor. I have no other choice until Lara returns."

"There are courses of action for your health. That is good. Executor of your estate? That seems extreme, but I will honor your wishes for the time being. Now what about Lara? What is the problem? I of course would like to help you if I can."

Forcibly calming himself and taking a breath, Thiago succinctly stated, "Lara essentially ran away four months ago. I have kept it out of the press, but have no leads on where she is. I am so worried, that I am starting to neglect the business and imagining all the worst for my princess."

He paused again, then continued, "I have Oscar on it, but he has found nothing of any substance. He tracked her on a flight to Argentina then totally lost her."

"Oh my! I am so sorry. Do you know what she took with her? Was there an event that caused her to leave? You two didn't butt heads, did you?"

Shaking his head and looking very sad, he responded, "She took two suitcases filled with clothes, her passport, her credit cards which she has not used since the purchase of the airline ticket, and a few thousand U.S. dollars cash.

"To be quite honest, we did have an argument. She wanted to try her hand at modeling and acting, but I could never allow my daughter to do that. I put my foot down and reminded her of the responsibilities to the company and our people. We stood toe to toe, with me giving orders and her saying she was grown and could make her own choices. I told her my expectations. My last words were to forbid her to pursue modeling and acting. She glared at me and told me I was impossible and then she ran from the library where we'd been talking to her room. When I got up in the morning, I didn't see her and figured she was cooling off. When I returned from work that evening, she was gone with no word to any of the staff. I then discovered the missing luggage and the other items."

Otto empathized, "you've had no word, no calls from her? Are you sure that she wasn't taken? How could she escape the scrutiny of her bodyguard? She adores you. I am surprised she wouldn't have at least called you to say she was alright."

With tears coming into his eyes, Thiago said, "Honestly she's been out-smarting her bodyguards over the years, though not in public. Even during her time at the university, she adhered to the security requirements. Oscar and I both believe she left voluntarily. The words were terribly ugly between us. I told her she would fail and not to do this then come begging for help from me. At one point during our argument, she said she didn't need me and could do this on her own."

"I understand. Sometimes when we are mad we say things that we would never otherwise say. I am sure it was the case on both sides of the argument. So Oscar has had no success. You believe she left on her own. Overall she has not been in the limelight and thus is not immediately recognized so no paparazzi interest, I would guess. How do you think I can help you?"

"Otto, I am confident that you have resources outside of the financial investments which we have always dealt with. Perhaps you can make some discreet inquiries. Keep an eye out for her. I do not want it in the press. It is far too private and that would really alienate her, I fear. We have been fortunate to not be a targeted family, as some of my associates are."

Otto sat back and thought for a few minutes. Could he use his resources to help here? It was different than other activities his team was involved with, but then again perhaps not so much. His team was the best at getting information, but to be discreet would take time. Perhaps JAC and Quip would have some ideas, he thought.

"Thiago, this is not an area in which I or my associates would normally get involved. However, I have known you for a long time and Lara since she was very little. I have a couple of folks that I might be able to have work on it. It will take time though, especially if you do not want the press involved.

"Doesn't she speak several languages? This is important to potentially discover where she might have traveled to. Do you have some current photographs of her? Exactly how much cash do you believe she left with and in which currencies? She aspires to be a model and an actress, right? As I recall, she is tall and thin but more proportioned than the typical anorexic runway model, with a face like an angel and with a slightly bronzed complexion and huge eyes. Did she do any acting in school?"

Thiago nodded and said, "She speaks fluently in languages that would allow her to easily fit in anywhere in North America or South America. She did not act in any school plays, but said her whole life was like playing a role. Sadly, though she inherited the looks of her mother, she also got her tenacity, or what you would call mule headedness from my side of the gene pool."

They both grinned, knowing that trait was well engrained in the both of them. It contributed to their success in business overall. Their discussion continued down the business path of the main objective for their lunch when it was originally scheduled. Otto wanted to gather his thoughts as well as give Thiago a chance to recover his composure after telling of the disagreement with his daughter. As they finished up their conversation, paid for their lunch, and readied to leave, Otto ventured forth with an offer.

"Thiago, I will have my team make some discreet inquiries."

"I understand, Otto, and I appreciate that it will take time. She could be any place and doing anything to reach her dream. Money is no object so please let me know your fees for this."

"Do not insult me with fees for doing a friend a favor. If the team incurs costs then you can reimburse for those, but no fees. You do have to make a promise to me for doing this." Otto knew that the longer she was gone the greater the risk at her recovery, and he wanted to push Thiago.

"Of course, anything! What do I need to promise?"

"That no matter how long it takes, and it could take some time to maintain your requested discretion, you will do what your doctors say so that you can see her when she is found."

"That is not fair. I can hardly control that."

"You will adhere to their requests, and I will have a doctor I know review the treatment recommendations as well. When she is found then you can readdress your will. Agreed?"

As they stepped outside, Thiago seemed reinvigorated, " Alright. I agree. Thank you, Otto. I will send some information to you. Please provide progress updates. Oscar is at your disposal if needed."

CHAPTER 1

We don't need no stinkin' badges

Juan and Carlos were fidgeting and distracted while waiting on the plane. Their home away from home did not provide much in the way of amenities, since they wanted as little attention as possible out here in the Chihuahuan Desert of Mexico. Besides, they didn't want to have an electricity bill for this unmarked landing strip they had spent so much time getting ready. The idea was to have it look deserted from the air as well as on the ground. Any time there was work to do, they showed up with their own water truck and portable generators. This allowed them to be self-sufficient for as many days as needed.

Carlos had become rather proficient at borrowing satellite communications time, so their voice and data connectivity never suffered because there was no phone line available. Actually, Carlos had been a telecommunications specialist in the military. He was quite clever at setting up complex signaling schemes that were encrypted and got bounced several times around his ground links to cloak the true location. When they sent a plane off or when they had a plane on approach, he insisted on radio silence. Being naturally cautious, he felt this minimized the possibility of the unnecessaries to triangulate their location based on radio communications traffic. That left them with a lot of time on their hands to worry about what might go wrong with the shipments.

Carlos was practical, thoughtful, and the consummate worrier of the two brothers. Juan, on the other hand, never showed up properly prepared for any situation. Thus, he improvised a lot to compensate for his cavalier approach to most everything. The result, however, gave him great adaptability to any given set of circumstances. His sense of humor, coupled with his knack of getting out of touchy situations, made him an excellent resource for this kind of work. Juan's natural abilities to adapt and excel at almost any sport, whether physical or social, made him the person everyone wanted on their team. Juan's charming wit and personality was always a hit with the ladies. This unfailing charm of his could usually be counted upon to get him out of difficulties, which he seemed to court more times than not. Born in Mexico, but educated in both the United States and Mexico allowed the brothers to work easily in either country. They preferred Mexico.

The rest of the ground crew in their private location in the Chihuahuan Desert of Mexico was comprised of Vaughn, Don, and Ron. They were referred to as the On-Brothers, though they weren't even closely related. They didn't quite seem able to make it with the ladies or possess the commonly accepted social behaviors. Indeed from time to time Carlos and Juan were asked if the On-Brothers were gay. They weren't, but the absence of social skills only left them each other to live with. Their favorite game was mental cruelty. They'd take turns belittling one another usually as a game of two against one. Their eccentricities could be entertaining or tiresome depending upon the circumstances.

Carlos had gotten into the habit of letting them know when they could devolve into their ritualistic verbal combat routine and when they could not. Whenever a landing was expected, the dialog became informational only among them, so that Carlos wouldn't lose his temper.

At one point Carlos and Don had been equal partners in the business. Don had zoned out from time to time, taking as much as six months off, leaving Carlos to run operations. Vaughn showed up one day after his marriage had failed and fell right in to the new line of work. His temperament was the opposite of Don's. Don was introspective, fairly well read, and when his pockets were full of money, he would simply leave if nothing was going on work wise. Don had come to Mexico seeking mystical enlightenment from the Yaqui Indians but stayed because of the peyote. One time he had even lived as a hermit in a cave along the Rio Grande and lived off the land wearing just a loin cloth. However after six months, he was driven to return to civilization primarily because he couldn't get his major food supplement, fudgesicles. Vaughn couldn't read very well so the material had to have lots of pictures of women and the more naked those were the better. Ron was like a puppy dog no one wanted, but for some reason he fit right in to round out the On-Brothers trio. The trio was mostly unfit and scruffy looking. Not candidates for inclusion in GQ magazine.

Carlos had an unusual birth defect. For all his planning and efforts to contain and control himself in a situation when he lost his temper, it triggered an adrenaline leak into his system which doubled his strength thus giving him the moniker Raging Bull. Juan loved to tease his older brother, but he had to be careful that he didn't push the wrong buttons on Carlos. The one time was quite enough and ever since then they'd worked together like well-oiled machinery. Carlos, at a lean 1.83 meters, muscular, black hair with a mustache, and Juan, at 1.52 meters, stockier but muscular, black hair with no facial hair, could easily be candidates for *GQ* magazine, when they were cleaned up. Neither of them had problems attracting females and thoroughly enjoyed them.

"Where the hell are they?" asked Carlos. "I don't know why I let myself get talked into using gringos for this operation. You know they can't be trusted! If they screw this up--"

Juan interjected, "Then we won't have to worry about them ever again. Look, you don't fly into the U.S. looking like us without attracting attention. They are wanted fugitives with nowhere else to go. They can't go back to where they came from, and we are the only ones who will work with them after the Mexican police started cleaning house. After the enemies they made at the Night Owl shoot out, their ONLY option is to work with us."

Juan looked up at the weather and in particular the clouds moving in and added, "I sure don't like the looks of the weather. These clouds have the look of *Nympho-Cumulus* all over them."

Carlos stared at Juan for a moment and said blankly, "….*Nympho-Cumulus?*"

Juan, not changing his studying of the cloud formations, said, "you know, fucking thunderstorms." To which Carlos rolled his eyes at being pulled into Juan's gag.

"But anyway, just so you know, I am glad we have that remote detonation device hidden in the plane as our failsafe. Good thinking, bro."

Carlos settled down a bit, based on Juan's statements. Juan was right, where would they go if not back here? JC and Robert were larger than life men who had played it fast and loose. The U.S. Federales were after both of them. If it hadn't been for Juan's plane and some low level flying, JC and Robert would be parked in the same cell block with Charles Manson and his friends.

JC was a small time crook who wanted to be a big time crook. At 1.835 meters tall and 113 kilograms, he was an imposing individual. His size, coupled with his hyper out-going and larger than life personality, made it seem like he almost sucked all the air out of a room when he entered. His jokes were desperately off color but his laughter was so contagious that everything seemed alright with everyone. He liked to pay for everything when he was out with the gang, and it earned him the nickname on-me JC. In fact he was so extravagant in his spending that he always needed more money, which led him into dealing drugs. His first wife didn't quite get the hang of his changed lifestyle and didn't want to go along that path.

The big score he needed to put himself into the larger than life role he envisioned came with a cash price he couldn't deliver. So JC, being the resourceful individual he was, killed two birds with a single stone. According to federal testimony, JC murdered his wife for the insurance money and used it to finance his first big drug deal. His second wife, who was almost the same age as JC's oldest daughter, didn't seem to mind JC's undocumented business activities. She thoroughly enjoyed spending the money it brought in. JC was always talking about his new acquisitions.

At dinner one night with 15-20 close friends, JC told everyone about the new Cadillac he had just ordered with every option possible.

JC told everyone, "you should see this new Caddy I have coming in. Man-o-man, it's got EVERY possible option you can think of! But the only one I couldn't bring myself to get was the automatic douche-bag. I don't want an automatic douche-bag."

His wife and daughter laughed the hardest at this as they did with all his antics.

JC's drug dealing connection was Juan out of Mexico City. They shared the same passion for flying, which is why Juan picked up JC one day at Dallas Love Field regional airport just one step ahead of the federales and flew him to Mexico. It was quite a haul that day since Juan also brought along another social climber, Robert.

Robert was somewhat quiet and withdrawn, almost moody. A moderately built ex-military gunnery sergeant and sharp shooter, there wasn't anything he didn't know about weapons and how to effectively use them. All Robert ever talked about was being in financial investments. Word was that after Robert left the service that is exactly what he did. He robbed banks, 20 to be specific. His assembled team would blow into a bank masked, heavily armed, hold a few hostages, and grab everything of value in under eight minutes. Then they'd take someone's car out of the lot and drive to where their car was located. The story goes that one of his team members got drunk one night and described in too much detail one of the robberies to a lady who was also an undercover cop.

The police broke in on Robert and held him at gun point while they searched his apartment. The SWAT team recovered several weapons and some C-4 explosives. One SWAT team member brought a locked brief case over to Robert and asked him to open it. Robert was being held down on his stomach with his hands cuffed behind him with two H-K semi-automatic weapons pressed to his head.

Sensing the irony of the situation, Robert told the guy, "you can open it if you'd like. I'd do it but I'm busy right now."

The guy said, "OK I will, but first let me bring it over here and put it next to your head" which he did.

Robert, not one to let the moment slip through his fingers, quickly added, "Hey man, before you open it can you put your fingers in my ears? I hate loud noises."

Robert was out on bail and trying to buy a drink at the bar with only dimes, nickels, and quarters after the police confiscated everything he had. That's when he bumped into *on-me* JC and Juan. Robert was due for sentencing the next day and was trying to have one last drink before he went in. When Juan and JC couldn't watch the pathetic activity of Robert trying to pay for a drink with loose coins, they both covered the tab.

However, Juan was never able to miss an opportunity to have a dig at some-one and, knowing a little about Robert, said, "Boy, some bank robber you are!"

The absurdity of the situation made everyone laugh and of course that was their evening toast at every round of drinks ordered. JC and Robert really seemed to hit it off as drinking buddies.

Juan sized up the bar crowd and knew something was wrong. He was pretty sure that his two new friends were being watched which meant so was he. But ever the party animal and with someone else to rock-out with, he ignored the feeling. The night got louder and louder. Juan even bought drinks for the DEA, the Feds, and the undercover police, pretending he was just being sociable to the crowd watching their antics. Apparently around midnight, a couple of small caliber weapons went off in the bar which quickly emptied the place.

Juan had staged the exit and took his two new friends straight to the fully fueled King Air twin engine parked at Love Field and promptly took off. He filed his flight plan while taxiing down the runway. He dropped from radar shortly after crossing the DFW city limits, and no one picked him up again until he was on the ground at the landing strip in the Chihuahuan Desert of Mexico. Juan was right. Robert and JC had no place else to go.

The On-Brothers came rushing in to say that a plane was on approach and so everyone went out to see if it was theirs or someone unwanted.

Carlos said, "Right, *saddle up!*" as he strapped on his favorite Colt 1911 semi-automatic pistol and grabbed his weapon of choice, an H-K semi-automatic assault rifle. Everyone else saddled up as well in case they needed to greet intruders.

Charles Breakfield – A renowned technology solutions architect with 25+ years of experience in security, hybrid data/telecom environments, and unified communications. He finds it intriguing to leverage his professional skills in these award-winning contemporary TechnoThriller stories. In his spare time, he enjoys studying World War II history, travel, and cultural exchanges everywhere he can. Charles' love of wine tastings, cooking, and Harley riding has found ways into *The Enigma Series.*

He has commented that being a part of his father's military career in various outposts, has positively contributed to his many characters and the various character perspectives he explores in the stories.

Rox Burkey – A renowned customer experience business architect, optimizes customer solutions on their existing technology foundation. She has been a featured speaker, subject matter expert, interviewer, instructor, and author of technology documents, as well as a part of *The Enigma Series.* It was revealed a few years ago that writing fiction is a lot more fun than white papers or documentation.

As a child she helped to lead the other kids with exciting new adventures built on make believe characters. As a Girl Scout until high school she contributed to the community in the Head Start program. Rox enjoys family, learning, listening to people, travel, outdoors activities, sewing, cooking, and imagining the possibilities.

Breakfield & Burkey – Combine their professional expertise, knowledge of the world from both business and personal travels. Many of the people whom have crossed their paths and are now a foundation for the characters in their series. They also find it interesting to use the aspects of today's technology which people actually incorporate into their daily lives as a focused challenge for each book in The Enigma Series. Breakfield & Burkey claim this is a perfect way to create cyber good guys versus cyber thugs in their award-winning series. Each book can be enjoyed alone or in sequence.

You can invite them to talk about their stories in private or public book readings. Burkey also enjoys interviewing authors though avenues like Indie Beacon Radio with scheduled appointments showing on the calendar on their website *www. EnigmaBookSeries.com*. Followers can see them at author events, book fairs, libraries, and bookstores.

The foundation of the series is a family organization called the R-Group. They spawned a subgroup, which contains some of the familiar and loved characters as the Cyber Assassins Technology Services (CATS) team. They have ideas for continuing the series in both story tracks. You will discover over the many characters, a hidden avenue for the future *The Enigma Chronicles* tagged in some portions of the stories.

Fan reviews seem to frequently suggest that these would make film stories, so the possibilities appear endless, just like their ideas for new stories. Comments have increased with the book trailers available on the Amazon, Kirkus, Facebook, and YouTube. Check out our evolving website for new interviews, blogs, book trailers, and fun acronyms they've used in the stories. Reach out directly at *Authors@EnigmaSeries.com*. We love reader and listener reviews for our eBook, Paperback, and Audible formats.

Other stories by Breakfield and Burkey in
The Enigma Series are at **www.EnigmaBookSeries.com**

We would greatly appreciate
if you would take a few minutes
and provide a review of this work
on Amazon, Goodreads
and any of your other favorite places.

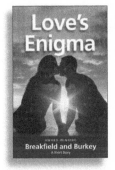

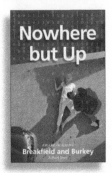
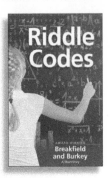

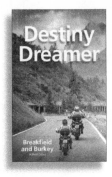

CPSIA information can be obtained
at www.ICGtesting.com
Printed in the USA
LVHW010102270722
724467LV00001B/45